TURNING
ANGEL

TURNING ANGEL

GREG ILES

HODDER &
STOUGHTON

Copyright © 2006 by Greg Iles

First published in Great Britain in 2006 by Hodder & Stoughton
A division of Hodder Headline

The right of Greg Iles to be identified as the Author of the Work
has been asserted by him in accordance with the Copyright,
Designs and Patents Act 1988.

A Hodder & Stoughton Book

1

A CIP catalogue record for this title is available from the British Library

Hardback ISBN 0 340 83370 X
Trade Paperback ISBN 0 340 83371 8

Printed and bound by Clays Ltd, St Ives plc

Hodder Headline's policy is to use papers that are natural, renewable
and recyclable products and made from wood grown in sustainable
forests. The logging and manufacturing processes are expected to
conform to the environmental regulations of the country of origin.

Hodder & Stoughton Ltd
A division of Hodder Headline
338 Euston Road
London NW1 3BH

Society is an artificial construction,
a defense against nature's power.

Camille Paglia

TURNING ANGEL

PROLOGUE

The rain kept falling, swelling the creek until it lifted the girl into its muddy flood. She swept down through the town, unseen by anyone as she passed the grassy mounds where three hundred years ago Indians worshipped the sun. She bobbed in the current beneath the Highway 61 bridge, naked and unbloodied, not yet gray, limp as a sleeping child. She rolled with the creek, which wound through the woods toward the paper mill and crashed into the Mississippi River in a maelstrom of brown waves. The girl made this journey alone and unknowing, but soon she would whip the town into another kind of maelstrom, one that would make the river seem placid by comparison.

She never meant to cause trouble. She was a quiet girl, brilliant and full of life. When she laughed, others laughed with her. When she cried, she hid her tears. She was blessed with many gifts and took none for granted. At seventeen, she had already brought honor to the town. No one would have predicted this end.

But then no one really knew her.

Only me.

CHAPTER

1

Some stories must wait to be told.

Any writer worth his salt knows this. Sometimes you wait for events to percolate in your subconscious until a deeper truth emerges; other times you're simply waiting for the principals to die. Sometimes it's both.

This story is like that.

A man walks the straight and narrow all his life; he follows the rules, stays within the lines; then one day he makes a misstep. He crosses a line and sets in motion a chain of events that will take from him everything he has and damn him forever in the eyes of those he loves.

We all sense that invisible line of demarcation, like an unspoken challenge hanging in the air. And there is some wild thing in our natures that makes us want to cross it, that compels us with the silent insistence of evolutionary imperative to risk all for a glinting shadow. Most of us suppress that urge. Fear stops us more often than wisdom, as in most things. But some of us take that step. And in the taking, we start down a path from which it is difficult and sometimes impossible to return.

Dr. Andrew Elliott is such a man.

I have known Drew since he was three years old, long before he was a Rhodes scholar, before he went to medical school, before he returned to our hometown of twenty thousand souls to practice internal medicine. And our bond runs deeper than that of most childhood friends. When I was fourteen, eleven-year-old Drew Elliott saved my life and almost lost his own in the process. We remained close friends until he graduated from medical school, and then for a long time—fifteen years, I guess—I saw him hardly at all. Much of that time I spent convicting murderers as an assistant district attorney in Houston, Texas. The rest I spent writing novels based on extraordinary cases from my career, which gave me a second life and time to spend with my family.

Drew and I renewed our friendship five years ago, after my wife died and I returned to Natchez with my young daughter to try to piece my life back together. The early weeks of my return were swallowed by a whirlwind of a murder case, but as the notoriety faded, Drew was the first old friend to seek me out and make an effort to bring me into the community. He put me on the school board of our alma mater, got me into the country club, talked me into sponsoring a hot air balloon and a Metropolitan opera singer during Natchez's annual festivals. He worked hard at bringing this widower back to life, and with much help from Caitlin Masters, my lover for the past few years, he succeeded.

All that seems a distant memory now.

Yesterday Drew Elliott was a respected pillar of the community, revered by many, held up as a role model by all; today he is scorned by those who venerated him, and his life hangs in the balance. Drew was our golden boy, a paragon of everything small-town America holds to be noble, and by unwritten law the town will crucify him with a hatred equal to their betrayed love.

How did Drew transform himself from hero into monster? He reached out for love, and in the reaching pulled a whole town down on top of him. Last night his legend was intact. He was sitting beside me at a table in the boardroom of St. Stephen's Preparatory School, still handsome at forty, dark-haired, and athletic—he played football for Vanderbilt—a little gray at the temples but radiating the commanding presence of a doctor in his prime. I see this moment as clearly as any in my life, because it's the instant before revelation, that frozen moment in which the old world sits balanced on the edge of destruction, like a china cup teetering on the edge of a table. In a moment it will shatter into irrecoverable fragments, but for an instant it remains intact, and salvation seems possible.

The boardroom windows are dark, and the silver rain that's fallen all day is blowing horizontally now, slapping the windows with an icy rattle. We've crowded eleven people around the Brazilian rosewood table—six men, five women—and the air is close in the room. Drew's clear eyes are intent on Holden Smith, the over-dressed president of the St. Stephen's school board, as we discuss the purchase of new computers for the junior high school. Like Holden and several other board members, Drew and I graduated from St. Stephen's roughly two decades ago, and our children attend it today. We're part of a wave of alumni who stepped in during the city's recent economic decline to try to rebuild the school that gave us our remarkable educations. Unlike most Mississippi private schools, which sprang up in response to forced integration in 1968, St. Stephen's was founded as a parochial school in 1946. It did not admit its first African-American student until 1982, but the willingness was there years before that. High tuition and anxiety about being the only black child in an all-white school probably held off that landmark event for a few years. Now twenty-one black kids attend the secular St. Stephen's, and there would be more but for the cost. Not many black families in Natchez can afford to pay five thousand dollars a year per child for education when the public school is free. Few white families can either, when you get down to it, and fewer as the years pass. Therein lies the board's eternal challenge: funding.

At this moment Holden Smith is evangelizing for Apple computers, though the rest of the school's network runs comfortably on cheaper IBM clones. If he ever pauses for breath, I plan to tell Holden that while I use an Apple Powerbook myself, we have to be practical on matters of cost. But before I can, the school's secretary opens the door and raises her hand in a limp sort of wave.

Her face is so pale that I fear she might be having a heart attack.

Holden gives her an annoyed look. "What do you need, Theresa? We've got another half hour, at least."

Like most employees of St. Stephen's, Theresa Cook is also a school parent. "I just heard something terrible," she says, her voice cracking. "Kate Townsend is in the emergency room at St. Catherine's Hospital. They said . . . she's dead. Drowned. Kate Townsend. Can that be right?"

Holden Smith's thin lips twist in a grimace of a smile as he tries to convince himself that this is some sort of sick prank. Kate Townsend is the star of the senior class: valedictorian, state champion in both tennis and swimming, full scholarship to Harvard next fall. She's literally a poster child for St. Stephen's. We even used her in a TV commercial for the school.

"No," Holden says finally. "No way. I saw Kate on the tennis court at two this afternoon."

I look at my watch. It's nearly eight now.

Holden opens his mouth again but no sound emerges. As I glance at the faces around the table, I realize that a strange yet familiar numbness has gripped us all, the numbness that comes when you hear that a neighbor's child has been shot in a predawn hunting accident, or died in a car crash on homecoming night. It occurs to me that it's early April, and though the first breath of spring has touched the air, it's still too cold to swim, even in Mississippi. If a high school senior drowned today, a freak accident seems the only explanation. An indoor pool, maybe? Only I can't think of anyone who owns one.

"Exactly what did you hear and when, Theresa?" Holden asks. As if details might mitigate the horror of what is upon us.

"Ann Geter called my house from the hospital." Ann Geter is an ER nurse at St. Catherine's Hospital, and another St. Stephen's parent. Because the school has only five hundred students, everyone literally knows everyone else. "My husband told Ann I was still up here for the meeting. She called and told me that some fishermen found Kate wedged in the fork of a tree near where St. Catherine's Creek washes into the Mississippi River. They thought she might be alive, so they put her in their boat and carried her to the hospital. She was naked from the waist down, Ann said."

Theresa says "nekkid," but her word has the intended effect. Shock blanks the faces around the table as everyone begins to absorb the idea that this may not be a conventional accident. "Kate was bruised up pretty bad, Ann said. Like she'd been hit with something."

"Jesus Lord," whispers Clara Jenkins, from my left. "This can't be true. It must be somebody else."

Theresa's bottom lip begins to quiver. The secretary has always been close to the older students, especially the girls. "Ann said Kate had a tattoo on her thigh. I didn't know about that, but I guess her mama did. Jenny Townsend identified her body just a couple of minutes ago."

Down the table a woman sobs, and a shiver of empathy goes through me, like liquid nitrogen in my blood. Even though my daughter is only nine, I've nearly lost her twice, and I've had my share of nightmares about what Jenny Townsend just endured.

"God in heaven." Holden Smith gets to his feet, looking braced for physical combat. "I'd better get over to the hospital. Is Jenny still over there?"

"I imagine so," Theresa murmurs. "I just can't believe it. Anybody in the world you could have said, and I'd have believed it before Kate."

"Goddamn it," snaps Bill Sims, a local geologist. "It's just not fair."

"I know," Theresa agrees, as if fairness has anything to do with who is taken young and who survives to ninety-five. But then I realize she has a point. The Townsends lost a child to leukemia several years ago, before I moved back to town. I heard that was what broke up their marriage.

Holden takes a cell phone from his coat pocket and dials a number. He's probably calling his wife. The other board members sit quietly, their thoughts on their own children, no doubt. How many of them have silently thanked God for the good fortune of not being Jenny Townsend tonight?

A cell phone chirps under the table. Drew Elliott lifts his and says, "Dr. Elliott." He listens for a while, all eyes on him. Then he tenses like a man absorbing news of a family tragedy. "That's right," he says. "I'm the family doctor, but this is a coroner's case now. I'll come down and speak to the family. Their home? All right. Thanks."

Drew hangs up and looks at the ring of expectant faces, his own white with shock. "It's not a mistake. Kate's dead. She was dead before she reached the ER. Jenny Townsend is on her way home." Drew glances at me. "Your father's driving her, Penn. Tom was seeing a patient when they brought Kate in. Some family and friends are going over there. The father's in England, of course, but he's being notified."

Kate's father, a British citizen, has lived in England for the past five years.

A woman sobs at the end of the table.

"I'm adjourning this meeting," Holden says, gathering up the promotional literature from Apple Computer. "This can wait until next month's meeting."

As he walks toward the door, Jan Chancellor, the school's head-mistress, calls after him, "Just a minute, Holden. This is a terrible tragedy, but one thing can't wait until next month."

Holden doesn't bother to hide his annoyance as he turns back. "What's that, Jan?"

"The Marko Bakic incident."

"Oh, hell," says Bill Sims. "What's that kid done now?"

Marko Bakic is a Croatian exchange student who has been noth-ing but trouble since he arrived last September. How he made it into the exchange program is beyond any of us. Marko's records show that he scored off the charts on an IQ test, but all his intelligence seems to be used only in support of his anarchic aspirations. The charitable view is that this unfortunate child of the Balkan wars has brought confusion and disruption to St. Stephen's, sadly besmirch-ing an exchange program that's only won us glory in the past. The harsher view is that Marko Bakic uses the mask of prankster to hide more sinister activities like selling Ecstasy to the student body and anabolic steroids to the football team. The board has already sought my advice as a former prosecutor on how to deal with the drug issue; I told them that unless we catch Marko red-handed or someone volunteers firsthand information about illegal activities, there's nothing we can do. Bill Sims suggested a random drug-testing program, but this idea was tabled when the board realized that positive tests would probably become public, sabotaging our public relations effort and delighting the board of Immaculate Heart, the Catholic school across town. The local law enforcement organs have set their sights on Marko, as well, but they, too, have come up empty-handed. If Marko Bakic is dealing drugs, no one is talking about it. Not on the record, anyway.

"Marko got into a scuffle with Ben Ritchie in the hall yesterday," Jan says carefully. "He called Ben's girlfriend a slut."

"Not smart," Bill Sims murmurs.

Marko Bakic is six-foot-two and lean as a sapling; Ben Ritchie is five-foot-six and built like a cast-iron stove, just like his father, who played football with Drew and me more than twenty years ago.

Jan says, "Ben shoved Marko into the wall and told him to apologize. Marko told Ben to kiss his ass."

"So what happened?" asks Sims, his eyes shining. This is a lot more interesting than routine school board business.

Clearly put off by the juvenile relish in Bill's face, Jan says, "Ben put Marko in a choke hold and mashed his head against the floor until he apologized. Ben embarrassed Marko in front of a lot of people."

"Sounds like our Croatian hippie got what he deserved."

"Be that as it may," Jan says icily, "after Ben let Marko up, Marko told Ben he was going to kill him. Two other students heard it."

"Macho bullshit," says Sims. "Bakic trying to save face."

"Was it?" asks Jan. "When Ben asked Marko how he was going to do that, Marko said he had a gun in his car."

Sims sighs heavily. "Did he? Have a gun, I mean."

"No one knows. I didn't hear about this until after school. Frankly, I think the students were too afraid to tell me about it."

"Afraid of what you'd do?"

"No. Afraid of Marko. Several students say he does carry a gun sometimes. But no one would admit to seeing it on school property."

"Did you talk to the Wilsons?" Holden Smith asks from the doorway.

Bill Sims snorts in contempt. "What for?"

The Wilsons are the family that agreed to feed and house Marko for two semesters. Jack Wilson is a retired academic, and Marko seems to have him completely snowed.

Jan Chancellor watches Holden expectantly. She's a good headmistress, although she dislikes direct confrontations, which can't be avoided in a job like hers. Her face looks pale beneath her sleek, black bob, and her nerves seem stretched to the breaking point. They must be, to bring her to this point of insistence.

"I move that we enter executive session," she says, meaning that no minutes will be taken from this point forward.

"Second," I agree.

Jan gives me a quick look of gratitude. "As you all know, this is merely the latest in a long line of disruptive incidents. There's a clear pattern here, and I'm worried that something irreparable is going to happen. If it does—and if it can be demonstrated that we were aware of this pattern—then St. Stephen's and every member of the board will be exposed to massive lawsuits."

Holden sighs wearily from the door. "Jan, this was a serious incident, no doubt. And sorting it out is going to be a pain in the ass. But Kate Townsend's death is going to be a major shock to every student and family at this school. I can call a special meeting later in the week to deal with Marko, but Kate is the priority right now."

"Will you call that meeting?" Jan presses. "Because this problem's not going to go away."

"I will. Now I'm going to see Jenny Townsend. Theresa, will you lock up when everyone's gone?"

The secretary nods, glad for being given something to do. While the remainder of the board members continue to express disbelief, my cell phone rings. The caller ID shows my home as the origin of the call, which makes me unsure whether to answer. My daughter, Annie, is quite capable of pestering me to death with the phone when the mood strikes her. But with Kate's death fresh in my mind, I step into the secretary's office and answer.

"Annie?"

"No," says an older female voice. "It's Mia."

Mia Burke is my daughter's babysitter, a classmate of Kate Townsend's.

"I'm sorry to interrupt the board meeting, but I'm kind of freaked out."

"It's all right, Mia. What's the matter?"

"I'm not sure. But three people have called and told me something happened to Kate Townsend. They're saying she drowned."

I hesitate before confirming the rumor, but if the truth hasn't already spread across town, it will in a matter of minutes. Our secretary learning the truth from an ER nurse was part of the first wave of rumor, one of many that will sweep across town tonight, turning back upon themselves and swelling until the facts are lost in a tide of hyperbole. "You heard right, Mia. Kate was found dead in St. Catherine's Creek."

"Oh God."

"I know it's upsetting, and I'm sure you want to be with your friends right now, but I need you to stay with Annie until I get there. I'll be home in ten minutes."

"Oh, I'd never leave Annie alone. I mean, I don't even know what I should do. If Kate's dead, I can't really help her. And everyone is going to be acting so retarded about it. Take whatever time you need. I'd rather stay here with Annie than drive right now."

I silently thank Jan Chancellor for recommending one of the few levelheaded girls in the school to me as a babysitter. "Thanks, Mia. How's Annie doing?"

"She fell asleep watching a documentary about bird migration on the Discovery Channel."

"Good."

"Hey," Mia says in an awkward voice. "Thanks for telling me the truth about Kate."

"Thanks for not flipping out and leaving the house. I'll see you in a few minutes, okay?"

"Okay. Bye."

I hang up and look through the door at the boardroom. Drew Elliott is talking on his cell phone at the table, but the rest of the board members are filing out the main door. As I watch them go, an image from our promotional TV commercial featuring Kate rises into my mind. She's walking onto the tennis court in classic whites, and her cool blue eyes burn right through the camera. She's tall, probably five-ten, with Nordic blond hair that hangs halfway to her waist. More striking than beautiful, Kate looked like a college student rather than a high school kid, and that's why we chose her for the promo spot. She was the perfect recruiting symbol for a college-prep school.

As I reach for the office doorknob, I freeze. Drew is staring at the table with tears pouring down his face. I hesitate, giving him time to collect himself. What does it take to make an M.D. cry? My father has watched his patients die for forty years, and now they're dropping like cornstalks to a scythe. I know he grieves, but I can't remember him crying. The one exception was my wife, but that's another story. Maybe Drew thinks he's alone here, that I slipped out with all the others. Since he shows no sign of stopping, I walk out and lay my hand on his thickly muscled shoulder.

"You okay, man?"

He doesn't reply, but I feel him shudder.

"Drew? Hey."

He dries his eyes with a swipe of his sleeve, then stands. "Guess we'd better let Theresa lock up."

"Yeah. I'll walk out with you."

Side by side, we walk through the front atrium of St. Stephen's, just as we did thousands of times when we attended this school in the sixties and seventies. A large trophy cabinet stands against the wall to my left. Inside it, behind a wooden Louisville Slugger with thirteen names signed on it in Magic Marker, hangs a large photograph of Drew Elliott during the defining moment of this institution. Just fourteen years old, he is standing at the plate under the lights of Smith-Wills Stadium in Jackson, hitting what would be the winning home run of the 1977 AAAA state baseball championship. No matter how remarkable our academic accomplishments—and they were many—it was this prize that put our tiny "single A" school on the map. In Mississippi, as in the rest of the South, sport overshadows everything else.

"Long time ago," he says. "Eternity."

I'm standing on second base in the photo, waiting to sprint for the tying run. "Not so long."

He gives me a lost look, and then we pass through the entrance and pause under the overhang, prepping for a quick dash through the rain to our cars.

"Kate babysat for you guys, didn't she?" I comment, trying to get him to focus on the mundane.

"Yeah. The past two summers. Not anymore, though. She graduates—was *supposed* to graduate—in six weeks. She was too busy for babysitting."

"She seemed like a great kid."

Drew nods. "She was. Even these days, when so many students are overachievers, she stood out from the crowd."

I could point out that it's often the best and brightest who are taken while the rest of us are left to carry on, but Drew knows that. He's watched more people die than I ever will.

His Volvo is parked about thirty yards away, behind my Saab. I pat him on the back as I did in high school, then assume a tight end's stance. "Run for it?"

Instead of playing along with me, he looks me full in the face and speaks in a voice I haven't heard from him in years. "Can I talk to you for a minute?"

The emotion in his eyes is palpable. "Of course."

"Let's get in one of the cars."

"Sure."

He presses a button on his key chain, and his Volvo's lights blink. As if triggered by a silent starter pistol, we race through the chilly rain and scramble onto the leather seats of the S80. He slams his door and cranks the engine, then shakes his head with a strange violence.

"I can't fucking believe it, Penn. It's literally *beyond belief*. Did you know her? Did you know Kate at all?"

"We spoke a few times. She asked about my books. But we never got beyond the surface. Mia talked about her a lot."

His eyes search out mine in the shadows. "You and I haven't got beneath the surface much either these past five years. It's more my fault than yours, I know. I keep a lot inside."

"We all do," I say awkwardly, wondering where this is going.

"Who really knows anybody, right? Twelve years of school together, best friends when we were kids. You know a lot about me, but on the other hand you know nothing. The front, like everybody else."

"I hope I see past that, Drew."

"I don't mean to insult you. If anyone sees beneath the surface, it's you. That's why I'm talking to you now."

"Well, I'm here. Let's talk."

He nods as if confirming a private judgment. "I want to hire you."

"Hire me?"

"As a lawyer."

This is the last thing I expected to hear. "You know I don't practice anymore."

"You took the Payton case, that old civil rights bombing."

"That was different. And that was five years ago."

Drew stares at me in the glow of the dashboard lights. "This is different, too."

It always is to the client. "I'm sure it is. The thing is, I'm not really a lawyer anymore. I'm a writer. If you need a lawyer, I can recommend several good ones. Is it malpractice?"

Drew blinks in astonishment. "Malpractice? You think I'd waste your time with bullshit like that?"

"Drew . . . I don't know what this is about. Why don't you tell me what the problem is?"

"I want to, but— Penn, what if you were sick? You had HIV, say. And you came to me and said, 'Drew, please help me. As a friend. I want you to treat me and not tell a soul.' And what if I said, 'Penn, I'd like to, but that's not my specialty. You need to go to a specialist.' "

"Drew, come on—"

"Hear me out. If you said, 'Drew, as a friend, please do me this favor. Please help me.' You know what? I wouldn't think twice. I'd do whatever you wanted. Treat you without records, whatever."

He would. I can't deny it. But there's more than this beneath his words. Drew has left much unsaid. The truth is that without Drew Elliott, I wouldn't be alive today. When I was fourteen years old, Drew and I hiked away from the Buffalo River in Arkansas and got lost in the Ozark Mountains. Near dark, I fell into a gorge and broke my femur. Drew was only eleven, but he crawled down into that gorge, splinted my leg with a tree limb, then built a makeshift litter and started dragging me through the night. Before he was done, he dragged me four miles through the mountains, breaking his wrist in the process and twice almost breaking his neck. Just after dawn, he managed to get me to a cluster of tents where someone had a CB radio. But has he mentioned any of that? No. It's my job to remember.

"Why do you want to hire me, Drew?"

"To consult. With the protection of confidentiality."

"Shit. You don't have to hire me for that."

He pulls his wallet from his pants and takes out a twenty-dollar bill, which he pushes at me. "I know that. But if you were questioned on the stand later—as a friend—you'd have to lie to protect me. If you're my lawyer, our discourse will be shielded by attorney-client privilege." He's still pushing the bill at me. "Take it, Penn."

"This is crazy—"

"Please, man."

I wad up the note and shove it into my pocket. "Okay, damn it. What's going on?"

He sags back in his seat and rubs his temples like a man getting a migraine. "I knew Kate a lot better than anyone knows."

Kate Townsend again? The sense of dislocation I felt in the boardroom was nothing compared to what I feel now. Again I see Drew sitting at the table, weeping as though for a family member. Even as I ask the next question, I pray that I'm wrong.

"Are you telling me you were intimate with the girl?"

Drew doesn't blink. "I was in love with her."

CHAPTER

2

My heart is pounding the way it does on the all-too-rare occasions when I run for exercise. I'm sitting in front of the St. Stephen's Preparatory School with one of the most distinguished alumni who ever attended it, and he's telling me he was screwing a high school student. A student who is now dead. This man is my lifelong friend, yet the first words that pass my lips are not those of a friend but of a lawyer. "Tell me she was eighteen, Drew."

"Her birthday was in two weeks."

I suck in my breath and close my eyes. "It might as well have been two years. That's statutory rape in Mississippi. Especially with the age difference between you. It's what, twenty years?"

"Almost twenty-three."

I shake my head in disbelief.

He takes my arm and pulls it toward him, forcing me to look into his eyes. "I'm not crazy, Penn. I know you think I've lost my mind, but I loved that girl like no one I've known in my life."

I look away, focusing on the playground of the middle school, where water has pooled on the merry-go-round. What to say? This isn't a case of some horny assistant coach who got too chummy with a cheerleader in the locker room. This is an educated and successful man in the grip of a full-blown delusion.

"Drew, I prosecuted a lot of child molesters in Houston. I remember one who had regularly molested an eleven-year-old girl. Can you guess what his defense was?"

"What?"

"They were in love."

He snorts with disdain. "You know this isn't like that."

"Do I? Jesus Christ, man."

"Penn . . . until you're in a situation like this, you simply can't understand it. I was the first to condemn that coach who got involved with that senior over at the public school. I couldn't fathom it then. But now . . . I see it from the inside."

"Drew, you've thrown your life away. Do you realize that? You could go to jail for twenty years. I can't even . . ." My voice fails, because it suddenly strikes me that I may not have heard the worst of what will be revealed in this car tonight. "You didn't kill her, did you?"

The blood drains from his face. "Are you out of your mind?"

"What did you expect me to ask?"

"Not *that*. And there's something pretty damned cold in your tone."

"If you don't like my tone, wait till you hear the district attorney. You and Kate Townsend? Holy *shit*."

"I didn't kill her, Penn."

I take another deep breath and let it out slowly. "No, of course not. Do you think she committed suicide?"

"Impossible."

"Why?"

"Because we were planning to leave together. Kate was excited about it. Not depressed at all."

"You were planning to run away together?"

"Not run away. But to be together, yes."

"She was a *kid*, Drew."

"In some ways. Not many. Kate had a different kind of upbringing. She went through a lot, and she learned a lot from it. She was very mature for her age, both psychologically and emotionally. And that's saying something these days. These kids aren't like we were, Penn. You have no idea. By fifteen they've gone through things you and I didn't experience until our twenties. Some of them are jaded by eighteen."

"That doesn't mean they understand what they're doing. But I'll be sure and run that argument past the jury."

Drew's eyes flicker. "Are you saying you'll represent me?"

"I was joking. Who else knows about this relationship?"

"No one."

"Don't be stupid. Someone always knows."

He sets his jaw and shakes his head with confidence. "You didn't know Kate. Nobody knows about us."

The naïveté of human beings is truly breathtaking. "Whatever you say."

Drew puts his big hands on the wheel and squeezes it like a man doing isometric exercises. In the small space of the car, his size is intimidating. I'm six-foot-one, two hundred pounds; Drew has two inches and twenty pounds of muscle on me, and he hasn't let himself slip much from the days he played tight end for Vanderbilt. It's not hard to imagine Kate Townsend being attracted to him.

"It comes down to this," Drew says in a steady voice. "The police are going to start probing Kate's life. And if they probe deeply enough, they might find something that connects me to her."

"Like what?"

"I don't know. A diary? Pictures?"

"You took pictures?" *Why am I asking? Of course they did. Everyone does now.* "Did you videotape yourselves too?"

"Kate did. But she destroyed the tape."

I'm not sure I believe this, but right now that's not the point. "What about Ellen?" I ask, meaning his wife.

His eyes don't waver. "Our marriage has been dead for ten years."

"You could have fooled me."

"I did. You and the rest of the town. Ellen and I mount a major theatrical production every day, all for the sake of Tim."

Tim is Drew's nine-year-old son, already something of a golden boy himself in the elementary school. Annie has a serious crush on him, though she would never admit it. "What about Tim, then? Were you going to leave him behind?"

"Of course not. But I had to make the break from Ellen first. I'll die if I stay in that marriage."

They always sound like this before the divorce. Any rationalization to get out of the marriage.

"I don't want to say anything negative about Ellen," Drew says softly. "But the situation has been difficult for a long time. Ellen's addicted to hydrocodone. She has been for six years."

Ellen Elliott is a lawyer who turned to real estate in her midthirties, a dynamo who focuses on the upscale antebellum mansions in town. Originally from Savannah, Georgia, she seems to have pulled off the rare trick of breaking into the inner cliques of Natchez society, something outsiders almost never accomplish. I've never known Ellen well, but the idea of her as a drug addict is hard to swallow. My mental snapshot is a sleek and well-tended blonde who runs marathons for fun.

"That's kind of hard for me to believe, Drew."

"You can't imagine Ellen popping Lorcet Plus like M&Ms? That's the reality, man. I've tried for years to help her. Taken her to addiction specialists, paid for rehab four times in the last three years. Nothing has worked."

"Is she clinically depressed?"

"I don't think so. You've seen her. She's wide open all the time. But there's something dark underneath that energy. Everything she does is in pursuit of money or social status. Two years ago she slept with a guy from Jackson during a tennis tournament. I literally can't believe she's the woman I married."

"Was she different when you married her? About the money and status, I mean?"

"I guess the seeds of that were there, but back then it just looked like healthy ambition. I should have seen it in her mother, though."

I can't help wanting to defend Ellen. "We all start turning into our parents, Drew. I'm sure you have been, too."

He nods. "Guilty as charged. But I try to stay self-aware, you know? I try to be the best person I can be."

And that led you to a seventeen-year-old girl? I have more questions, but the truth is, I don't want to know the gory details of Drew's personal life. I've heard too many drunk friends pour out the stories of how their lives fell short of their dreams, and it's always a maudlin monologue. The odd thing is that by almost anyone's estimation, Drew Elliott has led a dream life. But as my mother always said: *You never know what's cooking in someone else's pot.* And one thing is sure: whatever happens as a result of Kate Townsend's death, Drew Elliot's touchdown run through life has come to an end.

"I need to get home to Annie, Drew. Mia needs to leave."

He nods with understanding. "So, what about it? Will you help me?"

"I'll do what I can, but I'm not sure that's much. Let's see what happens tomorrow."

He nods and looks into his lap, clearly disappointed. "I guess that's the best I can hope for."

I'm about to get out of the car when Drew's cell phone rings. He looks at the LED screen and winces. "Jenny Townsend."

My chest tightens.

"She's going to want me to come by the house."

"Will you go?"

"Of course. I have to."

I shake my head in amazement. "How can you do it? How can you look Jenny in the eye tonight?"

Drew watches the phone until it stops ringing, then meets my eyes with the sincerity of a monk. "I've got a clear conscience, Penn. I loved Kate more than anyone on earth, except maybe her mother. And anyone who loved Kate is welcome in that house tonight."

Drew is both right and wrong. He will be welcome in the Townsend home tonight; in fact, of all the visitors, he will probably be the greatest comfort to Jenny. But what if Jenny Townsend knew that her personal physician had been having sex with her teenage daughter? That he was about to abandon his family and blow Kate's perfectly planned future to smithereens?

"I'll give you a call tomorrow," I say softly.

Drew catches hold of my forearm as I climb out, once more forcing me to look into his eyes. "I'm not out of my mind. It wasn't a midlife crisis that led me to Kate. I'd been starving for love for a long time. I've turned down more women in this town than you can imagine, both married and single. When I hurt my knee in that car accident last summer, I was home for six weeks. Kate was there every day, watching Tim. We started talking. I couldn't believe the things she talked about, the things she read. We e-mailed and IM-ed a lot at night, and it was like talking to a thirty-five-year-old woman. When I could walk again, I organized a medical mission trip to Honduras. Kate volunteered to come along. It was actually Ellen who suggested it. Anyway, that's where it happened. Before we returned to the States, I knew I wanted a life with her."

"She was seventeen, man. What kind of life could you have had with her?"

"An authentic life. She was only two weeks shy of eighteen, Penn, and she was going to Harvard in the fall. I've already taken the Massachusetts state medical boards. I scored in the top five percent. I've already put a deposit on a house in Cambridge."

I'm speechless.

"And now none of that will ever happen," Drew says, his face tight with anger and confusion. "Now someone has *murdered* her."

"You don't know it was murder."

His eyes narrow. "Yes, I do. It had to be."

I gently disengage my arm. "I'm sorry for your pain, man. I really am. But if it gets out that you were involved with Kate, you're going to be crucified. You'd better start—"

"I don't care about myself! It's Tim I'm worried about. What's the best thing I can do for him?"

I shake my head and open the door to the rain. "Pray for a miracle."

Mia Burke is sitting on the porch of my town house on Washington Street, a bulging green backpack beside her. I park by the curb, looking for Annie's smaller form, but then I see that the front door is open slightly, which tells me Annie is still sleeping and Mia is listening for her. Mia stands as I lock the car, and in the light of the streetlamp I see that, like Drew, she's been crying.

"You all right?" I ask, crossing the sidewalk.

She nods and wipes her cheeks. "I don't know why I'm crying so much. Kate and I weren't really close. It just seems like such a waste."

Mia Burke is the physical opposite of Kate Townsend. Dark-haired and olive-skinned, she stands about five-feet-two, with the muscular frame of a born sprinter. She has large dark eyes, an up-turned nose, and full lips that have probably sent a hundred adolescent boys into paroxysms of fantasy. She's wearing jeans and a LIFEHOUSE T-shirt, and she's holding a book in her hand: *The Sheltering Sky* by Paul Bowles. Mia has surprisingly eclectic taste, and this has probably confused the same boys who dream about her other attributes.

"You're right," I murmur, thinking of Drew with very little charity. "It is a waste."

"Did she commit suicide, Penn?"

It occurs to me that Mia's use of my first name might seem inappropriate to some people. It's always seemed a natural informality between us, but in light of what I now know about Drew and Kate, nothing seems innocent. "I don't know. Was Kate the type to kill herself?"

Mia hugs herself against the chill and takes some time with the question. "No. She always kept to herself a lot, especially this year. But I don't think she was depressed. Her boyfriend was giving her a lot of trouble, though."

"Kate had a boyfriend?"

"Well, an ex, really. Steve Sayers."

Steve Sayers, predictably, was the quarterback of the football team.

"I don't really know what the deal was. They dated for almost two years, then at the end of last summer Kate seemed to forget Steve existed."

Thanks to Drew Elliott, M.D. . . .

"The weird thing is, she didn't break up with Steve. She'd still go out with him, even when she obviously didn't care about him anymore. But she stopped having sex with him, I know that. And he was going crazy from it."

Mia's frankness about sex doesn't come out of the blue. We've had many frank conversations about what goes on beneath the surface at St. Stephen's. If it weren't for Mia's candor, I would have as little idea of the reality of a modern high school as the rest of the parents, and would be of as little use on the school board.

"Did Kate tell you she stopped having sex with him?" I ask.

"No. But Steve told a couple of his friends, and it got around. He thought she might be doing stuff with someone else. Someone from another school, maybe."

"What did you think?"

Mia bites her bottom lip. "Like I said, Kate was very private. She had this charming persona she could turn on, and most people bought into it. But that was just the mask she used to get through life. Deep down, she was somebody else."

"Who was she?"

"I'm not sure. All I know is that she was way too sophisticated for Steve. Maybe for any guy our age."

I look hard into Mia's eyes, but I see no hidden meaning there. "What made her so sophisticated?"

"Her time in England. After her parents got divorced, she went over to London and lived with her dad for a while. She went to an exclusive school over there for three years during junior high. In the end it didn't work out for her to stay, but when she got back here, she was way ahead of the rest of us. She was pretty intimidating with that English accent."

"I can't imagine you being intimidated."

"Oh, I was. But last year I started catching up with her. And this year I passed her in every subject. I feel guilty saying it now, but I felt pretty good about that."

Some of Drew's words are coming back to me. "You play tennis, don't you?"

"I'm on the team. I'm not as good as Kate. She was a machine.

She won state in singles last year, and she was on her way to doing it again this year."

"Didn't Kate play competitive tennis with Ellen Elliott?"

"Hell, yes. They won the state open in city league tennis."

"What do you think about Ellen?"

Mia's eyes flicker with interest. "Are you asking for the official line, or what I really think?"

"What you really think."

"She's a cast-iron bitch."

"Really?"

"Definitely. Very cold, very manipulative. How she treats you depends totally on who your parents are."

"How did she treat Kate?"

"Are you kidding? Like her personal protégée. Ellen was number one in Georgia when *she* played in high school. I think she's reliving her youth through Kate."

"How did Kate treat Ellen?"

Mia shrugs. "Okay, I guess. She was nice to her, but . . ."

"What?"

"I don't think Kate respected her. I heard her say things behind Ellen's back. But then everybody does that."

"What do you mean?"

"The women Ellen trains with for her marathons talk all kinds of shit about her when she's not around. They say she'll stab you in the back without thinking twice."

"So why do they hang around with her?"

"Fear. Envy. Ellen Elliott is hot, rich, and married to Dr. Perfect. She's the social arbiter of this place, in the under-forty crowd anyway. She has the life all the rest of them want."

"That's what they think."

Mia looks expectantly at me, but I don't elaborate.

"I think I know what you mean," she says. "I don't know what Dr. Elliott is doing married to her. No one does. He's so nice—not to mention hot—and she's so . . . I don't know. Maybe she fooled him, too."

"Maybe." Mia is too bright for me to question like this for long. "You probably need to get going, huh?"

She nods without enthusiasm. "I guess. I feel sort of weird, you know?"

"Because of Kate?"

"Yeah. But not the way you'd think. Her dying changes a lot of things for me. I'll be making the valedictory speech now, for one thing. And I wanted to do that. I have some things I want to say to our class, and to the parents. I didn't want to take any spotlight off of Kate by saying them in my salutatorian speech. Now I can say them, I guess. But I didn't want it like this."

"Well, you certainly earned it. Kate only beat you out by . . . what?"

"A sixteenth of a point on the cumulative." Mia smiles wryly. "She wasn't as smart as people think. She acted like she never studied, but she did. Big-time. I don't know why I'm telling you this. I guess I have some anger toward her. I'm not even sure why."

"Try to tell me."

Mia sighs and looks at the sidewalk. "Kate knew how to make you feel like shit when she wanted to. She would tear out your heart with a few words, then act like it was an innocent comment. She got Star Student because she outscored me by one point on the ACT, and she always made sure people knew that. But I outscored her by forty points on the SAT. You think she ever said one word about that?"

"What did you make?"

"Fifteen-forty."

"Wow. So you two were basically rivals, not friends."

Mia nods thoughtfully. "I'm more competitive than I should be, but for Kate, winning was an obsession. We were always the top contenders for everything. She was homecoming queen, I'm head cheerleader." A strange look crosses Mia's face. "I guess some people might say I had a motive for killing her, like that cheer-leader-mom thing in Texas."

"I don't think you have to worry about that. I've never heard anyone say a bad word about you."

An ironic laugh escapes her lips. "Oh, plenty gets said about me. But that's another story. And don't get me wrong about Kate.

She had a tough family life. Her dad was a real asshole. When she showed her vulnerable side, it was hard not to feel for her. Especially for me. But I had to deal with the same shit, and I don't use my intelligence to hurt people."

Mia gazes down Washington Street, one of the most beautiful in the city, and shakes her head as though dismissing some useless thought. Mia's father left her mother when Mia was two, and he's hardly seen his daughter since. Economic support was the bare minimum dictated by the courts, and even that came on a sporadic basis.

"As far as Kate dying," Mia says, "I guess I can't really believe it yet. It just doesn't make sense. It's so *random*."

"High school kids die in accidents like everyone else."

"I know, but this is different."

"Why?"

"After I called you, I got a few more calls. People are saying it wasn't an accident at all. They're saying somebody killed Kate. Did you know that?"

Could Drew be right? "Why are they saying that?"

"Some of the nurses at the hospital said it looked like Kate was strangled and hit on the head."

Despite my friendship with Drew, an image of him choking Kate fills my mind, and I shudder. "You know Natchez and gossip, Mia. Anything could have happened to Kate's body while she was floating down that creek."

"But why was she half naked? And why from the waist down? I suppose she could have been skinny-dipping, but with who? She wasn't with Steve—or at least he claims she wasn't. It makes me wonder if maybe Steve was right."

At this point Kate's classmates probably know twice as much about her death as the police department. "Right about what?"

"About Kate having another boyfriend. Someone none of us knew about. Someone who might get mad enough or crazy enough to kill her."

"Can you see Kate making someone that angry?"

"Oh, yeah. When Kate got on her high horse, she could piss you off beyond belief. And as far as making someone crazy—a guy, I mean—she was a very sexual person. We talked a few times about it. She really thought she might be a nymphomaniac."

"That term isn't even used anymore, Mia. A lot of girls first experimenting with sex probably feel that way."

She gives me a knowing look. "I'm not talking about experimentation. I'm no saint, okay? But Kate knew about things I'd never even heard of. She was as intense as any person I ever met, and she believed in giving herself pleasure. She, uh, this is kind of embarrassing, but she showed me a couple of toys once, and it shocked me. I know she freaked Steve out with some of the things she asked him to do, and that was over a year ago."

Sex toys? Drew's words come back to me with fresh impact: *These kids aren't like we were, Penn. You have no idea . . .*

"I know you want to look in on Annie," Mia says, picking up her backpack and slinging it over her shoulder. "I'll get out of your hair. Sorry if I was too frank about that stuff."

I step to my left and give her plenty of room to pass. "Don't worry. I've seen just about everything in my day."

She gives me a sly look that belies her age. "Have you? I figured you for a straight arrow. I asked my mom about you, but she won't tell me anything. She obviously likes you, but she gets all cryptic when I bring you up."

I feel myself flush. "Be careful driving. Your mind's not going to be on the road."

Mia takes her cell phone from her purse and holds it to her ear. It must have been set to vibrate. "She did? . . . No way . . . That's just *weird* . . . I will. Later." She puts the phone back in her purse and stares blankly up the street again.

"What is it?" I ask.

Mia's eyes betray a puzzlement I've never seen in them before. "That was Laura Andrews. Her mom's one of the nurses who tended to Kate. She just told Laura that Kate was raped."

"*What?*"

"She said Kate had a lot of trauma—down there, you know?"

My thoughts return to Drew. If Kate was raped, I hope he never has to know it. But of course he will, like everyone else in town. It suddenly occurs to me that by hoping to protect Drew from this knowledge, I'm assuming he is innocent of the crime. That's a dangerous assumption for any lawyer to make, but I've already made it. I simply cannot imagine Drew Elliott raping any woman, much less a high school girl.

"Let's hope that's not true," I murmur, recalling the shattered rape victims I tried to avenge as a prosecutor in Houston.

"Yeah," Mia echoes. "That's too horrible even to think about."

"So don't. Think about driving."

Mia forces a smile. "No worries. Do you need me tomorrow?"

"I may, if you can spare the time." I'm thinking of Drew and his request for help.

"Just call my cell."

She walks to her car, a blue Honda Accord, and climbs in. I watch to make sure she gets safely away, then walk up the steps into my house. As I close the door, my study phone rings. I trot to my desk and look at the caller ID: ANDREW ELLIOTT, M.D.

"Drew?" I answer.

"Can you talk?" he asks, his voice crackling with anxiety.

"Sure. What is it?"

"I'm at Kate's house. I just got a call on my cell phone."

"From who?"

"I don't know. But he told me to leave a gym bag with twenty thousand dollars in it on the fifty-yard line of the St. Stephen's football field. He said if I don't, he'll tell the police I was screwing Kate Townsend."

Shit. "You told me nobody knew about the affair."

"Nobody did. I have no idea who this could be."

My mind is whirling with memories of similar situations when I worked for the D.A. in Houston. "When does he want the money?"

"One hour from now."

CHAPTER

3

"Penn?" Drew says, breathing shallowly. "Are you there?"

My old friend's words have paralyzed me in the study of my house. "Twenty thousand dollars cash in an *hour*? At nine o'clock at night? That's crazy. That's impossible."

"No, it's not. I have the cash. We have a safe here in the house. Three, actually. One for documents, one for guns, one for cash and jewelry."

I should have guessed. Drew Elliott lives in a stunning Victorian palace sited on five acres in one of the affluent subdivisions near St. Stephen's, a mansion that contains every technological gadget known to man. "Do you think the blackmailer knows that?"

"He said he knew I had the money."

"Did you recognize the voice?"

"No. But it sounded like a black kid."

"A black kid? Are you sure?"

"Pretty sure. He asked for drugs, too."

"*Drugs?*"

"Prescription drugs. Painkillers. Anything I have. He said I should consider this drop as a down payment. His words. A sign of good faith."

"I hear something in your voice I don't like, Drew."

"I know what you're going to say, but—"

"You're not delivering that money, brother. You have two choices. Ignore the call, or phone the police and tell them everything right now."

Drew is silent for too long. "There's a third choice," he says.

"Drew, listen to me. There is no upside to paying this money. Just by showing up, you'd be admitting some guilt. You could also be taking your life into your hands."

"Because the caller could be Kate's killer? That's what you were thinking, right?"

He has me. "I guess so."

"That's what I'm thinking, too."

"Then you should call the cops. At this point, an act of God couldn't keep your affair with Kate from becoming public. You have to think damage control now. It's a hundred times better if the police learn the story from you than from someone else. Better for your family, too. Think of Tim."

"I have until tomorrow morning to make that decision."

"Don't assume that."

"Penn, the guy who called me probably murdered Kate. I want to see his face. I want to—"

"I know what you want to do. Forget it. Go home, mix yourself a stiff drink, and start thinking about what's best for your son. That ought to be a change."

Drew sucks in air as though I've knocked the wind out of him. "I know Tim needs me, okay?"

"You haven't been acting like you do. Tim would be lost without you. And if you really think Ellen isn't a good person, that's twice the reason to keep yourself out of jail."

More silence. "You're right. Goddamn it, I just need to do *something* about Kate."

"There's nothing you can do. It's time to suck it up and be a man. Kate's beyond help. She's gone. All you can do now is pick up the pieces of your own family."

"*Daddy?*" comes a small voice.

Glancing toward the hall, I see my daughter poke her head around the kitchen door frame. Annie is a physical echo of her mother, a tawny-haired beauty with eyes that miss nothing. This is both a blessing and a curse, as I am continually confronted by what is essentially the ghost of my dead wife.

"Annie's calling me, Drew. I need to go. You go home and calm down. I'll call you in a bit and we'll decide what you're going to do."

Silence.

"Drew?"

"I will."

"How's Jenny handling it?"

"It's destroyed her. I had to sedate her. She ought to be asleep soon."

"Jesus . . . okay. I'll talk to you later."

By the time I hang up, Annie is standing in front of me, her cheek pressing into my stomach. The one eye that I can see is full of sleep. She yawns, then says, "Where's Mia?"

"Mia had to go home, Boo."

"Aww. Mia's fun."

"I know. She'll probably be back tomorrow. She said you fell asleep during the movie."

"I guess I did. I already knew what was going to happen. Are you going to call Caitlin tonight?"

"Probably."

"Will you do it now?"

"Let's get you in the bed first. Then she can tell you good night."

Annie smiles, then tugs me toward the stairs. I follow, but she stops at the base of the staircase. "Will you carry me, Daddy?"

"Nine years old? You're pretty big to get carried these days."

"You can do it."

Yes, I can, I say silently, for some reason thinking of Annie's mother. Sarah will never carry her child up the stairs again. An ache passes through my chest, like the pain from an old wound, and then I sweep Annie up into my arms and march up the steep staircase to the second-floor bedrooms. The old Victorians in Natchez have stairs seemingly designed to keep pro athletes in peak condition. I turn into Annie's room, bend my creaking knees enough to pull back the covers, then slide her underneath them. She laughs and yanks the blanket up to her neck.

"Now call Caitlin!" she squeals.

I take my cell phone from my pocket and speed-dial Caitlin's cell phone. She's working a special assignment in Boston, as an investigative reporter for the *Herald*. I met Caitlin when her father, a newspaper magnate who owns the *Natchez Examiner* and ten other papers in a Southern chain, sent her down here to whip the *Examiner* into shape. We got close during my efforts to solve a decades-old civil rights murder and during the trial that followed. Caitlin grew to love Natchez—and me—but after the excitement of that trial faded, along with the glow of the Pulitzer she won for her stories covering it, she realized that Natchez might not be the most exciting place to spend your days, especially when you're under thirty and hungry for challenges.

After a year of living next door to Annie and me, Caitlin began taking assignments in other cities, mostly working on investigative stories for other papers in her father's chain. We've remained committed to each other, and to our plan of marrying one day. But following through with that plan would mean changes that Caitlin isn't ready to handle yet. Annie would begin to see Caitlin more as a mother, and would expect her to be around much more consistently. Caitlin has asked me about moving to a city—after all, I lived in Houston for fifteen years—but to my surprise, I find myself reluctant to leave the town where I grew to adulthood.

Caitlin's phone kicks me to voice mail. "This is Penn and Annie," I say. "We're trying to get a long-distance good-night kiss. Call us when you can."

"Voice mail," I tell Annie, trying to sound unconcerned. "She must be working."

"You should hurry up and marry her," Annie says. "Then she can be my real mom. Then she can live here."

I can't help but feel some resentment. When the *Herald* offered Caitlin a plum assignment investigating further sexual abuse in the archdiocese of Boston, she almost turned it down. The job meant at least two months away from Natchez, and though we talked about flying to see each other on weekends, we knew that probably wouldn't work out. But the offer came from a renowned editor for whom Caitlin had worked as an intern while at Radcliffe, and I sensed that if she said no, she would eventually resent it. I'm glad she took the assignment, but our fears about visiting have proved true. The sum of our recent contact? I've flown to Boston once, and she flew down to Baton Rouge for a weekend with Annie and me.

"She works this late?" Annie asks.

Lately it's become more and more difficult to reach Caitlin at night. "It's not that late for grown-ups. Maybe she's working undercover."

"Yeah, she does that sometimes," Annie says thoughtfully. "Like a spy."

"Yep. Now, shut those eyes."

Annie opens her eyes as wide as possible, then giggles like a two-year-old.

I poke her in the side. "You're a pain in the you-know-what."

More giggles. I give her a kiss, then walk into the hall and descend the long staircase. "See you in the morning!" I call.

"Not if I see you first!" she yells back.

In the kitchen, I raid the refrigerator and construct a colossal turkey po'boy. I only had a salad before the school board meeting, and I'm starving. To keep my mind off Drew and his problems I click on CNN, but there's no escaping. CNN makes me think of Caitlin, and thoughts of Caitlin bring me back to Drew.

The essential problem that has kept Caitlin and me from marrying is our age difference. At thirty-three, she is very much in the midst of proving herself in her chosen profession, which requires her to leave Natchez often. At forty-three, I've already succeeded in two different careers, and the only thing I have left to prove is that I can raise my daughter well. Having endured the problems that come with a ten-year age difference, I can't help but view Drew's dream of a real life with Kate as absurd. Did he plan to divorce Ellen and commute by air between Natchez and Boston in order to see Tim? He couldn't have continued practicing medicine in Natchez. The local society women would have risen as one to boycott his practice and ostracize the former darling of St. Stephen's Prep. How would Drew have introduced Kate to fellow doctors in Boston? *This is my wife. She just graduated—from high school.* Of course, Drew wasn't concerned about such mundane matters. He loved Kate, and the rest of the world could go to hell.

But now the world may have its way with him. As the CNN anchor reads a litany of global crises, I make a list of the threats Drew faces. First, statutory rape. Given the age difference between him and Kate, he could get twenty years in Parchman prison. And since Kate was his patient, he could lose his medical license. Even if he doesn't, the mere rumor of such an affair in Natchez could kill his practice. If Kate was raped, and physical evidence links Drew to her corpse, he could be charged with capital murder for homicide during the commission of another felony. In Mississippi, conviction for capital murder brings with it the very real possibility of death by lethal injection.

If Kate was in fact murdered, the police have a tough job ahead of them. By carrying her body to the emergency room rather than leaving it where they found it, the fishermen who found Kate deprived investigators of any chance to examine her body in situ. They might have lost or destroyed critical evidence. And since Kate was found wedged in the fork of a tree during high water, the actual crime scene is probably upstream somewhere along St. Catherine's Creek. With today's heavy rain, the police may never find out where she actually died.

Right now, detectives are probably focusing on the "helpful" fishermen, since these Samaritans may well have raped and killed Kate before taking her to the hospital. St. Catherine's Creek has never been noted for its fishing, and it's quite dangerous for boats during heavy rains. After interrogating the fishermen, the police will move on to Kate's mother, her boyfriend, and any close friends who might have information about her last hours. That could take much of the night, and will probably continue through tomorrow. If the blackmailer didn't exist—and if Drew is right about Kate not confiding their affair to anyone—Drew might just be safe.

But the blackmailer does exist, and my experience as a prosecutor tells me it's unlikely that Drew will escape entanglement in this case. If he had sex with Kate in the last seventy-two hours, she may have traces of his semen inside her. A phone call from the blackmailer to the police would focus their attention on Drew. Any confirming piece of evidence linking Drew to Kate in an inappropriate way would prompt police to request a DNA sample from him. That would bring disaster in three to four weeks—the time it usually takes to get the DNA results in a rush situation. And when the police start searching upstream in St. Catherine's Creek for the murder scene, they will eventually come to the bend where the two most exclusive subdivisions in Natchez come together. One of those subdivisions—Pinehaven—is where Kate Townsend lived. The other—just across the creek and through the woods—is Sherwood Estates, where Drew Elliot's Victorian mansion stands. In the absence of other evidence, this juxtaposition might not suggest anything, but if the blackmailer gets the rumor mill churning . . .

The microwave clock tells me forty minutes have passed since I last spoke to Drew. Feeling a little anxious, I pick up the kitchen phone and call his cell phone. He doesn't answer. I wait about a minute, then try again. Nothing. I hate to call his wife, given all that I've learned about their marriage, but I need to know that Drew is safely drunk somewhere, and not on his way to the St. Stephen's football field with a bag of cash.

"Hello?" says a groggy female voice.

"Ellen? It's Penn Cage."

"Penn? What's going on? Is Drew with you?"

I knew it. "No, I was actually calling for him."

"Well"—loud snuffling, rustling of cloth—"I thought I heard him pull up outside a while ago, but then he didn't come in. Maybe he's out in his workshop. He goes out there sometimes when he's feeling moody."

"Is there any way to check without you having to get up?"

"Intercom. Just a sec." There's a burst of static. "Drew? Drew, are you out there?"

More static. "He's not answering. He called a while ago and told me he was leaving the Townsends' house. Maybe he got called to the hospital on his way home. I think he's covering tonight."

"That's probably it. You get back to sleep, Ellen."

"Sleep. God . . . I had to take a pill to even have a chance at sleep. I was really close to Kate, you know."

"I knew you played tennis with her."

"That girl was gifted, Penn. I think she would have made the team at Harvard. God, wouldn't that have been something?"

"Yes, it would. I'm sorry, Ellen."

I hear a sound I can't identify. "We raise these children," she murmurs, "we pour everything into them, all our hopes and dreams, and then something like this happens. If I were Jenny Townsend, I'm not sure I could handle it. I might do something crazy. I really might."

"Well, I hope she finds the strength to deal with it."

"It's good to talk to you, Penn. We don't see you enough. You should come by for a drink. I really liked your last book. I want to talk to you about some of the characters. I think I recognized a few."

I give Ellen an obligatory laugh and ring off. *Where the hell is Drew?* I'm afraid I already know the answer. I start to dial my parents' house, but it's too late to ask my mother to come over. Instead, I dial Mia's cell. She answer after two rings.

"Penn?"

"Afraid so. Is there any chance you could come back for about an hour? Annie's asleep, but I need to go out."

"Um, I guess so. Is it important? Of course it is. You wouldn't call if it weren't."

"Are you with your friends now?"

"Such as they are. Everybody's pretty freaked out. But I'm not far away from you, actually. I can be there in five minutes."

"Thanks. I'll pay you double your usual rate."

"You don't have to do that. I'm on my way."

I hang up and walk back to my bedroom, the only one on the ground floor of the house. In the top of my closet is a nine-millimeter Springfield XD-9 with a fifteen-round clip. I carried a .38-caliber revolver in Houston, but recent experience taught me the wisdom of having a large magazine. I keep the weapon close, albeit with a trigger lock to protect Annie. Unlocking the guard mechanism, I slip the pistol barrel into the pocket of my jeans and grab a waterproof windbreaker from the closet.

Waiting on the front steps for Mia, I call Drew's cell phone again. When he fails to answer, I consider calling the police for help—but only for a moment. The risks to Drew are too great. When Mia pulls up to the curb, I give her a wave and walk to my Saab, hoping to avoid any explanations.

"Everything okay?" she calls.

I turn back to her. "Fine. Annie's still in bed. I just need to run an errand."

Mia nods, but I see suspicion in her eyes. I've never called her on such short notice before.

"What else have the kids been saying?" I ask.

"All kinds of things. But it's mostly bullshit. You know how people are. Like you said . . . Natchez."

"I should be back in less than an hour, but if I'm not, you can stay, right?"

"I'll be here when you get back."

I move toward my car. "I really appreciate it, Mia."

"Is that a gun in your pants?"

I look down. The butt of the Springfield is sticking up in front of my windbreaker.

Mia isn't looking at the pistol but at me, her eyes questioning. I start to give her an explanation, but nothing would really make sense. As casually as possible, I pull the tail of the windbreaker over the gun.

"Penn, are you okay?"

"Yes. Mia, you—"

"I didn't see anything," she says, her face radiating assurance. "I'm sure you know what you're doing."

If only that were true. "Keep a close eye on Annie."

"I will. Bye." She turns and hurries into the house.

I climb into my Saab and start the engine, wondering what kind of insanity I'll find when I reach St. Stephen's.

CHAPTER

4

Buck Stadium was called simply "the bowl" when I was a student at St. Stephen's, and the reason was plain. Back then, the stadium was only an oval hole in the ground surrounded by pine and hardwood trees. Spectators sat on its grassy sides to cheer during Bucks games, until enough money was raised to build rudimentary bleachers. Tonight three new school buildings stand on the south side of the bowl, and wide concrete steps march all the way down to the field. The bleachers are massive prefab units like those at college football stadiums, and huge banks of overhead lights can turn night into day at the flick of a switch. Fancy dressing rooms and a workout center stand on a terraced shelf halfway down the hill, and a blue rubberized track surrounds the football field. The year we fought our way to the state football championship, Drew and I practiced in a cow pasture filled with holes and played under dim "security lights" like the ones in supermarket parking lots.

Despite all the improvements, there's still only one narrow access road to the bottom of the bowl, which is probably why the blackmailer chose the football field to pick up his payoff. He can easily detect the approach of any police vehicles, and the surrounding woods offer infinite avenues of escape, once he crosses the Cyclone fence that surrounds the track.

I cut my headlights as I climb the main driveway of the campus, then park on the south side of the elementary school to remain hidden from the eyes of anyone in the bowl. With the Springfield weighting my right front pocket, I walk quietly along the side of the building toward the bowl.

Standing in the shadows beside the building is a Honda ATV, commonly called a four-wheeler in this area. The camouflage paint scheme, Vanderbilt bumper sticker, and gun boot mounted on the handlebars mark this four-wheeler as Drew Elliot's. Like most men in and around Natchez, Drew is an avid hunter. The only good news is that the gun boot contains a Remington deer rifle, which means Drew probably didn't go armed to deliver his payoff to the fifty-yard line below.

Twenty yards from the elementary school, the ground drops precipitously into the bowl. Transecting that space is the asphalt road that curves down to the track. Staying in the shadows by Drew's four-wheeler, I try his cell phone one last time.

There's no answer, but for a moment I think I hear the chirp of a ringing cell phone. Crouching low, I scuttle to the edge of the bowl and look down. It's like staring at a bottomless black lake. The light from the security lamps mounted on the stadium's press box dies after only a few yards. Whatever is happening on the floor of the bowl, I can't see it.

As I stare into the blackness, the whine of a small engine rises out of the hole. The whine seems to be coming toward me. Then a single headlight flicks on, cutting a bright swath down the length of the football field. Sitting at midfield is a small gym bag.

Where the hell is Drew?

What sounds like hoofbeats suddenly rises out of the bowl, followed by the sound of panting. I'm reaching for my Springfield when Drew's face appears out of the dark. He pulls up short, his eyes filled with shock.

"Penn? Come on!"

He races past me to the four-wheeler. Far below, the motorcycle stops beside the gym bag.

"What are you doing here?" Drew calls over his shoulder.

"Trying to keep your ass out of trouble!" I answer, dividing my attention between the distant motorcycle and Drew.

He cranks the ATV with a rumble, kicks it into gear, and lurches up beside me. "You can help me or you can stand here with your thumb up your ass," he says. "You've got three seconds to decide."

A high-pitched revving echoes out of the bowl, and then suddenly the headlight is tearing away from us again, back in the direction from which it came. Certain that nothing will dissuade Drew from pursuit, I hike my leg over the seat and clamp my arms around his waist. He hits the throttle, and the Honda flies over the lip of the bowl, descending as though in free fall.

"This is nuts!" I yell in his ear. "You know that!"

He grabs something from his pocket and holds it over his shoulder until I take it. It looks like a small kaleidoscope.

"What's this?"

"Night-vision scope! If he kills his headlight, keep that scope on him!"

Night vision? Why am I surprised? This is exactly the kind of useless toy that your affluent Mississippi hunter possesses. "Did you recognize the guy on the motorcycle?"

"He's wearing a helmet with a black visor. Gloves, too, so I don't know if he's black or white."

We hit the floor of the bowl with a bone-jarring impact, then zoom across the track onto the football field. A hundred yards ahead, the motorcycle slows to a near stop. He must be negotiating an opening in the Cyclone fence. Drew guns the ATV, and we hurtle up the football field at fifty miles an hour.

"What are you going to do if you catch him?"

"Ask some questions!" Drew shouts, pushing the Honda still harder. "Find out what he knows!"

The rest of Drew's words are lost in the roar of wind past my ears as we race toward the end of the bowl.

"Look!" he shouts, pointing at the almost stationary headlight. "We've got him!"

The smaller engine whines like a chainsaw, and then the headlight begins moving jerkily uphill.

"Fuck!" bellows Drew.

Suddenly the entire bowl is blasted by white light, as though God ripped back the night sky to expose a hidden sun. In the blinding light I see a narrow gap cut in the Cyclone fence. Drew steers toward it.

"You can't make it!" I scream, realizing the hole was cut for a motorcycle to pass through. *"Don't do it!"*

Drew jolts across the track with abandon, then—realizing he can't break the laws of physics—hits the brakes, throwing the Honda into a skid. The ass end of the four-wheeler spins forward, and suddenly it's me who's most likely to slam into the fence. But the grass is slick from rain. We spin once more, and then the front bumper of the ATV just kisses the loose wire of the Cyclone fence.

"Come on, baby," Drew pleads, trying to restart the engine, which died during the skid.

"Give it up, man. Let him go."

As the rattle of the motorcycle grows fainter, the steel fence post beside me sings as though struck by a hammer. Almost instantly that sound merges into a deafening boom that echoes around the bowl like cannon fire. Only then do I realize that the supersonic crack of the rifle bullet escaped me altogether. For a moment I wonder whether, despite the evidence of my eyes, Drew has drawn and fired his deer rifle at the fleeing motorcyclist. But he hasn't.

"Somebody's shooting at us!" I yell, clapping him on the shoulder.

"No shit!" he grunts, finally cranking the Honda to life. "Get off and hold the fence back!"

As I dismount the ATV, a second rifle shot blasts across the bowl. Drew yanks his own rifle from the boot and shoves it into my hands. "You know where the switch is? For the stadium lights?"

I nod blankly.

"Shoot back! Sooner or later, that asshole's going to hit one of us."

I scramble through the gap in the fence, move to the side of the opening, then lay the rifle barrel through one of the diamond-shaped holes in the fence and sight in on the staircase at the base of the press box. The switch box is mounted on the wall just above it. I see no one there, and I'm glad for it.

As Drew tries to bull the Honda through the gap in the fence, I draw a bead on the metal circuit box that contains the light switches. The Remington bucks against my shoulder three times before the blazing lights go dark.

"Get on!" Drew yells, the four-wheeler suddenly beside me in the darkness.

I shove his rifle back into the gun boot and climb onto the seat behind him, shocked by my exhilaration at having neutralized the threat from above. But the greatest threat to my safety probably wasn't the shooter in the stadium; it's the man whose waist I'm clinging to in the dark.

There's no path through the trees, but this doesn't deter Drew. He accelerates up the incline like a whiskey-crazed redneck in a mud-riding contest, dodging pines and briar thickets with inches to spare. As we crest the first hill, I feel the front wheels rise off the ground, and for a second I'm sure the Honda is about to flip backward and crush us, a manner of death all too common in Mississippi. But Drew stands erect and leans over the handlebars, restoring enough equilibrium for us to ramp over the hill and land in one piece on the other side.

To my surprise, he brakes to a stop and switches off the headlight. Now we face a darkness so deep, it makes the bowl seem hospitable by comparison. This is the darkness of the primeval forest.

"You'll never catch him," I say softly.

"Shhh," says Drew, killing the motor. "Listen."

Sure enough, somewhere below us and to our left I hear the faint protest of a small engine being pushed hard.

"He's running the creek bed," whispers Drew.

Drew is probably right, but that's no great help. "He could come up out of that creek in a dozen different neighborhoods," I point out. "We'll never get him now."

"Watch," says Drew, cranking the Honda again.

I hug him tight and clench my thighs around the seat as he flicks on the headlight and plunges down the hillside. He must have hunted these woods before. There's no other explanation for the speed with which he navigates the forest in the dark. We fly along one ridge as though pursued by the devil, then plunge down an almost perpendicular drop and splash into swiftly running water.

After struggling through the stream for a dozen yards, we climb onto a gravel-covered sandbar and race along the creek bed. All I can do at this point is hang on and pray that Drew knows where he's going.

Twice more I'm doused by creek water, but then I hear a whoop of triumph as he sights a solitary taillight ahead. Somehow—I can only assume it's because of superior knowledge of the terrain— Drew is closing the gap between us and the motorcycle. The note of the Honda's engine climbs in pitch as he pushes the ATV to its limit.

"Easy!" I shout. "You've got him now!"

"He's seen us! He's speeding up. If I push him, he might wreck."

"*We* might wreck!"

In thirty frantic seconds, Drew closes the gap to twenty-five yards. The taillight disappears as the motorcycle whips around a bend, but three seconds later we round it, too, and I sight the light again.

Suddenly the darkness gives way to a plain of white sand shining in the moonlight. The creek is a black snake slithering over it, and somehow the motorcyclist has reached the opposite side of that snake. Drew aims the Honda at the narrowest part of the stream. Instinct tells me this is a mistake, since shallows tend to be broad while narrows indicate deep-cut channels. But this is Drew's home ground, not mine. As the motorcycle escapes over the sand, Drew punches the gas, and we hit the narrows at thirty miles an hour.

It's like plowing into a guardrail. The rear end of the Honda flies over my shoulders, and the next thing I know, I'm sucking water and clawing mud. Knowing that the sinking four-wheeler could pin me to the creek bottom, I scrabble over the slime and burst up into the air.

I see no sign of Drew or the four-wheeler, only a cloud of steam rising from the water behind me. Diving back beneath the surface, I feel my way to the overturned vehicle and burn my forearm on the exhaust pipe. Then my hand closes on a bulging calf. Drew is pinned beneath the ATV.

Struggling around to the upstream side of the Honda, I plant both feet firmly on the creek bottom, then squat and grab the handlebars. Hoping the current will function like a second person, I heave upward and lunge downstream with all my strength.

The ATV rises about a foot, then stops.

I redouble my efforts, but the weight of the engine is just too much. As my back starts to give way, the main current of the creek suddenly lifts the ATV out of my hands and carries it several yards downstream. I fall and float behind it for a couple of seconds. Then I get my feet under me and turn, expecting Drew to break the surface.

He doesn't.

"Drew!"

Nothing but the sound of water.

I know a guy who snapped both femurs in a four-wheeler accident exactly like this one. And Drew took the brunt of the impact when we hit the creek. The water's not much more than four feet deep here, but the current is strong. If Drew was knocked unconscious, he could be thirty yards downstream already.

I take a deep breath and go to the bottom, then let the current carry me along. In less than ten seconds I collide with the ATV again. It's being dragged sluggishly down the creek. I'm feeling my way around it when a strong hand grabs my shirt and pulls me to the surface.

Drew looks wildly at me, his eyes white with fear. "Jesus, I thought you were hurt bad!"

"I was looking for you!"

His face is half covered with blood, most of it flowing from a cut above his eye. There's blood on his chest, too.

"Are you okay?" I ask.

He nods, then looks off into the woods. "That bastard got away, though."

Just as with Annie when she does something dangerous, my fear turns to fury as soon as I know Drew is all right. "What kind of juvenile bullshit was that? God*damn* it! You act like you're still in high school. *Junior* high!"

His head is cocked as though he's still listening for the motorcycle.

"He's gone!" I rail. "Your money's gone, too. And you damn near killed us to pay the bastard!"

Drew looks back at me, his eyes glinting with dark light. "I don't care."

"Why not?"

"Because that motherfucker killed Kate."

I start to argue, but something stops me. Maybe it's the strange light in his eyes. Or maybe it's the realization that he truly risked our lives to catch the guy on the motorcycle, something the Drew Elliott I know would not normally do. He's never been a hothead; he's a logical and intelligent man.

"How do you know the blackmailer is the killer, Drew?"

"Because he was there when Kate died. That's how he knows about us."

At the sound of certainty in Drew's voice, a new stillness settles over me. "How do you know he was there?"

Drew finally turns full on to me. His eyes are slits in the dark, his lips compressed. He looks like a man deciding whether or not to tell a priest the darkest secret of his life.

"Because I was the one who found Kate's body."

CHAPTER

5

Drew makes me wait until we have wrestled his four-wheeler out of the creek and stripped half the thing down before he'll tell me anything about finding Kate. He's one of those rare white-collar guys who actually knows how to fix things. He approaches machines with the same familiarity that he does the human body. Now he stands beside the steaming ATV, waiting for the air intake box to drain and the carburetor to dry. I'm sitting on a rotten log nearby, trying to catch my breath.

"All right, start talking," I snap.

He walks away from me and stares up the hill that the motorcycle disappeared over. With his rifle slung over his shoulder, he looks like a marine standing guard in some lost jungle. My Springfield is gone; it must have fallen out of my pocket at some point during our charge through the woods. Drew has promised to find or replace it, but at this moment a lost pistol is not my highest priority. I want to know what he held back from me earlier tonight.

"It was this afternoon," he says, still looking off into the dark. "Whatever led to Kate's death started this afternoon."

I remain silent, leaving him to fill the vacuum. I hope he doesn't take long. It's about fifty degrees, but with the wind hitting my wet clothes, it feels like deep winter.

"Kate was late getting her period," Drew says softly. "Only five days, but she was usually as regular as clockwork. She was worried."

So Drew has been sleeping with Kate for several months at least.

"I told her to buy a home pregnancy test, but she didn't want to. The truth is, I think she sort of hoped she was pregnant."

"Why?"

He turns to me, but his expression is indistinct in the moonlight. "Because that would have forced everything to a head. If she was pregnant, all would have been decided. She wouldn't have got an abortion. I would have asked Ellen for a divorce, and—"

"Would Ellen have given you a divorce?"

"I think so. It would have cost me dearly, but it would have been worth it."

"Go on."

"I was supposed to meet Kate tonight, after Ellen went to sleep. That's usually when we'd meet, during the week. She'd slip across the creek and come over to my workshop."

"Jesus."

"It was pretty safe, actually. Ellen never goes out there. She just calls on the intercom. Anyway, for some reason Kate couldn't wait until tonight."

"Maybe she took that pregnancy test after all."

He nods thoughtfully. "Maybe so."

"What did she do this afternoon?"

"She sent me a text message on my cell phone. It said, 'I really need to see you. The creek or the cemetery.' "

"The cemetery?"

"The city cemetery was our backup place. The creek meant St. Catherine's Creek. We met there a lot in the beginning, at the bend between Sherwood Estates and Pinehaven."

"You used cell phones to communicate?"

"Never directly. She sent me that message from a computer—

probably one at St. Stephen's. There was no traceable link to her cell phone."

Sherwood Estates and Pinehaven, the two most expensive subdivisions within the city limits. At the rear of each, wooded bluffs drop down to muddy, cane-covered flats that border the creek. During heavy rains, the creek rises several feet in hours and becomes a fifty-foot-wide torrent filled with logs and other debris.

"Kate would take her dog down there like she was exercising him," Drew says. "I'd just jog down there. If we needed to talk during the day, it was a good place."

"During the *day*? You're nuts. Why not just get her a cell phone in your name, or something like that?"

Drew shakes his head. "Too dangerous. In the past couple of months, I've had the feeling Ellen might be having me followed. It's very easy to eavesdrop on cell phones, and you can monitor their GPS position simply by calling a company that specializes in that. No warrant required."

"Okay. Go on."

"I don't know how long Kate was waiting at the creek. I got the text message at my office. It was time-stamped one fifty-four p.m. She was almost certainly at school then. She probably left the building at three. I left my office at three-thirty. It took me ten or twelve minutes to get down to the creek, I guess. I didn't park at home, because I was impatient. I parked at the back of an empty lot in Pinehaven and came in from the south."

"Did anybody see you?"

"I don't think so."

"But they could have. The blackmailers, for example. They could have seen your car and followed you."

"Maybe. But I don't think so. You can't see the back of that lot from the street."

I motion for him to continue.

Drew's voice drops in volume, forcing me to strain to hear him. "I saw her from forty yards away. She was lying on the creek bank with her head trailing in an eddy of water. I told myself it couldn't be her. My mind totally rejected the visual evidence. Cognitive dissonance, I think it's called. But at some level I knew. I sprinted up to her and looked down, and I just . . . she'd been wearing her tennis outfit. Her Izod shirt and sports bra had been pushed up to her neck, but she was naked from the waist down. There was fresh blood on the side of her head . . . petechiae around her eyes. I cradled her head and—"

Drew covers his mouth with one hand, unable to go on. A muffled sob comes from his throat. Then he speaks in a monotonic voice. "Her eyes were wide open, glassy, the pupils fixed and dilated. I was sure she was dead, but I tried to resuscitate her anyway. I gave her CPR for ten minutes, but I couldn't get a heartbeat."

"You didn't call 911?"

"I'd left my cell phone in my car."

I wonder if this is true. "Would you have called for help if you'd had it?"

"Hell, yes!"

"Was she still warm?"

Drew goes still. "Yes."

"Okay. So you knew she was dead. What happened then?"

"I went insane. I literally came apart. Suddenly everything I'd been holding inside for months just burst out of me. I was crying, talking to myself, screaming at the sky like Captain Ahab."

"Is this when you saw someone else there?"

"I didn't *see* anybody else. But there was someone there."

"How do you know?"

Drew clenches and unclenches his right fist. "I felt him."

"How?"

"The way you do in horror movies. Your scalp is itching and you start to sweat. You can feel someone looking at you."

This is a popular notion, but entirely untrue. Extensive experiments have proved this type of "intuition" false. "That was probably just paranoia."

Drew shakes his head with absolute conviction. "I've hunted all my life. There was a human being close to me in those woods. But he stayed concealed. He knew how to use cover, or I'd have seen him watching me."

I finally ask the obvious question. "If this is really how it went down, why wasn't it you who reported Kate's death?"

Drew looks at me as though puzzled about this himself. "It almost was. My first instinct was to cradle her like a baby and carry her up to my car. I was going to take her home to her mother and confess everything."

As reckless as this sounds, I sense that he's telling the truth. As a prosecutor, I heard many confessions in which murderers expressed this urge, and some even followed through with it.

"Did you actually pick her up?"

"No. It was at this point that I sensed the other person. I felt an urge to run, but I didn't. Only a coward would run, I told myself. I had to face the situation. But as I sat there staring at her blank eyes—eyes I'd looked into the night before as we made love, eyes so alive you can't *imagine* them—I started to see the situation from outside myself. What would I accomplish by confessing the affair? Kate was beyond help. If I confessed, I'd lose my medical license and probably go to jail. I might even be suspected of killing her. At that moment I honestly didn't give a shit about myself. But what would it do to my family? My parents? What would happen to Tim? I wouldn't be there to raise him. But worse, what would he think about me? He'd grow up believing I was a total shit, and maybe even a killer."

"So you left the scene?"

Drew nods. "I pulled Kate clear of the water, but I left her in the open so that she'd be easily found. I was going to make an anonymous call."

"Did you?"

A silent shake of the head.

"Why not?"

He bends down and examines the Honda's carburetor. "I'd been there for a while. I'm no detective, but I've read enough to know that you leave trace evidence everywhere you go. It was raining pretty hard. I figured the rain would wipe away any evidence that I was there by morning."

"That and more," I say softly, wondering more and more about Drew's actions. "It also washed away any evidence of the real killer. And it damn near washed Kate down to the Mississippi River."

He says nothing.

"You don't come out looking too heroic in this, buddy. A cop would be reading you your rights about now."

Drew looks at me with a direct gaze. "Probably so. But Kate wouldn't have wanted me to destroy Tim's image of me for the sake of her postmortem dignity."

"Her mother might have. You said the blackmailer sounded like a black kid. What would a black kid be doing down at St. Catherine's Creek? I don't remember ever seeing any down there."

"When was the last time you were down there?"

"When we were kids, I guess."

"That was thirty years ago, Penn. A couple of apartment complexes you think of as white have gone black in the past ten years. A lot of the kids play down there. Smoke dope, have sex, whatever."

"Do you think some random black kid would have recognized you?"

"Why not? I have a lot of black patients."

"But earlier you said that whoever was watching you was probably the killer."

"I think so, yeah."

"You think Kate was murdered by some random black kid?"

"Why not? Some crazy teenager?"

"We're talking about capital murder, Drew. Murder during the commission of a rape."

"Happens all the time, doesn't it?"

"It does in Houston or New Orleans. But Natchez is a universe away from there. Houston had two hundred and thirty-four homicides last year. I think Natchez had two. The year before that, nobody got murdered here."

"Yeah, but in the last twenty years, we've had some seriously twisted crimes."

He's right. Not even Natchez has gone untouched by the scourges of the modern era—stranger-murder and sexual homicide.

"Only now I'm thinking it wasn't one kid," he says. "We just got shot at while we chased the guy on the motorcycle. That means two people, at least. Maybe there were more. Maybe Kate was waiting for me at the creek, and it was just the wrong time to be down there. Maybe a crew of horny teenagers was down there messing around and they saw her. Maybe they decided they wanted her, whether she wanted them or not. Like that 'wilding' thing in Central Park, remember?"

I don't answer. As a prosecutor, I found that whenever a crime victim's relative suggested minority-assailant murder cases as parallels, I needed to look more closely at that person. What I've learned in the past five minutes has fundamentally altered my perception of Kate's death and Drew's relationship to it. When the school secretary interrupted the board meeting tonight, Drew already had a good idea of what she was about to say. When Theresa Cook choked out that our beloved homecoming queen was dead, Drew felt no surprise. Only hours before, he had been pounding on her chest and kissing her dead lips, trying to breathe life back into her body. I've never thought of Drew as duplicitous, but I guess we're all capable of anything in the interest of self-preservation.

"What happens now?" he asks.

"You tell the police about your involvement with Kate. If you don't, you're at the mercy of whoever was on that motorcycle. And his buddy with the rifle."

"What happens if I do tell the cops?"

"At the very least, you can count on a statutory rape charge from Jenny Townsend."

Drew shakes his head. "Jenny wouldn't do that."

"Are you crazy? Of course she would."

He steps closer to me, close enough for me to see his eyes clearly. "Jenny knew about us, Penn. About Kate and me."

I blink in disbelief. "And she was okay with it?"

"She knew I loved Kate. And she knew I was going to leave Ellen."

Every time I think I have my mind around the reality of this case, Drew moves the boundaries. "Drew, we're through the looking glass here. If you have any more earthshaking revelations, I'd just as soon hear them all now."

"That's the only one I can think of right now."

My mind is spinning with new permutations of motive and consequence. "A minute ago you said you were thinking of carrying Kate up to her mother and confessing everything. Now you tell me she already knew about you. Which is it?"

" 'Confess' was the wrong word. I meant tell Jenny how Kate died, that I'd found her. I felt it was my fault. I still do. I guess I said 'confess' because if I'd done that, everything would have become public."

I mull over this explanation. "Given what's happened, Jenny might change her mind about your relationship with Kate."

"We were fine tonight. That house was full of grieving people, but Jenny and I were the only two who truly knew what was lost when Kate died."

"Jenny doesn't know you were at the crime scene, does she?"

"No. But I'm probably going to tell her."

"I wouldn't rush into that. Even if she remains your biggest fan, if your affair with Kate becomes public, Jenny may feel she has no choice but to demand your head on a platter. If it were known that she sanctioned your relationship, she'd be crucified right along with you."

"Jenny's never been too concerned about the opinions of others."

"This is a little different than . . . Oh, hell, the point's moot anyway. If your affair becomes public, the police or the sheriff's department will probably charge you with murder. Spurred on by the district attorney, of course."

"Shad Johnson," Drew says softly.

Even the name makes my gut ache. Shadrach Johnson is a black lawyer who was born in Natchez but raised in Chicago. Five years ago, he returned to Natchez to run for mayor, an election he lost by 1 percent of the vote. A year later he won the post of district attorney, taking the office from a white man who had never distinguished himself in the position. The mayoral race Johnson lost happened to be going on during my investigation of the unsolved civil rights murder, and during the stress of that case, Shad revealed his true colors to me. The man has one interest—his own political career—and he doesn't care who he steps on, black or white, to advance it.

"Shad would charge you in a heartbeat," I murmur. "He has wet dreams about getting a case like this."

"Anything for headlines," Drew agrees.

I'm starting to think Drew may have been right not to call in the cavalry when he discovered Kate's body. My chivalrous side is revolted by his callousness, but the modern world is not a chivalrous place. In this world, no good deed goes unpunished.

"What will the blackmailers do now?" Drew asks.

"You gave them the whole twenty thousand?"

"Yeah. I thought about stacking some bills over a newspaper, but the geometry of the stadium wasn't right for that. I knew he'd have too much time to check the bag before I could get him."

"I'm surprised you didn't just take your rifle down there and shoot the guy when he showed up."

Drew looks uncomfortable. "I figured whoever it was would be watching me, looking for a gun, so I didn't take it down with me. I figured I could sprint back up to the four-wheeler before he got to the bag. I'd scanned the whole stadium with the night-vision scope before I went down, and I knew nobody was close to the fifty-yard line."

"Actually, you did make it in time to shoot him," I observe. "Only I showed up."

Drew nods, but I can't read his emotions. "So, what will our motorcyclist do now? Will he try to milk me or will he turn me in?"

"No way to know. But he knows one thing for sure after tonight. Blackmailing you is risky business. He probably didn't realize you were such a psycho."

"I think he'll keep playing me for a while. If he turns me in, he won't get another penny out of me. No more drugs either."

"You gave him drugs?"

Drew shrugs. "Just some samples. Nothing big. You know, that guy on the hill couldn't shoot worth a damn."

"He may not have been trying to hit us. Only to slow us down."

Drew snorts at the idea of such half measures.

"Can we get out of here yet?" I ask.

He leans over the ATV where the big padded seat usually sits and checks the rectangular box that holds the air filter. Then he snaps the seat back on, pulls out the choke, and turns the ignition key. The engine turns over a few times, dies. He tinkers with something, then turns the key a second time. This time the motor sputters resentfully to life. He nurses the throttle with a lover's touch, and soon the motor is roaring with power.

"Ready," he says with a satisfied smile.

The trip back to St. Stephen's is much more agreeable than the roller-coaster ride out here. If it weren't for the wind chilling my wet clothes, I might enjoy it. Several times we startle deer, which freeze in our headlight with wide yellow eyes, then explode into chaotic motion like panicked soldiers. All the way, we watch the ground for my Springfield, but we don't find it.

Drew brings us out of the woods on the high rim of the stadium, then drives swiftly around to the elementary school. I worried that there might be a police car waiting, but my car is still parked by itself in the shadows. A police patrol would probably be drawn to the glaring stadium lights before rifle fire. It's not uncommon to hear rifle shots on this end of town after dark, as poachers spotlight deer out of season.

"Did you drive all the way here on your four-wheeler?" I ask, getting off the ATV.

"No, my pickup is parked behind the main building."

"Do you need help loading this thing?"

"Nah, I've got some ramps."

I reach for the door to my Saab, then turn back to Drew. "When was the last time you had sex with Kate?"

"Last night."

"Did you wear a condom?"

He shakes his head. "She's on the pill."

"She got pregnant while she was on the pill?"

"It's highly unlikely," he says. "That's what I kept telling her. She always took it on time, so the chance of pregnancy was really nil."

Unless she got pregnant on purpose, I think, but I only nod and open my door.

"What is it?" Drew asks.

"By tomorrow, a sample of your semen is going to be on its way to a DNA lab somewhere. New Orleans is my guess. And if the cops get any reason to test your blood against that sample, you're going to look guilty of murder. There's only one way to prevent that perception, Drew."

"Tell the police I was having an affair with her?"

I nod again. "Right now. Don't wait five minutes."

He cuts the Honda's engine. "If I do that, the first thing they'll do is ask me for a DNA sample."

"It's still better than the alternative. You tell them first, they see you as trying to help. You don't . . . you're guilty as hell."

Drew ponders this. "If I were going to tell them, who would I call? The sheriff or the chief of police? Not Shad Johnson, right?"

Like many communities, Natchez has suffered from a long-running rivalry between city and county law enforcement. And Kate's body was found right at the border of the city limits, which could cause serious jurisdictional problems.

"Whoever you tell, it's going to get to Shad eventually. You might as well tell him first. The only way to play this kind of thing is get out ahead of it and stay there. If you volunteer the information, people can get angry, but they can't paint you as a liar. Think of Ted Kennedy at Chappaquiddick. Tell it now, Drew, before anyone beats you to the punch."

"Everything? Even that I found Kate's body?"

"I didn't hear that question, brother."

He looks confused. "What do you mean?"

"We have a saying in the legal profession. Every client tells his story once."

"Meaning?"

"The first and only time you tell your story is on the witness stand. That way—until that day—you have time to adjust the truth to emerging facts."

Disgust wrinkles his face.

"A cynical view, I admit," I tell him, "but experience is a hard teacher. If I hear you tell me one story tonight, I can't put you on the stand and let you tell a different one later."

"But I'm innocent," he says. "I told you that."

Drew's handsome face is a study in the complexity of human emotion. "Yes, you did. But you're not acting like a man with nothing to hide."

CHAPTER

Mia Burke's eyes go wide when I walk into the living room of my town house.

"God, what happened to you?" she asks.

"I got a little wet."

She rises from her chair and drops *The Sheltering Sky* onto an ottoman. "You're bleeding!"

"Am I?"

"Yeah."

She walks into the hall and motions for me to follow her to the bathroom. In the mirror over the sink, I see abrasions all over my neck and arms, and one long scrape on my left arm. The burn on my right forearm is red and throbbing.

"*Shit,*" she says softly. "Yuck."

"What?"

"Your back is worse than your front. It looks like you've got a bad cut under your shirt."

"Great."

"You'd better let me look."

I feel a little awkward in the bathroom with Mia. Two days ago I wouldn't have thought twice about it, but now . . . "Just pull it up and see if I need stitches."

She laughs at my cautiousness, then slowly lifts my shirt, which is stuck to my back. "It's a slash, really. It doesn't look too deep, but it's dirty. Are you about to get in the shower?"

"Yes."

"If I rub some soap into it, you can rinse it out in the shower. That should take care of it."

She slips around me and turns on the hot water tap, then rubs soap into a blue washcloth until she has a thick lather. "Are you going to cry?" she asks, holding up the cloth and stepping behind me again.

"Let's find out."

The soap stings like sulfuric acid, but Mia has shamed me into silence.

"Are you crying?" she asks, scrubbing like a hospital nurse. I can feel her pulling apart the skin to clean inside the cut.

"Thinking about it. What's Lifehouse?" I ask, remembering her T-shirt.

"A band, old man. You'd like them. I'll make you a disk." The humor disappears from her voice. "Did whatever you went to do work out all right?"

"Not as well as I hoped. But at least nobody got killed."

"That's good, right?"

"Right."

At last she removes the burning cloth from my back. "I'm going to leave the soap in there. If you want it to stop hurting, go take your shower."

"Thanks. I can handle it from here."

She laughs, her eyes flickering with humor despite the day's events. "Can you? Do you need me tomorrow?"

"After school, if you can make it."

"Okay. See you then."

She starts down the hall, but I call after her, "Have you heard anything else about Kate's death?"

Mia walks back to the bathroom door. "Steve Sayers and his dad are down at the sheriff's office right now, answering questions."

"Steve was Kate's boyfriend?"

"Figure of speech only."

"Do you know where he was this afternoon?"

"He told John Ellis he drove down to his dad's hunting camp near Woodville after school, to clean the place before turkey season."

Woodville is a small logging town thirty miles south of Natchez. "Alone?"

"That's what Steve told John. There may have been somebody down at the camp when Steve got there. I hope so, for Steve's sake."

"This time of year, I doubt it. So . . . Steve Sayers may not have an alibi."

Mia bites her lower lip and looks down the hall toward the front door. She's wearing small sapphire studs in her ears; I've never noticed them before. Suddenly she looks back at me, her dark eyes intense. "You don't really think Steve could have killed Kate, do you?"

"I don't know him. His parents either. What kind of boy is he?"

"He's okay. Kind of red, I guess. He's no brain surgeon. His dad's a game warden. What can I say? He's a jock of average intelligence."

"Violent?"

Mia shrugs. "He's been in a couple of fights, but then most of the guys I know have. The jocks, anyway."

"Has the sheriff's department talked to anybody else that you know about?"

"No. The police talked to Mrs. Townsend not long ago. That's what I heard, anyway. They asked for the names of Kate's closest friends."

"Do you know whose names she gave them?"

"No. The truth is, Kate didn't have any close friends. Not for the past year or so. I mean, we all thought of her as a friend, but nobody was really in her business, you know? Half the time, no one even knew where she was."

The police are going to find this fact very interesting. "Did you ever ask her where she was? Or try to figure out where she might be?"

"Not really. Steve did, of course. Like I told you, he always insisted she had some secret boyfriend, one she was ashamed for us to know about. But no one ever saw her with another guy."

I'm tempted to ask Mia if she ever saw Kate alone with Drew; she and her classmates might have seen them together and not thought twice about it. But there's no point in alerting her to the true nature of that relationship. "Was Kate tight with any of the black kids at St. Stephen's?"

Mia looks curiously at me. "Why?"

I'm not going to tell her about the blackmail call or Drew's assessment of the possible caller. "It might be important."

"Don't tell me they're going to try to railroad a black guy for this."

"Why do you say that?"

"Well, from what I've read, that used to happen all the time around here in the old days. You know how it was. That's why you took that civil rights case, right?"

"Yes and no. The truth is, I'm worried about 'them' railroading a white guy for Kate's murder. What about my question?"

"Well, we only have four black guys in our class. We're a pretty small class, so everybody knows everybody. But Kate didn't have any special thing with any of the black guys. You talking about sex?"

"Not necessarily. Any special relationship."

"I'll ask around, but tonight my answer is no."

"Okay." I pull the towel tight across the cut on my back. "Thanks for staying tonight. I'm going to hit the shower now."

She smiles and gives me a little wave. "Bye."

"Hey, did Caitlin call while I was gone?"

"No. No calls." Her eyes probe mine for a hidden reaction to this news.

"Thanks."

Her gaze lingers a moment longer, and then she walks down the hall to the front door. "Tell Annie I'll see her tomorrow afternoon."

"I will. Thanks again."

The front door slams.

* * *

I'm almost asleep when the telephone rings beside my bed. I'm too tired and sore to roll over and look at the caller ID. I took three Advil after my shower, knowing that without them I'd hardly be able to move in the morning. The answering machine can get this one for me.

"Penn?" Caitlin says after the beep, her voice sounding clipped and very Northern after Mia's soft drawl. "I'm sorry I didn't get your earlier calls. I was at a party for a reporter who's leaving the *Herald,* and the band was so loud I couldn't hear anything. I'm sure you're sleeping now. Look, I got a call from one of our reporters at the *Examiner.* She said a St. Stephen's girl named Kate Townsend was murdered today. Raped and strangled, she said, or at least that's what it looks like. No autopsy until tomorrow morning. Have you heard about that? I think I played tennis with this girl at Duncan Park. She was really sharp, going to Harvard, she said. Well . . . I guess I won't talk to you until tomorrow. I hope we can see each other soon. I know this sucks. I'm really getting a lot done, though. I may crack this thing soon. I hope the new book's going well. Talk to you tomorrow. I love you. Bye."

I was near to picking up the receiver when Caitlin signed off. I'm not sure why I didn't. But I can't help wondering why a Natchez reporter was able to get through to Caitlin when I wasn't. And half of her message was about Kate's murder, almost as if she were calling me to get details for a story. It's not that I don't want to share things with her. But I want her to be here to share actual experiences with me, not call for reports when things sound interesting.

A wave of relief goes through me when the phone rings again. I roll over onto one elbow and answer.

"Hey, babe," I murmur. "Sorry. I was half sleep before."

"Penn?" says a male voice.

"Yeah, Drew. What is it?"

"I was surfing the Web, and I found a site maintained by the Mississippi Supreme Court. They've got the whole criminal code posted there. And from what I can tell, statutory rape only applies to girls under *sixteen,* not eighteen."

I blink in the darkness. "Are you sure? I remember the statute pretty well. Of course I learned it before moving to Texas for fifteen years. The legislature could have changed it."

"Here's the applicable language. 'The crime of statutory rape is committed when any person seventeen years of age or older has sexual intercourse with a child who: one, is at least fourteen but under sixteen years of age.' There are qualifications, but they all deal with even younger victims and the age difference between victim and perpetrator. It also says, 'Neither the victim's consent nor the victim's lack of chastity is a defense to the charge of statutory rape.'"

"They must have changed the statute," I say in disbelief. But even as relief courses through me, a sense of foreboding rises in my mind. "Drew . . . I think I read somewhere that some states were moving in this direction because there were so many suits being brought by parents who hated their daughters' boyfriends. You've got two seventeen-year-olds having consensual sex. The guy turns eighteen and bam, the girl's parents try to lock him up for statutory rape."

"So, I'm in the clear?"

"Under that statute," I say uneasily. "But somehow I don't think you're out of the woods yet." *What is it?* I wonder, searching my memory for the source of my anxiety. "There's definitely a sexual harassment issue here, but of course that's a civil matter. It's criminal charges we're worried about, felonies in particular." Suddenly, a voice is sounding in my head, the voice of my old boss, the district attorney of Houston: *lascivious touching or handling of a minor . . . contributing to the delinquency of a minor, and then the big one, sexual—* "Drew, are you still at your computer?"

"Yes."

"Look up sexual battery."

I stare up at the dark ceiling, listening to the clicking of keys and praying that my instinct is wrong. "What does it say?"

"Just a minute. Okay . . . uh . . ."

"Read it aloud."

"Here . . . 'A person is guilty of sexual battery if he or she engages in sexual penetration with (A) another person without his or her consent.' I'm okay there."

"Keep reading."

" '(B) a mentally defective, mentally incapacitated, or physically helpless person. (C) A child at least fourteen but under sixteen years of age, if the person is thirty-six or more months older than the child.' Thank God."

Drew sounds so relieved that I'm tempted to let him hang up and get a good night's sleep. But I'm almost certain that bad news is coming. "Keep reading."

"Okay. There's a second paragraph. 'A person is guilty of sexual battery if he or she engages in sexual penetration with a child under the age of . . .' "

His voice falters. "Drew?"

"Eighteen," he whispers. "It says eighteen here."

"Keep reading."

"Oh, God. Oh, no."

"Please read it for me."

" '. . . if he or she engages in sexual penetration with a child under the age of eighteen years if the person is in a position of trust or authority over the child including without limitation the child's teacher, counselor, *physician,* psychiatrist, psychologist, minister . . .' "

Drew's voice sounds like that of a man being sedated before an operation, a monotone fading into nothingness. "You can stop, Drew."

He continues as though he can't hear me over the print screaming from his computer monitor. " '. . . priest, physical therapist, chiropractor, legal guardian, parent, stepparent, aunt, uncle, scout leader or coach.' "

"Drew, listen to me. Are you listening?"

Out of a deep well of silence comes a single sob.

"Drew, it's *all right.* I know you're feeling terrible guilt right now. Seeing it written down like that, you may feel for the first time that you're guilty of a crime."

"She's dead," he says in a shattered voice. "And if I hadn't crossed this line with her, she'd be alive right now."

"You don't know that. You're not God. Listen to me, buddy. I love you. I love you, and I respect you. You're just human, like the rest of us."

"Wait a minute," he says wetly. "I'm looking for the penalty."

"Don't. Leave that for tomorrow."

"I need to see it."

No, you don't, I say silently. *It's going to be thirty years—*

"Jesus Christ. It's thirty years."

"That's not going to happen, Drew. I promise you that."

"Oh my God," he says with fresh dread.

"What? What is it?"

"For a second offense, it's *forty* years. Timmy would be—"

"Turn off that computer! That's not the real world, Drew."

"Are you sure?"

"Hell, yes. I was a prosecutor for fifteen years. That's why you wanted my advice about all this, remember? And my advice is to go to sleep and let me do the worrying for you. That's what you're paying me for."

"Twenty bucks doesn't pay for much worrying."

I don't reply for some time. Then I say, "You saved my life. And you risked your own to do it. If you hadn't, my daughter would never have been born. That buys you a lot of worrying."

"You never asked for this."

"No, but I can handle it. You've got to stay in control for me, though."

"You're not leaving town or anything tomorrow, are you?"

"No way. Now, what are you going to do about the blackmail issue? Are you going to come clean with the cops?"

"After what we just learned? I don't know."

"You're a smart guy, Drew. Let's talk about probability."

"Okay."

"How often did you see Kate? I don't mean platonically. How often were you alone with her, intimate with her?"

"Every day. Or night, rather."

Unbelievable. "For how long?"

"For the last seven months, I guess. Ever since the mission trip to Honduras. After that, we couldn't stand to be apart."

"Get out ahead of this thing, Drew. It's your only chance."

"I hear you."

I let the silence do its work for a while. "Do you?"

"It's Tim that's holding me back. I don't want him to have to know about this if he doesn't have to. I don't want him to have to go through the grief he'll get at school because of it. I don't even want *Ellen* to have to deal with it, now that Kate's dead. There's just no reason anymore."

"Yes, there is. This thing is beyond your control now. No matter what you do, it's eventually going to come out."

"I'm not so sure. If Kate said she didn't tell anybody, she didn't."

"Then who's blackmailing you?"

"Kate's killers."

I grunt noncommittally. "*I'm* not so sure."

"I know. But I am." He breathes steadily into the phone. "Thanks for tonight, Penn. I mean it."

"Night, buddy."

The open line hisses in my ear.

I hang up.

CHAPTER

7

Drew's blackmailers lost no time making him pay for his indecisiveness. At 11:10 the next morning, I was helping my mother paint some bookshelves in her garage when my cell phone rang. The screen showed Drew as the caller. I walked out of the garage under the pretext of getting better cell reception, then answered by saying, "Are you as sore as I am?"

"You were right," he said. "I'm fucked."

A current of anxiety shot through me, but experience kept my voice calm. "What's happened?"

"I just got off the phone with Shad Johnson. He got an anonymous call this morning."

"Let me guess. The caller said you were having an affair with Kate Townsend and that you might have killed her."

"Yep."

"Did he give any details?"

"Johnson didn't say so."

"What did Shad ask you during the call? Did he ask straight out if the accusation was true?"

"No. He basically said, 'Doc, I hate to have to call you about this, but I got this call with an accusation, and I wouldn't be doing my duty if I didn't ask you about it.' He was pretty friendly, actually."

"Shad Johnson is not your friend."

"I understand that. I was just giving you his tone. He said he wanted to give me a chance to deny it as soon as possible, so that it doesn't become any kind of thing."

" 'Thing'? That was his word?"

"Yeah."

"It's already a *thing*, Drew. You can bet your ass on that. Did you flat-out deny that you were seeing Kate?"

"No."

I sighed with relief.

"I acted stunned," he said, "which I was. I told him I was too shocked even to respond to such an outrageous accusation, that Kate was a close friend of our family, and that we'd been shattered by her death. Shad said he understood. He said he'd like to talk to me about it at his office. He said I might have information about Kate that could help them piece together a better picture of her than they have now."

"What did you say to that?"

"What could I say? I told him I wanted to do everything I could to assist the investigation."

"Okay. When is this meeting?"

"Lunch today. Fifty minutes from now."

Shit. "Was it a short call? Long? What?"

"Short."

"That's because Shad got what he wanted. He thinks he's going to question you on his territory."

"He's not?"

"Not unless you're a complete moron—which, after last night, I'm starting to believe."

"Penn—"

"Damn it, why didn't you volunteer the information last night like I told you to?"

"You know why! I didn't want Tim and Ellen to have to deal with it if they didn't have to."

"Well, now they have to."

"What do I do, Penn?"

"You really need a lawyer now."

"I told you that last night."

"And I told you I wasn't your guy. Not for this."

"The meeting's in fifty minutes!"

I bowed my head in resignation. The odds of finding a Natchez lawyer qualified to take that meeting were low, and the odds of adequately briefing one in time were nil. "Where are you now?"

"At my office. Seeing patients."

"You're off at twelve?"

"Yeah."

"You just had an emergency."

Drew was silent for a moment. "I'm skipping the meeting?"

"I'm going in your place."

"Is that the best thing?"

"We need to get some idea of what Shad is thinking. I'd also like to know what the autopsy turned up. Shad probably has the pathologist's report in hand by now."

"I don't want to think about that. This is Kate we're talking about."

You'd better get used to it. "Sorry. Now . . . we have a tricky little problem to deal with. Think before you answer me, okay?"

"Okay."

"The first thing Shad is going to ask me is where you were when Kate was murdered. He won't be obvious about it, but he'll ask. And I happen to know you were at the murder scene. Where did you go *after* you left the creek?"

"Home."

I was silent long enough for Drew to realize that if he was lying, he had better come clean then or stick with his story. "Was Ellen there?"

"No. She was at her sister's place."

"What about Tim?"

"The maid had taken him to his music lesson."

"So nobody can verify that you were home?"

"I answered some e-mails soon after I got there. Couldn't we use those?"

"Maybe. But depending on how narrow a window they've established as time of death, the e-mails probably won't put you in the safety zone."

"Tim got home around five, and Ellen about six."

"Okay. It's also possible that someone saw your car parked in that vacant lot in Pinehaven. For that reason, and for others I can't predict now, I may decide I need to tell Shad the truth. Everything. Today. The affair, the blackmail, everything."

Drew said nothing.

"In fact, the more I think about it, the more I think coming clean may still be the best option we have. Even lying by omission digs a hole they can bury you in later."

A woman on Drew's end of the line called out a blood pressure reading. Drew lowered his voice. "You're my lawyer, Penn. I trust your instincts. Say whatever you think you need to. I'm innocent— of murder, anyway—and I'm not going to hide anything except to protect my son."

What could I say to that? "I'll call you when the meeting's over. Keep your cell phone wired to your hip, and don't answer any calls until you hear from me. Don't talk to *anybody*."

"I won't."

I hung up and turned back to the garage. My mother was watching me with a quizzical look on her face. In that moment I realized just how far my life had already slid off its accustomed track. After dropping Annie at school this morning, I drove down to the football field and searched it for my lost pistol. Failing to find it, I went up to the high school and told Coach Wade Anders to keep an eye out for it. Anders is the athletic director of St. Stephen's, and he promised to have his assistants search the bowl again before any kids were allowed into it. He also asked if I knew anything about the switch box for the stadium lights being shot up. I told him I didn't, but that I'd send someone to install a new box as soon as possible. He looked at me in silence for a little while, then nodded as though we shared a special understanding. Like everybody, Anders was building up capital where he could.

The lost gun problem didn't end there. The land that Drew and I chased the blackmailer over is owned by a group of investors who use it as a hunting camp. I called the doctor who heads the group to tell him I might have lost a pistol on their land, and to ask his members to keep an eye out for it. When he asked what I was doing on their land, I made up a story about a troublesome armadillo rooting up the St. Stephen's football field—an armadillo I chased onto their land in my single-minded quest to kill it. Remarkably, he laughed as though he understood completely.

"Mom, I'm sorry," I said, "but I need to go take care of something."

"Is everything all right?" she asked, her eyes making it clear that she knew better.

"Yes."

"It's not Annie, is it?"

"No, no."

"Are you and Caitlin all right?"

"We're fine, Mom. This is just some legal business."

She went back to painting the shelves with long, smooth strokes of her brush. At sixty-eight, she works with the strength and flexibility of someone twenty years her junior. Being raised in the country does that for some people.

When I arrived at the house this morning, Mom held up the newspaper and asked me about Kate's death. Thankfully, Caitlin's staff had reported only the known facts, which left my mother as curious as the rest of the town. And like most of the town, Mom believes Drew Elliott hung the moon. She often says that Drew is the only "young" doctor who practices medicine with the conscientiousness of my father. What would she say if she knew that he was sleeping with Kate Townsend until the day she died?

"Be careful," Mom called as I walked to my car.

"I will," I called, thinking that was good advice to follow when dealing with Shadrach Johnson.

* * *

The district attorney's office is on the third floor of the water-works building in Lawyer's Alley, across from the massive city courthouse. In a town filled with architecturally significant build-ings, the waterworks is nothing special, a three-story concrete block with one glass-brick corner enclosing the staircase. I park under the courthouse oaks and cross the street, waving at one of my parents' neighbors as she walks into the DMV office.

There's no receptionist behind the door on the ground floor, just a staircase. As I climb the stairs, my errand weighs heavy below my heart. I've got to tell Shad Johnson the truth as I know it—up to a point, anyway. Drew had sex with Kate the night be-fore she died, so I have to assume that the state pathologist has al-ready recovered his semen from her body. And while no judge would order Drew to take a DNA test based solely on an anony-mous telephone call, Shad may already have more proof connect-ing Drew to Kate.

Last night, Drew told me he'd been intimate with Kate for the past seven months. How many seventeen-year-old girls could sleep with a forty-year-old man that long without telling a single friend about it? If Kate told her mother about the affair, why not her best friend? And with Kate dead at the hands of a killer, how long will it take Jenny Townsend—however much she may like Drew—to tell the police what she knows? Shad may already have proof of the affair; he may have called this meeting simply to see if Drew will lie about it, using the lesser crime of sexual battery as a litmus test for deception before questioning Drew about the murder. I did the same thing many times as a prosecutor.

When I reach the third floor, a heavy female secretary with dyed-orange hair and a flower-print dress gives me a quizzical look from behind a glass partition. Five years ago Shad had a male fac-totum who dressed like Malcolm X, but he vanished shortly after Shad's mayoral defeat. This woman was obviously expecting Drew, who is known on sight by most Natchezians. I'm pretty well-known myself, but in a small town no one ever quite attains the celebrity of the best doctors. My father is testament to that fact. He can't walk twenty yards in Wal-Mart without being stopped by adoring or inquisitive patients.

"I'm Mr. Johnson's noon appointment," I tell the secretary.

"No, you're not."

"You expecting Dr. Drew Elliot?"

She looks confused. "That's right."

"I'm his attorney."

Her lips form a perfect O, just like they do in cartoons. "You're Penn Cage."

"I am. I'm Dr. Elliott's attorney."

The expression of surprise morphs into an uncertain glare. "I know about you."

"Your boss and I once went a few rounds over a civil rights murder."

She picks up the phone and begins speaking in a hushed tone.

My statement about the civil rights murder is true. The irony of that case is that I, the white lawyer, was crusading to solve the twenty-year-old murder of a black man, while Shad, the black politician, was trying to bury the case to keep from upsetting the white voters he needed to win the mayor's office.

The secretary hangs up and buzzes me through the door. "End of the hall," she says curtly.

As soon as I enter the blandly painted corridor, a door at the far end opens and a black man a few inches shorter than I peers out, an expression of annoyance on his face. "Son of a bitch," he says without a trace of Southern accent. "I was having a good day until now."

"Hello, Shad."

The district attorney shakes his head, then walks back into his office, squaring his shoulders for combat as he goes. I follow him inside and wait to be invited to sit.

As usual, Shadrach Johnson is dressed to the nines in a bespoke suit and Italian shoes. His hair has a little more gray in it than the last time we locked horns, but his eyes still flash with quick intelligence. My first impression of him was of a brash personal injury lawyer, and nothing in the intervening years has changed that. Shad's jutting jaw greets the world with a perpetual challenge, his eyes project arrogance and mistrust, and his shoulders stay flexed under the weight of an invisible yet enormous chip.

"Your buddy's not playing this right, Cage," he says, taking a seat behind an enormous desk that looks like an antique. "An innocent man doesn't send his lawyer to speak for him in a situation like this. Have a seat."

Go for it, I tell myself. *Turn on the gravitas and recite the lines you rehearsed on the way over: This is a very serious matter, Shad. Dr. Elliott was indeed seeing the dead girl, but he did not kill her. You and I have to set aside our personal history and help the police to find a dangerous killer. Dr. Elliott wants to assist the investigation in every way, but he also wants to keep this unfortunate matter from escalating into something that could ruin reputations and break up families unnecessarily.*

I was prepared to say those things, but now that I'm actually facing Shad Johnson, something stops me. It all seemed so clear in the car: pay the short-term price for a long-term gain. But this office, as modest as it is, gives me the old feeling I had when I worked for the D.A. in Houston. Irrevocable decisions are made in this room, decisions about who will be punished and who will not. Who will spend decades in prison? Who will die at the hands of the state? For any prosecutor, Drew Elliott would be a juicy target, but for a man like Shad Johnson—a man who dreams of being governor and more—Drew is a prize elephant.

There's no doubt that Drew would look better to a future jury if he told the truth now. But what other consequences might result? Natchez is a small town, and when small-town cops are handed a likely suspect, they don't look too hard for another. Truth be told, city cops aren't much different. And confessing to the affair with Kate would immediately open Drew to a sexual battery charge that Shad could use to jail him, should he choose to. No, better to keep my cards close to the vest.

"That's a lot nicer desk than the one the last D.A. had," I observe, stalling for time as I take the chair opposite Shad.

The district attorney can't help but brag; it's his nature. "I got it out of storage from the old Natchez Museum," he says, rubbing the finely grained wood. "It came from the attic of one of the antebellum homes. Longwood, I think. Ironic, isn't it? Me working at a cotton planter's desk? I had it appraised. It's worth sixty grand."

I give Shad a level gaze. "I hope you're not one of those people who knows the price of everything and the value of nothing."

Shad's eyes narrow. "What are you doing here, Penn? Where's Dr. Elliott?"

"He had an emergency at his office. He had to stay and handle it."

"Bullshit. Your client's scared. His dick's got him tangled up in a capital murder case, and he's terrified."

Shad must have more than the anonymous call in his pocket. "How do you figure that?"

"Did Elliott tell you about the call I got this morning?"

"He said you mentioned an anonymous caller who told you some story about him being intimate with Kate Townsend."

"That's right. And the good doctor did not deny it."

"Did he confirm it?"

"That's what this meeting was for. For him to confirm or deny. Now he's sent you in his place. The big-time mouthpiece. I didn't think you practiced anymore."

"I wasn't practicing when I took the Del Payton case either."

Shad looks like he just bit into something sour. My punishing Del Payton's murderers after Shad had resisted reopening the case cost him just enough support in the black community to take the mayoral election away from him. But that's old news. I've got to get a handle on his present intentions before I paint myself into a corner.

"Shad, let's—"

"Stop," he says, jabbing a forefinger at me. "You're here because you want something."

He's right. "I would like to know what was discovered during Kate's autopsy."

Shad studies me for several moments. "And you think I'm just going to give that to you?"

"If you continue to pursue my client, I'll get it one way or another. Why don't we try to foster a spirit of cooperation here?"

"You haven't done any cooperating with me so far." He lifts a sheaf of fax paper off his desk and flips to the last page. "But I'm feeling generous. What do you want to know?"

"Time of death?"

Shad shakes his head. "We'll pass on that for now."

"Cause?"

"Strangulation. There was also head trauma that might have killed the girl if she hadn't been strangled first."

"Interesting. There are rumors going around town about rape. Nurses at the hospital did some talking. Was the girl raped or not?"

"The pathologist says she was."

"Genital trauma?"

Shad nods slowly.

"Did they recover semen from her?"

"Affirmative. Both holes."

His crudeness is meant to shock, but I saw too much rape and murder in Houston for this to bother me. "So, the killer had some time with her."

Shad shakes his head, a strange smile on his face. "Not necessarily. The pathologist already ran serology on the semen samples. They came from two different men."

A glimmer of hope sparks in my soul. "Multiple assailants?"

"You could read it that way."

"What other way is there? You have a different scenario in mind?"

"After the call I got this morning, you can't blame me for speculating a little."

"I'm listening."

Shad leans over his desk and steeples his fingers. "Let's say Dr. Elliott was having an affair with this high school girl. In his mind, it's true love. Then he finds out his prom queen's been sharing the poonanny with somebody else when he's not around. Her old boyfriend, say. The doc finds out, and he flips out. Maybe Kate is cruel about how she tells him—you know some women. So, your client starts choking her, trying to make her shut up. Before he knows what he's doing, he's shut her up for good."

"By that scenario, the girl wasn't raped at all."

Shad waves his hand as though at a minor annoyance. "Rape is a subjective finding in a dead girl. She's not accusing anybody. So she had some genital trauma. Rough consensual sex can cause that. Hell, I've had women get mad if I *didn't* traumatize them down there."

"You're reaching, Shad."

He settles back in his chair. "I don't think so. I'll tell you something else for free. The St. Stephen's homecoming queen was pregnant."

Shit. "How far along?"

"A little over four weeks. And *that*—according to the laws of the great state of Mississippi—makes this a double homicide, Counselor." Shad arches his eyebrows in mock concern. "The community's going to be very upset by that idea, the murder of an unborn baby. You know, I can see some people speculating that Dr. Elliott was just playing with this poor girl—getting a little on the side—and when she turned up pregnant, he saw his nice little life crashing down around him. He saw thirty years in Parchman for having sex with a juvenile patient, so he killed her."

I suddenly see a glimpse of the future. This case is going to trial, and Drew Elliott will be the defendant, whether he deserves to be or not. Thank God I didn't march in here spouting his secrets. "The public shouldn't be able to make that kind of speculation," I say evenly, "because they shouldn't associate my client's name with this case in any way."

Shad smiles and shakes his head. "We've got a simple situation here, Counselor. Somebody is making telephone calls saying your client was screwing the dead girl. I can't control that caller's actions. So you've got to assume that Dr. Elliot's name is going to be in the street soon. The best thing Drew can do for himself is provide us a DNA sample and clear his name as quickly as possible. If his DNA doesn't match what the pathologist swabbed out of the girl, nobody can ever say a word against him."

Check and mate. If I'm going to come clean about the affair before the trial, now is the time. But the truth as I know it will only lend credence to Shad's first scenario—murder committed in a jealous rage.

"You asked about time of death," Shad reminds me. "If you'll tell me where Dr. Elliott was during the hours surrounding it, I'll give you the time of death."

"No deal. We're getting way ahead of ourselves."

Shad's eyes glint with a predator's love of the hunt.

"What about the fishermen who found the girl's body?" I ask, trying to take Shad's mind off Drew's alibi. "Have you ruled them out?"

"They're down at the hospital providing DNA samples as we speak. They couldn't wait to do it."

Damn. "And Kate Townsend's boyfriend?"

"Steve Sayers? Same deal." Shad taps the cherry desktop with manicured fingernails. "The boy's alibi is a little weak, but he couldn't wait to get over to the hospital and give blood. He offered to whack off in a cup right here in my office. Says he hasn't had sex with the victim in months. Seems Miss Townsend just up and stopped putting out, no explanation. And before that, she was as hot as they come, according to the Sayers boy. Kinky, he said." Shad gives me a cagey look. "You think she got religion?"

I keep my face impassive.

Shad smiles and leans back in his chair. "The bottom line is this: I need DNA from everybody who might have known the Townsend girl in the biblical sense. And any reasonable man would have to include your client on that list. Now, everybody *but* your client is chomping at the bit to give me said sample. Your client, on the other hand, has sent his celebrity mouthpiece down here to talk for him. So I'll ask you straight out, is Dr. Elliott going to provide a DNA sample to the state in the interest of expediting this investigation? Or is he not?"

I choose my words with great care. "No judge would order my client to give a blood sample on the basis of an anonymous call alone."

Shad concedes this with a slight inclination of his head. "That may be true. But in the interest of protecting the community, what innocent man would object to it?"

"In a perfect world, I'd agree. But if it got out that you asked Drew Elliott to give a DNA sample in connection with this murder—and it *would* get out, if he complied—the rumor alone could destroy him. It's practically a child molestation charge. The stigma would never go away."

"You can't keep his name out of this mess, Cage. Our mystery caller didn't telephone just me this morning."

I cover my mouth and swallow hard. "Who else?"

"Sheriff Byrd and the chief of police. Our caller's a persistent fellow. He seems to believe strongly in his cause."

"Did you trace the source of the calls from phone records?"

"They originated from a pay phone on the north side of downtown."

"The black section?"

Shad inclines his head again.

This fits what Drew told me about the blackmailer's voice. "Did the police fingerprint the phone?"

"They're working that angle, but no matches yet." Shad suddenly gives me a look of honest puzzlement. "The thing is, Penn, accusing Dr. Elliott of this affair seems so out of left field, it's hard to imagine anyone making it up. You know? If it's not true, who would even *think* of it?"

"Somebody who hates Drew Elliott."

Shad turns up his palms. "From what I gather, the good doctor hasn't got an enemy in the world. Everybody talks about him like he's a saint."

"There's a reason for that. He's a genuinely good man."

Another beatific smile. "Then he's got nothing to worry about. The way I see it, providing a DNA sample is about the *only* way Dr. Elliott is going to be able to preserve his sterling reputation."

"There's no way I'm letting Drew go down to the St. Catherine's Hospital lab for a DNA test. The man's on staff there, for God's sake. Word would shoot through that building in less than an hour. By nightfall, everybody in town would know about it."

Shad leans back and speaks in a cold voice. "I'm sorry to hear that. Because if he doesn't, I'll be forced to consider other alternatives."

"Such as?"

"Well, I've been sitting here thinking about that. One thing, it's the first week of the month. That means the grand jury's in session. Probably will be for two more days. They might be real interested in hearing about this situation. About the anonymous call, and about the strange coincidences, like how Dr. Elliott lives upstream on that creek where the girl's body was found. They might just decide they want a DNA sample from the doctor on their own."

Jesus. "That's unethical, Shad. You'd be perverting the purpose of the grand jury. It doesn't exist to investigate crimes. And for your information, at least a thousand people live upstream on that creek, maybe more."

Shad's eyes brim with confidence. "Just a thought, Counselor. But emotions are running high in this town. People want a brutal killer like this caught and punished. That's my sole interest here. And I'm not going to let the fact that your client is white and rich stop me from getting to the bottom of this poor girl's death. That kind of miscarriage of justice stopped the day I took over this office."

Like a chess player experiencing a flash of insight, I suddenly see a dozen moves down the board. And what I see sends a rush of adrenaline through my veins. This conversation isn't about murder at all—it's about politics. I should have realized that before I walked in the door.

The mayoral election Shad lost five years ago was the most hotly contested in Natchez history. He lost to Riley Warren, a two-term white incumbent with a flamboyant style and a love for backroom business schemes that earned him the nickname Wiley. While some of those schemes benefited the city, others weighed it down with suffocating debt, and by the end of his term—last summer—even Wiley's supporters suspected that he'd enriched himself more than the city he was elected to serve. Shad might have defeated Warren then, but he was only halfway into his first term as district attorney. It wouldn't have looked good for him to resign after the promises he'd made to rectify "racial inequalities" in Natchez's criminal courts.

Despite dwindling support, Wiley Warren ran for mayor a third time. His enemies polled local worthies in search of an opposition candidate—myself included. Like most who were asked, I declined to enter the fray. Ultimately, Warren's enemies ran a rather dim bulb named Doug Jones against their nemesis, and despite Jones's utter lack of distinction or vision, he handily defeated Warren in the primary. The only black candidate to step forward was a funeral director with a checkered past, a man with enemies of his own in the black community. Black turnout was low on election day, and Doug Jones won by a 58 to 42 percent margin. The newly Honorable Mayor Jones took office and promptly became the invisible man. If he took no bold new initiatives for the city, neither did he make any tragic mistakes. He managed this by doing almost nothing at all. But shortly after Christmas he finally did do something: he held a press conference and announced that he had been diagnosed with lung cancer and would resign his office within ninety days.

That was two months ago.

If Mayor Jones pulls the trigger within the next four weeks, as promised, then the chief executive office of the city will be up for grabs. Local election rules dictate that once the mayor's office is vacated, a special election must be held within forty-five days. Sitting here in this office, I realize just how important that fact is to Shad Johnson. If Shad were to convict a rich white doctor of capital murder, he could pronounce his election promises to the black community fulfilled and enter the mayoral race with a united front behind him—something that didn't happen five years ago.

The seemingly boundless confidence in Shad's eyes triggers another revelation: he doesn't even have to *convict* Drew. Even if Shad loses, he wins politically in the black community, just for making the effort. He can always blame a courtroom loss on the white man's secret manipulation of the system.

I look Shad hard in the eyes but speak softly. "You're going to run for mayor again."

He blinks like a reptile basking in the sun. "No comment, Counselor."

"You think putting Drew Elliott in Parchman is your ticket to a unified black electoral base."

Shad attempts to dispose of my theory with a wave of his hand. "Our business here is to rule out Dr. Elliott as a murder suspect— if we can—so that my officers can get on with the investigation of this heinous crime."

Spoken as though for reporters. My new understanding of the political situation has sent my mind racing down a dozen different paths, but I'm not here to figure out the future of Natchez. I'm here to protect Drew Elliott.

"All right," I say in a tone of surrender. "What about this? Dr. Elliott has a laboratory in his office. Send over a couple of police officers right now, during his lunch hour. His lab tech can draw the blood you need—do a buccal swab, whatever—and the cops can attest that it's his. The chain of custody remains intact, and so does Dr. Elliott's reputation."

Shad nods. "I can live with that."

I look at my watch. "I'd better call him."

"I thought he had an emergency."

"He's probably handled it by now." I get up and offer Shad my hand.

He takes it, but he squeezes gently rather than shakes, then withdraws his hand. "I hope your boy comes up clean, Penn. If he doesn't . . ."

"He will."

Shad looks surprised by my statement. But I was talking about Kate's murder, nothing else.

I'm almost to the door when he says, "Penn, about the mayoral situation."

I turn and regard him steadily. "Yes?"

"I heard some local power brokers asked you to run against Wiley Warren last year."

"That's right. I wasn't interested."

"Not interested in running against Warren? Or not interested in being mayor?"

"Both. Neither."

Shad studies me with unguarded curiosity. "The town's in a lot different place than it was a year ago."

"You're right, I'm sad to say."

It kills him to ask the next question. "Are you still not interested?"

I turn up my palms, then smile easily. "No more than you. Have a good day, Shad."

Outside the D.A.'s office, I stand in the sun and stare across the street at the courthouse. Somewhere inside, a simple white man named Doug Jones is wrestling with his fear of death and deciding when to resign the office of mayor. I'm surprised he's waited two months, given the gravity of his diagnosis. I watched an uncle die of lung cancer, and I've forgotten neither my horror nor his pain. But while Mayor Jones struggles with his mortality, Shad Johnson watches from across the street like a hungry vulture waiting to draw life from death. My new appreciation of Shad's deeper motive has clarified Drew's situation.

If Shad can get sufficient evidence, he will rush Drew to trial in record time, hoping to convict him—or at least garner a week's worth of headlines—before Mayor Jones resigns. But Drew's legal jeopardy is not the sole reason for my interest in Shad's political intentions. For the past six months, despite my decision not to seek the office of mayor a year ago, I have been pondering the idea of entering the special election.

My reasons are simple. One month into Doug Jones's administration, the International Paper Company—the largest employer in the county—announced that it would close its Natchez mill after fifty years of continuous operation. The shock to the community still hasn't passed. Closure came swiftly, and about a month ago the severance pay of former employees began to peter out. So did their heath insurance benefits. And IP was merely the last in a short but devastatingly complete line of local manufacturing companies to shut down. Triton Battery. Armstrong Tire and Rubber. Johns-Manville. That leaves tourism the only industry pumping outside dollars into Natchez. And tourism is a seasonal business.

In a single year, Natchez has been transformed from a fairly healthy city into a community on the edge. We've lost more than five hundred families in the wake of the IP closure, and more are leaving every week. In 1850, Natchez boasted more millionaires than every city in America except New York and Philadelphia, the money flowing in as cotton flowed out by the hundreds of thousands of bales. But as the soil was slowly depleted, cotton farming moved north to the Delta, and Natchez entered a period of decline. Then in 1948, oil was discovered practically beneath the streets. By 1960, the year I was born, the city was flush with millionaires again, and Natchez became a truly magical place in which to grow up. But in 1986, the price of oil crashed, and the Reagan administration sacrificed domestic oil producers in his battle to win the Cold War. The number of local oil companies dwindled from sixty to seven, and by the time the price of oil began to climb again, there wasn't enough industry left to exploit what remained of our depleted reserves. Without visionary leadership, Natchez will soon shrink to a quaint hamlet of ten or twelve thousand people—mostly retirees, service workers, and people on welfare—and the thriving city of twenty-five thousand that I grew up in will be only a memory.

When I first heard about Doug Jones's terrible diagnosis, I sensed the hand of fate offering this city a final opportunity for salvation. And to my surprise, I felt a powerful surge of civic responsibility swelling in my heart. Shad Johnson will tell voters he felt a similar call to public service, but I know him too well to believe that. Five years ago, he left his Chicago law firm to return to Natchez and run one of the most cynical campaigns I've ever witnessed on either a local or national level. I'm proud that my efforts in the courtroom helped snatch victory from his grasp, but it was black voters who ultimately did that. Enough of them saw through Shad's theatrical skills to tip the balance against him. They closed their eyes, gritted their teeth, and voted for what they hoped was a harmless white man. But as Shad himself said earlier, Natchez was a different city a year ago. Now we are in crisis. And a man who does nothing during a crisis is as bad as a man who causes one.

As I stare at the great white courthouse, my cell phone rings. I climb into my Saab and answer.

"Are you out of the meeting?" Drew asks in a tense voice. "Did you see the autopsy report?"

No questions about his future, only about what happened to Kate. Is that because he loved her so dearly? Or because he has something to fear? "She was strangled, Drew."

"That's what I thought," he says quietly. "From the petechiae around her eyes. Was she pregnant?"

"Yes. Four weeks along."

A sharp intake of breath. "That's why she was so desperate to see me. Jesus, what about—"

"Stop talking, Drew. We can go into details later. Right now we have a problem. The district attorney wants a sample of your DNA."

Silence.

"The pathologist found semen inside Kate's body." There's no point in telling Drew that the pathologist found the semen of two different men, and in two different locations. "Of course, I expected that, given what you told me about the previous night."

"I'm listening."

"Shad wants to prove you murdered Kate. He wants to prove it badly."

"Does he really think I'm capable of that?"

"All men are capable of that, Drew. We can talk about Shad's motives later. Right now, under these circumstances, giving him the sample is the best thing you can do. It'll buy us three or four weeks while the lab does the test. And time is what we need more than anything right now."

"Why?"

"Because the police may have caught the real murderer long before the test is completed, or even begun. And by that point, it won't matter nearly so much that you were having sex with Kate Townsend. In fact, if Shad gets a confession from someone else, I might be able to persuade him to cancel the test altogether. You'd probably have to make a massive contribution to his next political campaign"—which will be sooner than anyone suspects—"but I think you could live with that."

"Okay, fine. But what about the autopsy? What else did the report show?"

"*Later.* Shad wanted you to waltz into the St. Catherine's Hospital lab and give the blood sample, but I worked out a compromise."

"Which is?"

"Can you trust your lab technician?"

"Susan? Sure. She's been with me nine years."

"Good. Because in the next hour, a couple of cops are going to show up at your office and watch Susan draw some blood from your arm."

"Okay."

"And, Drew?"

"Yes?"

"From now on, don't answer any questions from anybody without talking to me first. Nothing. You got that?"

"Okay."

"You'd better get things straight with Susan."

"I will. Are you going to be here when they draw the blood?"

"Is your office empty during lunch?"

"Like a cemetery."

"All right. I'll come by and make sure they don't hassle you for pubic hairs or anything like that."

"Thanks."

As I hang up and start my car, a tall, big-bellied white man wearing a brown uniform and a gray cowboy hat swaggers by my car and turns into the doorway of the district attorney's office. He is Billy Byrd, the sheriff of Adams County. As Sheriff Byrd pulls open the D.A.'s door, he glances back at me and gives me a superior smile, as though he already knows exactly what transpired in the office upstairs a few minutes ago. And of course he does.

Welcome to Mississippi politics.

CHAPTER

8

Shad's emissaries arrive at Drew's medical lab before I do. But they're not cops, as I expected; they're sheriff's deputies. I can tell by the big yellow star on the door of the white cruiser parked outside. This tells me that in the investigation of Drew Elliott, the district attorney has chosen to align himself with the fat man in the cowboy hat who walked by my car a few minutes ago, rather than with the chief of police, who by any standard of common sense should be handling this matter.

Drew practices in a suite of offices maintained by Natchez Doctors' Hospital, which is located behind the cluster of primary care clinics that feed patients to the main facility. The front door of Drew's office is unlocked. I enter to find his waiting room dark. There's light in the corridor beyond it, but the door to the hall is locked. After I bang loudly, a young woman's face appears behind the receptionist's window. She waves, then buzzes me into the corridor.

Drew's lab is right across the hall, a brightly lit rectangle containing centrifuges, microscopes, and expensive blood chemistry machines. Against the far wall, a blue phlebotomist's chair stands beside a white refrigerator. Drew himself is reclining in the chair, one shirtsleeve rolled up past his elbow.

I step in and find two deputies standing with their backs to the wall opposite Drew. They look uncomfortable. I recognize one of them. Tom Jackson was the top detective at the police department until the sheriff hired him away, which wasn't hard to do. The county pays cops about five thousand a year more than the city does. Jackson is as tall as Drew, and his handlebar mustache gives him the look of a cowboy in a Frederic Remington painting. He gives me a friendly nod, but his partner—a short, black-haired man with pasty skin—doesn't even acknowledge me.

"Tom," says Drew, "this is Penn Cage, a buddy of mine."

"I know Penn," Jackson says in a deep voice.

Both deputies must know why I'm here, but Drew seems to want to preserve the illusion of a friendly get-together. He nods past me, and I turn to see the white-uniformed woman who let me in. She's in her midthirties, with short brown hair and a heart-shaped face distinguished by intelligent brown eyes.

"Penn, this is Susan Salter, my med tech."

"Nice to meet you, Susan."

She manages a slight nod; she looks the least comfortable of us all.

"Well," says Drew, "let's get this over with."

Susan takes a long white box from a cabinet and looks at the deputies. "You said four tubes?"

"That's what our evidence technician told us," says Tom Jackson. "I guess they want to make sure they don't have to ask for more blood later."

Susan removes four vacuum tubes with purple stoppers from the box and lays them flat on one arm of the chair. Then she straps a Velcro tourniquet around Drew's left biceps and slaps his antecubital vein three times. A vein like a rigid blue pipe stands up at the place where Drew's arm muscles insert at the inner elbow. Susan pushes the stopper end of one of the tubes into a Vacutainer syringe, then with a single deft motion pricks the needle into Drew's vein and presses the stopper of the tube down onto the rear of the needle with her thumb.

A fountain of dark blood begins filling the tube, sucked inward by the vacuum inside it. The short deputy looks away.

"I need to use the restroom," he mumbles.

"Down the hall to your right," says Drew.

The deputy disappears. As Susan replaces the full tube with an empty one, I realize her hands are shaking. She's playing out a scene she couldn't possibly have imagined an hour ago. How much has Drew told her? I wonder.

"Tom?" I say, taking advantage of the other deputy's absence. "What do you figure the time of death was?"

Jackson looks warily at me. "You don't know?"

"The D.A. wouldn't tell me."

He sighs and shakes his head. "People are acting mighty squirrelly about this case. I'd like to help you out, though."

"Will you?"

"Well . . . we know the girl didn't leave the school until three. The fishermen say they found her about six-twenty."

"What did the body temperature tell you?"

Jackson glances uncomfortably at the door. "I don't know about all that. I heard they're not sure how long she was in the water."

"Best guess?"

The short deputy walks through the door, looks at Jackson, and smiles. It seems a strange thing to do, but it shuts Jackson up.

When the four tubes lie full of blood on a table and the tourniquet has been removed from Drew's arm, Tom steps forward with a plastic evidence bag and holds it open. Susan drops the tubes inside. Drew shakes his head, looking more than anything like an innocent man doing his best to humor overzealous cops.

"That it, guys?"

Jackson nods. "That's it, Doc. Sorry to bother you with this."

"How long do you think it will take to get the DNA results?" I ask.

"Usually takes a month, at least," Tom replies. "They'll probably rush this, considering the situation. But two and a half weeks is the fastest I've ever seen. Out of New Orleans, anyway."

This is exactly what I expected.

Drew stands and offers Tom his hand, and Jackson gives it a strong shake. In all likelihood, Tom is a patient of Drew's. But when Drew offers his hand to the shorter deputy, the man turns without a word and leaves the lab. Tom shrugs sheepishly, then follows his partner out.

Drew looks at Susan. "I guess I screwed up your lunch hour."

She forces a smile. "That's okay. I'm not hungry."

Drew gives me a pointed glance, and I realize he needs to speak further with Susan in private.

"I'll give you a call later," I tell him, starting for the door.

"Wait," he says. "Have you had lunch yet? I'm starving."

"I was about to get something."

"Why don't we eat together? We ought to talk about a couple of things."

I don't want to risk talking about this situation in public. "Tell you what, I'll grab some food and come back here. We can eat in your office."

Drew looks dismayed, but then he seems to get it. "Okay. See you in a few minutes. No hamburgers."

I leave the office and go out to my car, my mind on Susan and her ability to keep quiet. I feel like Thai food, but the only Thai restaurant is downtown, and it would take too long to get there and back to Drew's office. The only options on this side of town are fast food and Ruby Tuesday's. I pull into the drive-through lane at Taco Bell and order a couple of zesty chicken bowls, some tacos, and two Mountain Dews, which the restaurant delivers in record time. Then I pull back onto the bypass and get into the turning lane for Jefferson Davis Boulevard, the street that leads to Drew's office.

While I wait for the light to change, the blare of a police siren pierces my ears. Several vehicles behind me pull onto the grassy median, and then a police car with blue lights flashing screeches to a stop behind me. With nowhere else to go, I shoot across two on-coming lanes of traffic and pull my right wheels onto the curb of Jeff Davis Boulevard. The squad car roars past me.

This kind of thing is pretty unusual in Natchez at midday. Maybe that's what triggers my intuition, but in any case I hit the accelerator and take off in pursuit of the squad car.

The blue lights swerve into a parking lot on the right side of Jeff Davis Boulevard. Sure enough, it's Drew's office. *What the hell could have happened so fast?* I wonder, skidding into the lot behind the police car.

And then I see.

A muscular man in a blue cap is brandishing a wooden baseball bat at Drew, who stands in a half crouch with his hands held out from his body. Susan Salter is screaming at the man to put down the bat.

Two uniformed cops leap from the squad car. As one draws a can of pepper spray from his belt, I see two other men lying on the ground not far from the man with the bat. One rolls over onto his back, clutching his bloodied face in pain.

"Drop that bat!" yells one of the cops, who's holding a deadly steel baton called an asp.

The man with the bat jerks his head toward the cop, and at that moment I realize something alarming: the blue cap he's wearing is a St. Stephen's Bucks baseball cap, which almost certainly makes him not a man at all, but a boy. From the rear, his size and muscularity gave him the appearance of an adult. But when I read the letters on the back of his jersey—SAYERS—everything clicks. The boy with the bat is Steve Sayers, Kate Townsend's ex-boyfriend.

"Why are you pointing that at me?" Sayers screams at the cop, his eyes blazing with anger or fear and maybe both. *"He's* the one! Look what he did!"

Steve points to the men on the ground, and I recognize one of them as a St. Stephen's senior. *What the hell is going on?* As the cop yells again for Sayers to drop the bat, Steve swings the Louisville Slugger in a great roundhouse arc. Drew ducks beneath the whistling wood, and Steve keeps spinning. As the bat comes around a second time, Drew springs forward and snatches it from Steve's hands.

"Get back, Steve!" he shouts. "I don't want to fight you!"

But Sayers is beyond rational thought. He lunges for Drew's throat, his eyes filled with rage. With a lightning motion, Drew thrusts the fat end of the bat into Steve's midsection. There's an explosive grunt, and Steve folds over the bat and drops to his knees, sucking for air. In the same moment, a cloud of pepper spray envelops Steve and Drew. Steve screams, and Drew begins clawing at his eyes with his free hand.

"That's enough!" I yell at the cop. "That's Dr. Drew Elliott! I'm his attorney. There's no more danger!"

"Drop the bat, Doctor!" the cop yells at Drew again.

"Drop it, Drew!" I shout.

But Steve Sayers isn't done. Somehow he gets to his feet and charges Drew like a blind bull. Drew must be blind himself, because he takes the brunt of the charge in his belly. From reflex he pops Steve across the upper back with the bat, and this time the boy drops to the cement and stays there. Drew tosses the bat away and holds up his hands in surrender.

The cop with the pepper spray takes a pair of handcuffs from his belt, rushes up to Drew, and cuffs his hands behind his back.

"I was defending myself!" Drew protests, tears streaming down his face. "Penn, these kids attacked me. I tried to talk to them, but they wouldn't listen!"

"He's telling the truth!" shouts Drew's med tech, stepping forward.

The other cop has cuffed Steve Sayers and is now checking the other boys on the ground.

"What happened here, ma'am?" asks the first cop.

Susan Salter swallows and tries to collect herself. "Dr. Elliott and I were just standing here talking, and these kids drove up and started cursing. They picked the fight. I have no idea why. It was crazy! Dr. Elliott did everything he could to avoid it."

"What's your name, ma'am?"

"Susan Salter. I'm Dr. Elliott's medical technologist."

The cop turns to me. "You're Dr. Elliott's lawyer?"

"Yes, I am, Officer. Penn Cage. As you saw, my client was clearly defending himself. But as serious as this looks, it's still misdemeanor assault, and I very much doubt that my client will press charges. He knows these boys, and I'm sure it was all a misunderstanding. Isn't that right, Drew?"

Drew looks in my direction with tears streaming down his face. "Uh . . . that's right, Officer. We were just horsing around, and it got out of hand."

"Bullshit!" yells one of the boys on the ground. "That bastard tried to kill us! He broke my fucking nose!"

The cop points at Steve Sayers. "In that kid's hands, a baseball bat is a deadly weapon. It looked like aggravated assault to me."

The cop is right. Steve Sayers is at least six-foot-one, and he has the hyperinflated musculature I associate with the use of anabolic steroids. All three boys do, come to think of it, which makes me think of Marko Bakic and his little drug business at St. Stephen's.

"Aggravated assault is a felony, Officer," I say evenly. "Steve's a good kid. There's no reason to put a felony arrest on his record."

"Everybody wait right here," says the cop, who looks young enough to be a rookie. He's not going to make decisions involving prominent citizens without some advice from a superior. As he goes back to his squad car to use the radio, I turn to one of the seniors on the ground. "What the hell were you guys doing?"

"Kiss my ass!" he barks. "That bastard needs his ass kicked. Fucking cradle-robber. Pervert."

Then it hits me: *They know about Drew and Kate.*

I'd like to question Drew, but the second cop is standing too close to him. I try to catch Drew's eye, but the pepper spray has rendered those organs useless for the time being.

When the young cop returns from his car, he walks right past me, informs Drew that he's under arrest for aggravated assault, then begins reading him his Miranda rights. The other cop takes his cue and does the same to Steve Sayers.

"What are you guys doing?" I ask in the calmest voice I can muster. "Dr. Elliott was clearly defending himself. You heard what he said during the fight."

"Judge'll decide that," says the young cop. "Step back, sir."

"The most you can arrest him for is simple assault."

"I'm just doing what the chief told me to do."

"The chief of police told you to do this?"

"That's right. You got a problem, take it up with him."

"I'll do that," I reply, but what I'm thinking is, *Son of a bitch! This situation is becoming more political by the minute.* The police chief should have ordered the patrolman to let Drew go, or at most to arrest him for simple assault, then release him on a recognizance bond. An arrest for aggravated assault can only mean one thing: the chief wants Drew and Steve in his custody. And the only reason I can see for that is the long-running turf war between the police department and the sheriff's office. In the arena of that conflict, the police chief has been handed a gift from the gods. He can now hold Sheriff Byrd's two main murder suspects in his jail for at least one night.

The boys cuss and spit at Drew as the cops haul them to their feet. One's face is a mass of blood below the nose; the other's left eye is already swelling shut. For a man defending himself against three assailants, Drew did a lot of damage.

A second squad car pulls into the lot. As the police herd their charges into the cars, I promise Drew I'll meet him at the station. Then I pull Susan Salter into the courtyard of Drew's office building. She's hyperventilating now, and her tears are flowing nonstop.

"I don't understand!" she says in a stunned voice. "This morning everything was fine, and now . . . everything's upside down! It doesn't make any sense. How could they think Dr. Elliott could do anything against the law?"

Is she talking about the fight? I wonder. *Or about Kate's murder?* I take hold of Susan's thin wrists and speak in a reassuring voice. "Listen to me, Susan. I don't know how much Drew told you about his situation, but I do know this: he trusted you with his life. He told me you'd worked for him nine years, and that he had absolute confidence in you. What you just saw will be the talk of the town by tonight. If you add to that talk, it can only hurt Drew. Do you understand?"

She sucks her upper lip into her mouth as though thinking hard, then nods and wipes her nose. "Don't worry about me saying anything. I hate gossip. That's why I quit the hospital. All they do over there is cheat on their spouses and gossip about it afterward. I think they like the talking better than the cheating."

"Will you tell me what you saw in the parking lot?"

She nods helpfully. "It happened just like I said. We were standing there talking about recombinant DNA, and this big pickup truck screeched to a stop beside us." She points at a jacked-up orange pickup parked thirty yards away. "There were three guys inside. They looked like high school kids, but big, you know? I think Dr. Elliott knew them, because he waved and spoke to the driver. But then a guy jumped out of the backseat and started screaming at Dr. Elliott."

"What did he scream?"

"Curse words, mostly."

"Try to remember exactly."

Susan has a primitive Baptist's reluctance to utter profanity. " 'You motherfucker,' I think he said first. 'You sick motherfucker. It was you. It was you all along.' "

Oh wow. This is only a preview of the community reaction to Drew's secret private life. "Did Drew say anything back?"

"No. He looked too shocked to speak."

"Go on."

" 'You need your ass kicked,' I think the boy said next, and then he jumped at Dr. Elliott like he was going to hit him. Dr. Elliott called him by name then. He told Steve to calm down and get back in the truck. But the kid just threw up his fists and kept jumping forward like he was going to hit Dr. Elliott. I was kind of freaked out, but not really scared at that point. It was so *weird*. But then the other two guys jumped out of the truck."

"Is that when the bat came into it?"

"No. That only happened after Drew knocked the other two guys down."

"Who threw the first punch?"

"The first kid. Steve."

"Did Drew fight back?"

"Not at first. He kept trying to calm Steve down. But after Steve hit him five or six times, Dr. Elliott shoved him backward. Steve fell down, and I think that really embarrassed him. He screamed for the other guys to help, and at that point the other two guys jumped Dr. Elliott."

"What happened then?"

Susan shakes her head as though in wonder. "I'm not really sure. I mean, it happened so fast. It was like Dr. Elliott knew how to fight and they didn't. They were really mad, and they were screaming and throwing punches everywhere, but it looked sort of like my husband wrestling with my ten-year-old son. The second it got serious, it was like, *over.*"

"How did the baseball bat come into it?"

"Steve went down first, but while Dr. Elliott was handling the other two, Steve grabbed the bat from the truck." Susan shakes her head as if reliving the fight. "It was *scary.* I've never seen Dr. Elliott like that. I saw him once at the hospital picnic. He played softball with his shirt off, and he was like, *ripped,* you know?"

"I know. I grew up with him."

"But he wasn't that competitive, not like the other guys. He was just out there for fun. But today . . . Dr. Elliott did everything he could to stop that fight, but once he knew it was going to happen, he just *switched on.* I've never seen anything like that."

I can understand Susan's awe. Steve Sayers and his buddies have been pumping iron seriously for two or three years. But their steroid-plumped muscles are no match for the speed and strength that genetics bestowed upon Drew Elliott at birth. And their teenage anger couldn't begin to compare with the deadly resolve of a man who sensed he was fighting for his life.

"But in your mind, it was the other guys' fault?" I ask.

"Oh, totally. Absolutely. They wanted a piece of Dr. Elliott, and they pushed him until they got it. Dear Lord."

"All right, Susan. Will you be okay if I go on to the station now?"

She nods uncertainly. "I think so. Thanks for staying with me."

"Glad to do it. And you're not going to talk to anybody about this? Other than the police?"

"No, I understand." She looks suddenly upset again. "Mr. Cage, is Drew going to be all right?"

The look in Susan Salter's eyes tells me she's more than half in love with her boss, but I don't even want to go there. I nod at her as though any other outcome would be impossible. "You take care, okay?"

"I will."

As I hurry back to my Saab, one thought fills my head: *How did Steve Sayers find out that Drew was involved with Kate?* But once in the car, another, more frightening thought takes its place: *Who else knows about it?*

CHAPTER

9

Natchez police headquarters is a one-story building sandwiched between a Pizza Hut and an abandoned strip mall on the north side of town. The PD used to be downtown, but that more stately building was razed to make room for a modern juvenile justice center. By the time I arrive at the station, both Drew and Steve Sayers have been processed and taken to detention cells in the rear of the building. The other two high school boys were booked on simple assault and now await their parents in holding cells; a six-hundred-dollar bond will free them.

I demand a meeting with the chief of police, and almost immediately I'm escorted to his office. Chief Don Logan sits waiting for me behind his desk. He's a thin man in his forties who looks more like an engineer than a policeman. His spartan office reflects his reputation as a managerial type. Chief Logan has family photos on his desk, and more computer manuals than law enforcement texts on his bookshelves. He's known for being careful about procedure, so it's all the more surprising that he's made the political move of arresting Drew.

"Hello, Chief Logan," I say equably.

He regards me coolly over a steaming cup of coffee. "In my

seven years as chief," he says, " I've never seen anything like the furor over this situation. I understand the emotional side, of course. A pretty young girl, so much potential. A prominent physician suddenly associated with her murder. But people are losing their perspective over this thing. There's a mob mentality developing out there. Nobody seems to want to let matters take their normal course. To let the system work."

"Including the district attorney?" I prompt.

Chief Logan raises one eyebrow, but he doesn't take the bait. "I'm sure you're wondering why we've charged your client with aggravated assault."

"You read my mind, Chief."

"I'm going to lay my cards on the table, Penn. We have a troubled history with the sheriff's department. You know all about it, I'm sure. The city of Natchez is under the jurisdiction of the police department, but technically, the sheriff has jurisdiction over the entire county, which includes the city. In general, we have a working agreement whereby we work crimes inside the city limits and the sheriff takes the county."

"But?"

Logan takes a sip of coffee. "But Billy Byrd is a political animal. And when a high-profile case comes along, the sheriff believes it's his God-given right to storm in and take over the investigation. Billy ran roughshod over the last police chief, and he's tried to do the same to me on occasion. He's actually had his deputies try to arrest one of my officers at a couple of crime scenes. They almost came to blows. I've requested several legal opinions from the attorney general's office in Jackson, but nothing they send us is ever definitive enough."

"I understand your problem. I dealt with some of the same issues in Houston."

Chief Logan nods as though encouraged. "I'm glad you do. Because today I'm drawing the line. Kate Townsend's body was discovered just within the boundary of the city, which alone makes it our case. But she almost certainly died farther upstream in that creek, which removes any doubt whatever about jurisdiction."

Sheriff Byrd won't see it that way. "You're preaching to the choir, Chief. Tell me about the assault charge."

"Since that's a felony charge, Dr. Elliott and the Sayers boy will have to spend the night in this building. I'll have a chance to talk to them without any interference from Sheriff Byrd. Now, as Dr. Elliott's lawyer, you can stop me if you want to. But know this: my sole interest is in solving Kate Townsend's murder. I'm not railroading anybody to judgment in order to grab some headlines, here or anywhere else."

This is good news indeed.

"If Dr. Elliott's guilty," Logan goes on, "then he should be punished to the fullest extent of the law. But if he's not, the man deserves some protection." The chief shakes his head. "Drew's reputation will be blown to hell by suppertime tonight, and as far as I can tell, there's nothing against him but some anonymous phone calls and a fistfight."

"Which he didn't start," I point out.

The chief waves his hand as though shooing away a fly. "The judge will throw out the assault charge tomorrow morning. The bottom line is, I think Dr. Elliot's safer in my jail than anywhere else in this town tonight."

I sit back in my chair and study the chief. He's the first rational man I've spoken to in some time. "I hear you loud and clear."

"I don't have isolation cells here," he says, "but I do have some eight-man units that are empty. I've put Drew in one and the Sayers boy in the other. They'll be safe and relatively comfortable until tomorrow."

I try to suppress a smile at the thought of Shad Johnson learning about this development. "Have you spoken to the D.A. about this assault arrest?"

Chief Logan looks out his solitary window and gives a long-suffering sigh. "I try very hard to get along with the district attorney. But I have a feeling Mr. Johnson isn't going to like this one bit." He looks back at me, his dark eyes hard with conviction. "You know what? Tough titty. This ain't right, and I ain't going along with it. There's not a damn thing Mr. Johnson can do about this arrest before tomorrow, unless he wants to call a judge and have Dr. Elliott released on the strength of the D.A.'s word. And given Mr. Johnson's main political support base, I don't think he'll want to do that."

I stand and shake hands with Logan. "I'm quite satisfied that procedure has been followed, Chief. Do you have any problem with me speaking to my client before I go?"

"I'll have him brought to the visitors' room."

On my way out, I stop and turn back. "Do you know Kate's time of death yet?"

Logan watches me in silence for a few moments. Then he says, "From the body temperature—which they did take when the fishermen got her to the ER—the M.E. figures she died between three and five-thirty p.m."

"That's pretty exact."

Logan nods. "They know she left the school alive at two fifty-five, and she hadn't cooled much by seven-thirty, when they took the temp. The M.E. says he feels pretty confident about that window."

"Does he have any idea how long she was in the water?"

"It's hard to say, given how quickly everything happened. If he did know that, we might be able to figure out how far upstream she died. But that creek moves very fast in flood. She wouldn't have to be in it long to be swept miles downstream. And remember, Kate was found at six-twenty. No matter what the M.E. says, a maximum of only three hours and twenty minutes could have passed after death, even if someone strangled her the minute she walked out of St. Stephen's. I don't think the body temperature is going to tell us what we want to know, Penn."

"Okay. So as of now, suspects need alibis from three p.m. to five-thirty."

"Yep."

"Thanks, Chief."

He smiles. "You didn't hear it from me."

Five minutes later, Drew is escorted into the tiny visitors' cubicle and seated behind a glass partition with a metal screen in it. He looks pale and drawn, and his eyes have the dull sheen I associate with lifers in the Walls unit at Huntsville, Texas, where I used to spend quite a bit of time. Has thirty minutes in a cell done this to one of the toughest friends I ever had?

"When am I getting out, Penn?"

"Not until tomorrow, I'm afraid."

I expect anger, but Drew hardly reacts. Maybe his listlessness is a symptom of grief. Maybe the attack by the St. Stephen's teenagers has punctured his illusions about his relationship with Kate—or maybe his image of himself as a good man.

"Chief Logan's done you a big favor," I explain. "He's isolated you from Sheriff Byrd, who would love to use you to grab some headlines. He's also put you at more of a remove from Shad Johnson, who wants to use you as a stepping-stone to higher office. Both men would like to interrogate you at their leisure, but I doubt either one will be bothering you in here."

"You never gave me the details of Kate's autopsy," Drew says, his eyes boring into mine.

"I gave you the main points. The rest is medical jargon."

His eyes don't waver. "Don't bullshit me. Don't try to spare me."

I focus on some dried pink bubblegum on the glass between us. "The pathologist thinks she was raped."

"Based on?"

"Genital trauma."

Drew looks confused by this. "Go on."

"They found semen from two different men inside her body."

He closes his eyes like a man fighting bone-deep pain. "Why didn't you tell me that before?"

"I wanted you sane when the deputies came to collect your blood."

He shakes his head as though I've betrayed him.

"Drew, I have to ask you this. Is there any chance that Kate was having consensual sex with someone else besides you?"

A slow blink. Then an odd smile. "You still don't get it, do you? Kate loved me. She loved me *absolutely*. If you'd told me earlier that they found two different semen samples inside her, I could have told you right away that she'd been raped."

"Well . . . I wish there were some way to prove absolute love. Because I think the D.A. is going to paint you as a jealous older man who went crazy when he found out his teenage mistress was sharing her natural bounty with someone else."

Drew's mouth wrinkles with disgust. "I don't care what he does."

"You'd better start. You'd better give the whole situation some serious thought tonight. Try to conjure up some idea of who might have wanted to rape or kill Kate. Because the fact that she was pregnant means that you could be charged with double homicide."

Drew's blue eyes are impenetrable to me. After a time, he says, "What happens tomorrow?"

"Tomorrow I'll have the assault charge against you dismissed. You don't want to charge Steve Sayers for attacking you."

"No."

"All right—"

"Fuck!" Drew exclaims, his face suddenly flushed. "What about *Tim?* He's going to see the newspaper. Kids are going to tell him his dad's in jail!"

I wish there was something I could do to ease Drew's mind about his son, but there's not. "Tim's going to have a bad time throughout this thing," I say evenly. "You have to accept that. I'll get you out as early as I can tomorrow, and you can talk to him yourself."

Drew shakes his head, his eyes flicking back and forth in helpless rage.

"Something else you'd better get used to," I add. "Steve Sayers and his buddies are a pretty typical example of how the people in this community are going to feel about you for a while."

Drew's eyes fix upon me. "All I care about is Tim. You get me out so I can help him understand this. After that, I'll find out who killed Kate."

There's an undertone in Drew's voice that sends a tingle along my forearms. It's the emotionless timbre of the man who put down three muscle-bound jocks without breaking a sweat. He said,

"After that, I'll find out who killed Kate," the same way he might say, "After dinner, I'll take out the garbage."

I nod and stand in the little cubicle. "I'll see you in the morning."

Drew leaves the visiting room without a word.

By the time I pick up Annie from school, I've taken several cell calls, and my phone is still ringing. Most of the calls have been from school parents, pumping me for information about Drew and Kate. But a few were more serious, and more disturbing.

One was from Holden Smith, the president of the St. Stephen's school board. Holden had heard a distorted version of the afternoon's fight from Steve Sayers's father, and he was livid at Drew. About the only fact he had right was that Steve and Drew were being held in jail on felony assault charges. I did my best to explain that Drew wasn't at fault, but Holden didn't buy my argument.

"That's not even the *point*," he said. "We've got a member of the school board brawling with three of our students! That's simply unacceptable. Drew should know better than to let something like that happen."

"I told you he tried to stop it, Holden. The fight couldn't have been avoided."

"Okay, okay, but look what the fight was *about*. Everybody in town knows Drew was having sex with Kate Townsend, and that he might even have killed her. Do you—"

"Nobody knows that!" I snapped. "That's pure speculation!"

"So what! Do you realize what that kind of rumor will do to St. Stephen's? To our public image? Do you know what kind of *lawsuits* we're going to get over this?"

"What are you telling me, Holden?"

A brief silence. "We want Drew off the board."

"Who's 'we'?"

"Everybody!"

"You want him to resign?"

"If he doesn't, we'll vote him off tonight in a special session. We have no choice."

"That's bullshit. The board could give Drew its qualified support, based on his years of dedication to the school. Did that thought enter anyone's head?"

"Don't even pretend that's an option," Holden said in a dismissive voice. "You know how this town works. And that brings up another issue. What about you, Penn? Are you Drew's lawyer now?"

"I'm not sure."

"Well, if you are, you're not going to be able to remain on the board, either."

Holden was right about that. As a board member, I'll be named in any civil suit arising out of the present situation. I can't remain on the board and also defend Drew in a civil or criminal proceeding. Of course, resigning would cut off my flow of inside information, but I wasn't about to align myself with gutless Holden Smith.

"Drew and I will both resign," I said with disgust. "You'll have our letters in the morning."

"We'd prefer to have Drew's tonight."

I hung up on him.

While I drove along in a funk, Caitlin called me from Boston. Apparently, a reporter for the *Natchez Examiner* had called her and delivered a summation of the rumors spreading across town. Caitlin was stunned that I was being mentioned as Drew Elliot's lawyer. She knows Drew, but only superficially, and she has no special reason to believe he's innocent of the crimes being attributed to him.

"Exactly when were you going to tell me you were representing Drew?" she asked. "Or were you going to tell me at all?"

"I'm not sure I'm going to represent him."

"I thought you didn't practice anymore."

"Drew is a lifelong friend, and he needs help. Right now, I'm acting primarily as a friend." This wasn't strictly true, but I've been deceiving myself as well as Caitlin about that. "When I see how this develops, I'll make a decision about the legal side of things."

"Penn, why didn't you tell me about all this last night?"

Caitlin sounded hurt, but she hasn't been very communicative to me about her recent situation either. "I couldn't get you on the phone last night. You were at your party."

"You could have called me this morning."

"Yes, but you already had reporters working the story. You may even end up working it yourself."

"We've been in that situation before, and we handled it fine."

"But not without tension."

A little laugh. "Tension's okay. We can live with tension. It's deception we can't live with."

"I agree."

More silence. "What's that supposed to mean?"

"I just agreed with you."

"You had a tone."

"No tone. Look, things are breaking fast on this. I'll call you tonight and give you a better idea of where I stand, okay?"

Her sigh told me she was far from happy with this arrangement. "Did Drew kill her, Penn? I'm asking as your lover, not a journalist."

"You know I can't answer that. Even if I knew the answer."

"But he was involved with her?"

"You won't report my answer?"

"No."

"Yes. He was in love with her. But I don't think he killed her."

"Classic midlife crisis?"

"I don't think it's that simple. Drew says he and Ellen have been living a charade for ten years. He was starved for affection, and he finally found exactly what he was missing. And now here we are."

"What about the two semen samples—"

"No more," I cut in. "I'll talk to you tonight."

"I love you," Caitlin said after an awkward silence.

"You too."

When Annie gets into the car, I set my phone on silent. I also keep quiet about the fact that I've spoken to Caitlin. Annie would want to call her back immediately, and I don't want to deal with that right now. Annie says she needs to go to Walgreen's for some school supplies, so we make a run to the drugstore, one of my few sources in town for iced green tea. By the time we get home, my phone shows eight missed calls. While I scroll through the list, an incoming call pops up. It's from Sonny Cross, a sheriff's deputy assigned to the Mississippi Bureau of Narcotics. Sonny has two young boys at St. Stephen's, and through me, he's spoken to the board a few times about Marko Bakic, our Croatian exchange student. Sonny suspects that Marko has gotten involved in the local drug trade, but so far he's been unable to prove it.

"Sonny," I say. "What's up?"

"I'm calling to give you a heads-up," Cross says in his laid-back, urban-cowboy voice.

"Marko Bakic again?"

"Among other things. Last night there was a big party out at Lake St. John. A rave. There was a lot of X there, and a lot of St. Stephen's kids, too."

Lake St. John is a horseshoe lake about thirty miles up the Mississippi River, on the Louisiana side. It's thronged with Natchez natives in the summer, but this time of year, most of the lake houses are deserted.

"Was it only St. Stephen's kids?"

"No, thank God. The Catholic school and the Baptist boys were well represented."

"Did you bust the party?"

"No. We didn't find out about it until it was over. Whoever organized it did just what they do in the cities. The kids get word over their cell phones to go to such and such a place. When they get there, they find a sheet of paper taped to a pole with a coded message, a rhyme only the kids will understand. After they get led around to four or five different spots, they know where the rave is, and they know whether they're being followed or not."

"I know the routine."

"Word is, these raves have been going on for a couple of months now. Different location every time. And I'm hearing our boy Marko is behind them."

"Great."

"Yeah. You know, most of the X in Mississippi gets brought up from the Gulf Coast. The Asian gangs down there control the trade. And Marko's been down to Gulfport and Biloxi a couple of times that I know about. I wanted you to know we're going to be stepping up surveillance on him."

"I appreciate it."

"I just want to try to minimize the damage to St. Stephen's if we have to take Marko down. You know, once you get X into a community, you usually get LSD, too. It tends to be cooked and sold by the same crews. One of my sources said some kids may have been doing acid last night at the lake party. And check this, Marko bought out a roadside fireworks stand and put on a psychedelic show at the end of the night. Sailed out on a party barge and let off five grand worth of rockets."

"Sorry I missed it. But where does a poor exchange student get the money to do that?"

"That's no mystery, bubba. It's proving it that's the bitch."

"Hey, do you know where Marko was yesterday between three and five-thirty?"

Sonny Cross laughs darkly. "Already thought of that, my man. Checked it out, too. Marko was with Coach Anders from three until nearly six."

"At the school?"

"No, at Anders's house. Wade has just about wangled the kid a football scholarship at Delta State. Just what the world needs, right? One more soccer-style kicker. Anyway, I called Wade, and he told me he worked the phone for the kid about an hour. Marko was right there with him, doing homework. Then Wade tried to help Marko with his chemistry." Cross laughs again. "The blind leading the blind. Anyway, no luck there."

"Thanks, Sonny. I really appreciate the information."

"Sometimes I think you're the only one. You ask me, some of those people on the board have their heads most of the way up their asses."

"To be honest with you, I'm resigning from the board tomorrow. But I'll do all I can to help with the Marko situation."

Silence. "Can you tell me why you're resigning?"

"It's the Drew Elliott thing."

"Huh. I don't see why you'd have to resign because of that. But you know more about it than I do. I hate to see you go, man."

"Thanks. I'll keep you posted."

"You ask me, Drew Elliott is a stand-up guy. Like the old-time docs. He actually gives a shit how you're doing."

"I think you're right. Look, I hate to go, but—"

"One last thing, Penn. That Townsend girl wasn't the all-American, lily-white virgin some people are making her out to be."

Suddenly my haste is gone. "What do you mean?"

"I've done a lot of surveillance in this town. And I've seen Kate Townsend in some places good girls just don't go, if you get my drift."

"I'm not sure I do."

"She hung with some pretty bad company sometimes. And she's no stranger to drugs."

"Weed? Or worse?"

"Worse, I think."

"This might be really important, Sonny. Important to Drew. Where exactly have you seen Kate?"

"Brightside Manor."

This is the last thing I expected to hear. The Brightside Manor Apartments are a dilapidated group of buildings on the north side of town, the closest thing to a slum inside the city limits. Its occupants are poor and black, and the complex is named frequently in the newspaper as the site of crimes from domestic abuse to shootings. "What the hell was Kate Townsend doing there?"

"I'm not sure. But I've spotted her there several times over the last few months. I've even got videotape of her going in and out. About once a month, now that I think about it."

"You think she was buying drugs?"

"Maybe. I wasn't going to bust her to find out, being who she was. But the thing is, girls like Kate Townsend get their drugs from friends, not dealers. And looking like she did, Kate wouldn't have to *buy* drugs at all, you know?"

"I'm listening, Sonny."

"Well, Brightside Manor is where Cyrus White lives."

"Who's that?"

"The top drug dealer in the city of Natchez. And its Cyrus's building that I've seen Kate go in and out of."

"Jesus."

"That's why I say she wasn't buying weed. If Kate Townsend was visiting Cyrus White to get drugs, she was there for some heavy shit. Powder cocaine, or maybe even heroin."

Every new sentence out of Cross's mouth freaks me out more. "Do we have heroin in Natchez?"

"Brother, every town has every drug. You just have to know where to look."

"Wonderful. Do you know anything else about Kate?"

"No. But I've got a theory, if you want to wrap your mind around something scary."

"I'm listening."

"She's wasn't going there to buy *anything*. She was there to see Cyrus."

"You mean . . ."

"That's what I mean. Cyrus has a real taste for white girls. A well-documented taste."

Kate Townsend doing a drug dealer? "That sounds too crazy, Sonny."

"Cyrus ain't your average drug dealer. In past years, most Natchez dealers were punks barely out of their teens. Cyrus is thirty-four and smart as a whip. By the time I heard he was in business, all his competition had been wiped out. Ruthlessly. But I couldn't pin a thing on him."

Cyrus is thirty-four . . . Drew is forty. Did Kate have a thing for older men in general?

"Cyrus is a veteran of Desert Storm, if you can believe it," Sonny continues. "He was in the air force. I've been trying to bust him for over a year, but nothing sticks. He's the Teflon nigger."

Sonny's use of the N-word is completely unself-conscious. He belongs to that group of Southerners who modify their vocabulary

by the company they're in. Around whites he knows—and probably suspects he's busting—Sonny says "nigger" without even a
shading of caution. Around strangers, he's as politically correct as
the next guy. But there's no question how he really sees the most
frequent targets of his profession. There's also no question that his
prejudice is part of what makes African-Americans his primary
targets, rather than the Kate Townsends of the world. But that
prejudice isn't unique to redneck sheriff's detectives in Mississippi.
It thrives in the blood of the American judicial system, all the way
up to Washington.

"Does Sheriff Byrd know about Kate's connection to Cyrus?"
I ask.

The narcotics agent doesn't answer for some time. Then he says,
"It's not that I don't trust the sheriff, Penn. I just don't like him
messing around in my cases until it's time to move on something.
He can be a disruptive influence."

"I hear you, Sonny. I appreciate you telling me all this. Anything
else you get on Kate, please let me know."

"Will do. And I'll do anything I can to help out Dr. Elliott."

I hang up, my mind spinning with the new information. How
well did Drew really know Kate? Did he see her as an all-American,
lily-white virgin, as Sonny described her? Or did he know about
her shadow side? If not, that hidden part of her life might hold the
key to the second semen sample found in her corpse, and thus the
key to freeing Drew.

It's that question that occupies me as I sit at my dining room
table with Annie in the fading light of dusk. Annie is doing her
homework, and now and then she throws a question at me, more
out of boredom than from needing help. I'm supposedly working
on my new novel, but what I'm really doing is trying to tease out
the secret threads of Drew's and Kate's lives. My new awareness of
Cyrus White has completely changed my perspective on Drew's situation.

One thing that keeps coming back to me is Drew's assertion
that the blackmailer who called him that first night and told him
to leave the money on the football field "sounded like a black

kid." I doubt that a thirty-four-year-old war veteran would sound like a kid, but sometimes people's voices surprise you. Heavyweight champion and convicted rapist Mike Tyson sounds like a five-year-old boy when he speaks. But the more likely answer is that a big-time drug dealer like Cyrus White probably has dozens of kids working for him. And that's who he'd get to make a call like that.

It wasn't just money they wanted, I recall with sudden clarity. The blackmailers wanted drugs from Drew, as well. But does that point toward Cyrus White? Why would a drug dealer ask for drugs? As I ponder this question, my front doorbell chimes. I'm not expecting anyone, but given all that's happened today, there's no telling who it might be.

When I open the door, I find the last person I would have expected. Jenny Townsend, Kate's mother. Jenny is tall and clear-eyed like Kate, and she's holding a worn Jimmy Choo shoe box in front of her.

"Hello, Penn," she says in a controlled voice.

"Jenny," I say awkwardly. "Will you come in?"

She takes a deep breath and seems to gather herself before answering. "No, thank you. I saw Annie through the window. I know you're busy."

"It's all right. Really."

"No," she says, shaking her head. "I don't think I could take it. I used to help Kate with her homework just like that, after her father left."

What does one say at these moments? There's nothing appropriate, so I remain silent. Jenny actually looks grateful that I'm not forcing her to make small talk.

"I've heard a lot of rumors today," she says with obvious difficulty. "Some were pretty terrible. One was that you're representing Drew Elliott."

So, that's what this visit is about. "Drew is an old friend, Jenny. You know that. I can't begin to imagine what you've gone through, but I feel obligated to try to help Drew through this."

"Oh, you misunderstood me," she says. "I didn't mean that you representing Drew was terrible. In fact, I was glad to hear that.

That's why I brought you this." She gestures with the box but doesn't quite offer it to me.

"What is that?"

"Kate's things. Her private things. I haven't looked at all of them. I'm not sure I could bear it, and it wasn't meant for my eyes anyway." Jenny brushes a strand of hair out of her eyes, then flinches at some inner pain. "Katie kept this hidden in the attic. There's a diary, some souvenirs, and some computer disks. I think that's where she kept her pictures of Drew. I think some of them are probably . . . intimate pictures."

"I see," I say softly.

"Penn, I don't know what happened to my daughter yesterday. The police tell me she was raped and murdered. I don't know anything for certain right now, but I *do* know—or at least I believe— that Drew could not have hurt my Katie."

A flood of relief washes through me. "I'm so glad to hear that, Jenny. I believe the same thing."

"That's why I'm leaving this box with you."

I nod but say nothing.

She looks down at my welcome mat and speaks with a new tension in her voice. "The police and the sheriff's department have gotten more aggressive with their questioning. They want to search my house from top to bottom for clues to Kate's 'recent lifestyle.' I don't want them to see what's in this box." Jenny looks up, her chin quivering. "Those men have no right to invade my daughter's privacy. This is a difficult thing for me to do, Penn. If it turns out that Drew did harm Kate, perhaps without even meaning to, this box contains the only physical evidence of their relationship."

"Maybe you should keep it, then."

She shakes her head. "I can't. And there's no one else. I have no close family here, and even if I did, I wouldn't trust them with it. I'm not even sure I trust myself with it. That's why I'm not putting it in a safe-deposit box. I'm trusting you because of who you are and who your father is. Your father was my doctor when I was young. Tom Cage has more integrity than any man I've ever known, and I don't think the apple fell far from the tree. I respect what you did in solving that old civil rights murder, for not giving a damn what people around here thought about it." I start to interject, but she motions for me to be quiet and pushes on. "I don't know what's going to happen about Katie in the next few weeks, but if somewhere along the way you come to believe that Drew hurt my baby, I expect you to make sure that the right people see what's in this box."

I nod slowly, not quite believing that this is happening.

Jenny holds out the box. "I want you to give me your word as a gentleman, Penn. I know that word is sort of outdated, but I still believe it applies in some cases."

"You have my word, Jenny."

Even as I accept the box and cradle it under my right arm, I wonder what I'm doing. How can I defend Drew in court if I've vowed to make sure he is punished if he turns out to be guilty? Maybe that's why I'm taking the box. Maybe it's my way out of defending Drew at trial.

"Daddy?" Annie calls from the living room. "Who is it?"

"I'm going to run on," Jenny says.

"I don't know what to say, Jenny."

She turns away, walks to the top step, then looks back. "The district attorney told me Kate was pregnant. It must have been Drew's baby."

I nod slowly.

"Do you think he would have married her, Penn? Tell me the truth."

"Jenny, that's the one thing in this whole mess that I'm absolutely sure of. He'd have married her tomorrow if he could."

She tilts back her head and blinks away tears, then gives me a shattered smile and hurries into the night.

In the silence on my front steps, I feel tears coming to my own eyes. How did we bring ourselves to this pass? Jenny Townsend in her solitary grief; Drew sitting alone in jail; Kate Townsend lying dead on a slab somewhere in Jackson, an ugly Y-incision stitched into her torso; an empty chair at Harvard that will now be filled by some luckier kid who will never know what tragedy brought him or her there. Did all this result from Drew's forbidden love of Kate? Or do I trace it back to Drew's wife and the hydrocodone addiction that Drew says killed their marriage? Or—

"Daddy?" Annie calls from the door. "Can't you hear the phone?"

"No, Boo," I say softly. "I'm coming."

I walk to the kitchen and pick up the telephone. "This is Penn."

"Penn? Walter Hunt."

It takes me a moment to switch gears. Walter Hunt is an accountant who lives in Sherwood Estates, and a neighbor of Drew's. He has two kids in St. Stephen's.

"What can I do for you, Walter?"

"Nothing for me, but I thought you'd like to know—Ellen Elliott is piling up furniture and all kinds of stuff in her front yard. Looks like Drew's stuff to me—golf clubs and skis—guns, too. To tell you the truth, it looks like she's building a bonfire."

Jesus Christ. "Thanks, Walter. I'm on my way. Where's Tim?"

"Timmy's over here with us. My wife went over and slipped in their back door."

"Don't let anybody call the police. I'll be there in no time."

"Hurry, Penn. Ellen's so toasted, she can barely walk."

CHAPTER
10

I'm sitting on my front steps with Annie, waiting impatiently for Mia Burke to arrive. Annie is playing Scooby-Doo on her Game Boy Advance. I'm trying to focus on the perfume of a white narcissus, which blooms liberally on Washington Street this time of year, but at this moment it's hard to enjoy anything. My mind won't leave the Jimmy Choo shoe box I just hid atop the armoire in my upstairs guest room, the box that contains the secret history of Kate Townsend's life with Drew. I shudder to think what would be happening now if the police had discovered that box during a search of Jenny Townsend's house. The only thing keeping me from going through Kate's personal things right now is my fear that Ellen Elliott may do something to hurt Drew as badly as she can out of revenge.

After failing to reach Ellen by phone, I called Mia, who agreed to watch Annie until I get back. Before she hung up, Mia told me she had something to tell me about "the Kate situation," but she refused to say more on her cell phone. Since Mia is plugged into the high school information grid, she may know things that I or the police couldn't discover in a year of asking questions.

Annie looks up from the glow of her Game Boy and fixes me in a serious gaze. "Daddy, everybody keeps asking me why I wasn't in the pageant this year. Why can't I tell them?"

I take a deep breath and sigh. The Confederate Pageant has been the center of white social life in Natchez for the past seventy years. Replete with hoop skirts, sabers, and rebel uniforms, this celebration of pre–Civil War life in the Deep South is one of the most politically incorrect spectacles in the United States. Yet it remains an institution that most of the affluent children in town participate in—as velvet-clad toddlers dancing around a Maypole, clean-cut high schoolers waltzing with flattered tourists, or intoxicated college kids trekking home three times a week during March to don Confederate regalia and march to the strains of "Dixie" as members of the "Confederate Court." Being asked to take part in the pageant is a mark of social distinction—based largely on one's mother's or grandmothers' service to one of the powerful "Garden Clubs"—and certain roles confer star status on those offered them.

Annie has already played starring roles in the pageant, and this year she was offered a spot in "The Big Maypole," one of the vignettes with roles for fourth-graders. This made my mother happy, but I was ambivalent about it. Mom believes Annie will be damaged more by not participating in the pageant with her friends than by acting in a racially questionable production whose subtleties she can't even understand. "After all," she asked, "what harm did it do you? You were in the pageant from the age of four to twenty, and you're as liberal as they come." I laughed, but Annie proved her wrong. A nine-year-old with black friends can easily grasp the issues, and when I explained them to Annie, she asked me to decline the role for her, which I did. I also asked her not to make a big deal of it at school, since so many kids in her class would be taking part.

"But I *mean*," Annie says in an exaggerated voice, "what's the point of not doing something if you don't tell people why you're not doing it?"

As usual, she sounds five years older than her true age, and also as usual, she's right. If you're going to try to change things by example, you have to let people know what you're doing and why, even if you're only nine.

"You're right, punkin. Go ahead and tell them why you're not doing it. But you'd better expect some strong reactions, maybe even from your teacher. Things change slowly around here."

She nods seriously. "I'll think before I talk."

I wish some adults I know would do that. "Good girl."

"Dad?" Annie asks in a tone of some anxiety.

"Yes?"

"Timmy's mom came and picked him up early from school today."

Images of Ellen Elliott fill my mind again. "Did anyone say why?"

"No. But I heard some teachers talking in the hall. They said Dr. Drew was in some kind of fight, and that he'd done something bad."

Damn gossips. "Did they say what he'd done?"

"No. But one of them called him a bad name."

"Which teacher did that?"

"Mrs. Gillette."

A cranky old sourpuss. I silently mark Mrs. Gillette down for further attention. "Dr. Drew hasn't done anything for kids to worry about. You don't pay any attention to people gossiping, okay?"

"I know. I just wanted to tell you, 'cause Timmy's seemed really sad lately."

As I put my arm around Annie and hug her tight, a pair of headlights comes up Washington Street at slightly over the speed limit, then slows and darts to the curb in front of our house. Mia jumps out of her Accord with a smile on her face and a CD case in her hand.

"We're gonna do some *dancing,* girl!" she says to Annie, popping out her hip in a move that seems to travel up her spine and out to her stiffened fingers by some occult law of physics.

Annie leaps to her feet. "What kind of dancing?"

"Cheer dancing!"

Annie claps and hugs Mia's waist. She's practically jumping out of her skin with excitement. This type of giddiness a father simply cannot generate—not in my experience, anyway.

"Run inside and put this on your boom box," Mia says, cutting her eyes at me. "I'll be right there."

"Hurry!" Annie says, taking the disk and disappearing into the house.

"What is it?" I ask quickly. "What do you know?"

Mia's smile vanishes. "Do you know about the grand jury?"

"Tell me."

"This afternoon, four girls in my class got subpoenas to appear before the grand jury."

My chest tightens. "Appear when?"

"This afternoon. It already happened."

"Damn! Did they tell you what they were asked?"

"I haven't talked to them myself, but I heard they got questioned by the district attorney, the black guy who ran for mayor last time."

"Shad Johnson."

"Right. All I know is that it was about Kate and Dr. Elliott."

"This is unbelievable. Shad actually used Drew's name?"

"I don't know for sure. I can try to find out."

"Please. No one's supposed to talk about what happens in the grand jury room, but that's probably all those girls are talking about." *Along with half the grand jury members,* I add silently.

"Oh, definitely. They're major mouths."

"Do you think they knew anything intimate about Kate?"

"No. I don't even know why those four got subpoenas."

"Shad's taking potshots. That's all he knows to do. And he's abusing the hell out of the grand jury system."

"How?"

I click the button on my key ring, opening my car door. "A grand jury isn't an investigative body. It's constituted to decide whether people should be tried for a crime or not, based on evidence uncovered by law enforcement. Shad's using the grand jury to bypass some important legal protections."

"Like?"

"Like not questioning juveniles without their parents present. Police officers can't do that. Shad could also call Drew in there and question him without an attorney present. But he has no grounds whatever to do that. Drew hasn't even been charged with murder. If Shad brought his name up to the grand jury, the only justifiable reason would be in connection with the fight this afternoon. But Drew hasn't even been *arraigned* on that charge."

"Everybody's talking about that fight," Mia says. "I heard Dr. Elliott busted Steve up pretty bad. I saw the other two guys myself, Ray and Jimmy. They looked like they'd been hit by a truck."

"The fight happened at lunchtime. Why weren't those guys in school?"

"They ditched. Most of the seniors ditched today. A lot of them were scheduled to be questioned by the police or by sheriff's deputies, and the rest just used that as an excuse."

"What are people saying about Drew?"

"The word is mixed, believe it or not."

"Really?" I want to ask more, but something tells me that Ellen Elliott can't wait. "I've got to run, Mia. But I want to hear about this when I get back. And please find out all you can about what happened in the grand jury room."

She holds up her cell phone. "No problem. See you when you get back."

The front lawn of Drew's house looks like a garage sale from hell. The grass is littered with tennis rackets, golf clubs, water skis, guns, cameras, and assorted furniture. Books and clothing lie strewn around the yard, most notably a tuxedo draped over a weight bench and a formal gown hanging from a low oak limb. I have to steer around a shattered flat-screen TV to negotiate the pebbled driveway.

As I get out of the car, the front door of the massive Victorian bangs open and Ellen staggers into the yard carrying a compound bow. I hold up both hands to show I'm not a threat. Ellen has killed more than a few deer with that bow, and she's quite capable of taking me out with a razor-tipped broadhead.

"Ellen!" I call. "It's Penn Cage."

"You're not welcome," she says in a flat voice. "You're the wrong kind of lawyer. Go home."

She's wearing some sort of floral housecoat that's falling open from the waist up. Her usually well-coiffed hair hangs in limp strings around her face, and her eyes are puffy and red. Only her dark tan communicates any impression of health, but that's an illusion purchased at the local spa.

"I'd really like to talk to you, Ellen."

"So would half the town. My so-called friends, especially. They want to express their sympathy. *Right.* Those jealous bitches are so giddy with glee they could just *shit.*"

Ellen is clearly drunk. Maybe not on alcohol, though. Maybe it's hydrocodone, as Drew warned me last night. Or maybe both. She flings an arm toward the street.

"Look at them! Vultures, every one."

Across the street, the porch lights of two houses are burning brightly. Looking closer, I see neighbors standing in little knots in the yards, staring unabashedly at Ellen and me. I can't make out Walter Hunt, but he must be there.

Ellen tosses the bow into the yard, takes two steps toward me, and gives me a withering glare. "Well? Is it true? Are you representing Drew?"

"I'm just trying to be a friend, Ellen."

"A friend," she says skeptically. "Yeah, I'll bet. I know how you guys stick together. You probably knew about it all along, didn't you?"

"About what?"

"Little Katie-poo, of course. The backstabbing slut."

"Absolutely not."

She gives me a knowing gaze. "Be honest, Penn. You didn't sit around over a couple of scotches while Drew told you how great it is to squeeze a pair of seventeen-year-old tits again?"

"I had no idea anything like that was going on, Ellen. That's God's truth."

She waves her hand dismissively and turns away from me. "Whatever. You're probably doing Mia over at your place every chance you get."

"*What?*" My face heats with anger. "Are you out of your mind?"

"Come on," she says, looking back over her shoulder. "As much as

Caitlin is out of town? I know these girls, Penn. I hear them talk. They're nothing like the girls I went to school with. No guilt, no repression. Those days are *gone*, honey. These girls are the lucky ones."

"How so?"

She gives me an intoxicated smile. "You know what the difference is between then and now, babe?"

"What?"

"These days, good girls *do*."

I hold up my hands in a beseeching gesture. "Ellen, I'm just here to offer any kind of help I can."

She swings her head around and belly-laughs as though I've just told a dirty joke. "Get real, Penn! You're here for *damage control*. Admit it. You want to know what I've told the cops, or what I might tell them tomorrow."

Is that really the reason I've come? I wonder. I'd like to think I'm the gentleman that Jenny Townsend believes I am, but maybe Ellen is right. "I won't deny I'd like to know that. It could have great impact on Drew's future."

Ellen grins slyly. "You bet your ass it could. He's sweating it over there in jail, isn't he?"

"Have you seen him?"

Another preening smile. "Yes, I have. And it was pretty goddamn satisfying. It's a new experience for him, I'll tell you that. Jail is about the last place our golden boy ever thought he'd wind up. But that's where he belongs, if you ask me. It'll give him a little *perspective*. Remind him of what's important in life."

"Which is?"

"Family. *Sacrifice*. That's what it comes down to in the end. You can do what you want to do, or you can do what's right. And the two aren't ever quite the same."

"I'm not sure that's always true."

Ellen gives me a piercing look. "You know it is."

"I was thinking of my wife."

A shadow of regret crosses her face. "I'm sorry. Sarah was as good as they come. But Drew *ain't*. I used to think he was, once. But he's just like the rest of them."

"The rest of who?"

"*Men,* sugar." A wild light flashes in her eyes. "When it's all said and done, they only care about one thing."

"What's that?"

Ellen thrusts out her left hip and slaps her rump. "Dipping their wick in a piece of ass that's attached to a smiling, subservient, and preferably *young* woman. And if not young, then different from what they're used to. *Capisce?*"

Her gesture has caused one surgically enhanced breast to fall out of her housecoat. When she sees me looking, she does nothing to cover herself. "See what I mean?" she drawls. "Nothing stirs a man's loins like a little *strange,* right, Penn? Oh, I know the story well." She covers herself with a jerk of her gown and surveys the wreckage of her husband's possessions.

"Ellen, if you want to be crude about this, let's be crude. What happened to you and Drew is simple. He was unhappy, and his dick led him astray. You're worldly enough to understand that."

"Oh, I understand *that* all too well. I went astray myself one night in Jackson with a darling little tennis pro." Her eyes flicker at a memory that cuts through her chemical haze. "But that's not what this affair was about. No, sir. This was *love,* capital *L-U-V.* Didn't Drew tell you? This was soul mates, poetry-and-candlelight, I-want-to-have-your-baby-and-do-mission-work-together-in-Peru stuff."

Drew, you stupid asshole, I curse silently. *Couldn't you keep your mouth shut? Did you think you'd confess your secret dreams about your mistress, and your wife would understand?* Like many men who have come to the point of needing a lawyer, Drew Elliott is his own worst enemy. And thanks to him, there's not much I can accomplish here.

"Ellen, let me just say this. Because of Kate's death, Drew's smallest actions—and yours—could have far more serious consequences than you might imagine. We've got a politically motivated district attorney who'd like nothing better than to convict a rich, white doctor for murder."

"Yes, we do," Ellen drawls. "That black boy is definitely hungry for some white meat. And he's got his eye on Drew, all right. He already asked me to come down and talk to the grand jury."

My blood pressure plummets. "What did you tell him?"

"I'd think about it."

"Did Shad threaten to subpoena you?"

"He's not that stupid. Shadrach was sweet as pie, honey. He knows he can't force a wife to testify against her husband."

A wave of relief rolls through me, but Ellen instantly dashes it. "Don't look *too* secure. Shad may not have to worry about that problem too much longer."

I don't want to encourage her by asking, but I have no choice. "Why not?"

"Tomorrow I'm driving up to Jackson and hiring the meanest divorce lawyer in the state."

"Ellen, you don't—"

"Don't what?" She cocks her perfectly plucked eyebrows. "Do you have a *comment*, Counselor? Do you think I'm un*justified* in this course of action?"

I shake my head slowly. "It's your life. I'm just sorry to hear this. I think something brought you and Drew together all those years ago, and there has to be something left of that. Tim, at the very least."

For the first time I see tears in her eyes, little silver drops that she quickly wipes away. "I used to think there was," she says in a hoarse voice. "But I was a fool. And whatever hope I had left, Drew just crushed in about as public a way as he could. I couldn't go back to him now if I wanted to."

"Ellen—"

"Don't talk to me about swallowing my pride for Tim's sake! I don't like the taste of it! I'm not going to watch Drew *mourn* that little bitch for the rest of my life. Timmy's better off with me alone than with a father who'd run off with his goddamn babysitter."

There's nothing more to be said. Ellen is dead set on a scorched-earth campaign, and the only thing that could possibly change that is time. Time and maybe sobriety. I get into my car, back away from the gingerbread castle, and head home.

CHAPTER

11

When I get back home, I'm ordered to sit down and watch a performance by Annie and Mia. Given that I've been gone less than thirty minutes, the dance is truly amazing. Mia moves with the bone-snapping precision of a girl in a hip-hop video, which doesn't surprise me, since I've seen her do the same as a cheerleader at St. Stephen's football and basketball games. What amazes me is Annie. She's only nine years old, yet she mimics Mia's moves as though she's wired to the older girl's brain. She doesn't quite have Mia's precision, but the flexibility and rhythm are there. It's only a matter of practice. Her mother was a great dancer, too, and even after five years, the memory brings a lump to my throat. When they finish dancing, I jump to my feet, yelling and clapping in approval. Annie glows with pride, and Mia watches her with real affection.

"Bath time," Mia says, doing a quick sequence of moves to keep Annie's attention.

"Aww," Annie moans. "I'm clean!"

"That's bull!" says Mia, laughing. "We just sweated two gallons, at least. Your armpits are already stinky. I smell them from here."

Annie sniffs cautiously beneath her left arm. "Uh-*uh*."

"Uh-*huh*. Get going, Stinky!"

Annie giggles and then cartwheels into the hall. "Will you still be here when I get out?"

Mia shakes her head. "I've got way too much homework to stick around here. I'm gone as soon as your dad pays me."

"Are you coming back tomorrow?"

Mia looks at me.

"Absolutely," I tell them, knowing I'm bound to be caught up in Drew's mess, whether I want to be or not.

As Annie's footsteps fade down the hall, Mia takes a seat on the ottoman in front of my chair and pulls the elastic band from her ponytail. Dark hair cascades around her shoulders. She puts the band between her teeth and shakes her head, then gathers her hair again and binds it into a looser ponytail.

"I talked to Stephanie James," she says. "She's one of the girls who got questioned by the grand jury. She said the D.A. didn't use Dr. Elliot's name at first. He kept asking if Kate had ever confided anything to Stephanie about an 'older man.' After Stephanie said no about ten times, Johnson got really aggressive. He acted like she knew about the affair but was holding back on purpose. Stephanie said she actually started crying. She also said she knew several people sitting in the chairs out there. The grand jury members. Some of them were St. Stephen's parents."

"Great."

"Is it bad?"

"Oh, it's bad."

"What can I do to help?"

"Nothing, I'm afraid. But you've been a huge help already."

"I don't feel like I have. Dr. Elliott's in trouble, and I really like him. He helped me with my science fair project last year. He was really nice."

I start to ask if she ever sensed any improper attention from Drew, but then I decide against it. As if reading my mind, Mia says, "No, I never got a hint of weirdness from him. I never even caught him looking at my butt, which most older guys do every time I turn around."

I can't help but laugh at Mia's awareness of the reaction her body causes in men. I've admired her derriere myself on occasion. "You told me you've heard mixed reactions about Drew and Kate. Tell me about that."

"Well, from the parents it's all bad, of course. They blame him totally for the affair. Some of them say Kate always looked old for her age—and acted a lot older—but they say that's no excuse."

"But the kids are different?"

Mia tilts a flattened hand back and forth to indicate ambivalence. "The girls, mostly. The guys are calling him a perv and talking all kinds of shit about what they ought to do to him. But the girls understand it."

"Why?"

She smiles to herself. "I think a lot of them have fantasized about doing the same thing Kate did."

"Are you serious?"

"Hell, yeah. Make out with a hot guy like Dr. Elliott?"

"But he's twenty years older than they are!"

"So?" Mia looks genuinely puzzled.

"So . . . I don't know." Ellen Elliot's words come back to me in a rush: *These girls aren't like the girls I went to school with . . .* "You tell me."

"I think you'd be surprised at what we talk about," Mia says with a sly smile.

Water gurgles through the pipes in the wall. Annie has started her bath. "For instance?"

"Um . . . the hot dads list."

"The what?"

"The *hot dads* list. That's the fathers of kids at St. Stephen's who still rank as hot."

I shake my head in wonder. "Who keeps this list?"

"The senior girls, mostly. Some juniors. It's not written down or anything. Just something we talk about. Dads we'd hook up with if we got the chance."

"And Drew was on this list?"

"The very top."

"Really?"

"Oh, yeah. You're on it, too."

My face reddens.

"I'm not saying you're on *my* list," she says with an apologetic smile. "But I've heard a lot of girls name you."

"And these girls think it was okay for Drew to be sleeping with Kate?"

"Pretty much. I mean, Kate wasn't going to be with some high school boy, anyway. If Dr. Elliott was unhappy—and anybody who knows his wife knows he had to be—then what happens is what happens, you know? It's natural."

"Adultery is natural?"

Mia shrugs. "It is to these girls. Half of them come from broken homes. More than half, probably."

God, what have we come to?

"And the guys are only acting so pissed because they're scared," Mia goes on. "They know they can't possibly compete with a guy like Dr. Elliott, even on their own primitive level. I mean, look what he did to the jocks who tried to beat him up. So they say he's pervy and all. But every one of those guys would do that or worse if they thought they could get away with it. So would the fathers who are trash-talking Dr. Elliott. Some of the most self-righteous of those guys give me looks that totally creep me out when I run by them in tight shorts. They practically drool on me."

I'm not even sure I want to know more at this point. The girls defending Drew aren't doing so on the basis of forgiving human frailty; they're saying you can't blame a guy for doing something most other men would do if given the same chance. Morality doesn't even come into it. "What do *you* think about Kate and Drew?"

Mia bites her lip and takes some time to think. "It makes me sad for Timmy."

"Do you know him?"

"Yeah. He's a sweet kid, he really is. And his life is going to *suck* for a while."

For some reason, my mind jumps off track to one of the phone calls I got this afternoon. "What do you know about Marko Bakic?"

Mia's face closes almost instantly. "Why do you ask?"

"His name has come up in connection with some things."

"What kind of things?"

"Drugs."

She nods almost imperceptibly.

"Are you nodding because you know Marko's involved in drugs?"

"Just keep talking. I'll answer what I can."

What the hell? "Do you know anything about a rave party out at Lake St. John last night?"

"Maybe."

"Were you there?"

She looks at her fingernails. "Maybe."

"Was there a lot of Ecstasy there?"

"There could have been."

"What about LSD? See any of that?"

Mia draws her legs up beneath her and sits Indian-style on the ottoman. She's wearing loose gym shorts over a skintight Nike running suit. With her careful expression, she looks like someone judging a gymnastics competition.

"In what capacity are you asking these questions?" she asks with a strange formality. "Is it just for your personal interest? Or are you asking as a member of the school board?"

I'm not sure myself. "A concerned parent, let's say. I know something about X and LSD from my work in Houston. And I'm getting the feeling that I need to know more about Marko Bakic, if I want to protect the students at St. Stephen's."

Mia slowly shakes her head. "I can't say much about that subject."

"Why not? Are you afraid?"

Another long pause. "It wouldn't be cool. A lot of people could get in trouble."

"What's your personal opinion of Marko?"

Her jaw muscles work beneath her tanned cheeks. "He's a psycho. I'm serious, Penn, he's completely amoral. Right and wrong don't register in his mind. But he covers it well. He's smooth. A lot of people think he's fun."

"But not you?"

"I think he's a self-absorbed prick. I used to think he was fun. He had me snowed like the rest. Not now, though. I saw through him."

"Do you want to tell me about it?"

"Not really."

"Okay."

Mia gets to her feet and looks at me with her wide, dark eyes. "If you're going after Marko, be careful."

Her severe gaze unsettles me. "What do you know, Mia? It sounds like I need to hear it."

"Marko's not like the rest of us, okay? We're soft. *American.* Marko grew up in a war zone. His root directory is fucked up. That's all I know to say. And he hangs with some bad people. If you're going to mess with him at all, you want somebody like Dr. Elliott around. Somebody who can get radical if things get out of hand."

"Understood. Tell me, have you ever heard of Cyrus White?"

She mulls over the name. "No. Who is he?"

"A drug dealer. Don't ask around about him. I'm serious, okay? He's not a Nancy Drew project."

Mia looks offended. "I know when to talk and when to shut up."

"I'm sorry."

She takes her CD out of the boom box and walks past me to the door.

"I haven't paid you yet," I remind her.

"You can catch up tomorrow." She reaches for the doorknob, then looks back at me. "I heard Ellen Elliott freaked out. Is she really dumping her husband's shit all over the lawn?"

I shrug noncommittally.

"I also heard you were over there."

The cell phones of Mia and her friends are like native drums on a Pacific island. Every significant event is instantly known by the tribe.

"I guess Ellen thinks he did it, huh?" she asks.

"Did what?"

"Got Kate pregnant, for one thing."

I close my eyes in dismay. If this is public knowledge already, Drew is so screwed, it's beyond belief.

Mia says, "Do you think Ellen believes her husband killed Kate?"

"Of course not."

"Some people are going to think that."

"Probably so."

"Except for the pathologist finding two guys' stuff inside her, right? That makes it more complicated."

"Jesus, Mia, is there anything you don't know?"

"Not much." She gives me a sad smile. "Sometimes I wish I knew a lot less than I do. I wonder what that would be like."

"They say ignorance is bliss."

"Not ignorance. Innocence. That's what I was talking about. Innocence."

Mia sighs, then passes through the door to the street.

CHAPTER

12

I'm standing outside my daughter's bathroom door, feeling strangely adrift between two extremes. Splashing behind this door is Annie, at nine years old still truly innocent, while driving away from my house is Mia Burke, an eighteen-year-old who knows far more about the adult world than I would ever have guessed yesterday. How long will it be before that world begins chipping away at Annie's innocence? And how will she react when it does? How will *I* react?

An image of Kate Townsend suddenly fills my mind. Mia said there was no way Kate was going to "be with" a boy her own age. Did Drew Elliott seduce and corrupt that girl? Or was it the other way around? No jury would ever see it that way, of course, but right now I'm only interested in the truth. And my best shot at discovering it may be opening the shoe box hidden atop the armoire in my guest room.

After walking softly down the hall, I climb onto a chair, pull down the shoe box, and carry it to the bed. The scent of perfume wafts upward when I pull off the lid, exposing a jumble of letters, cards, ticket stubs, USB flash drives, videotapes, and various other knickknacks. There's cloth in the bottom, which turns out to be a pair of men's bikini underwear.

Beneath the briefs lies a photograph printed on computer paper. It shows Drew and Kate standing in front of a mirror—a hotel bathroom mirror is my guess. They're naked and laughing, and Drew has his right arm around Kate's waist. Kate is holding her right arm high in the air, and in the upper corner of the mirror I can just see the blue star of the flash from the camera she's holding. Drew's stomach muscles stand out in rigid relief, and Kate's breasts are firm and erect. Her torso is marked with small red ovals, probably caused by the recent pressure of Drew's fingers. It's disquieting to see Kate this way after seeing her mostly from a distance: on the tennis court in conservative whites or wearing a cheerleader uniform on the gym floor.

"Daddy?" calls Annie. "Are you up here?"

"Yes!" I call toward the hall. "Are you ready to get out?"

"Almost!"

"Just call me when you're ready!"

As I stare at Kate's body, something else catches my eye. At the bottom of her shoe box lies a multicolored schematic of the London Underground. Picking it up, I realize that the map is actually the jacket of a thin hardcover book. A journal. And written on the first page in a flowing female hand are two paragraphs:

> *This is the journal of Katharine Mays Townsend. My father gave me this book of blank pages when he left for England this time—for my seventeenth birthday. He told me that this time of my life is precious, that I will never be so filled with possibility, and that I should record everything I think and do. Right now I'm more of a mind to record everything HE does and, more importantly, does NOT do, so that he might finally recognize himself for what he is and is not. But I doubt even that would do it. Denial is a powerful thing.*
>
> *I've always been told that I'm a special girl, though not by the person I most needed to hear it from. But I do believe I'm unlike most of the peers I know at this point in my life. For that reason I shall record my thoughts and deeds, and if*

someone digs up this book a thousand years from now, they will find an accurate record of what was in the head of a materially spoiled but emotionally starved American girl of the 21st century.

   Hello, whoever you are!

I flip quickly through the pages, conscious that Annie could walk in at any moment. Some are covered with tight blocks of script, others with hastily scrawled paragraphs. Doodles and caricatures adorn many pages, illuminating the journal as the work of a talented artist. I can hardly suppress my excitement. The last year of Kate Townsend's life is right here, page after page of it, and I'd like nothing more than to read the journal from cover to cover right now. But that will have to wait until Annie is in bed.

   Still, I can't resist a quick look.

Suspending the diary by its front cover, I let it fall open to its natural breaking point. It opens to a two-page spread lined with four columns. The columns on the left-hand page are headed "Hook-ups" and "Real Hook-ups." The columns on the right-hand page are headed "Rejected" and "Rejected by." These two pages, I realize, are where Kate Townsend believed she saw herself most clearly, not through the lens of the effusive praise she must have heard every day, but measured by her physical acceptance or rejection by the people around her. Like most of us, sadly, this beautiful and brilliant girl defined herself more by who desired her rather than by any internal sense of self. But that weakness may be Drew's good fortune. I eagerly scan the columns, searching for information that might somehow help to free him.

HOOK-UPS
David Adams, K
Peter Smith, K (Emerald Mound)
Johnny Wingate, K
Jack B., K
Henry F., K (St. James Park)

Jed Andersen, K, B
Patrick Schaefer, K, B, F
Chris Vogel, K, B, F
Geoffrey, K
David Quinn, K, B
Chris Anthony, K, B, F, O (the Pavilion)
Carson, K, B, O
Win Langston (the sand bar), F
Jody (first bj)
Michael (went down on me)
Gavin Green (Junior trip)
Walter Wenders (69) (I actually came)
Spencer D.
Turner (Queen's Ball)
Andy Winograd
Steve
Kane J.

REAL HOOK-UPS
Andy, V
Steve, V, 69, O/A
Sarah Evans, OV,V/V (weird)
Drew (EVERYTHING)
Shit, shit, shit, shit!

REJECTED
Timmy Livingston
Walter Taunton
Billy
Neil (hot, but too young)
Jack D.
Ricky
Dr. Davenport (yuck)
Chris Farrell
Cyrus (shit, close one!)
Tyler Bradley

Mr. Dawson, PERV!
Mark Wilson (gross)
Bass Player, Blue Steel (2 Goth!)
Jeanne Hulbert! (2 butch)
Andy
Coach Anders! (I think)
Martin
Sarah Evans (stalker!)
Gavin

REJECTED BY
Point guard, Jackson Academy
Jay Gresham
Mr. Marbury
Laurel Goodrich
Dr. Lewis
Morgan Davis (25)
Lead singer, Wings of Desire

Several names jump out at me as I scan the list, most of them high
school boys who attend St. Stephen's. With some entries I recognize
surnames only; they probably belong to boys from the other local
high schools. But some of the names truly shock me, as they seem to
belong to adults. Under the "Rejected" column is Coach Anders, the
athletic director of St. Stephen's. Wade Anders is thirty years old and
divorced, with two kids of his own at St. Stephen's. Kate's parenthetical notation seems to indicate some uncertainty about whether
Anders made a pass at her or not, and I can only hope it was her
imagination. Mr. Dawson—the "perv"—is also a teacher at St.
Stephen's. He's taught religion for one year, and now it's likely to be
his last. I have no idea who "Dr. Davenport" is. Ditto for "Mr. Marbury." But they apparently had close contact with Kate, perhaps
during her time in England. And Sarah Evans, a recent graduate of
St. Stephen's, is listed under both the "Real Hook-ups" and "Rejected" columns. There's also a female listed under the "Rejected
by" heading. Apparently Kate liked to experiment.

But the entry that stops my breath is under the "Rejected" column: *Cyrus.*

There's no surname listed, but the parenthetical, "Shit, close one!" seems to indicate some anxiety on Kate's part that set this encounter apart from the others. She clearly felt less in control with "Cyrus" than with the other males she rejected. I can't be sure that this Cyrus is Cyrus White, the drug dealer Sonny Cross warned me about, but I know of no Cyrus who attends St. Stephen's or any other local school. At least Cyrus isn't listed on the "Hook-ups" page, which tends to discredit Sonny's theory that there was an ongoing sexual relationship between Kate and the drug dealer.

Studying the list in more detail, I can only hope that it's comprehensive. The letters following the names seem to be a simple code signifying a graduated scale of sexual activity. I saw many similar codes during my time as a prosecutor in Houston, usually in the private documents or computer records of men. "K" probably stands for Kissed. "B" . . . Breasts? "F" probably stands for "fingers" or some variant thereof. The "69" and "bj" are self-explanatory. The letters following the entries under the "Real Hook-ups" heading are a bit surprising in their explicitness, but Mia did tell me that Kate was highly sexual. My guess is that "V" stands for vaginal intercourse. O/A must signify oral/anal contact. And the "EVERYTHING" following Drew's name I can only guess at.

More than anything, I wish Kate had dated these entries. I'm sure Mia could give me at least a vague time frame, but I can't afford to show her this journal—not yet, anyway. I need to read it from cover to cover, then load the computer disks and peruse everything on them. I hope Kate didn't password-protect them, but I suspect she did. Even standing naked before a bathroom mirror, she radiates the self-possession of someone well practiced at protecting herself.

Staring at the photo in a kind of trance, I experience a rush of intuitive knowledge so powerful that, while I realize that facts could prove me wrong, I feel viscerally sure they will not. I race downstairs to my study, Annie's voice pursuing me down the stairs. I call out reassurance, but I keep running.

In the study, I go to my bookshelves and pull out a folding map of Natchez. It's a simple thing, a free handout produced for tourists by the Chamber of Commerce, but it's proved invaluable to me during the writing of my last two novels. Spreading it open on my desk, I orient myself to Highway 61, then search for the Brightside Manor Apartments, the reputed lair of Cyrus White. I find them in short order, on the north side of town, near where the old black high school used to be. To the west of the apartments lies Lynda Lee Mead Drive, a street named for a Natchez-born Miss Mississippi who became Miss America. But to the east of them—my heart thumps against my sternum—to the east lies open land transected by a curving blue line.

St. Catherine's Creek.

I close my eyes and breathe something very like a prayer of thanks. Though Brightside Manor is several miles from where Drew found Kate's body—and even farther from where Kate's corpse was discovered by the fishermen—the apartments stand a mere forty yards from the creek into which her body was dumped. *This* is something that will sway a jury, if not the district attorney. One glance at this map shows that Cyrus White could easily have raped and murdered Kate Townsend in his apartment, then dumped her body into the flooded torrent behind it with the near certainty that she would be swept far downstream from the crime scene, if not all the way to the Mississippi River.

"Daddy?" Annie calls faintly.

Remembering the nude photo lying on my bed, I leave the map and sprint back up the stairs. From the reverberation of Annie's voice, I can tell she's still in the bathroom. "I'll be here in a minute, baby," I promise, looking in through the steam. "I'm doing something."

Annie smiles up from the tub. "I'm fine. I just wanted to know where you were. I heard you running."

"Everything's okay."

I hurry back to the bedroom and pick up the photo of Drew

and Kate. *What were you doing at Cyrus White's apartment?* I ask silently.

It takes a few moments for my ringing cell phone to register. When I pick it up, the caller ID says MIA. I'm almost afraid to answer and find out what new tragedy she's discovered. "Hello?"

"Nancy Drew here," she says in a deadpan voice. "Remember I told you I wanted to do what I could to help Dr. Elliott?"

"Yes."

"Well, I got to thinking about what you told me about Shad Johnson hijacking the grand jury."

"Yeah?"

"So I decided to take a ride down to his office."

"You knew where it was?"

"I figured it would either be in the courthouse or in Lawyer's Alley. I didn't have to look very hard. Except for the bars and Pearl Street Pasta, the waterworks building was the only one downtown with lights blazing inside."

"That's the D.A.'s office, all right," I say, not interested enough by Mia's amateur detective work to remove my gaze from Kate's body or my mind from the juxtaposition of Brightside Manor and St. Catherine's Creek.

"Well, that's not all I saw," she says.

"No?"

"You sound distracted. What are you doing, watching soft porn on Cinemax?"

"Sorry. What else did you see?"

"Two people walking into the first floor of the waterworks building. They used the D.A.'s door, and they looked pretty friendly."

"Did you recognize them?"

"Sure did. One was the sheriff, Billy Byrd."

My chest tightens. "And the other?"

"Judge Minor."

Holy shit. Kate's nude body is forgotten.

"Got your attention now?"

"You do indeed." Arthel Minor is one of Natchez's two circuit

court judges. He was among the first African-Americans in Mississippi to be elected to the position after Reconstruction. As a circuit
court judge, he has a 50 percent chance of handling the Kate
Townsend murder case when it comes to trial. And like both Shad
Johnson and Billy Byrd, Arthel Minor is known to have higher political aspirations.

"How did you recognize Judge Minor, Mia?"

She laughs. "I served on the Mayor's Youth Council this year. I
spent a couple of hours talking to him. He had me rolling on the
floor with his jokes."

This girl is good. "Can you see what they're doing now?"

"Not from where I'm sitting, which is at the malt shop drinking
a Parrot Ice. But I can get back there in about a minute."

"Hang on a second. I need to think."

"Don't strain yourself."

The image of Shadrach Johnson, Sheriff Billy Byrd, and Judge
Arthel Minor meeting together after business hours sends a cold
shot of fear through my veins. It might seem natural that these people should meet and discuss an investigation in progress. But in fact,
this kind of meeting never happens. Contrary to what we see on television, the investigation of a crime is handled almost solely by police officers. After adequate evidence has been obtained, the case is
then handed over to the district attorney, who takes it to a grand
jury. If the grand jury binds the accused over for trial, there's a preliminary hearing before a municipal court judge. Only then does a
circuit judge enter the picture. What Mia has described is a meeting
that, while legal by the strict letter of the law, is very dangerous to
the integrity of the legal system, and more particularly, I fear, to my
friend Drew Elliott. Together, those three men could investigate
Drew's life, try him for murder, and sentence him to death.

"Mia, can you come back here and watch Annie for an hour? I
know I'm taking advantage, but can you do that?"

"I guess I'd better. The Ivy League isn't cheap, you know."

"You're two minutes away, if you punch it."

She laughs. "More like one."

"Annie's still in the bathtub. I'll meet you at the front door."

CHAPTER

13

There's an empty parking space in front of the D.A.'s private entrance. I park and ring the bell, but no one answers. Banging on the door produces no response, either. I call Shad's office from my cell phone, but all I get is a recording saying that the office is closed.

Even angrier than when I left the house, I walk around to the alley behind the waterworks. In the shadows between the buildings, I can hardly see my hand in front of my face. But on the third floor, bright fluorescent light spills from a row of casement windows.

Shad's office.

A ladder dangles from a landing on the building across the alley. *Fire escape.* One minute of careful climbing puts me on a third-floor landing, where I smell the aroma of seafood cooking in the restaurant on the next block. I can also see directly into the office of the district attorney. What I see brings acid into my throat.

Shad Johnson is pacing around his office in a brilliant blue suit, while seated at his desk is Arthel Minor. To ensure impartiality, circuit judges are supposed to be assigned cases by a simple system of rotation, but in practice cases are often steered to certain judges by crafty lawyers. It's pretty clear to me which judge will be assigned Kate Townsend's murder case. Beyond Judge Minor, leaning against a filing cabinet on the far wall, stands Billy Byrd, the redneck sheriff of Adams County. This is the most unlikely lynch mob I ever heard of, but there's no doubt in my mind about their intended function.

Two bricks lie on the landing at my feet. I'm tempted to hurl one through Shad's window, but that would probably put me in jail for the night. Instead, I pick one up and start banging the metal railing of the fire escape. The clanging echoes through the alley like hammer blows in a blacksmith's shop.

Shad soon comes to his window. I keep banging, and Sheriff Byrd appears at the next window in the row. Then Judge Minor materializes behind him. The sheriff motions angrily for me to stop.

I don't.

Sheriff Byrd clearly does not recognize me. But now that I have the group's attention, I hold up my cell phone, shake it theatrically, then dial Shad's office again. They all turn away from the windows. Finally, Shad answers his phone.

"Hello?"

"*Who's making that goddamn racket?*" I yell.

"What?" Shad asks in a flabbergasted voice. "Who is this?"

"Penn Cage, you unethical prick. Go downstairs and let me in."

"Is that you banging on that fire escape across the alley?"

"You bet it is. And now that I've caught you three in the act, there's no point trying to hide. Open up."

Shad slams down the phone.

I scramble down the ladder and race around to the D.A.'s door. Sheriff Byrd stands waiting for me, one hand on the gun in his belt and a seething anger tightening his jaw muscles.

"What the Sam D. Hell do you think you're doing?" he growls.

"I'd like you to answer the same question." I push past him and take the stairs two at a time, preferring to confront the judge before the others. But when I reach Shad's office, Judge Minor is nowhere in sight.

Now Shad sits behind his antique desk, watching me like someone looking at a dangerous mental patient.

"Where's Judge Minor?" I demand.

The district attorney doesn't answer.

"He didn't make it downstairs that fast unless he sprinted, and that's a little undignified for a judge—even one of questionable integrity. Is he hiding in another office?"

"What are you doing here at this hour?" Shad asks, slowly getting himself under control. "What are you talking about?"

"I'm talking about the third co-conspirator in this little lynch mob."

Shad's mouth drops open. "You'd better choose your words with more care, Counselor."

"I said exactly what I meant to say."

"Did you now?" Sheriff Byrd asks from behind me, huffing from the exertion of climbing stairs.

"What else did I see through those windows?" I ask. "The circuit judge, the sheriff, and the district attorney all huddled in a room after dark. The irony is exquisite."

"What irony's that?" asks the sheriff, who wouldn't know irony if it hit him over the head.

"If Shad and Judge Minor weren't black—and if this were forty years ago—what else could I conclude but that I was seeing a lynching in the making?"

"You don't know what you're talking about," Shad says finally.

"Do you deny that you three were discussing Drew Elliott before I showed up?"

Sheriff Byrd starts to deny it, but Shad holds up a hand to silence him. "Why should I deny that?"

"Because it isn't exactly standard procedure for a murder investigation."

"Dr. Elliott isn't a standard murder suspect. Neither was Kate Townsend a standard victim. She was practically a celebrity around here. And that's what we were discussing. The whole town's turned upside down from the rumors going around, and we wanted to make sure we were all on the same page."

"That's called collusion, Shad."

"It's none of your damn business what we're doing up here," says the sheriff.

I focus on Shad. "You know a meeting like that borders on being unethical. Drew hasn't even been charged with murder. The circuit judge has no place whatever in this matter. Not at this time."

"*Borders* on," Shad echoes, tilting his head to indicate the equivocal nature of this point. "This is a special case, Penn. And we all agree that it needs to be expedited as quickly as possible."

"That's exactly the wrong thing to do. You need to proceed methodically, follow precedent, and leave no stone unturned in your investigation."

Sheriff Byrd leans against the filing cabinet again and regards me with disdain. "My mama always told me the worst vice is *ad*-vice."

"I know your mama," I tell him. "I think most people would agree she could have used a little advice herself along the way."

Byrd comes off the file cabinet with stunning speed, one fist clenched and the other hand on his gun.

"Billy!" Shad yells. "He's just trying to bait you."

"You smug son of a bitch," Byrd says in a murderous tone. "Just keep on with your shit. See what happens."

Shad lays his palms flat on his desk. "Penn, you'll get your chance to weigh in on these issues during the trial. But for now—"

"The *trial*? You've found nothing so far that indicates Drew should even be indicted. You've hijacked the grand jury to question minors without their parents present. You've started rumors that have already gone a long way toward ruining Dr. Elliott's career. Half the town already thinks he's guilty of murder, and he hasn't even been *charged*. And what do you have, really? A rumor that he was having sex with Kate Townsend. That's light-years away from capital murder!"

Shad seems unfazed by my impassioned outburst. "Are you finished?"

"For the moment."

"Then why don't you try listening for a change?"

"I'm all ears."

"Dr. Elliott is in deep trouble, and it has nothing to do with the meeting you just witnessed. Let me review the evidence for you. First, the anonymous call that started this thing."

I start to argue, but Shad silences me with a shake of his head.

"That call was too strange to ignore. If you were the D.A., you would have handled it just as I did. You'd have called Dr. Elliott into your office. In any case, that anonymous call certainly led somewhere, didn't it?"

"Damned straight," agrees Sheriff Byrd.

Shad looks embarrassed to have Byrd's support. "Second," Shad goes on, "the preliminary serology on the semen samples. Based on the lab findings, one of those two samples is very likely to be confirmed as belonging to Dr. Elliot when the DNA analysis comes back—which won't be as long as you think. Third, that particular semen sample wasn't taken from the Townsend girl's vagina, but from her rectum."

The hair along my forearms stands up. When Shad told me yesterday that Kate had semen "in both holes," I naturally assumed that the unknown sample—the one unknown to me, that is—was the one swabbed from her rectum.

"That rather prurient fact," Shad says with authority, "bolsters my theory that Dr. Elliot's intercourse with the victim was an act of vengeance if not outright rape. A 'grudge-fuck,' I believe it's called."

I can't even begin to deal with the implications of this new information in this room. "But at our first meeting, you told me the trauma was vaginal, didn't you?"

"I believe I said 'genital.'" Shad looks down at some papers on his desk. "There was labial swelling, some vaginal abrasions, but also anorectal swelling with small tears inside the anus."

I take a moment to process this. "Which semen was deposited first? That found in the vagina? Or the anal sample? Even if you assume Drew had anal sex with Kate, he could have deposited that semen up to seventy-two hours before she was swabbed, while the sperm found in her vagina could have been deposited just prior to death."

Shad shakes his head, and I detect something like smugness in his eyes. "We'll never know that," he says. "Since the girl was DOA, she wasn't swabbed until the next morning during the autopsy in Jackson. The sperm in both samples were dead. One of the disadvantages of investigating crime in a small town."

"What else do you have?" I ask quietly.

"Fourth," Shad enumerates. "Fingerprints. Sheriff Byrd's detectives found Dr. Elliot's fingerprints all over Kate Townsend's bedroom and private bathroom."

Drew, you stupid bastard, I curse silently. "How do you know those prints are Dr. Elliot's?" I ask the sheriff. "Given your relationship with the PD, I can't believe you went to the city jail to print him, or even that you asked the police to fax theirs over to you."

Sheriff Byrd gives me a superior smile. "One of my deputies took some prints from the doc's private bathroom when they went to his office to collect his blood."

Now I remember. The short, unpleasant deputy excused himself to "use the restroom" while Susan Salter pulled Drew's blood. The little son of a bitch.

"What else?" I ask, working hard to hide my dismay.

"Phone records," Shad says. "We've got Kate Townsend's cell phone records for the past year. The past few months are clean, but if you go back to this past summer, it gives Dr. Elliott some problems."

"Of course she called Drew," I say. "She was the family babysitter."

Shad grins good-naturedly. "You're going to dig the hole deeper if you don't keep your mouth shut. Why don't you listen to what I have to say?"

He's right. If Drew were a normal client, I'd stand here with my mouth shut. But I feel compelled to defend my friend, even when I don't know exactly what he has or hasn't done.

Shad dons a pair of reading glasses and examines a piece of

paper with tiny type on it. "I wouldn't have found it odd if the girl called Dr. Elliott's home a few times, or even more than a few. But she didn't do that. She called his medical office and his cell phone almost exclusively. She did it often and at very odd times. Like three o'clock in the morning. And the calls lasted a very long time." Shad looks at me over the lenses of his glasses. "Hours."

I struggle to hold my poker face.

"But the real kicker," Shad says with obvious relish, "is that she didn't just call him direct. She bought third-party phone cards at Wal-Mart and dialed into an 800-number switchboard before calling his cell phone. That's a standard method of trying to disguise phone calls—particularly in extramarital affairs." He glances at Sheriff Byrd. "Computers are a wonderful thing, aren't they?"

Byrd chuckles.

The only positive I can see is that they seem to have no record of Kate using computers to text-message Drew. Certainly they've checked his records by now. Perhaps those digital connections are not so easily traced. "What else?"

Shad removes his reading glasses and meets my gaze. "A classmate of Kate Townsend's saw her changing cars with Dr. Elliott in a public parking lot."

"What do you mean, 'changing cars'?"

"You know exactly what I mean. Both of them parked their cars in a public lot, and when they thought no one was looking, Kate climbed into Dr. Elliot's car and they drove away. A female St. Stephen's student told that to the grand jury this afternoon."

My stomach rolls over.

"This girl also said that it looked like Dr. Elliott and the girl were fighting."

"How long ago did this supposedly happen? And where?"

Shad shakes his head, his eyes twinkling. "Sorry, Counselor. Can't tell you everything. That wouldn't be right."

Shad's litany of evidence like this would titillate and possibly sway a jury—until they realized that he was proving the wrong point.

"Fine," I say. "Drew looks like a dog for carrying on with Kate

Townsend. But you're no closer to murder than you were ten minutes ago. All you've given me is evidence of an extramarital affair, most of it circumstantial. This isn't a divorce case, Shad."

He nods as if in agreement. "You're right about that. But you're wrong about what I've shown, and you know it. I've presented you with direct evidence of sexual battery, a serious felony."

Shad's heading right where I didn't want him to go.

"Dr. Elliott was Kate Townsend's personal physician," he says, "a position of trust defined by statute. Having consensual sex just once with a juvenile female patient will buy him thirty years in the pen. And I figure Dr. Elliott probably repeated that offense a hundred times or more."

"Open-and-shut case," says Sheriff Byrd.

I give Shad my coldest stare. "You don't give a damn about Drew having sex with that girl. If you charge him on that offense, it's pure politics, and everyone in town will know it."

"How do you figure that?"

"You're singing your song about positions of trust and underage sex. You want to go out to the public school with me tomorrow and start questioning seventeen-year-old black girls? You want to ask them if any of their coaches have rubbed their shoulders after practice? Or maybe rubbed some more intimate parts, as defined in the statute on sexual battery?"

Shad has gone still as a bust in a museum.

"You want to go over to the junior high and start asking fifteen-year-old black girls how many of them are sleeping with adult men? That's statutory rape, open and shut. Hell, you could fill up both jails in an hour. But you won't do that, will you? You'd lose votes faster than if you put on a KKK sheet and hood. Don't pretend that public morals or public safety have anything to do with this case, okay? You want to convict a rich white man to further your political ambitions. End of story."

I turn to Sheriff Byrd. "I don't know why you're part of this, but I'm going to find out. And don't think I'll hesitate to go to the media with the whole stinking mess. You've already ruined my client's reputation. I've got nothing to lose."

Both men are staring at me with more anxiety than anger. Sheriff Byrd walks over to a chair and takes a seat beside Shad. The district attorney rises from his chair, comes around the desk, settles his butt on it, and smiles as though this whole confrontation is just a misunderstanding between friends.

"Penn, you were a prosecutor for fifteen years. The evidence I've laid out tonight is just what we've uncovered in the first forty-eight hours. Can you imagine what else there is to find? You know Dr. Elliot's DNA is going to match what we took from that girl's rectum. And at that point—forget any future evidence that comes in—at that point, just about any jury in this state will be ready to fry his ass and not lose a minute's sleep over it."

I let his last sentence hang in the air. This is the kind of logic that condemned many an innocent black man not so many years ago.

"There's just one problem with your scenario, Shad. A tiny little hole that a second-year law student could drive a cement truck through."

"What's that?"

"The second semen sample. You're completely ignoring it. Who else had sex with Kate Townsend? Who raped her? That's what you should be trying to find out."

"On the contrary," he says, "that's the cornerstone of my case. Dr. Elliott murdered Kate Townsend in a jealous rage over what he perceived as infidelity on the girl's part."

"Then who's the mystery man? If the semen in her vagina wasn't deposited during a rape, why hasn't the guy come forward?"

Shad glances at Sheriff Byrd as if deciding how much to reveal. "I think it's a kid," he says finally, "just like the deceased. A kid who's scared shitless, and with good reason. He doesn't want to jump into the middle of a capital murder case. Also, he's probably scared of Dr. Elliott. Maybe he saw Elliott kill the girl. If so, he's got to figure, 'If he killed *her,* he'll damn sure kill *me* to keep me quiet.' Or the kid may have told his parents what he saw. *They* may be keeping him from coming forward. These days, a lot of parents would do that."

"Everything you just told me is pure speculation."

Shad shrugs. "Maybe so. But it's the kind of speculation juries like."

He's right. And although he might have some difficulty getting this speculation into the record in a normal courtroom, he'll have no trouble with Judge Minor. Good old Arthel will give Shad all the rope he needs to hang Drew with innuendo.

"Come on, Cage," says Sheriff Byrd. "You know as well as I do that most murder victims are killed by people they know, and know well. Same with rape."

"You're absolutely right. Are you satisfied that you're aware of everybody Kate Townsend knew well?"

"We're getting there."

"So you know all about Cyrus White."

Byrd's eyes narrow, but Shad looks blank.

"What are you talking about?" asks the sheriff.

"I'm talking about regular contact—regular and *documented* contact—between Kate Townsend and Cyrus White. And I'm not talking about casual encounters in the mall. I'm talking about her visiting his crib in the Brightside Manor Apartments."

"Stop right there," Shad says irritably. "Who the hell is Cyrus White?"

"Only the biggest drug dealer in the city of Natchez."

Shad glances at Byrd. "Is that right?"

The sheriff nods reluctantly.

"Why haven't I heard of him before?"

I can't resist answering. "The voters of this city would probably like to ask you the same question, Shad."

The sheriff gives me a dark look, then cuts his eyes at Shad. "You don't know who Cyrus is because he's never been arrested. Where did you get your information, Cage?"

Since I can't betray Sonny Cross, I barb my evasion with a point. "From the same person who told me Cyrus was sexually obsessed with Kate Townsend."

"Bullshit."

"Cyrus has a serious jones for white girls, Billy. That seems like the kind of thing you ought to know about, given the circumstances of this case."

"Cyrus is black?" Shad asks. "I mean, if he lives in Brightside Manor, I guess he must be."

"He's black," the sheriff confirms. "But he doesn't always stay at Brightside. He has safe houses and apartments all around town. The crib at Brightside is just one of them. Cyrus moves around a lot."

"Where was this guy when the murder happened?" Shad asks.

Sheriff Byrd looks at me again but says nothing.

"He doesn't know," I tell Shad. "Billy figured he could nail Dr. Elliott on circumstantial evidence alone, and since that's what you want him to do, why look any further? Right, Sheriff?"

"Screw you, Cage. Don't tell me how to run my business."

"Somebody needs to. Has it seeped into your brain yet that St. Catherine's Creek runs *right behind* Brightside Manor?"

Sheriff Byrd's mouth falls open. He looks like a largemouth bass that's been hooked deep in the gut.

"That's what I figured." I turn to Shad. "Ain't it a bitch? You were all ready to rush a pillar of this community to execution to make yourself look good for an election, and now Cyrus White drops out of the woodwork. Nailing a black drug dealer for killing a white girl won't buy you much capital with black voters, will it? In fact, it might hurt you some."

Shads eyes are no longer focused on me. They've moved off to the middle distance as he makes lightning calculations about the political ramifications of all this.

"Ask yourself this, Shad," I say softly. "On one hand, you've got a distinguished physician who's never been in trouble in his life. He was having sex with an underage girl, but he was in love with her and ready to marry her. *That's* the guy you've got sitting in jail. On the other hand, you've got a notorious drug dealer who violently wiped out all his competition, who is known to have been sexually obsessed with the murder victim, and who lives on the creek into which the body was dumped. Now—which suspect would a reasonable man conclude is the most likely killer?"

Shad swallows audibly. The sound gives me great satisfaction.

Sheriff Byrd stands up straight and tries to stare a hole through me. Except for the paunch, he looks a lot like the black-hatted gunfighters in the old Westerns my dad and I watched when I was a kid. "Tell me where you got your information about Cyrus and the Townsend girl," he says, taking two steps toward me.

"Sorry, Sheriff. If I told you *everything*, that wouldn't be right, would it?"

Shad speaks in a cold voice. "Tell him, or I'll charge you with obstruction of justice."

"You call what I saw when I walked into this office justice?" I laugh outright, then turn and walk to the door. "I'll see you boys tomorrow, after you've taken a DNA sample from Cyrus White. And be sure to inform the newspaper, the grand jury, and Judge Minor that you have a second suspect. Or I'll have to do it for you."

"Hold it, Cage," Sheriff Byrd warns. "We're a long way from done here."

I keep walking.

"You can't get out," Shad calls after me. "The downstairs door is locked."

He's right. "Then get your ass down there and open it. Or I'll smash it open."

"Do that, and I'll arrest you," threatens the sheriff, his voice edged with hatred.

It's times like this that I think the judicial system should be entrusted solely to women. "Arrest me, and I'll make you look like the biggest asshole in the county on the front page of tomorrow's paper. And that's saying something."

Billy Byrd looks like he's about to stroke out.

"Open it for him," Shad says softly. "Here are the keys."

I walk downstairs without waiting for Billy. He'll be ready to kill me by the time he reaches the ground floor, but right now I don't give a damn.

I stand at the glass door, listening to his boot heels hammer the steps and the keys jangling in his hand. He stops behind me but makes no move to open the door.

"You're writing mighty big checks with that mouth of yours," he says in a low voice.

I turn and face him, my jaw set. "What did Shad buy you with, Billy? Whatever it was, it must have been big. I know you don't sell cheap, especially to a black man. They've never been your kind of folks."

Byrd's trigeminal nerve twitches his cheek. "Be careful, boy."

"Of what, exactly?"

The smile that cracks his face is like another man's grimace.

"Don't you wish it was forty years ago?" I say softly. "So you could just put two in the back of my head and say I assaulted you? Or maybe that I tried to escape?"

The smile leaves Byrd's lips. "Sometimes I think they had it right back then, yeah."

"Open the door."

The sheriff tosses Shad's keys onto the floor and walks back up the stairs.

I unlock the door, toss Shad's keys into a trash can in the corner, and walk out into the night.

As I stand in the street looking at the hulking white courthouse, everything I didn't know about Drew rushes through my mind with dizzying speed. His fingerprints in Kate's bedroom. Kate's cell phone records. A witness seeing Drew and Kate changing cars in a parking lot. Each of these facts is another stone in the pile that could eventually bury Drew at trial. Not evidence of murder, of course, but evidence of depravity to a conservative jury. And Shad was right about one thing: if the semen found in Kate's rectum turns out to match Drew's DNA, Shad's theory of rape and murder as revenge is going to sound a lot more plausible. No member of a Mississippi jury will want to believe that a high school senior was practicing anal sex for recreation. I'm not sure I believe it myself. If it weren't for Cyrus White's relationship with Kate—and the location of the Brightside Manor Apartments—I'd be damned frightened right now.

My cell phone rings. The caller ID says MIA, but when I answer, all I hear is sobs.

"Mia? Is that you?"

She's crying, I'm sure of it. My heart bounds into high gear. "Is Annie all right?"

"Yes, but something terrible has happened!"

"Tell me."

"Chris Vogel is dead."

Chris Vogel is a junior at St. Stephen's and the star of the basketball team. I saw him two days ago, shooting three-point shots in a neighbor's driveway downtown. "Are you sure?"

"Positive. Everybody's talking about it."

"How did he die?"

"He drowned at Lake St. John."

Lake St. John. The same lake where the X-rave was held last night. I climb into my Saab, crank the engine, and pull into the empty street. "When did this happen, Mia?"

"Tonight."

"Do you have any details?"

"More than I want. Apparently, Chris never came back to town after the party last night. He and Jimmy Wingate ditched school today. Everybody figured they had hangovers, because they wouldn't answer their cell phones. But apparently they stayed up at the Wingates' lake house. They just didn't want word to get back to the teachers where they were. They stayed drunk and probably worse, given the shit that was up there the other night."

"You mean drugs."

"Mm-hm."

"How do you know all this?"

"Christy Blake called and told me about Chris, but as soon as I hung up with her, I called Jimmy Wingate. We were good friends when we were little. He's in bad shape. Seeing Chris drown really messed him up."

I want to know more, but I'd rather hear it face-to-face. "I'll be home in three minutes. Tell me when I get there, okay?"

Mia sobs into the phone. "Please hurry."

I hang up and press down on the accelerator. I've never seen or heard Mia lose her composure before. But tonight it's no wonder.

Death is difficult enough for adults to deal with, but for adolescents it can be a paralyzing shock. Flushed with hormones and in the best physical shape of their lives, they view death as a shadowy event that waits incomprehensibly far in the future. The sudden loss of one of their own—particularly a school hero like Chris Vogel—punctures their illusions of immortality. *You are not immune,* says Fate, speaking with utter permanence.

Two high school kids dead in two days? muses a voice in my head. *In a school with only five hundred students? How could they not be connected?*

CHAPTER

14

I'm parked outside my house on Washington Street, trying to reach Sonny Cross, the narcotics agent who told me about Cyrus White. Mia stands in the open door, her worried face illuminated by the porch light. Someone answers in a voice so soft as to be almost inaudible.

"Sonny?" I ask. "Are you asleep?"

"On surveillance," he whispers. "Hang on."

I hear the sound of heels on pavement—probably Sonny's snakeskin cowboy boots—and then he speaks in a normal voice. "You must have heard about the Vogel boy."

"Yeah."

"Things go to shit in a hurry, don't they?"

"Do you think his death was drug-related?"

"Definitely. The kid with him admitted they'd done three tabs of acid in the past twelve hours. I was there when they questioned him."

"Did he say where they got it?"

"Claims they found it in a bag by the lake road."

"This is Jimmy Wingate?"

"Yeah."

"Were his parents there?"

Sonny chuckles dryly. "Oh, yeah. Jimmy's old man threatened to beat the crap out of him if he didn't tell us the truth, and the kid *still* wouldn't talk."

"You think they got the acid from Marko Bakic?"

"Who else? But nobody's admitting that. These kids either love Marko or they're scared shitless of him."

"Maybe both," I suggest. "Marko knows nothing about American football, but he won the South State football playoff for St. Stephen's by kicking the winning field goal. I wouldn't think that would be enough to keep kids quiet when a childhood friend dies, though."

"Yeah, well, time's on our side, bubba. Let Chris's death really sink in, and somebody'll get mad enough or upset enough to talk."

"I hope so. St. Stephen's can't take much more of this."

"Natchez can't take much more," Sonny mutters.

"Could the LSD have come from Cyrus White rather than Marko?"

"You can bet it went through Cyrus's hands before it got to Marko. Just like it went through the Asians' hands before it got to Cyrus. I suppose some other white kid could be buying from Cyrus, but it wasn't until Marko got to St. Stephen's that this shit started showing up there."

"Look, Sonny, I had to mention the Cyrus-Kate connection in front of Sheriff Byrd. I kept your name out of it, but I did tell him the contact was documented. He may be able to figure out where it came from based on that."

"Ah, shit, don't worry about it. Byrd can't afford to fire me. I make him look too good. I gotta go, Penn. Later."

I hang up and get out of the car. As I walk up the steps, Mia runs forward and hugs me, then sobs against my chest. "What's happening? Everything's gone crazy!"

"Calm down," I tell her, trying to separate us, then giving up and stroking her hair the way I do Annie's when she's upset. "It's going to be all right."

She pulls away and stares at me, her eyes sparkling with tears.

"No, it's not. You know it's not. Don't tell me things are okay when they're not. My dad does that."

The dad who left when she was two. "I'm not saying things are okay, Mia. I'm telling you I'm going to make them right."

"How? You can't bring Chris back to life."

"No. All I can do is try to keep what happened to Chris from happening to anybody else."

She lays her head on my chest again. I let her alone for a bit, trying not to feel too awkward with her body pressing against mine. Then I separate us.

"Where's Annie?"

"In bed."

"Good. Do you feel like telling me what you know now?"

She wipes her eyes and nose. "My eyes are swollen. That always happens when I cry. I know I look like shit."

"It's okay. Just tell me what happened."

She disengages from me, sits on the top step, and hugs her knees. "About seven tonight, Chris bet Jimmy Wingate he could beat him across the lake. Swimming, right? As cold as it is at night, and that's the wide part of the lake, too. Jimmy didn't want to do it, but Chris was wasted and kept calling Jimmy a pussy. I can just see it. Chris is such a redneck sometimes. So they tried it. No life jackets, pitch black. They were about halfway across when Chris got into trouble. He just stopped swimming and tried to float. He told Jimmy he was watching the moon, that the moon was changing colors every second."

They'd done three tabs of acid in the past twelve hours, Sonny said.

"Jimmy tried to get him to keep swimming," Mia continues, "but it was like Chris couldn't hear him. Jimmy was treading water, and he knew he couldn't last long. When he finally got Chris to start swimming again, Chris started puking. After that, Chris couldn't keep himself afloat. Jimmy wasn't sure which bank they were closer to, so he tried to pull Chris back to the pier where they'd started. He barely made it forty yards before he was exhausted." Mia is rocking steadily now. "He had to let Chris go, and he barely made it back himself. He was crying like a baby when he told me this."

"Things *have* gone crazy," I murmur.

"Did I help any?" Mia asks.

"What?"

"About Shad Johnson. Did I help Dr. Elliott by seeing Shad with the judge and the sheriff?"

I reach down and squeeze her shoulder. "You helped a lot. I really appreciate it."

"Can you tell me about it?"

"I wish I could, but—"

"You don't trust me."

"It's not that. It's just . . ."

She looks up, her eyes hurt. "If you really trusted me, you'd tell me."

I sit beside her on the steps. "Drew's situation is about more than a crime, okay? It's political. The D.A. wants to convict Drew to prove that a rich white man won't be treated any better than a poor black one in this town."

"That sounds like a good thing."

"If that were the real reason he was doing it, it would be. But it's not. Shad wants to be elected mayor. And if what he really wanted was to bring this city back to life, I'd support him. But that's not what he wants. He wants a stepping-stone to bigger things. He wants personal power. And he's willing to railroad Drew to get it."

Mia turns to me and smiles through her tears. "That wasn't so hard, was it?"

"No."

She raises a forefinger and pretends to zip her lips. "It's in the vault."

"*Seinfeld*?"

She laughs. Then she begins to cry again.

"Did you know Chris well?" I ask.

"Since nursery school."

This doesn't surprise me. I started at St. Stephen's when I was four years old. Fourteen years later, most of the people I graduated with were children I'd played with in nursery school. I knew them as well as I knew my own family, and many of them I still do. That's one of the things that makes this shrinking town worth saving. Some of the best parts of American life that have vanished elsewhere still thrive here.

"I still want to help," Mia says. "I mean it. Even if you think it's dangerous. School's boring me to death. I'm just counting the days until graduation. I want to do something that matters. Especially now."

I stand and pull her to her feet, then look hard into her eyes. "Who brought the LSD to the party?"

She goes still, her eyes locked on mine.

"Was it Marko?"

"I don't know. Not for sure."

"Would you tell me if you knew?"

"I don't know."

"What would keep you from it? Loyalty to your friends? To Marko? Or is it fear of Marko?"

She closes her eyes, then opens them again. "I'll think about that, okay? I'm not sure myself."

"Fair enough."

"I'd better go now."

I try to give her a smile of encouragement, but it fails.

"Will you hug me once more?" she asks in a small voice.

I start to, but something stops me.

"Never mind," she says, her mercurial eyes quick to recognize my hesitation. She walks down the steps and to her car, not once looking back.

"Be careful, Mia."

"Don't worry. I can take care of myself." She slams her door and pulls away, leaving me feeling like a complete asshole.

CHAPTER

Closeted in my downstairs bedroom with Kate's shoe box, I remove her journal again and prop myself up in bed. I already tried without success to view the contents of the three Lexar flash drives from the box. Each flash drive is protected by a security program that requires a password even to view file names and types. I'll have to ask Drew tomorrow if he knows any of Kate's passwords. If Kate stored intimate photos on the drives, maybe he was privy to that information, so that he could borrow the drives sometimes and view them. If not, I'll have to hire a professional hacker to open the files.

After adjusting my reading light, I reread the opening passage of Kate's journal, then wade into the body of the work. Her voice seems mature for her age, which I would expect from a senior bound for Harvard. But there's something else here, an unguarded honesty I didn't expect. I've been sent many manuscripts by published and unpublished writers over the years, and one thing I've learned is that people who write unflinchingly from the heart have the capacity to move us, where more polished craftsmen often fall short.

Kate's journal begins in the early summer of last year. As I read the early entries, my hunger to know more about her more recent months causes me to skip ahead. What quickly emerges from the pages is a picture of a girl maturing very fast, changing from a bored overachiever concerned with the social politics of high school to a fully engaged young woman ready to ditch the standard plan in order to be with the man she loved. By the time I've skimmed to the halfway point, I find myself mourning Kate Townsend more deeply than I would have thought possible.

Realizing that I might have missed important information in my haste, I go back and start again, this time folding down the corners of pages that seem representative of the arc of her final year, and also of those that hold information that might be helpful in defending Drew.

There's the early stuff, where Kate was still a part of the high school as most adults imagine it. Drew was recuperating from a knee injury, and thus home all day with Kate and Timmy.

6/3

Mia got voted head cheerleader today. Makes me wish I never even tried out. Well, she deserves it. She actually seems to give a damn about the stupid games, or at least about cheering. I'm not sure why I tried out except that it's what you're supposed to do. I'm such a retard. It's too late to quit now though. Damn, damn, damn.

6/18

Steve and I went to the lake today. He was really moody. He keeps asking me what I'll do if I get into Harvard or Princeton. As if I would turn one of them down! It's so obvious that we're going to split up when that time comes. I don't know how I can keep playing this role until then. I already can't remember what made me date him in the first place. I mean the physical element is still there, but aside from that, it's hell. He can't carry on a conversation that's not about baseball or deer hunting or what so-and-so looks like. And he's so VAIN. I don't think he's ever passed a mirror without *looking into it. He's always fixing his hair and asking me how it looks. He's such a <u>girl.</u> Nobody would believe it, but he is. God, I want a guy I can talk to. I hope like hell the guys at college are different. The ones at colleges around here sure aren't, though; they're the Steves that left high school two or three years ago. <u>Please</u> let me get in early decision.*

6/29

Played tennis with Ellen Elliott after work today (6–2, 6–1). She was <u>so</u> pissed. I wonder if they still make love. I really doubt it. Mom told me she heard that Ellen cheated on him a couple of years ago. Why would she do that? She's got a guy most women would give their left ovary for and she's cheating with some stupid tennis pro? Is there something I don't know about Drew? Is he terrible in bed? Brilliant and interesting but incompetent between the sheets? No way. That can't be it. They sleep in different rooms now. He says it's because of his knee, but I'll bet that dates back to the tennis pro. I bet I know why she did it, too. I've seen the insecurity in her, that need for constant reassurance. Like the breast implants. <u>Way</u> too big. Don't ever let me be that pathetic.

7/1

Drew talks to me like an equal. None of the condescending crap I get from most adults around here. That drives me <u>batshit.</u> Most of them haven't read a book in twenty years other than John Grisham or Nora fucking Roberts. The other day I made an allusion to John Updike and Mrs. Andersen thought I was talking about an <u>actor.</u> Hello?!!! Sometimes when his knee is really hurting, Drew asks me to read to him. I love it! He lies there on the sofa just looking at the ceiling. He lets me pick what I want to read, too. I read him a play by Paddy Chayefsky, one of Kesey's books. Part of <u>Goat.</u> An essay by Ayn Rand. He asks me where I come up with this stuff. Nabokov would be too obvious, but once I tried to embarrass him by reading an incestuous sex scene from Anaïs Nin. He *kept a straight face for about five minutes, then closed his eyes. When I got to the really explicit part, he started to snore. I really thought he'd fallen asleep! Bastard!*

7/28

Ellen won't look me in the eye when we're in their house. On the tennis court we're fine, but if she comes home while I'm keeping Tim, she won't meet my gaze. It's weird. It's like she sees me as a threat. I go out of my way to speak to her, but she cuts every conversation short. Has she caught Drew looking at me when I'm not looking or something? Has he <u>talked</u> about me to her? Maybe she feels I'm usurping her position with Timmy. If it weren't for Drew, I'd want out of there.

8/9

Drew's knee has gotten a lot better. He's talking about going on the mission trip to Honduras after all. Ellen told me I should go along, that it's the kind of real-world experience that a lot of the kids going into the Ivy League may already have had. I mean, <u>what?</u> When I asked why <u>she</u> doesn't go, she told me once was enough. She apparently got a case of dysentery in the Dominican Republic, and that killed her desire to help "the unfortunate" in any way except by writing a check. If he's serious about letting me come, I'm going to do it! Why not? I'd love to see Honduras, and I'd really love to be with him somewhere without Ellen and Timmy. Just to see how we are.

On August 18, Drew and Kate flew to Honduras along with a team sponsored by a local church.

8/21

This is a journey into the unbelievable. Never have I seen people so poor, so sick, so helpless. Yet never have I seen smiles so broad, eyes so bright, or heard laughter so pure.

I've shot a hundred pics already. My admiration for Drew grows every day that I watch him work. There are five other doctors with us—some of them specialists—but somehow Drew is the de facto leader of the team. I've watched the other doctors gape in awe as he works. Yesterday he removed four cancerous masses from a miner's neck. Two of the other doctors warned him not to do it. They said the patient needed a hospital and general anesthesia. Drew said the guy would never get either, and that the cancer would probably cut off his air supply within a month. The operation took place under a tarp stretched over a picnic table. Drew injected the man with lidocaine, told him to be still, then cut on him for about an hour. He had to inject more lidocaine throughout the procedure, but the miner just smiled and murmured encouragement all through the operation. He somehow knew Drew was his last, best hope. I know one thing now: that's the kind of man I want. Not a doctor, necessarily, but a man who'll take risks to do what he knows is right. Who won't be paralyzed by anxiety or rules or anything else. I want someone who <u>acts.</u> When Drew walked out of that tent, I waited until no one was around and then hugged him as tight as I could and told him I thought he was wonderful. Corny, maybe, but I don't care. Anybody with eyes to see would have said the same.

8/22

Today I asked Drew if he believed in God. I mean, this is a mission trip, right? But it doesn't seem to me that he's into all the praying and Bible stuff the others talk about every night. He told me he doesn't believe in the conventional concept of God. He said the idea of a God that watches the sparrow fall, that intervenes in human affairs, that rewards the faithful and punishes the wicked is a wishful fantasy. I asked him about life after death, and he just shook his head. "Come on," I said. "What happens after you die?" He looked at me like he was a thousand years old and said, "Kate, when you die, you're dead." I think he's watched a lot of people die in pain. "So this is all there is?" I asked. He nodded and said, "All we'll ever know as individuals, anyway." "Then I guess we'd better do all we can to be happy," I said (which I believe). He looked so sad then, but he said, "I think you're right." And then I made this colossal blunder and said, "Are you happy with your wife?" I NEVER meant to say that. I meant to say, "Are you happy with your LIFE," but it just came out, and I let it stand. He looked at me for a really long time without saying anything, and then he turned away. And then I knew. I guess I'd always known. He wasn't happy, and he hadn't been for a long time. And I wanted to make him happy, wanted it in a way I never wanted anything before. I wondered what would make him happy, and whether maybe I could. I knew then that I'd do whatever it took to take away the pain and loneliness in that face.

The mission team soon returned to Natchez, but too much had happened to go back to the way things were before.

8/27

It finally happened! We were talking in his workshop (fourth time I sneaked out) and it was really hot. His air conditioner was broken. I said we ought to go over to the Johnsons' pool, since they're out of town. Drew was worried at first, but then he said yes. We slipped through the trees and then across the open grass to the edge of their pool. He looked at me like he was unsure what to do, so I went first. I took off my top and my shorts, and then I walked into the water. I turned back and watched him strip to his underwear—boxer briefs. I couldn't stop shivering. I'd seen him in just tennis shorts before, but this was different, because we were alone. We swam for a while, keeping our distance, talking from a few yards apart. But then finally we came together, and he held me while we talked. He moved out to where the water was about five feet deep, and I wrapped my legs around him and laid my head on his shoulder. We talked for a long time, and then we stopped talking. I asked if he wanted to kiss me. He didn't say yes. He just raised my head, looked into my eyes, and did it. My whole body was quivering. I'd waited SO LONG for that moment. His kiss was so tender and knowing, not like Steve's at all, not like anyone's (except maybe Sarah Evans's—which is weird because Drew is so masculine). And then he said, "I want to see you." I knew what he meant, so I slipped my bra straps down and then my whole bra. He looked at my breasts as though appraising them, and then he covered my nipple with his mouth and I started to lose track of everything. I literally melted into the water. I felt him against me down there. After a while he made this shocked sound, and then he told me to put my hand down between us. That kind of scared me, but I let him pull my hand down. The pool water was cold, but between us the water was very warm, like someone was peeing in it. I thought for a minute that maybe he _was_ peeing, and that he was weird about that or something, but then he said, "It's you, Kate. That's _you._" And I blushed so deeply, because I realized it was. Drew held me tight and pulled me against him—still with his shorts on—and started moving against me. Then he whispered in my ear, "Is it all right if I climax?" I literally could not speak. I just nodded into his shoulder. And then he did. There was this explosion of air from his lungs, not grunting or anything like Steve. And then he just shivered the length of his body. I was crying, but not from sadness. I was overwhelmed. I wanted to look in the water, but I didn't. He walked to the shallows then, still holding me up, then he walked up out of the pool like I was a little girl. He carried me over to this big padded chair the Johnsons have on their patio and laid me down in it, and then we did it for real. God. When I think about it now, sitting here in the cold air-conditioning, all I can really remember is clinging to him and feeling things I'd never felt before. I kept thinking, "He's *married, stupid!" but I didn't stop or tell him to. After he fi-nally stopped moving, I tried to sound calm when he talked to me, but I wasn't. I was freaking out. My heart was just pounding, but I didn't want him to know. I'm <u>still</u> shaking. It's 6:30 a.m and <u>I don't want to go to work!</u> How can I look at Ellen now? If I go late, I won't have to see her. She'll be playing tennis or getting her hair done or some-thing. And Timmy, God, this is going to be <u>so</u> hard. And so <u>weird.</u> I feel guilty, but that's only part of me. The other part can't think of anything but him. Last night . . . wanting it again, that ineffable closeness. I can't believe that was our first time. Where do we go from here? I hope he's okay with it, not freaking out because I'm so young. He looked SO HAPPY. I think he was crying at one point, but I didn't want to say anything. He needed me so badly. Have to sleep some now.*

9/7

Two lives. That's what I'm leading. It's the strangest expe-rience ever. I have a day self and a night self, and the two never flow together. During the day, Drew is a vague feeling, always there yet indistinct, a heaviness in my stomach, a tin-gle in my forearms. Life goes on around me and with me, yet the Real Me is hibernating. I can't eat—a new experi-ence! I've always eaten ravenously, but now I can't eat any-thing. The excitement and anticipation fill me in some way I've never been filled before, turning my heart into a huge balloon that presses down my stomach and rises into my throat. Is this what love is? When I first see him, that bal-loon rises so high into my throat that I can't speak. But the sleep deprivation is starting to get to me. I feel like I'm hal-lucinating sometimes. If I don't get some rest, Mia's going to take valedictorian, and I can't afford to lose that until I hear something from Harvard. Maybe I should quit the cheer-leading squad. That wouldn't affect my transcript, and I could take naps in the afternoon. Maybe . . .

As I read on, Kate's amazing self-awareness shows me how Drew could become so captivated by her.

9/18

I know some people will say I'm looking for a father figure, and my first instinct would be to say, "Bullshit. I already have a father. He just happens to be a prick." But really, what if I am? What if one of the needs Drew fills for me is a protective presence who takes care of certain things? What's wrong with that? Everyone needs some of that, and I was certainly shortchanged in that department growing up. If Drew is happy being that for me, and if he makes me happy by being that, where's the fault in it? A lot of people would be happy to tell me, of course, but screw them. What do they know? Half of conventional married couples end up divorcing, so there. Is this relationship going to stunt my emotional growth or something? No. Most people who'll criticize us probably stopped growing themselves years ago—emotionally and intellectually—especially in THIS TINY TOWN.

After two months of nightly rendezvous, Kate has developed into an accomplished lover, and her hunger seems to have no bounds. Yet just as in the past, she continues to measure herself against others.

11/5

Tonight I had eight orgasms in two hours. Two clitoral, six vaginal. Drew is amazing. Or maybe I am. Do other women respond like this? I hope so, for their sakes. But I know Ellen never did. And I know my girlfriends don't. Except maybe Karen Carr.

11/17

Drew wants to test my testosterone level. He thinks a libido like mine has to be driven by something other than the normal hormonal flow. I think he must be right, with the crazy things I want. There's still so much I haven't shown him! Sometimes we get to a place where it hurts me, but instead of wanting it to stop, I want it to intensify. Once when I was on top, his hand was on my breastbone and it slipped up around my neck. I pressed it there with both hands to show him what I wanted. He squeezed for a little bit, but he didn't really cut off my air. I wanted to tell him that Steve used to do that for me (at my request, of course) but I felt too weird to say it. Drew would probably understand, but I'm not sure. If I tell him how that gets me off, he might think I'm messed up somehow. Of all the things we've done, he's never suggested anything that involved pain. I could tell him I read somewhere that some people like oxygen deprivation when they climax (he probably knows that already), and try to get to it that way. I could say Karen told me about it. I don't know. Maybe I am sick or something. But if I want it, it must be natural, so what's wrong with it?

All I can think about after reading that entry is the autopsy report. *Cause of Death: Strangulation.* Could it be that Kate wasn't murdered at all? That she died during what was, for her, normal sexual activity? I'm still wondering this when the name I've been searching for leaps off the page as though written in letters of fire.

11/18

Tonight I met Cyrus face-to-face. Can't talk about why, even here. He wasn't at all what I expected. He looks young and old at the same time. His face is young but his eyes are old. He reminds me of Drew that way. Cruelty and kindness living in the same soul. I found myself wondering who would win if he and Drew had to fight to the death. Like that stupid Mel Gibson movie: "Two go in, one comes out!" And what would they fight over? Me, of course. A scary image. But it turns me on, too, in a weird way. Seriously turns me on.

12/15

Fuck, fuck, fuck! <u>No letter from Harvard!</u> Clearly I didn't make the cut for early decision. After school, Mrs. Parrinder pulled me aside and told me Mia got into Brown. That's probably true. I remember Brown had the same ED notification date as Harvard. That's weird, too, because Mia's so straight compared to me. You'd think <u>I'd</u> be going to Brown and she to Harvard. Of course she claims she didn't even apply to Harvard, but I know that's bullshit. She had the SATs, and who wouldn't apply who had a chance of getting in?

12/18

Tonight Drew and I talked about maybe bringing someone else into our lovemaking. He says he's never done that before, and I like the idea of making him experience something he never has. <u>I've</u> sure never done it. The only girls I know who have are sluts who pulled a train when they were drunk or something. Or Susie Drane, who let Chris and Chip both do her on the football field one night. Ugh! The obvious question: should the "third" be a guy or a girl? When Drew asked what I thought, I said "girl" to make it seem less threatening, but the truth is, I'd rather it be a guy. I'd <u>love</u> to see Drew do things to a guy, and vice versa. But I also want to know what it feels like to be completely full. When I finally admitted that, Drew didn't seem threatened by it. But clearly there are problems with this kind of thing. Do you pick a friend you both know really well? Or a total stranger you know you'll never see again? A stranger reduces the emotional risks but increases the medical ones. The easiest way to start would be Sarah Evans, of course, since I've already been with her. But when Drew asked if we could trust her to keep quiet, I realized I wasn't sure. Sarah's been kind of stalking me lately, and this would make that worse. Drew said maybe the best thing would be to try a couple, a guy and girl at the same time. That way we'd all have the same things at risk, and nobody would feel left out of the sexual stuff. I asked Drew if there was a *woman he fantasized about having, or if he had a friend he could trust to try something like this. I was afraid he was going to say, "Mia Burke." But he really surprised me. He said maybe Penn Cage, the writer. Drew trusts him, and Penn's girlfriend (fiancée?) is like 33 and hot. Caitlin Masters is her name. I played tennis with her once at Duncan Park. She's from Boston, and she dresses sort of risque sometimes, so maybe she'd be into something like this. It seems weird even to be writing about this, but if it's something you desire, what are you supposed to do? Pretend it never popped into your head? Drew said we shouldn't rush it, though, and I think he's right. There's time for all this.*

While the shock of reading this passage settles over me, I see Cyrus's name lower down the page.

12/23

Cyrus wants me. And he's so fucking open about it! Far more open than Drew ever was. Maybe it's a racial thing, just to be out with it like that. Or maybe he's just used to getting whatever girl he wants. He kept pulling on his package while he talked to me, just like the black guys on MLK Street. Like I wasn't seeing it or like he didn't give a shit if I did. It's such a double standard! What if those guys' wives and girlfriends walked around rubbing their clitorises (clitorisae?) all the time? They'd flip out! All that practiced cool would evaporate in about two seconds. And somewhere behind that double standard is the belief that "It's different for men." That men need it more, think about it all the time etc." IF ONLY THEY KNEW!

A month passes without major changes in Kate's pattern. Then Cyrus reappears, like a supply ship that arrives once a month.

1/14

Cyrus is definitely getting to be a problem. Tonight he walked me into a corner and murmured stuff right in my ear. He asked if I had "something against niggers." His word, not mine. I told him I didn't, but that I was in love with someone else. He asked who. "Some gay-ass white boy?" he said. God, I wanted to tell him about Drew. That would have made him step back! He just stared at me like a wild man, like he blames me for driving him crazy. Then he touched my right breast—not too hard, just a tweak to my nipple. I was wearing a bra, thank God, because my headlights definitely came on, from fear, I'm sure. He could probably see them, but too bad. He's making himself crazy. I just hope I don't have to do this much longer. But it's all in a good cause, right? At least I see it that way. The cops definitely wouldn't.

This passage makes me think Kate *was* seeing Cyrus to buy drugs. I'm ecstatic to find evidence of Cyrus's obsession with Kate; I only wish I could show selected portions of this journal to Shad Johnson. A dangerous game.

2/3

Tonight I told Drew that the best kisser I ever knew was a girl. Have to be honest, right? Nothing ever aroused me faster than Sarah Evans's tongue in my mouth. It anticipated every want before I even wanted it. Drew asked if she kissed me "down low" better than he does. Again, yes, but I think she had an unfair advantage! She knows the territory better than any man could. At least Drew doesn't freak out like other guys about other sex I've had. (How can he though, he's been with like 22 women—21 before he got married.) Of course I've never cheated on him. That would probably be different. In fact, I know it would. I never want to find out! I never want to see him truly angry!

As I read the last line again, I know I can never show this journal to Shad. Here is the smoking gun that the D.A. would give anything to be able to read aloud to a jury.

By mid-February, Kate is growing less obsessed with sex and more concerned with the future of her relationship with Drew.

2/19

I've always heard people say, "Youth is wasted on the young," but I didn't understand that until I'd been with Drew awhile. Now I look around and see people my age living from moment to moment, jumping from thing to thing without thought. On one hand it's beautiful to be completely in the moment, but it's also like being less alive, almost living like an animal, without past or future. Except people aren't truly like animals, because they're haunted by insecurity. Kids don't realize how much freedom they have to screw up, over and over if they need to, because that's the true gift of youth—time. The need to be accepted drives everyone to crazy extremes, even adults. But in my peers it's almost a manic need. And girls are the WORST. It isn't even acceptance that most of them want, but ATTENTION. My god, the things they'll do to get it. Alter their voices, act out, give blowjobs to guys they barely know, "Look at me! Look at me! Notice me!" I talked to a couple of friends about it, but of course they think I don't understand their problems. They all say I'm so beautiful and smart and assume I've never had to deal with self-doubt. A couple of years ago I was a pathetic wreck, I just hid it better than most. Guess I learned that from Mom. Thanx, Mom, if you ever read this.

2/24

Mom knows! Oh, my God. I don't know how I'm going to tell Drew. I'm only writing because Drew didn't get on the computer. Hurry up! He's going to freak, but I have to let him know somehow that it's all right. I can't believe it. All that anxiety I've had about Mom finding out, and she's known for TWO WEEKS. She's played it <u>so cool.</u> She wouldn't even tell me how she knows, but she acted like she's seen us together or something. Maybe she followed me *over there. Maybe she walked in on us here and didn't tell me. It's so weird. She said she knows I think I'm in love with him, but that's only natural since I'm so young and he's such a good guy in so many ways. She's really concerned with Drew's feelings, I think, and she wants to talk to him. Actually, now that I think about it, Drew will be glad it's come to this. I mean, I think he will. I guess I should look at this as a test. If he panics and doesn't want to talk to her, then he's not serious about wanting to be with me. I'm just a* diversion. *God, that would kill me! But if that's how he reacts, I've got to face it.*

2/26

Every time I go to Cyrus's I tell myself it's the last time. But then I have to go again. It's just taking so LONG. Longer than Drew's worst estimate. Sometimes I feel stupid for waiting, but that's par for the course, I guess. I should talk to some other mistresses about this. I'm sure we're a silent sisterhood, suffering alone, yet all dealing with the same issues. I feel your pain, girls!

3/4

Mom and Drew talked tonight! He actually came over to our house at 10:30, and the two of them talked in the kitchen for like two hours. I went over to Lessley's before he got there, because Mom wanted to see him alone. She called me home at one a.m. She had tears in her eyes when I walked in, but I think she was happy. I asked her what was wrong, and she said, "I don't know why I'm crying." And I said, "What happened? Tell me!" She just hugged me and said, "He really loves you, honey. He loves you in a way no one ever loved me. You're very lucky in that. You're just unlucky in the circumstances." She said a lot more, but I can't sit still to write it! I'm going over to Drew's in twenty minutes. Oh My God. I can't wait *for him to talk to Dad! He's one person the great David Townsend sure won't intimidate. I think Mom wants to see that encounter too. It makes me realize how Daddy has used his education and his gender to intimidate us. I want to see what he's like when that advantage is neutralized by superior strength and intelligence. Hell, yeah!*

3/14

Mom's been worrying lately. She trusts Drew. She even worries for him. Her main worry is Timmy, I think. She doesn't know whether Drew's love for me is strong enough to make him leave Tim. I understand Drew's conflict, though the irony is devastating. Because one of the things I love about him is that he's NOT like my dad. Yes, he could divorce Ellen, but he could never abandon Tim. He'll always be the father he needs to be, and that's just something I'm going to have to deal with. I mean, I love Timmy too, even though he isn't mine. And Drew and I can have our own after a while, anyway. It's going to be all right. I know it is.

3/19

Got my acceptance letter! YEAH! Now I get to drop the "H-bomb" like all the other Ivy League brats. And now I'm second-guessing myself, of course. Before I got in, I thought I wasn't good enough for Harvard. Now it's like . . . maybe it's too cliché for me. It's like Woody Allen said, "I'd never want to join a club that would take me as a member." Plus, I saw the same juvenile shit in Cambridge that I did when I visited Ole Miss. Stop overanalyzing! You got what you wanted. Live with it!

Then Kate's final entry:

3/31

Five days now. Never been this late before. Drew told me to get a test at the pharmacy, but I've been too nervous. I don't want to know yet. There's so much stress already, I don't want to add my being pregnant to it. Drew doesn't

*need that. Neither does Mom. Neither do <u>I.</u> But I keep
thinking about that senior party at the lake, when I got so
drunk. I know I missed my pill that day, and maybe even the
day after. Shit, what if I <u>am?</u> I always thought I'd get an
abortion, but now that it's real, that's not such an easy call. I
mean, what if I had the baby? Drew already told me that it's
my decision, he won't pressure me either way, and I know
he means it. In some way it would be such a relief. My future would be decided, at least in that way.*

 *Drew's been talking to a med school friend about practic-
ing medicine in Boston. He said he already took the boards
or whatever. He was saving that as a surprise, but I think he
wanted to ease my worry about the future. He definitely
loves me. He's shown me so many times, in so many ways. If
a baby comes, <u>so be it.</u> That child would be the two of us
alive in the world as one, and <u>how can that be bad?</u>*

With that the journal ends.

Less than twenty-four hours later, Kate Townsend was dead.

I close the book and drop it onto the floor beside my bed. I'm
too tired to try to analyze what I've just read. I switch off the ringer
on my phone, turn off my reading lamp, and roll onto my stomach.
As sleep slowly takes me, one aspect of the journal remains at the
forefront of my thoughts: Kate's voracious sexuality. Seventeen
years old, and already she was considering the risks and rewards of
a ménage à trois with a stranger. More disturbing still, in light of
the way she died, was Kate's desire to be choked during sex. This
opens up so many possibilities that I must wait until I've rested to
consider them. But one thought refuses to leave me alone: it now
seems less impossible than it did yesterday that Kate Townsend
could have died at Drew's hands.

CHAPTER
16

Annie leans over the front seat of my car, kisses me, then climbs out and runs into the St. Stephen's middle school. From habit, I wait until she disappears from my sight before driving on. It's a primitive instinct, like the one that made Annie keep a hand in contact with me for over a year after her mother died, even while she slept.

As the line of cars moves slowly past the high school, Holden Smith steps from beneath the overhang and motions for me to pull over. When I do, he comes to the window with a big smile and tells me he's scheduled an emergency board meeting to deal with the aftermath of our two student deaths. Yesterday he practically demanded my resignation along with Drew's; today—with the *Examiner* offering up Cyrus White as a possible suspect—he's saying the board was hasty in suggesting I resign. Holden sounds positive that Chris Vogel drowned because of Ecstasy or LSD. And while no one has fingered Marko Bakic as the source of those drugs, Holden seems quite prepared to expel our troublesome exchange student without any proof. I reiterate my intention to resign, but I also agree to appear at the meeting, primarily in order to gather the most information possible about the events surrounding Chris

Vogel's death. I feel Holden's relief as he pumps my hand in farewell.

"Chickenshit," I mutter as he walks away.

I pull out onto Highway 61 and head into town. The first order of the day is getting the assault charge against Drew dismissed. As I pass the hospital, my cell phone rings. It's Don Logan, chief of the Natchez Police Department.

"Are you getting your buddy out of jail this morning?" he asks.

"I'm on my down there now."

"Well, his situation has worsened a bit since last night."

My pulse quickens; something serious has happened. "How so?"

"This morning we searched the woods upstream from where we found the Townsend girl. We started at dawn, and we moved pretty fast along both banks. We had a little dispute with the sheriff's department, but I won't go into that now. The point for you is that when we reached the woods between Pinehaven and the creek, we found Kate's cell phone."

There's a hitch in my breathing. "And?"

"It's one of those camera phones. She had some pictures stored inside it. One of those pictures shows Dr. Elliott asleep on a bed. In the nude."

Even though I'm driving, I waver like a man losing his balance. "Does the district attorney know about that picture?"

"Yes, sir. He does."

While I work through the implications of this development, Chief Logan speaks again. "Penn, between you and me, I've got a source over at the sheriff's department. She tells me that Dr. Elliott is going to be arrested by a couple of deputies as soon as he leaves this building."

Jesus. "On what charge?"

"Sexual battery is what I heard. But I'm thinking murder."

"If the D.A. wants Drew charged with another crime, why doesn't he just have you charge him?"

There's a long silence before Logan answers. "The D.A. would tell you it's because murder is a state crime, and a defendant accused of it has to be held in state custody. But if you ask me, it's because Billy Byrd is a lot deeper in Shad Johnson's pocket than I am or ever will be."

This leaves me both angry and uncertain about what to do. "Has Drew been scheduled for arraignment?"

"Eleven o'clock."

"I may let him attend that proceeding after all. I'll let you know well before then what I'm going to do."

"I'd appreciate it. Things are getting mighty interesting down here."

"Don, have you turned up anything on Cyrus White?"

"Nothing at all. It's like he's vanished off the face of the earth."

"I'd say that makes him look more than a little guilty."

"I agree. But maybe he's just paranoid. Maybe he doesn't believe Shad Johnson's promises of fair treatment for blacks in the judicial system."

"Was that humor, Don?"

"Don't forget to call me."

Chief Logan hangs up.

Even before I lay my phone on the seat, one certainty settles into my bones. Despite what I told Shad and Sheriff Byrd about Cyrus White last night, Drew is going to be charged with capital murder. It seems unbelievable, but worse has been done in this town in the name of politics. Another certainty quickly follows the first: Drew needs a real lawyer, not a former prosecutor-turned-novelist who's too close to the case. He needs a top-flight defense attorney with years of experience, one with the credentials to neutralize the subliminal cards that Shad Johnson will bring to the table. That means a local attorney who is black and preferably female. Several black attorneys practice in Natchez, but the only one I know well practices civil law. I need a wise counselor to help me choose my candidate.

I slow down and make a U-turn, then head back south. My father's office is less than a mile away. For forty years, he has treated more black patients than any white doctor in town, and he knows many of them like family. If anyone can tell me about the black lawyers in town, it's my dad. I call ahead and ask for Esther Ford, his physician's assistant. Esther has very little formal training, but after forty years of working at my father's side she knows more about primary care medicine than many interns. When she comes on the line, I ask if Dad can spare me fifteen minutes. She laughs and simply hands the phone to him.

"What's up, Penn?" Dad asks in his resonant baritone.

"I need to see you for a minute. I've got an emergency."

"A medical emergency?"

"No, but almost as bad."

"Does it have to do with Drew Elliott?"

"How'd you know?"

"When I made rounds this morning, that's all anybody was talking about in the doctors' lounge."

"What were they saying?"

"That Drew's been screwing the Townsend girl. That she got pregnant, and he snapped and killed her."

"Great."

"I figure if any of that's true, it's the first part. The rest I can't see. Drew Elliott is the best young doc I've seen in my career, and I'm not talking about technical skills. He cares about people. Any man can be led astray by his willie, but Drew Elliott committing murder? No way."

"I wish more people felt that way."

"People turn on you fast. It's human nature."

My father once learned this lesson in a very painful and public way. It took me almost twenty years to pay back the man who tried to ruin him. "Dad, I need some advice, and I need it fast."

"Shoot."

"I need the best black lawyer you know."

"To defend Drew?"

"You got it."

"You're the hotshot lawyer. Why ask me?"

"You know why. I want him local, and I'd actually rather have a her. Does anybody in town fit the bill?"

"Hang on, I'm thinking."

"Take your time." I hear Esther talking in the background.

"I only know of three black female lawyers in town. I've heard good things about two of them, but that's not who I'd hire if Shad Johnson was trying to nail me to the barn door."

"Why not?"

"I'm not sure. You asked my opinion, I'm giving it to you."

"Fair enough. What about men?"

"We ought to ask Esther."

"I'd go to her if I was sick, but not for this."

More silence. Dad calls out a medication and dosage to someone. "Penn, I'm at a loss here. When I think of local lawyers—black or white—and then I think of the situation Drew is facing, I just come up blank."

"I know what you mean."

"Sorry I can't be more help."

"It's okay. I'll just—"

"Wait a minute!" Dad says in an excited voice. "Hell, I should have thought of that first thing."

"What?"

"Not what—*who*."

"You have someone in mind?"

"The smartest lawyer for a thousand miles around, if you ask me. No offense."

"Who are you talking about?"

"Quentin Avery."

Images of a tall black man in a black suit arguing before the Supreme Court fill my mind. In some of those old news photographs, the "Negro lawyer"—as the captions referred to him then—stands beside Thurgood Marshall. In others, beside Robert Carter and Charles Huston. I even remember Quentin Avery standing shoulder to shoulder with an angry-looking Martin Luther King, Jr.

"Quentin Avery," I echo. "I knew he owned a house out near the county line. But I didn't think he spent much time there."

"Quentin travels a lot, but he's been staying out there most of this past year. He's sort of a recluse now. I've been treating him for diabetes and hypertension."

"How old is he?"

"Mm, two or three years older than I am. Seventy-four?"

"What kind of shape is he in?"

"Mentally? He's writing a law textbook. And in conversation, he's so quick I can barely keep up with him."

"What about physically?"

"He lost a foot a couple of months ago—diabetes—but he still gets around better than I do. He's like a spry old hound dog."

"What made you mention him? I mean, Avery is a legend. Why would he take a case like this?"

Even as I ask this question, a possible answer comes to me. Quentin Avery might be a legend of the civil rights movement, but time has not increased his stature. The moral leadership he demonstrated in the sixties and seventies seemed to vanish in the 1980s, when he began handling personal injury cases and class action lawsuits against drug companies. This giant who argued landmark cases before the highest court in the land was suddenly trying accident cases in Jefferson County, Mississippi, the predominantly black county famed for its record-breaking punitive damages awards, most of them based on the prejudices of the African-Americans who filled the jury box each week. Recently, federal prosecutors began reviewing many of those awards, and initiating action against both jury members and the attorneys involved.

"Oh, I don't think he'd take the case," Dad replies. "Although you never know what will interest Quentin. But you can bet he knows the perfect lawyer to get Drew out of this jam."

"Does Avery know who I am?"

"Sure he does. Quentin wasn't in town when you solved the Del Payton murder, but he followed it from New Haven. He was teaching law at Yale then. He said he admired you for bringing Leo Marston to justice after all those years. I think he's read a couple of your books as well. Maybe he was just being nice, but that's not Quentin's style."

"Should I just call him out of the blue?"

"You could, but he probably wouldn't answer. Why don't you

let me call first? I've got a good idea of your situation. If Quentin's willing to help, he'll call you."

"Good enough. But time is critical."

"I got that, son."

Someone is beeping in on my phone. It's Chief Logan again. "I've got to run, Dad."

"Go. Bring Annie by to see us soon."

"I will." I click the phone to take the incoming call. "Chief?"

"Penn, somebody just told Billy Byrd that he saw Dr. Elliott's car parked in a vacant lot in Pinehaven on the afternoon of the murder. That lot's adjacent to St. Catherine's Creek, and not a quarter mile from where we found Kate Townsend's cell phone."

"Mother*fucker.*" Drew's recklessness is going to damn him in the end. "Is that the worst of it?"

"Afraid not. This witness says he saw Drew's car at about three forty-five p.m. Kate Townsend's cell phone records show that she answered a text message from a girlfriend at three twenty-two p.m. We found her cell phone in the woods less than two hundred yards from where Drew's car was parked. That means they were in very close proximity to one another within twenty-three minutes. That's provable, Penn. What a jury would read into that, you know better than I."

I can't believe this. "Is there anything else, Don?"

"My source says Sheriff Byrd's planning to arrest your man for capital murder. She even heard that with the D.A.'s help, Byrd might try to take Drew right out of my custody."

Astonishment paralyzes me.

"Penn, are you Drew's lawyer or not? He doesn't seem too sure himself."

"I guess I am for the moment."

"What do you want me to do if Byrd shows up and tries to take him out of here? I've called the attorney general in Jackson for an opinion, but all I got was the same old runaround. Goddamn lawyers . . . pick any dozen of them and you won't find a pair of balls in the bunch. No offense."

"None taken," I mutter, searching desperately for a solution.

"What do you want me to do?"

Desperate times, desperate measures . . .

"Penn?"

"Charge Drew with capital murder."

The silence on the other end of the line is absolute. "On my own authority?"

"You know what the evidence is. You've got the girl's cell phone. Charge him with murder right now. Don't wait. Do it the second you hang up."

"I take back what I said before. You've got a pair of balls on you, all right."

"Will you do it, Don?"

"I'll do it. But you'd better get your ass down here in a hurry."

CHAPTER

17

Drew is a sobering sight today. Gone are the Ralph Lauren khakis and Charles Tyrwhitt button-down he wore to work yesterday morning. Now he wears the orange-striped prison garb I usually see on inmates picking up trash around the city. His handsome face is shadowed by thirty hours' growth of beard, but it's his eyes that unsettle me most. They're no longer the eyes of an accomplished physician in command of his surroundings; they're the haunted eyes of a man who realizes that the world he once bestrode with confidence may soon contract to an eight-by-ten-foot cell.

"Tell me you have some good news," he says.

"I do. But it's not all good. You'd better put your game-face on."

He blinks slowly. "Give me the bad first."

"The police found Kate's cell phone in the woods not far from her house." I lower my voice to a whisper. "Also not far from where you told me you found her body."

He watches me without speaking for a while. "What's so bad about that? Had she tried to call me or something?"

"I don't know. But she had some pictures stored in her phone. Explicit pictures."

Another slow blink. "Pictures of what?"

"You. Unclothed."

Drew closes his eyes but says nothing.

"I saw them. One looks like your penis, another looks like your ass. What I remember from the high school dressing room, anyway."

"Do any show my face?"

"Yes. In one you're sleeping naked."

"Goddamn it. I told her to erase that stuff." He grits his teeth and shakes his head, but it's hard to be angry at a dead girl. "Is that all the bad news?"

"No. Someone saw you park your car in that vacant lot near the creek after all. Honestly, that's the most damning piece of evidence they have, because unlike the rest, which only prove an affair, that puts you close to what they may eventually prove was the crime scene."

Drew lays his elbows on the narrow ledge on his side of the visiting window. "What about the good news?"

"We're not done with the bad yet."

"Shit."

"The semen that the serology tests say is yours wasn't swabbed from Kate's vagina. It came from her rectum."

Drew looks at me like a man offended by a personal question. "What are you asking me, Penn?"

"Is your DNA going to match that semen when the big test comes back?"

He looks away, then back at me. "Kate liked to finish that way sometimes, okay? I don't know why, but she got a lot of pleasure from that. I did, too, obviously. We probably did that . . . one out of every four times."

I don't speak for a while. I'm trying to judge his honesty about a subject on which Drew is the only living authority.

"Why?" he asks. "Did somebody make a big deal of that?"

"Kate was in high school, Drew. *Everybody's* going to make a big deal out of that. It's going to make you look a lot more guilty of rape to a lot of people."

"That's crazy. It was her idea. Ellen and I never had anal sex."

"Because you never asked, or because Ellen refused?"

He stares at me with wide eyes, then hangs his head. "I see what you mean."

"The autopsy report says Kate had both vaginal and anal trauma indicative of rape. Would you have traumatized her back there?"

"No way. She relaxed totally during that act. If she was traumatized back there, whoever raped her did it."

I think about this for a while. "Did Kate ever ask you to choke her during sex?"

His head pops up. "No. Why?"

I lower my voice to a whisper. "Did you know Kate kept a journal?"

Drew glances at the door behind him, then turns back to me and nods.

"Kate's mother brought that to me, with some of her other personal things. She didn't want the police to find them."

"That's good. I told you Jenny understood."

"Kate wrote in her journal about wanting you to choke her. Apparently Steve Sayers used to do that to her, and at her request."

Bewilderment. "She never told me that. And she never asked me to do it."

I'm almost afraid to ask the next question. "Did you two ever bring anyone else into your bed?"

"Did she write that we did?"

I'm tempted to lie and try to trap him, but I don't. "She wrote about wanting to do it."

Drew looks like he might be about to ask me what she wrote about that subject. But then he says, "She did want to. We might have done it in the future, but . . . no, we never did."

"Kate had three miniature flash drives in the box with her journal. The USB type. Lexar."

"Did you open them?"

"I couldn't. They're password-protected."

He looks intrigued but offers nothing.

"Do you know the passwords to those disks?"

"No."

"They're high-capacity drives—five hundred twelve meg. I'm

thinking they have digital photos on them. If it turned out that she had some pictures of other men—even one other man—that might really help you."

Drew is no longer looking at me. "I don't know her password," he says. "Not even for her e-mail account. She was private about stuff like that."

"Okay. Let's try a little good news—although on a personal level, you may see it as bad. Have you seen the morning paper?"

"No."

"Have you ever heard the name Cyrus White?"

Drew looks blank. "No. Who is he?"

"A black drug dealer."

No reaction.

"Kate had some contact with this guy," I go on. "Regular contact. She visited Cyrus every month or so at the Brightside Manor Apartments."

"Brightside Manor?" Shock now. "What the hell was she doing there?"

"Nobody knows. I got this from Sonny Cross, the narcotics agent. Keep that to yourself, by the way. Sonny says it's unlikely that Kate went there to buy drugs, because girls like Kate don't need to buy drugs. Guys will give them whatever they want. Did you ever see Kate get high?"

"Hell no," Drew says distractedly. He's obviously preoccupied with this new information about his mistress. "Kate hated drugs. I think she tried grass when she was fifteen, but she didn't like what it did to her head." He scratches his shoulder as though to kill a bug under his clothes. "But why else would she go to a place like that?"

I try to choose my words carefully, but there's no way to sugar-coat this. "Sonny suggested that she might have gone there solely to see Cyrus."

Drew pales. "You're out of your mind. Or Cross is. What does that redneck know about Kate anyway? He's never spoken to her in his life."

"He apparently knows more than you do about at least one

part of her life, as hard as that may be for you to swallow. We don't have time for hurt feelings, Drew. We need to figure out what the hell Kate was doing at Brightside."

Drew shakes his head again, but whether from anger or puzzlement, I can't tell.

"This isn't some twenty-year-old punk we're talking about," I explain. "Cyrus is a thirty-four-year-old veteran of Desert Storm. He runs the serious drug trade for the whole city. He has ties to Asian gangs on the Gulf Coast, and he ruthlessly wiped out his competition here when he went into business."

Drew turns up his palms. "I don't know what to say, okay? This is totally out of the blue for me. Is there anything else you can tell me?"

"According to Sonny, Cyrus has a taste for white girls."

I see fury building in Drew's face, and a new tension gathering in his heavily muscled shoulders.

"Stay calm, buddy," I say quietly. "In the journal Kate kept a list of guys she'd hooked up with. Guys and girls."

Drew looks more interested than surprised. "Tell me."

"She listed people she'd made out with, people she'd rejected, and people who had rejected her. Under the heading of guys she'd rejected was the name Cyrus. Beside this name—in parentheses— she wrote: 'shit, close one!' In another part of the journal she wrote that Cyrus had come on to her pretty strong during one visit. He backed her into a corner and fondled her breast."

A steely calm emanates from Drew's eyes. "Get me out of here, Penn."

"I can't do it. You're going to be charged with murder this morning. And at my request."

His mouth drops open.

"It was that or let Sheriff Byrd arrest you. For some reason I don't yet understand, Billy's acting as a monkey's paw for Shad Johnson. So it was basically a choice of jails. The other one's nicer, but this one's safer—for our purposes anyway."

"This is bullshit," Drew says. "You get me out of here now. I'll find out what this Cyrus was doing with Kate."

"That's not going to happen. With Shad pushing this thing, bail will be denied."

"Where's Cyrus now? Have the police talked to him? Have they taken a blood sample from him? That's got to be who raped Kate at the creek."

"Possibly," I concede. "I hope it was."

"Son of a *bitch!*" Drew explodes, slapping the ledge. "Do you realize where Brightside Manor is?"

"About forty yards from St. Catherine's Creek."

"Exactly! And the creek was in flood. He could have killed her there and dumped her body in the creek!"

"I thought of that last night. Only it seems unlikely that Kate's body would wash up within a couple of hundred yards from her house."

"Not really," says Drew, shaking his head. "That's a dogleg bend with a lot of obstacles that trap floating objects. Kate wasn't far from a fallen tree, now that I think about it." His eyes bore into mine. "You didn't answer my question. Where's Cyrus now?"

"Nobody knows."

Drew stares at me like a madman. "You're shitting me."

"No. And until the police find him, question him, and take blood from him, you're going to sit right where you are now. So settle down and get ready to tough it out."

"Tell me you're not serious."

"I am. And don't even think about doing anything crazy, Drew. I know inmates escape from the outdoor area of this jail with embarrassing regularity. I also know that if you got out of here and tracked down Cyrus White before the police, he'd be dead. But that would be the worst thing you could do. We need a confession from Cyrus. Failing that, we need a DNA match to the other semen sample taken from Kate's body."

The coldness in Drew's eyes could freeze desert sand. "They can match DNA to a corpse as easily as they can to a live body."

"Promise me you won't try it. Or I'll tell Chief Logan to put you in lockdown around the clock. He'll do it if I ask him."

Drew's hands are shaking.

"Promise me," I repeat. "Or this is the last time you'll see me in here."

After some time, he nods. I stand and reach for the door behind me. "One more thing."

He looks up with burning eyes.

"You need a real lawyer now. A top-notch criminal defense attorney, preferably black and female."

Drew says nothing.

"That's nonnegotiable," I tell him. "Understood?"

He waves his hand in a gesture of dismissal. He could care less about lawyers at this point. His mind and will are totally focused on one thing.

Cyrus White.

I'm sitting in Chief Logan's office when Sonny Cross calls my cell phone and delivers the next bombshell. "Penn, do you know Jim Pinella?"

"The oil man?"

"That's him. He's got a son at the Catholic school. A junior. Michael. Mike, they call him."

"I've met Mike," I reply, vaguely recalling a tall, thin boy who acted in a play at the Little Theater.

"Well, the kid was just beaten within an inch of his life."

A surreal feeling envelops me in a bubble, blurring Chief Logan and everything else in the office. "Who did it?"

"Some black guys. It happened outside the Brightside Manor Apartments."

"Brightside Manor? What the hell was a white kid doing over there? Buying dope? Or was this another mystery visit like Kate Townsend's?"

"Mike wasn't buying dope," Sonny says curtly. "Where are you now?"

"The police station."

"I'm on Liberty Road. Can you meet me in the parking lot of First Baptist Church?"

"Does this concern Drew?"

"I'm not sure, but it damn sure concerns St. Stephen's."

"I'll be there in five minutes."

CHAPTER

18

The First Baptist Church is a massive monument to the Southern Baptist sensibility. Built on forty-eight acres of pristine meadow sold by the devout owner of the antebellum mansion next door, the towering church complex manages to look both smug and sober at the same time. Today it's quiet, but usually the grounds echo with the screams of basketball from the church's gymnasium or the crack of softballs from the emerald diamonds in back.

I'm parked by a bronze bell in the front parking lot, waiting for Sonny Cross to arrive. Like so many parts of Natchez, the contrasts here are stark. On this side of the highway stands Devereaux, a nationally famous gem of Greek Revival architecture surrounded by oaks shrouded in Spanish moss. On the other side sit an aging Pizza Hut restaurant, a Coca-Cola bottling plant, and somewhere in the clapboard houses behind them the fossilized shell of the Armstrong Tire plant, once one of the most powerful economic engines in the city.

Sonny Cross's Ford Explorer turns into the entrance of the church's broad drive. As I watch him approach, I recall visiting the Coke plant as a child. Its interior was a cavernous, open space filled with rattling, clanking machinery. The most awe-inspiring contraption in the place pulled empty green bottles along a conveyor belt, jetted ten ounces of fizzing, caramel-colored elixir into each bottle, then sealed each one with a silver cap. I could have watched that machine for hours. The icy Coke I was handed as I left that building was the best-tasting drink I ever had in my life. But that place exists only in my memory now. Today that Coca-Cola building bottles nothing. It merely serves as a hub from which trucks distribute cases of aluminum cans throughout what remains of the city I remember. We don't make anything anymore.

"Hey," Sonny calls from the window of his Explorer. "I only got a couple of minutes. You hear there's an emergency school board meeting tonight?"

The drug agent has light blue eyes, a blond mustache, and a mullet hairstyle that belongs onstage with Lynyrd Skynyrd. Cross seems to fancy himself a sort of *Miami Vice* cowboy, favoring snakeskin boots and turquoise jewelry.

"I heard about it," I confirm.

"You gonna be there?"

"Unless you tell me I shouldn't."

"No, you should. The deadheads who've been asleep at the switch all this time are finally calling me about Marko Bakic."

"Let me guess. Bill Sims."

"He's one of them."

"What does Mike Pinella getting beat up at Brightside Manor have to do with St. Stephen's?"

"Maybe nothing," says Sonny, his face hardening in anger. "Or maybe a lot. This past October, Mike started getting into pot. He'd never tried it before, but since all his friends suddenly decided weed was the thing to do, Mike went along. He got steadily deeper into it, but the deeper he got, the more unhappy he got. He's a Catholic kid, and he had a lot of guilt. Still, he went to that X-rave two nights ago where Marko shot off all the fireworks."

"At the lake," I murmur, orienting myself.

"Right. Anyway, Mike grew up downtown, on the same block with another kid you know a lot better."

"Who's that?"

"Chris Vogel."

The boy who drowned in Lake St. John last night . . .

"When Vogel drowned, something snapped in Mike. I know this kid pretty well, okay? His younger brother is friends with my oldest son, and I worked for his dad a couple of summers out of high school. So, after Mike heard Vogel drowned, he called me up. He told me he was really upset, and he didn't want to see anybody else get hurt. He said he knew where Chris had got the acid that killed him. He told me he was willing to testify against the guy who sold it or set him up for a bust, whichever I wanted. He just needed to get some things straight before he told me what he knew. I pressed him, but he wouldn't budge on that. That was this morning, Penn." Sonny takes a deep breath. "Now he's lying in the ICU at the hospital. His jaw's broken, his hands, too. He can't tell me what he knows, and he couldn't write it down either, as hard as he tried. I sat there watching tears roll down that boy's face while he struggled to do it."

The reality of this is difficult for me to accept. What could the skinny kid I remember from that play have to do with drug dealers? But of course that's all too easy to answer. It's my heart that won't accept it. It's something I'd rather not believe could happen in Natchez. "Who beat him up, Sonny? Cyrus's people?"

"Had to be." Cross is clenching his side-view mirror so hard that his knuckles are bone white. He doesn't even seem aware that he's doing it.

"Didn't you tell me you thought it was Marko who supplied the drugs for the lake party?"

Sonny nods.

"Do you still feel that way? Or do you think it was Cyrus?"

"When you get right down to it, is there any difference?"

"From the school's point of view, there's a big difference. From Mike Pinella's? None."

"I try to go by the letter of the law," Sonny says quietly. "But sometimes . . . in this business . . . I just want to fuck somebody up. You know?"

"I know. When I was an assistant D.A. in Houston, I saw things nobody should ever see. And I dealt with cops who saw a lot worse than I did on a daily basis. Sometimes I wanted to pick up a gun and go out there myself. But you can't do that."

Sonny fixes me with a no-bullshit stare. "The way I heard it, you have done that. And more than once."

"Only in defense of my family," I say softly. "That's where I draw the line."

He looks away for a while, seemingly at the church steeple, then turns back to me. "How do you define 'family'? Because I'm not Mike's biological father, I don't have a responsibility to protect him?"

"You can't protect Mike now. He's already been hurt."

"And the others like him? They're part of this community, Penn. Part of this town we call ours. Those kids aren't family?"

"They are. But you can't do whatever it is you're thinking about doing. That's a tribal reaction, Sonny. I've felt it myself. Drew's walking the same razor's edge you are. He'd like to break out of jail and take Cyrus White apart piece by piece. But you can't give into that urge. Not yet, anyway. Give the law a chance to work."

Sonny's mouth wrinkles with contempt. "You talking about Shad Johnson?"

"Yes. And Sheriff Byrd and Chief Logan."

The drug agent hawks and spits on the asphalt. "That's what I think of Sheriff Byrd these past couple years, and I work for the man."

"I don't know what to tell you, Sonny. You're part of the system. Make it work. But please, anything you find out about Marko, pass it on to me before tonight's meeting. Six p.m."

Sonny pulls a tin of Skoal from his shirt pocket, dips his thumb and forefinger into the snuff, then packs it between his lower lip and gum. "I got some things working," he says, putting the Explorer in gear. "I'll let you know something, one way or another."

"What do you have working?" I ask anxiously.

He winks and grins. "Don't ask, don't tell, right? Later, bud."

The Explorer's tires squeal as Sonny skids around the silent bell and roars back toward the highway.

* * *

The early afternoon passed without surprises. Shad Johnson cussed out the chief of police for arresting Drew, but he did nothing else about it. The whereabouts of Cyrus White remained unknown. My father spoke to Quentin Avery, but the famed civil rights lawyer did not promise anything beyond "giving some thought to your son's situation." I picked up Annie from school at three and drove her to softball practice at Liberty Park. I often stay and watch her practices, when I'm not drafted into coaching myself.

She's hitting well today, but her fielding is less than spectacular. The coach ends practice early for some reason, and Annie walks over with a dejected expression on her face. I'm about to console her when my cell phone rings. The ID says it's my father.

"Hey, Dad. What's up?"

"Quentin Avery just called me."

A fillip of excitement runs through me. "Yeah?"

"He says he's bringing a lawyer by my office, one who'd be perfect for defending Drew. He wants you to meet him. Can you get away?"

"Hell, yes. What time?"

"Daddy, you're cursing again," Annie reminds me.

I smile and tug on her ponytail. "What time?"

"Now. Quentin already had an appointment to get his foot checked, so I guess he figured he'd kill two birds with one stone."

"Who's the lawyer?"

"He didn't say."

"Okay, fine. I'm on my way. I just have to drop Annie off."

"Was that Papa?" Annie asks when I hang up.

"How did you know?"

"By the way you talk to him. It's different than when you talk to me."

Annie has more intuition than I ever did. "You're just like your mother, girl."

All the humor goes out of her face. "Am I really?"

"You are. Just like her."

After we get in the car and start toward the highway, Annie

says, "You and Caitlin haven't been talking much lately, have you?"

"No. She's pretty busy up in Boston."

Annie mulls this over. "It sure seems like it. But I thought she'd come down and visit us more often."

"I did, too, punkin. So did Caitlin. Work is something adults don't have a lot of choice about sometimes." *Although in this case that's not true.*

"Can I ask you something personal, Daddy?"

"Sure, Boo."

"Is Mia too young for you?"

The question leaves me speechless.

"I mean, I know she is," Annie goes on, "but she seems really mature for her age, and I really like her a lot. She doesn't seem at all like the other high school kids, you know? She reads the same kind of books you do, and she's really pretty, and—"

"Annie."

My daughter's eyes go wide, as though she's hoping for good news but expecting bad.

I reach over and squeeze her hand. "Mia's got a lot to do before it's time for her to settle down, baby. She has to go to college and figure out what she's going to do with her life. Just like you will in about ten years."

"Nine years," Annie corrects. "I'll be eighteen in nine years. I just thought she'd be a cool mom, that's all. For somebody, you know?"

"I think you're right." I lean over and hug her to my chest so she can't see the tears welling in my eyes. My daughter so desperately needs a maternal figure, and I have failed to provide one. Right now—for the first time, really—I feel true anger at Caitlin for spending so much time away. I don't think she was honest with me or with herself when she took her latest "temporary" assignment.

"I need to run down to Papa's office for a while, Boo. I'll see if I can get Mia to sit, okay?"

"Okay," she says in a bored voice, as though seeing Mia holds no excitement whatever.

I take out my cell phone and speed-dial Mia's number.

CHAPTER

My father's private office is a library devoted to medicine and military history. Scale models of World War Two tanks and planes stand beside ships from the Napoleonic era, and hand-painted lead soldiers guard every bookshelf in the room.

"How's Drew holding up?" Dad asks from behind his desk. My father is six feet tall with white hair, a silver beard, and piercing eyes that have witnessed most of the ways the human body and soul can fail.

"It's hard to tell."

"Did that drug dealer named in the paper kill Kate Townsend?"

"I honestly don't know."

"You don't look very confident. What's your worst fear, Penn?"

I haven't really thought about it that way. "To anyone but you, I'd have answered it's that Drew will be wrongfully convicted of murder."

"But to me?"

I close my eyes, and when I speak, the truth emerges as though by its own decision. "It's that Drew might have killed Kate without meaning to. The girl was highly sexual, despite her youth, and she liked to be choked during sex. She died of strangulation. It doesn't take Sherlock Holmes to see the possible link."

"But Drew denies anything like that?"

"Yes."

A buzz sounds from Dad's phone, and Esther tells him she's on her way back with Quentin Avery.

"Where's Annie right now?" Dad asks.

"I had Mia meet me outside and take her home. I didn't know how long we'd be."

He looks past me and rises from behind his desk, his eyes twinkling. "There's Quentin! Come in here, man."

I turn and face the door. Often, when I meet someone I've seen only in pictures or on film, I find the actual human being to be much smaller in reality. That's not the case with Quentin Avery. The famed lawyer may be over seventy, but he still carries the charismatic aura of a man who once strode boldly across the national stage. Despite the loss of his foot, he still stands six-feet-four, and he wears his white hair in a tight Afro hairstyle. His eyes have a greenish tint, and his skin is lighter than that of most Natchez blacks, but it's darker than Shad Johnson's, which is so light that some people have called him "more white than black." But Avery's appearance means nothing in the end. This man standing in my father's office has argued multiple cases before the United States Supreme Court—argued and *won*. He has counseled presidents on civil rights issues, most notably JFK and Lyndon Johnson. He has struck fear into the hearts of white supremacists and corporations across the country. He has taught death penalty law at the Yale Law School. He has profoundly changed legal precedent, and by so doing, has done what few of us ever will: he has changed the world.

"My friend's gonna be a little late," Quentin Avery says by way of greeting. "My apologies, gentlemen."

I imagined that he would speak precisely, the way so many black leaders of his generation strived to do. But Quentin Avery seems to have retained his Southern accent. His rich baritone rumbling in the lazy drawl of a manservant has probably caused many an opposing lawyer—not to mention judges—to underestimate him over the years. I offer him my hand.

"Penn Cage, Professor."

Avery smiles an easy smile, then takes my hand in a grip of steel. "Just plain Quentin works for me. Mind if I sit down? My foot may be gone, but it still throbs something terrible on occasion."

"Take the couch, Quentin," says my father, coming around his desk. "Penn, you sit back here. I'd love to hear this, but I've got patients to see. I'll kick you out if I need to."

"Thank you, Tom," Avery says, settling into the leather sofa opposite Dad's desk.

I sit behind the desk and wait for the legend to speak.

"Your father told me a little about your problem," he says. "And based on what he said, I have a good lawyer in mind. Local, too, though not female. Black lady lawyers are still in short supply in Mississippi. But my protégé is tied up downtown. Why don't you tell me a little more about your case? I ought to be able to tell you whether he can help you or not."

As I summarize the events of the past few days, Quentin Avery watches me with eyes that miss nothing. I tell him about Drew finding Kate's body, the anal sex angle, the blackmailer, Cyrus White, even the nude photos in the cell phone. Now and then Avery's eyes narrow or his lower lip pushes out, but he doesn't break my flow with a single question. I suspect he's learning as much about the situation by the way I describe it as he is from the facts. I conclude my briefing by telling about the witness coming forward and placing Drew's car in the vacant lot near the creek. The only detail I omit is Jenny Townsend leaving Kate's private effects with me. Until I know that Quentin Avery's "protégé" intends to handle Drew's defense, I can't afford for anyone to know that shoe box exists.

"So, what do you think?" I ask.

Avery sighs thoughtfully. "I can tell you're worried for your friend."

I nod assent.

"You're right to look for another lawyer for him. You have no business handling this case."

He seems to be waiting to see if this offends me. It doesn't.

"You're way too close to your client. The man saved your life. You played on the same athletic teams for years. From what you've told me about him, Dr. Elliott is a larger-than-life kind of man. A hero, in some ways. That's why it's so hard for you to accept that he killed her."

I open my mouth to argue, but Avery holds up a hand that could easily palm a basketball. "I'm not saying he did it, Penn. But somewhere down deep in your soul, you're afraid that he did."

I remain silent, but my opinion of Quentin Avery's instincts just went up.

"I don't care whether he killed that poor child or not," Avery goes on. "And it's critical that his lawyer be just as detached. That's the only way he can defend Elliott to the best of his ability. You know that, of course. It's just tough to remember when you're that close to a defendant."

"You're right. What do you think about the facts?"

"Facts?" Avery snorts. "What facts? The police haven't even found the crime scene yet. Everything the D.A. has is circumstantial, and most of that doesn't point to murder. Now, I'm not saying that the evidence he does have wouldn't predispose a jury against Dr. Elliott. A Mississippi jury hears everything you've told me? They're surely going to believe he could have done it. And if they find out Dr. Elliott was down in that creek with his hands on her dead body, they're gonna vote guilty. *Unless* you can prove that big, bad Cyrus White raped and killed her."

"That's a pretty tall order, it seems to me."

Quentin nods. "Even if that other semen sample matches Cyrus's DNA, all you've done is prove that Cyrus had sex with her." He sniffs and gives me a little smile. "Of course, the jury's gonna make all the difference in this trial. White folks are gonna come on preconditioned to believe that a depraved nigger dope dealer wouldn't hesitate to rape and kill a tasty young thing like Kate Townsend. Black jurors will feel exactly the opposite. Odds are, you'll get a racially mixed jury. That's good for Dr. Elliott, because this is capital murder. All it takes to acquit is *one* juror with reasonable doubt." Avery grins, his teeth astonishingly white. "It'd be a mighty poor lawyer who didn't think he could persuade one juror that a fine, upstanding healer like Dr. Elliott just *might* not have done it."

For the first time in days, I feel a surge of real hope. "I feel stupid for sounding so pessimistic. I think it's because I know that the D.A., the sheriff, and the judge are so dead set on convicting Drew."

Avery nods sagely. "Cause for concern. And to tell you the truth, that's why I was willing to get involved in this case."

"I don't understand."

"Shad Johnson," he says with obvious distaste.

"Do you know him?"

"We've met a few times. I know his people."

His people. This means family, stretching back for an unknown number of generations. "How do you feel about him?"

"I think he's dangerous. Not only to Dr. Elliott, but to every black man, woman, and child in this town."

I'm dumbstruck. "What do you mean?"

"There's a crisis in black leadership in this country, Penn. The leaders of my era are relics of another age. A lost age, I'm sorry to say. Martin, Malcolm X . . . Fannie Lou Hamer, Medgar . . . they're dead as the dinosaurs. You've basically got three types of black leaders today. There's the managerial type, who pretends race isn't even an issue. He wants a large white constituency, but he also wants to keep the loyal blacks behind him. He's pragmatic—and not a bad leader—but he tends to suppress the best type by claiming that going mainstream is the only solution for blacks. Then you have your black protest leader. He's black, loud, and proud. He casts himself in the image of Malcolm and Martin, but deep down he's nothing like them. He uses the ideals of those great leaders only to get what he really wants: personal status and power. Marion Barry, Al Sharpton, Louis Farrakhan—the list is endless. They're flashy, flowery, and dangerous. They deceive the mass of black Americans by tapping into their emotions, but they use that support only in service of egotistical ends. You won't see these men wearing the simple black suits and plain white shirts that Martin and Malcolm wore. They want to be players, and they love dressing the part. True protest leaders are humble men, Penn. They value wisdom, not media consultants."

"That sounds a bit like Shad Johnson, but not completely."

"Shad is schizophrenic," says Quentin Avery. "He began as the first type, but failure has pushed him into becoming the second."

I'm about to ask what the third type of black leader is when Quentin says, "Shad actually despises his own people. Did you know that? Not all of them, but the ones who most need help. He blames them for their own misfortunes, just like white racists do."

I nod. "I've heard Shad speak disparagingly of local blacks. He actually used the term 'bone-dumb bluegums' in front of me once."

Quentin bends over to rub his phantom foot. "That doesn't surprise me at all. There's a lot of self-hatred at the root of that language. He's anti-Semitic, too. He maintains close ties with Louis Farrakhan. It's sad to see in a man of Shad's intellectual gifts."

"Are you all right?" I ask, as Avery seems to be in some distress.

"I'm fine. Damn diabetes." He straightens up. "The thing is, Penn, to be a genuine black leader, you've got to love that lazy, weak-minded brother fishing on the highway bridge with a cane pole in the middle of the workday. If you don't, you ain't gonna help nobody."

I remain silent, trying to decide if I agree with him.

"It's like Jesus," Avery muses. "Jesus loved the harlot and the sinner. You want to save a whole people, you got to start at the bottom, not in the king's antechamber. Or in the mayor's office, as it were."

Does Avery know that Shad has his eye on the mayor's office again? "What's the third type of black leader?"

A look of regret settles into the lawyer's face. "The prophetic leader. That's Martin, Malcolm . . . Ella Baker. Or James Baldwin, in the intellectual sphere. Jesse Jackson's the only recent political leader who had an opportunity to fill that role, but he faltered after 1988. The current generation has produced *no* leaders of this type, much less of that caliber. I'm watching Barak Obama, but I'm not sure yet. The reasons have more to do with the pervasiveness of mass market culture and the failure of the black middle class than with any personal failure." Avery waves his hand. "But that's not why we're here. I only mention this because it underpins my feelings toward the district attorney."

He reaches into his shirt pocket and removes an expensive-looking cigar, which he puts between his teeth but does not light. "The minute I heard Mayor Jones was terminally ill, I knew Shad would declare for mayor again. Five years ago, he left Goldstein, Henry, in Chicago—that's a top firm, with many influential black lawyers—and he left there bragging how he was gonna come down South and win the mayor's office, then use that as a stepping-stone to the governor's office in Jackson. From the governor's office, Shad figured, he could reach the Senate. After that, who knows? But he failed his very first test. Wiley Warren beat him, even with all the black celebrities Shad flew down here. Well, young Shadrach wasn't *about* to go back to Chicago with his tail between his legs. So he ran for D.A. and won. But that's not what he wants. No, sir. He wants what he told his partners he was coming down here to get. Now, this town desperately needs a good mayor. But Shadrach Johnson isn't it. Last time out, he promised a color-blind meritocracy and a rejuvenated city. That didn't get him the mayor's chair, so this time he's putting out the word that he's stepping to an all-black band. Every city position will be filled by a black candidate, qualified or not. Friends are good, family's better. He's gonna give whitey a taste of what it's like to be on the bottom. A lot of local blacks will vote for Shad just because of skin color, but that would be a mistake."

"I understand your feelings about Shad, Quentin. But I don't think a courtroom defeat in this case will be enough to keep him out of the mayor's office."

"You're right about that. No, I'm relying on Shad to do the critical damage himself."

"What do you mean?"

Avery gives me a rogue's smile. "Let's say, God forbid, that Dr.

Elliott did kill that poor girl. And let's assume that a mountain of evidence piles up that seems to prove that he did. Penn, I believe that even in that circumstance, Shad won't be able to let well enough alone. He won't trust in the evidence. He'll do something unethical—maybe even illegal—to stack things in his favor. To make the verdict a lock. And you'll be right there to expose him. Then *my* personal end will have been accomplished."

A surge of optimism courses through me, but just as quickly it dissipates. "Quentin, I'm very encouraged by this meeting. But I'm also worried. You understand the overall situation much better than I do, but the guy you brought me here to meet knows nothing yet. And time is a factor in this case. Shad's in a big hurry."

"The guy I brought you to meet knows more than you think."

"How's that?"

Avery takes the cigar out of his mouth and smiles. "He's sitting right in front of you."

It takes me several moments to absorb the full implications of this. "Are you telling me you plan to defend Drew at trial? Personally?"

"I do."

"Because of Shad Johnson."

"That's right. But my motive shouldn't bother Dr. Elliott too much. He's gonna get a better defense than he ever dreamed."

I sit silently, trying to take this in. "I know you're right about that. But . . ."

"What?"

"Drew doesn't seem to grasp the jeopardy he's in. Or doesn't care much, if he does. I think Kate's death put him into some kind of shock, and he hasn't come out of it yet."

Avery chuckles softly. "Don't worry. When he sees those twelve supposed peers sitting in the jury box staring at him like he's Charles Manson, it'll sink in. In a big damned hurry, too."

The realization that a legend like Quentin Avery has taken up the cross I thought I was going to have to bear alone brings relief unlike any I've experienced in years. "I tell you, Quentin, I feel like a new man."

"Don't celebrate yet. I've got a feeling we got more bad news coming."

"What kind?"

"Evidence. Evidence that won't help the doctor any."

I nod slowly. "I hope you're wrong."

"Sometimes I am. But it happens less and less, the older I get."

From anyone else's lips this would sound arrogant, but from Quentin Avery it doesn't.

"It's one of the paradoxes of old age," he adds. "Your prick gets weaker but your reasoning gets stronger." He laughs richly. "The two must be related. Maybe intelligence is more a matter of focus than anything else."

"You could be right."

I drop my palms flat on the desk with a slap. "What do you want me to do?"

He ticks off a list on his long fingers. "Reserve some rooms at the Eola Hotel. A suite for me, plus four or five regular rooms for offices and overflow. I'll need a retainer of sixty thousand dollars, and another fifty thousand deposited in an account for expenses. That's just to start."

"Consider it done," I say, praying that Ellen Elliott doesn't have control of Drew's liquid assets.

"That's what I like," Quentin says, "a man who knows what talent is worth."

"It's easy when it's somebody else's money."

"You've got a point there."

"What about me personally? How do you see my role?"

The old lawyer purses his lips like a man trying to figure out the function of an unfamiliar machine. "Let's call you my chief investigator. You've shown a flair for it, which is only what I'd expect from a former prosecutor. Come to think of it, you're the enemy by constitution. But I'd rather have you inside the tent pissing out."

Without preamble, Quentin Avery lifts his cane and struggles to his feet—or to his foot, I guess.

"Let me walk you to your car," I offer.

"No, thanks. I've got somebody to do that."

Nevertheless, I accompany him to the waiting room. Avery walks with great purpose despite his limp. When we open the door, a beautiful black woman of about forty stands and starts forward.

"Is this your daughter?" I ask, as she holds the front door open for us.

They both laugh.

"Doris is my wife," says Quentin, limping outside. "Penn Cage, Doris Avery." He winks at me. "Now you see why I spend so much time at home."

"Yes, I do," I say awkwardly, wondering if Quentin has more sympathy for Drew than I thought. At probably thirty-five years older than his wife, he must view a separation of twenty-three years as relatively minor.

As though reading my mind, Quentin says, "Kate Townsend was seventeen; we can't let ourselves forget that."

"No," I agree.

"Sexual battery is a statutory offense," he says gravely, "and Dr. Elliott could well get thirty years for it, no matter what happens with the murder case."

"I understand."

"*But*"—Quentin winks at me—"if any lawyer can talk a jury into a little human understanding on the issue of younger women, I'm your man."

I can't help but laugh. "I'll bet you are."

We proceed slowly to the parking lot, Doris supporting Quentin's right side by bracing his right arm. She looks strong, with taut calves showing beneath her skirt.

"Now that we've got things settled," Quentin says, "I have one question for you, Penn."

"Shoot."

"What's the real reason you're not handling this case? Your friend's life is at stake, and you've got the chops to defend him. I *suppose* you might have the good sense and detachment to realize you shouldn't handle it, but I don't think that's it." He looks hard into my eyes. "About the only reason I can see you giving it up is that you know he's guilty."

I shake my head. "That's not it. The truth is, I'm thinking of running for mayor myself in the special election. And if I go to war with Shad to defend Drew—and lose—I'll lose the election, too. So . . . maybe the future of the town is more important to me than Drew's fate, as terrible as that sounds."

Quentin Avery appraises me for several moments. Then there's a wrinkling around his eyes, a glint in his pupils, and finally his lips break open to reveal his shining white teeth. "Boy, you're gonna put a big old kink in Shad's world, aren't you? He's gonna want to kill you before the month is out."

Doris stops us at a shining new Mercedes and opens the passenger door.

"What do you think about me running for mayor?" I ask.

Quentin shrugs. "Don't know you that well yet."

"Fair enough. What do you think about another white mayor instead of a black one?"

The renowned lawyer chuckles and looks down into the valley of kudzu behind my father's office. "What I'd like to see is a *good* mayor. This town's in a world of hurt, and it's got no time for racial ideology. It's got no time for anything but getting down to the business of business. Maybe you're the man for the job, and maybe you ain't. All I know is, you're the man who put Del Payton's killer behind bars, and that's more than I could do back in 1968." He grins. "So I'm willing to give you a *look,* anyway."

Quentin climbs into the passenger seat, settles himself, then peers up at me. "I sense you've got a question for me, too. Maybe more than one."

He's right. I want to ask him why he seemed to abandon the civil rights movement in the 1980s and '90s to pursue personal injury and class action cases, which greatly enriched him but did little for the people he professes to love. But I don't dare offend him. Drew can't afford to lose a lawyer of this caliber, not with the system already aligned against him. "I'm just trying to get my mind around all this," I reply, not untruthfully.

"No, you've got questions," insists Avery. "But we'll be seeing a lot of each other in the coming days. After you get your confidence up, you can grill me to your heart's content." He faces forward and laughs. "Tell your daddy I'll see him later in the week."

Doris Avery closes the door, then takes me by the upper arm, pulls me to the rear of the Mercedes, and speaks in a low but intense voice.

"I want to make you aware of something, Mr. Cage."

"Please call me Penn."

"All right, Penn. Quentin's in a lot worse shape than he pretends to be. Diabetes is a terrible disease, and it's taken more away from him than a foot. A lot more than he'll admit."

Doris Avery's eyes are wet with private pain, but she doesn't cry. "I'm not going to tell him not to take this case. But I'm telling *you*—don't push him too hard. I've already got a lot fewer years to spend with him than I'd like. And he gave far too much of himself over the years to people who didn't appreciate it to kill himself doing the same thing now."

"I hear you, Mrs. Avery."

She nods once, then turns and walks to the driver's door. Then she smiles, just a little. "You can call me Doris from now on. Good day to you."

CHAPTER

20

Driving up the curving entrance to St. Stephen's Prep, I realize I've given Sonny Cross all the time I can afford. I voice-dial his cell phone as I park in front of the high school. He answers after five rings.

"Yeah?"

"It's Penn, Sonny. It's six p.m. I'm about to go into the board meeting. You have anything for me?"

A squawk like a muffled yell comes through my phone. A cut-off grunt follows.

"Soon," hisses Cross.

"Sonny? What the fuck was that?"

"Don't know. Must be your cell phone. I'll call you back as soon as I can."

Something's going down, but I don't have time to press him on it. "You've got nothing on Marko Bakic?"

"Right. As of now."

"Don't forget to call me."

The St. Stephen's boardroom looks just as it did on the night I learned Kate Townsend was dead. The ten faces gathered around the rosewood table are more than somber. It's as though some cat-astrophic threat faces the entire town, and we are meeting to consider extreme responses. Holden Smith opened the meeting before I arrived, making it clear that my status in this group is now equivocal. Only the headmistress, Jan Chancellor, looks happy to see me arrive.

"Sit down, Penn," says Holden. "Afraid we had to start without you."

I sit but don't respond.

Jan Chancellor says, "The board has just scheduled a memorial service for Kate and Chris tomorrow."

"Where?"

"The school gymnasium," says Holden. "Chris was Methodist, but Kate was Presbyterian. And we wanted to do it during school hours. Better not to try to transport all the kids out to a church. We can do it right here."

"Did you talk to Jenny Townsend about this?"

"I'm going to inform her as soon as the meeting's over."

Typical. As if the board's decision should rule everyone else's life. "Okay. So why am I here?"

Holden's voice takes on an almost feminine tone of irritation. "The next order of business is the expulsion of Marko Bakic."

"Expulsion and deportation," grunts Bill Sims. "It's time for that little bastard to go back where he came from."

"On what grounds are you expelling him?" I ask.

"They don't really have anything specific," Jan informs me. "Just a catalog of smaller infractions. Detention-type infractions."

"Which I seem to remember he served detention for," I think aloud, noting Jan's use of "they."

"Exactly," she says, turning to Holden and Bill. "If you want to expel Bakic, you're going to have to do it arbitrarily."

"Fine," says Sims. "He's a damn Croatian. What can he do about it?"

"He can sue you and this school," I say in an even voice. "Our insurance would cover it, but the publicity would eat us alive. You'd wake up every day and read the words 'illegal drugs' and 'St. Stephen's Prep' in the same article."

"He's not even an American!" blurts Smith.

"That makes no difference. The foreign prisoners being held at

Guantánamo are suing the federal government for unlawful imprisonment, among other things. American lawyers are lining up down there to represent them."

"Bullcrap!" Sims bellows. "That's just *bull*crap. That's what's wrong with this country."

"No, that's one of the things that's right with it."

Sims glares at me, then looks at Holden Smith as if to say, "What the hell's *he* doing here anyway?"

"I'll tell you something else," I go on. "You pulled the trigger too fast on Drew. The more I find out about Kate's death, the more certain I am she was raped and murdered by someone else."

"Who?" asks someone down the table. "That drug dealer mentioned in the paper?"

"I can't discuss that here."

"We're in executive session," says Holden. "No one's keeping minutes. Nothing will leave this room."

"That's the funniest thing I've heard all year. I don't remember one sensitive topic discussed in this room that I didn't hear about two days later from someone who shouldn't have known a damned thing about it. Everyone in here talks out of school, to belabor the expression, and I'm not blowing Drew's defense to hell to satisfy the curiosity of this group. I just want those of you who condemned Drew for murder the minute you heard about him and Kate to know you were wrong."

"But he *is* guilty of the affair," insists Holden. "Correct?"

"If he is, you know what that makes him?"

"What?"

"As human as the rest of us."

Holden looks genuinely hurt. "Penn, you're taking this personally. We all like Drew. We all respect him, apart from this, of course. But the damage that's already been done to this school because of his involvement with Kate is incalculable. And what about the damage to Kate herself?"

"Honestly? I'm not sure how all that shakes out yet. What if Kate was already in deep trouble? What if Drew was a stabilizing influence in her life?"

"You're saying that having sex with a forty-year-old man stabilized Kate's life?"

"No. But being loved by him might have. Holden, the total tonnage of what we don't know about these kids' lives would sink an ocean liner."

The board president blows out a stream of air like someone resigning himself to ambiguity. "Penn, you obviously know a lot more about this situation than we do. What do you recommend?"

"Regarding Marko? Watch him closely, that's it. If someone steps forward and says they saw him bring drugs to that lake party, that's a different matter. A police matter. The lake party happened off school grounds, of course, but since it's a criminal offense, I think we could justify immediate expulsion under our zero-tolerance policy. But so far, nobody's come forward. And now that the Pinella kid has been beaten up, I doubt anyone will."

"Was Marko responsible for that?" asks a woman at the far end of the table.

"I don't know, Jean. Look, even if Marko is selling drugs to our kids, he's not the one bringing them into the city. Illegal drugs are an industry, and in this case they start down on the Gulf Coast and flow northward. Certain people here wholesale it to other people—possibly Marko—who then retail it to users, like a small number of our students. Marko's only part of a very long chain. We don't yet know who might have thought they had reason to beat up the Pinella boy."

"But Marko is the link that most affects this school," Holden says. "Until he showed up, we didn't have a problem."

"Not a *visible* problem. Every high school in America has a drug problem, Holden."

"Should we test some of our students for Ecstasy and LSD?" asks Sims, reviving an idea we killed months ago.

Now I'm losing my patience. "Bill, if you're worried about the school's image, that idea is about as stupid as it was when you brought it up a couple of months ago."

Sims reddens but doesn't respond.

"What we need to do is calm down and let the police and the

judicial system work. If you want Marko on a plane back to Croatia, you may get your wish sooner than you think."

"What do you know?" Holden asks eagerly.

"I know that the best thing we can do is let things take their course. Now, do you need me for anything else?"

Jan glances at Holden. "Penn, we'd like you to remain on the board. This body was premature in asking you to step down."

"I agree, Jan, but I can't do that."

"Are you officially Drew's lawyer?" asks Holden.

"I haven't decided yet. But it makes no difference. This body has given up any moral right to leadership that it had before this crisis started. Most of you are here because you have your own private agendas, which may or may not be in the best interest of the school as a whole. One of our most distinguished and generous alumni is in trouble—he may soon be fighting for his life, in fact— and you abandoned him without even hearing his side of things. So, I bid you good night."

I stand and walk to the door.

"Penn, wait!" Holden calls.

"Let him go," snaps Sims. "Goddamn bleeding heart lecturing us like that."

As soon as I clear the door, I find myself jogging toward my car. My frustration is about to boil over. I climb in and start the car but leave the engine in Park. I'm not even sure where I should go now.

When my cell phone rings, I assume it's Jan Chancellor trying to get me to return to the board meeting. But my caller ID says SONNY CROSS.

"Sonny?"

"Yeah. Sorry I couldn't talk before. I've got what you need now. Man, you're not gonna *believe* it."

"What?"

"Marko, Cyrus, Kate . . . I understand everything now. And, boy, have I got something to help Drew."

"Tell me!"

"Not on your life. Not on a cell phone."

"Where are you?"

"My house. Beau Pré Road. You know where that is?"

"Yeah. What's the house number?"

"Two seventy-one."

"I'll be there in ten minutes." I pull into the southbound lane of Highway 61 and press the accelerator to the floor.

CHAPTER

21

A few miles south of Natchez, Kingston Road forks away from Highway 61 and curves through rolling land that a century and a half ago made up thriving cotton plantations populated with hundreds of slaves. Beau Pré Road is a serpentine offshoot of Kingston Road, lined with one-story houses and aluminum trailers, some with bass boats sitting in their front yards. The houses are set far apart, with small ponds, outbuildings, and dog runs in the overgrown border land between lots.

It's full dark as I round a long curve that should carry me to Sonny Cross's house. From what the drug agent said in our brief cell phone conversation, it sounded like he's discovered the holy grail of this case. My greatest hope is that he can prove that Cyrus White murdered Kate. Scanning the homes flashing past on my left, I see two gold numbers tacked to the wall of a house trailer.

Two sixty-nine.

I ease my foot off the gas and coast around the tail of the curve. A lone porch light appears in the trees to my left. Then the beam of my headlights hits a rutted dirt driveway that intersects Beau Pré Road on my left. As I turn onto the dirt, a yellow rectangle of light appears beneath the porch light. The black silhouette of a man walks into the rectangle, then passes through it, and the orange eye of a cigarette bobs along the driveway at a height of about six feet. When I reach the cigarette, I stop my car, turn off my engine, and get out.

Sonny Cross takes a deep drag off his cigarette. The orange glow illuminates his haggard face and glints off a silver stud in his left ear. Despite the fatigue in his face, I see excitement in his eyes.

"How much do you want to know?" he asks.

"Everything."

"Don't be so sure. This is *Dirty Harry* stuff."

"Tell me everything, Sonny."

Another long drag. Smoke drifts into the night as he speaks. "I was pretty upset this afternoon. You saw it when we talked. I couldn't just sit around waiting for something to break."

"What did you do?" I ask, my gut tightening in anticipation.

"I decided to have a little talk with Marko Bakic. I picked him up outside the Wilsons' house, easy as pie. Then I took him to, uh . . . an undisclosed location, where we had a frank and honest exchange of views."

"A willing exchange of views?"

Sonny chuckles softly. "There might have been a little duress."

"Jesus, what did you do to the kid?"

"I just asked him some questions. But young master Bakic indicated an unwillingness to cooperate. He emphasized this with some well-chosen sarcastic remarks. He seemed quite pleased with himself, all in all. So I stuck my gun in his mouth."

I shake my head in disbelief.

"To tell you the truth," Sonny reflects, "even that didn't rattle him much. I think that boy saw a lot of shit over in Bosnia, and guns by themselves don't scare him. I don't think he believed I'd really use it."

"You didn't, did you?"

Cross shakes his head slowly. "No. But I convinced him I would."

"How did you do that, exactly?"

An unguarded smile. "Some things we must pass over in silence, my son."

"Was that what I heard when I called you before the board meeting? You torturing Marko?"

"No. That was somebody else."

"Who?"

"One of Cyrus's guys."

I'd like to sit Sonny down and have a talk with him about the niceties of the Constitution, but right now I have a different priority. "Enough foreplay, Sonny. Give me what you got."

"Marko's basically Cyrus's punk, okay? He registered in the student exchange program hoping to get New York, L. A., or Miami. Instead, he got Natchez, Mississippi. Imagine his dismay. Marko saw himself as the next *Scarface,* a young Al Pacino coming to America to take over the drug trade. But when he got here, he didn't find Robert Loggia, an old dealer soft and ready to fall. He found Cyrus White, a kind of nightmare he'd never seen before. Cyrus recognized something in Marko, though, maybe because they had both seen war up close. He saw Marko's ambition, and he used that to open up new markets. *White* markets. Through the older brothers and sisters of our high school kids, Marko made contacts in the white fraternities at LSU, Ole Miss, USM, Millsaps, Louisiana Tech . . . you name it. This network is far more extensive than I imagined. The Asians on the Gulf Coast wholesale to Cyrus, massive shipments moving north by several different routes. When it gets here, Cyrus sends out his boys to supply Baton Rouge, Jackson, Oxford, Ruston, Hattiesburg—all the markets Marko opened up. It's a massive operation, Penn. Mind-blowing, really."

The drone of an engine echoes through the trees, then a pair of headlights sweeps past us in a long arc.

"Why are we out here?" I ask.

"My kids are inside," Sonny explains. "My ex-wife hears any more about this cowboy shit, she'll be asking the judge to modify our custody agreement. Mosquitoes getting you?"

"I'm good. Go on. You said you had something that would help Drew."

Sonny grins. "I know why Kate Townsend was seeing Cyrus. She was buying Lorcet from him. You know what that is?"

"Pain pills, right? Like codeine?"

"That's right. She tried to buy it from Marko first, but he doesn't keep Lorcet in stock. It's more of an adult drug. The kids don't use it much. Anyway, Marko goes to Cyrus and asks for some, but Cyrus won't hand it over just like that. He's curious by nature. He wants to know why Marko suddenly wants hydrocodone."

The word "hydrocodone" triggers something in my mind, but I'm too interested in what Sonny discovered to ponder it.

"Marko tells Cyrus he's going to use the Lorcet to buy the finest piece of ass in the city. Cyrus asks who he's talking about. Dumbass Marko tells him, and that was that. Cyrus knew damn well who Kate Townsend was. Her picture's been in the newspaper about twenty times over the past couple of years. Tennis, swimming, her scholarship to Yale."

"Harvard."

"Wherever. Cyrus told Marko that if Kate wanted Lorcet, she'd have to come to him to get it. Personally. *That's* how all this started."

"I don't get it," I say softly, suddenly afraid that I do. "Drew told me Kate never used drugs."

"Then she was buying them for somebody else."

Another set of headlights appears in the distance, moving slowly this way.

"Tell me about Kate and Cyrus."

Sonny watches the lights come and go. "Once a month or so, Kate would tell Marko she needed a new bottle. She was buying at the rate of a hundred a month. A hundred pills, I mean. She bought a hundred and fifty per visit, the last couple of months."

"Would the medical examiner have tested for hydrocodone in Kate's body?"

"They always do toxicology in a young girl like that, because suicide is so common. I already checked. No hydrocodone or metabolites in Kate. No drugs at all."

"What about the sex angle? Did Marko say Kate and Cyrus hooked up?"

Sonny nods emphatically while drawing on his cigarette. "No, but this is even better. Once Cyrus got a look at Kate, he couldn't stop thinking about her. Marko said every time Cyrus saw him he asked about her. Who she was talking to? Who she was fucking? Who had she fucked in the past? What music did she listen to? Everything. Every last detail. The guy was obsessed."

"But Marko didn't think they ever had sex?"

"No. She just drove Cyrus nuts, the way women like to do." Sonny gives me a conspiratorial smile. "Marko thinks Cyrus killed her, man."

A rush of excitement goes through me, but I try to stay calm. "Can he prove it?"

"No. But here's the gold, man. Here's something you can throw right in Shad Johnson's face."

I feel blood pounding in my ears. "What?"

"You know what that crazy Cyrus was doing?"

"How could I know, damn it?"

Sonny laughs at my impatience. "He was tracking her cell phone. He wanted to know where she was all the time, right? Well, there are companies you can pay to digitally ping some- body's cell phone every fifteen minutes. As long as the target per- son's cell phone is on, this company can give you their GPS coordinates every quarter hour, and they'll never know it." Sonny cackles with glee. "It doesn't even *cost* that much. These compa- nies are all over the Internet, Penn. Paranoid spouses keep them in business."

I don't even bother telling Sonny that I knew about this technol- ogy. "If I can prove that Cyrus was tracking Kate's cell phone, es- pecially on the day she died . . ."

"It's looking like something just might stick to the Teflon nigger this time. And get this: Marko says whenever Kate left the apart- ment, Cyrus would be crazy mad. He told Marko he didn't think it was him being black that bothered her. It was that he sold drugs. Which was crazy to him, since she was there to *buy* drugs."

"Drugs she wasn't taking," I murmur, my mind on Drew's words in his car on the night he told me he was involved with

Kate: *Ellen's addicted to hydrocodone. . . . You can't imagine Ellen popping Lorcet Plus like M&Ms?* "Goddamn it," I whisper.

"What is it?"

"Nothing."

"Don't bullshit me, Penn. If it's something I need to know, tell me."

"It's not," I assure him, wondering if Drew could really have sunk that low. "Give me the rest of it, Sonny."

"You've got most of it. Except that Marko's scared shitless."

"Why?"

"Because Cyrus doesn't need him anymore. Now that Cyrus has the contacts at the colleges, Marko's just one more middleman he doesn't want to pay."

"That's good," I reason, thinking like a prosecutor. "Maybe Marko will testify against Cyrus to save his ass."

Sonny grins. "He's considering that as we speak."

As we stand in the silent darkness, I realize it's not silent at all. The high-pitched drone of crickets is almost a scream, and a spring breeze rattles the millions of oak leaves surrounding us. Across the road, a car engine starts, and a pair of headlights clicks on.

"Slut," Sonny mutters.

"Who? Kate?"

"No. My neighbor's got a teenage daughter over there, about fifteen. There's a different boy over there every week. I've even seen a couple of black boys pick her up. One jig from the Catholic school showed up at my front door saying he was looking for a girl named Karen—that's this girl. I said, 'The only black girl on this road lives about three miles down that way.' " Sonny laughs. "He didn't know what the hell to say."

The screech of a screen-door spring silences the crickets, and the yellow rectangle appears again on Sonny's porch. Then a little boy's voice calls into the night.

"Are you coming back in, Daddy?"

Sonny turns back to the house and yells, "Just a couple of minutes, Kevin."

Across the street, the car pulls slowly into the road. It's a Lexus sedan, an older model but still expensive for Beau Pré Road. As I watch, the window on our side slides down, and the car slows as though its driver wants to ask for directions. He's probably reluctant to pull into Sonny's driveway without an invitation, so I start toward the road.

As I walk, I see a glint of metal in the open window. In one paralyzed moment adrenaline floods my body. I've been shot at before, and despite the darkness, I know what I'm looking at. *"Get down, Sonny!"* I scream, diving to the ground.

Night vanishes in a starburst of white light and thunder, the explosions coming too quickly to count. *Automatic weapon.* As the seconds dilate, I whip my head toward Sonny, who for some reason is still on his feet, standing in full view of the gunman.

He's returning fire at the Lexus. Orange flame leaps from his pistol, but the reports are lost in the roar of the machine gun. I look back at the Lexus, and for one instant a screaming Asian face is revealed by a perfect circle of light. Two holes appear magically in the door below the face. Then another fusillade of bullets erupts from the rear window. An explosive grunt sounds behind me.

Sonny's hit!

As the spinning tires scream, I roll back toward Sonny Cross. He's lying on his back, his eyes wide, his mouth gasping for air. His right arm jabs his gun toward me.

"Take it!"

I do. But by the time I come to my knees with the pistol raised, the Lexus is fishtailing up the road. I empty Sonny's clip at the fleeing car, then drop the gun and fall to my knees beside him. The blood on his white knit shirt tells me he's been hit at least three times in the torso. His chest rises and falls erratically, and the wheezes coming from his throat and chest tell me death isn't far away.

"My kids," he says in a guttural voice. "Check on . . . my boys."

"You first, Sonny." I pull my cell phone from my pocket, but as I dial 911, the front door of the house bangs open again.

"Daddy? Daddy, where are you?"

Panic in the voice. "Daddy's still out here!" I shout. "He's fine! He's coming in just a minute. Go back inside, boys!"

"911 dispatcher," says a woman's voice in my ear.

"This is Penn Cage. I've got an officer down at two seventy-one Beau Pré Road. Multiple gunshot wounds. I need an ambulance, stat. Now, connect me to the sheriff's department."

Up on Sonny's porch, two small silhouettes stand wavering in the yellow rectangle.

"Sheriff's department," says another woman.

"Deputy Sonny Cross has been shot at his home. Multiple gunshots. Repeat, Deputy Sonny Cross. Get some paramedics out here. He's critical. The shooter's fleeing the scene on Beau Pré Road, headed toward Highway 61. It's a black Lexus with at least three people inside. An older-model Lexus. You need to set up roadblocks immediately. The shooter is Asian, repeat, Asian ethnicity. Call Sheriff Byrd at home. Tell him Penn Cage reported it."

"Hold on, Mr. Cage," says the dispatcher.

"I can't. Two seventy-one, Beau Pré Road."

One of Sonny's children has left the porch and ventured about half the distance to his father. "Daddy?" he calls tentatively.

Even in his distress, Sonny manages to shake his head. "Don't let them see me like this. Don't—" A gout of blood erupts from his throat.

I jump up and run to the boy, snatching him into my arms and trotting back to the porch, where his brother waits. When I set him down, I try to reassure them both, but the faces in the glow of the porch light already know the worst. I drop to my knees and grasp a thin wrist tightly in each hand. "Are either of you hurt?"

"No, sir," says the oldest, who looks like he might be eleven. "Should I get my gun?"

"Where's my dad?" asks the other, who's eight at the most. Tears are running down his face.

"Your daddy's hurt, boys. But he's going to be all right. The ambulance is on the way. I want you to go inside and call your mom. Tell her she needs to come right over here. Do you understand?"

"Yes, sir," says the older, who I now remember is called Sonny, Junior.

The younger boy doesn't want to go, but Junior grabs his wrists and pulls him inside. I race back to the end of the driveway. For the first time, I notice a light lying on the ground beside Sonny. It's not a flashlight. It's a spotlight mounted beneath the barrel of his pistol. He must have flicked it on before he opened fire on the Lexus. That was the circle of light that showed me the gunman's face. It may also have been what guided the shooter's bullets to Sonny's chest.

"*Penn?*" Sonny chokes, his hand grabbing at the air. "Are you there?"

"I'm here, buddy." I use the gun light to illuminate my face. "You hang on."

His desperate eyes lock onto mine. "My boys?"

"They're not hurt. They're both fine, and they know you're fine."

Somehow Sonny laughs, a wry sound that turns into a terrible coughing fit. "Not . . . fine," he rasps. "Not gonna make it this time around."

"Bullshit." I take his hand and squeeze tight.

"Asian," he whispers. "Shooter was Asian."

"I saw him."

"I'm cold, man. Just like the damn movies. Just like . . ."

"The ambulance is on the way, Sonny. Hang tight."

"Too far. Know . . . response time. Tell 'em save the gas." With a sudden surge of strength, Sonny Cross raises his other hand, rolls into me, and grips my biceps like a claw. His eyes are straining out of their sockets, like the eyes of a dying martyr exhorting his torturers to have faith. "It's yours now, Penn. Cyrus . . . Marko . . . you gotta finish it. Do what you have to do . . . hear me?"

"I can't do what you did today."

He falls back on the ground, his eyes half shut now, but his grip still strong. "Chris Vogel," he croaks. "Mike Pinella . . . Kate. How many others? Family, man . . . all family."

"I hear you, Sonny."

His next words ride a deep exhalation of the kind I've heard too often before. "Tell Janie I'm sorry, man. Tell her . . . I never meant—"

This time the silence is absolute. Not even the crickets disturb the transit of Sonny Cross's troubled soul as it departs for wherever it is bound.

A high-pitched sob sounds behind me. I turn and see the two boys standing six feet away. They look at me, then run to their father and collapse with their heads on his chest. Then the crickets resume, and the high note of a siren wails Sonny Cross's benediction.

CHAPTER

22

By the time I reach the city jail, I've told the story of Sonny Cross's death three times: first to sheriff's deputies, then to sheriff's detectives, and finally to Sheriff Byrd himself. Part of me wanted to hold back what Sonny told me about Kate visiting Cyrus, but I couldn't in good conscience do that. All I could do was withhold my near certainty that Kate was buying those bottles of Lorcet for Ellen Elliott.

I also gave up the information Sonny tortured out of Marko, and that seemed to go a long way toward convincing Sheriff Byrd that Kate's death might be more complex than a matter of a jealous older man. The fact that Cyrus had been tracking Kate's GPS location through her cell phone was particularly convincing. Once Byrd and I were alone, I told him exactly how Sonny had extracted this information, and that this made it unusable in court. Nevertheless, I had a feeling that Marko Bakic was in for a long night.

Sheriff Byrd ordered roadblocks set up on all routes leaving the city, but his dragnet didn't catch the black Lexus. Either the killers slipped out of town before the roadblocks were set up, or they were still hiding somewhere in the city, waiting for things to cool down. An army of deputies raided Cyrus's known safe houses and rousted all their drug snitches, but nothing has produced results. Like the Asian killers he probably summoned here, Cyrus White has vanished.

Piled on the shock of watching Sonny die, the ordeal of being grilled for two hours exhausted me, and I was tempted to go home to bed. But I had to know one thing before I could sleep. Was I right about Kate's errands to Cyrus?

Tonight the bench on the other side of the glass in the visiting cubicle is empty. Drew finally walks in and sits down, no guard visible behind him. His eyes have the empty look of a man in a fugue state.

"Sonny Cross is dead," I tell him.

Drew tilts his head to the left as if to say, "What does that have to do with me?"

"He told me some things before he died. Like why Kate was visiting Cyrus White."

Now he's interested.

"Kate was buying Lorcet from him, Drew. A hundred pills at a time."

Drew's eyes close.

"Lorcet is hydrocodone, right? The drug Ellen is addicted to?"

He nods slowly, then hangs his head.

"Don't make me drag it out of you, Drew. I need to know."

He opens his eyes and lays his forearms on the little window ledge. "I didn't know she was getting it from Cyrus. I had no idea."

I'm stunned by the amount of anger that erupts from within me. "What *did* you know, man? Why was Kate buying the drugs at all?"

Drew's right cheek twitches as though in response to an electric shock. "I told you how bad Ellen's addiction was. Four times through rehab, and still she couldn't kick it. I'd prescribed the absolute limit to keep her out of withdrawal. The DEA was watching me all the time. A lot of doctors are hooked on Lorcet, so they monitor those prescriptions closely. Anyway, Ellen finally stole one of my pads and forged some prescriptions. She got away with it a couple of times, but then she got caught. If Win Simmons at Rite-Aid hadn't called me instead of the police, she'd have been in deep trouble."

"How did Kate come into it?"

"We were deeply involved by that time. She saw how upset I was the night of the prescription incident, so I told her what had happened. I was in pretty bad shape myself. I couldn't concentrate at work. I was afraid to leave the house for fear of what Ellen might do. She refused to go back into rehab. She was drinking heavily to mask the withdrawal, and that made her violent. Then, in the middle of this nightmare, Kate showed up one night with a bottle of Lorcet Plus. One hundred ten-milligram pills in a phar-macist's bottle." Drew shakes his head as though in awe. "It was like salvation. I asked where she got them, and she just said, 'From a friend. Don't worry about it.' Of course I *was* worried, but Kate wouldn't tell me any more. She said it was no big deal to get Lorcet, half the town was popping them. She needed five hundred dollars to cover the cost, but she said she could get whatever I needed, whenever I needed it, no risk at all. I know how terrible this sounds, but . . . it made life bearable at last. I had the DEA off my back, and Kate was happy that I could relax and pay attention to her."

"Yeah, it was perfect," I say bitterly. "Except that Kate was risking her freedom every time she made a pickup for you. Jesus, Drew. Do you realize how sleazy this is?"

He bows his head again.

"I can understand you falling in love with Kate, okay? She was a beautiful girl, full of promise, a lot like you when you were eighteen. And I understand the temptation to consummate those feelings. It takes serious effort for me not to just sit and stare at Mia sometimes. But this is different. You risked that girl's future to make life a little easier on yourself. That's low, man. That *sucks*."

"I know it."

"Is that all you have to say?"

He turns up his palms. "What can I say? Do you think words really matter at this point?"

He's right about that. "You realize that Cyrus may have killed Kate?"

He nods almost imperceptibly.

"And that Cyrus would never have gotten within a mile of her if—"

"I've already gone farther down that road than you ever will," Drew says softly. "The irony is that if Cyrus did kill her, that will free me from jail. But it can't free me from my own judgment—or yours—or worst of all, my son's. And whether you believe it or not, those judgments will be harder for me to bear than a life sentence in Parchman prison. If I caused Kate's death, I will live in hell until the day I die."

I study him without speaking. I've heard many people say this kind of thing over the years. And they do suffer—usually for a month or two. Then they thank the stars for their freedom and happily go back to their old ways. I don't think Drew is like those people. He is quite capable of torturing himself for years. But that doesn't make what he did any less reprehensible.

"If Cyrus killed her, that may free you on the murder charge," I tell him. "But you still may do thirty years for sexual battery. And if a jury ever finds out about this little drug arrangement, you can count on it."

His eyes lock onto mine. "Did you tell anyone about it?"

I wait before answering, watching him for signs of self-concern. "Not yet."

He doesn't react. He doesn't even thank me. He seems resigned to whatever fate awaits him.

There's a soft knock at the door behind me, and then someone pulls it open. Looking back, I see Chief Logan gazing down at me, his dark eyes sober.

"I need to see you a minute, Penn."

Drew glances up at him. "Hey, Don."

Logan doesn't even look in Drew's direction. The days of special treatment for the police chief's doctor are over.

I get up and follow Logan to his office. He sits behind his desk, puts his face in his hands, and rubs his temples with his thumbs.

"What's happened?" I ask. "Have you found Cyrus?"

"No." He looks up. "But somebody did."

"What do you mean?"

"Cyrus has been hiding in a safe house downtown. North Union Street. Fifty minutes ago, a car pulled up to it, and a guy wearing black from head to toe got out holding two pistols. One was silenced. He shot the two guards on the porch, but nobody heard him. One of those guys is still alive, but they already shipped him to University Hospital in Jackson with a severe head wound. He's unlikely to make it."

My stomach has gone hollow. As Chief Logan speaks, I flash back to my years as an assistant district attorney in Houston. This kind of thing happened all the time there. But *here,* in my hometown? A placid little city that wouldn't even be called a city anywhere but Mississippi? This kind of crime is as alien as a terrorist attack.

"After the gunman took out Cyrus's guards," Logan goes on, "he walked calmly through the house, shooting people as he went. Cyrus was in a back bedroom with a girl. With that silencer, I doubt he heard anything but grunts and muffled cries. Maybe a scream. When Cyrus walked out, the shooter nailed him five times with the second pistol. Then the shooter dropped both guns and walked out like he didn't have a care in the world. He even left the car out front."

"Was it a Lexus?"

"My first thought," says Logan. "But no, it was a Camry with Adams County plates. It was stolen a few minutes before the crime."

"This was obviously a professional hit."

Logan nods. "Just like Sonny Cross."

"Anybody say the shooter was Asian?"

"He wore his mask the whole time, and he never said a word."

"The guy who shot Sonny wasn't wearing a mask."

"I know." Logan takes a pen from a mug that reads *TALLADEGA!* and starts tapping it on his desktop. "The total body count from this little encounter is five wounded and three dead. Probably four by morning."

I shake my head, not quite able to accept that my strongest alternative suspect in Kate Townsend's murder is dead. "Did you learn anything about Kate's murder from the survivors?"

"My detectives are still over at the hospital questioning them. But so far, all we've got is computer matches on the shooter's handguns."

"That fast?"

Logan nods, his face unreadable. "The silenced one was stolen from a residence in Biloxi a few months ago."

Biloxi . . . gambling capital of the Gulf Coast. Also the base of the Asian drug gangs. "Well, that sure tells us something."

The chief is watching me closely. "The other handgun was bought and registered right here in Natchez, two years ago."

A chill of anxiety runs along my skin. "Who bought it?"

"Drew Elliott. And it's never been reported lost or stolen."

I feel as though my body mass has doubled. Breathing is difficult, and the idea of moving seems impossible. "Drew's been in jail all night. Right?"

Logan sighs. "As best I can determine, yes. But I wasn't here myself. And there's no closed-circuit camera in his cell."

Again I remember the escapes I've read about in the *Examiner*. For some reason, inmates at the city jail are allowed to exercise in a fenced area behind the station, and more than a few have disappeared from this flimsy enclosure. "He couldn't have gotten out for like forty minutes and then come back, could he?"

"I don't think so, Penn. But I can't be certain."

"Christ, Chief."

Logan looks up at me, his eyes filled with regret. "That's not really my main concern, to be honest. I'm more worried that Drew used his cell phone to hire this done."

I struggle not to let Logan see how much this possibility worries me. "Who could Drew call that could have found Cyrus? Both you and Sheriff Byrd have guys working around the clock, and they couldn't find him. How could Drew?"

"Granted," says Logan, but he still looks unconvinced.

"The theory that Drew slipped out and did the shooting himself has the same flaw," I point out. "How would he know where to find Cyrus?"

"You told me Kate Townsend visited Cyrus regularly."

"But only at Brightside Manor."

Logan raises his eyebrows. "Are you sure?"

I'm not sure. "Don, let's be realistic. This had to be the Asian crew that popped Sonny Cross."

"I hope so. Because I gave Drew access to his cell phone when I shouldn't have. And I sure regret that now."

"This was some kind of drug hit. It had to be."

"Like I said, I hope so. But you've got one more problem."

"What?"

"We recovered another pistol at the scene. You'll be interested in that one, too."

"Why?"

"It's a Springfield XD-9. And it's registered to you."

It takes all my composure to keep my mouth from falling open. "I can explain that, Don."

Logan nods, but he looks far less confident in me than he has for the past couple of days. "I hope so, Penn. Because this looks bad. Really bad."

"I lost it the other night, chasing a guy who tried to blackmail Drew. Two guys, actually."

Logan shakes his head, clearly furious that I've been holding back information. "Why didn't you report it lost?"

"Because I lost the gun on hunting camp land. Dr. Felder's camp, right behind St. Stephen's. I knew if anybody found it, it would be a hunter from that club. I called Dr. Felder the next day and told him to warn his members to be on the lookout for it. I also told Coach Anders at St. Stephen's to watch for it, just in case I lost it on the field. I searched the field and the track myself but found nothing. One of the blackmailers must have picked it up. That's the only explanation."

"Okay. I'll call Dr. Felder tomorrow and try to verify that."

Two days ago, Chief Logan wouldn't have had to make such a call. My word would have been enough. "I can't believe this," I murmur.

"What?"

"That Cyrus is dead. I needed him alive to save Drew. I needed a confession from that son of a bitch. I mean, DNA might prove that Cyrus had sex with Kate, but it can't prove he killed her. It can't even prove he *raped* her. And now we'll never know what Cyrus knew about her last hours, if anything. Barring the discovery of an eyewitness who saw Cyrus kill Kate, Drew is going on trial for murder."

The chief's gaze is not without sympathy. "Don't give up hope yet."

"Why not? Have you found a witness?"

Logan's eyes shine with knowledge I can't read. "Cyrus was hit five times," he says. "That's what two witnesses told my detectives. But when my patrolmen responded to the 911 call, they didn't find his body."

"*What?*"

"There was nothing but some blood where the witnesses said he fell."

I stare at Logan in disbelief. "Do you think the wits lied to you? I mean . . . Christ, was Cyrus really shot at all? Could the whole thing have been staged to make us believe he's dead?"

"This is real life, Penn. Forget that TV shit. The girl Cyrus was in bed with made the 911 call, and she's not part of his crew. She's a white girl from Morgantown. On the 911 tape you can hear a black guy screaming at the girl to hang up, then the phone goes dead. I doubt Cyrus's guys would even have called 911. Anyway, the girl told us Cyrus was wearing a bulletproof vest. His homeys confirmed that he owns one. Kevlar with ceramic inserts."

I'm trying to visualize the scene. "Even if that's true, why would Cyrus be wearing it in his bedroom?"

"Expecting a hit, maybe? Cyrus heard about Sonny and got scared?"

The prospect of Cyrus alive and breathing has me wired with

excitement. "Have you covered all the hospitals? Of course you have. I don't know—"

"Penn," the chief cuts in.

"What?"

"I'm going to interrogate Drew. Right now. I'm assuming you want to be present?"

Suddenly, and for the first time, I view Don Logan as a potential enemy. "Don, Drew was in your custody while these shootings occurred. I think we'd better wait until—"

"I'm going in there," Logan says in a voice edged with steel. "You can take it up with the Supreme Court later, but right now I'm going to do what I have to do. I've been more than fair with Drew, but he hasn't reciprocated. And I've had enough of people getting hurt and killed in my town. Kids are dying, and Drew knows more than he's saying. More than he's saying to me, anyway."

I hold up my hands in supplication. "Let me call his attorney first. That's all I ask."

Logan looks at me like I'm crazy. "*You're* his attorney. I just told you I'd let you be present."

"I'm not Drew's attorney, Don."

"Who the hell is?"

"Quentin Avery."

Logan freezes in his chair. "You're kidding, right?"

I shake my head. "You know who Avery is?"

"Yessir, I do." The chief stands and removes his gun belt. Every move communicates an attitude of defensiveness. "And I'm not waiting around for that SOB to make a federal case out of this. As far as I'm concerned, you're all the lawyer Dr. Elliott needs. The interrogation starts in one minute."

He walks past me without meeting my eyes.

"Don, wait," I plead.

"Fuck you."

CHAPTER

23

When I called Quentin Avery to tell him about Drew's impending interrogation, I got his wife instead. Doris Avery was reluctant to bring Quentin to the phone, but I heard him protesting in the background, and then his rich voice came down the wire from the far northern edge of the county.

"What are you pulling me out of bed for, Penn Cage?"

I quickly related everything that had happened since we last talked. Quentin sounded intrigued by the attack on Cyrus, and still more by his disappearance. But he wasn't worried about Drew being interrogated by Chief Logan. If I felt nervous, he said, I should observe and make sure that Drew answered only questions pertaining to Cyrus's death. Quentin's nonchalance worried me. I felt that he was misreading Drew—whom he still had not met—and that Drew's belief in his own innocence might cause him to make statements against his interest in the legal sense.

But Quentin turned out to be right. Chief Logan got nothing out of Drew other than a denial that he'd been involved in the attack on Cyrus and his guards. Drew appeared even more shocked than I to hear of the attack, but he was very interested in Cyrus's escape. Like me, Drew raised the possibility that Cyrus might be attempting to fake his own death. As Chief Logan tried to shoot down this theory, I decided that if Cyrus was trying to fake his own death, he'd done it without premeditation, by simply taking advantage of a tragic but fortuitous event. But Drew seemed committed to the theory that the entire attack had been orchestrated by Cyrus to rid himself of his own men—potential witnesses against him—and then "die" to escape being punished for Kate's murder. "What better way to avoid prosecution?" Drew challenged Logan. "Cyrus is probably on his way to Chicago or Los Angeles by now."

Logan ended his interrogation no wiser than he'd begun it. I warned Drew not to answer any more questions without myself or Quentin present, promised to visit him in the morning, then let Chief Logan walk me to my car.

"Something's not right, Penn," he said. "I don't know whether it's Drew or something I don't know about yet. But something's deeply wrong in this town."

"Maybe something's been wrong for a while, Don. Maybe it's just coming to the surface at last."

"You talking about drugs?"

"And the other things tied up with it. Race problems, teenagers in trouble, big enough money to draw out-of-town predators."

"What about this Marko kid?" Logan asked. "What's his story?"

"You didn't have him on your radar before this?"

"No."

"He's a Croatian exchange student who wants to be Al Pacino."

"What?"

"Nothing. Just something Sonny Cross said."

Chief Logan looked like he wanted more information, but I was too tired to tell what I knew about Marko Bakic. "What's your problem with Quentin Avery, Don?"

The chief took out a cigarette and lit it. After a couple of drags, he said, "Avery sued my uncle in a personal injury case. Danny Richards. Uncle Danny owned a trucking company. They hauled pulpwood, mostly. Well, one of his drivers was drunk one Friday. Black, of course. Some of those guys buy two cases of beer in the morning and drink all day up in the cab. It's crazy, of course, but how you gonna stop them? Uncle Danny checked his drivers lots of times, but you can't be up in the trucks with them all the time. Anyway, this particular driver overcorrected on a turn and spilled a load of logs on a housewife coming back from the grocery store. Paralyzed her. Avery took the case and pushed it to the limit. The driver didn't have anything but a mountain of debt, so he spent a few years in jail, then got out. He's driving log trucks again."

"And your uncle?"

"Avery shut him down. All the assets of his company were seized to pay the punitive damages. The case was litigated in Jefferson County, of course. Uncle Danny killed himself two years later. Drove into a bridge piling, stone sober in broad daylight, one-car accident."

"I'm sorry."

Chief Logan blew out a long stream of smoke. "That motherfucker comes into my station, he'd better hope there's people around the whole time. Otherwise, he just might slip on a banana peel."

I waited for more, but the chief added nothing to his story. It's an ancient rule: lawyers make enemies. "I'll see you, Don."

He dropped his butt and ground it out on the pavement. "Yeah."

As I drive away from the police station, my mind constructs a montage of images I never saw in life but which I now know happened: Cyrus White being attacked by a black-masked killer; the ethereal Kate Townsend walking alone into the Brightside Manor Apartments to score drugs for her married lover's wife. And playing beneath these images like the black-and-white filmstrips of carnage I saw in driver's education class, the death of Sonny Cross, my own personal nightmare of muzzle flashes and panic and black blood. My feelings about Sonny remain mixed. He was

a flawed man, but he did his best to protect his hometown from a
scourge he knew more intimately than most of us. It was an obligation he felt deeply, and as he died, he passed part of that obligation on to me, like a falling soldier passing a regimental banner to
a comrade.

Reflecting on the hurricane of violence that began spinning
through my town two days ago, I ask myself what lies in the eye of
that storm. And the answer that comes to me is simple: *Marko
Bakic.* Given what I told Sheriff Byrd tonight about Sonny's interrogation of Marko this afternoon, Marko is probably sitting under
a hot light down at the sheriff's department right now. But maybe
not. Billy Byrd has a lot to deal with tonight.

Dialing Directory Assistance on my cell phone, I request the
home phone number of Paul Wilson, the retired professor who
sponsored Marko in the student exchange program. It's after
eleven, but Paul keeps late hours. I've seen him jogging with his
dog after midnight in his subdivision. I know this because I often
keep late hours myself, especially when I'm writing. After Paul's
phone rings five times, I start to hang up, but then the professor
answers in a wide-awake voice.

"Penn Cage! What's up, fella?" Paul is a Yankee, and he obviously saw my name on his caller ID.

"Hey, Paul. I know it's late, but I was wondering if I could talk
to you for a minute."

"It's not late over here. Janet and I were just having a glass of
pinot noir and watching Puccini on PBS."

A hysterical laugh almost escapes my mouth. Paul has instantly
fulfilled my stereotypical image of him. I've heard that he and
Janet drink a lot of wine, and I know from talking to him that he
listens to too much NPR.

"Have you heard from the police tonight?" I ask.

There's a brief silence on Paul's end. "As a matter of fact, the
sheriff called. He was quite rude, actually."

"Are they questioning Marko now?"

"No, Marko's out on a date."

"I didn't think kids went on dates anymore."

Paul laughs. "They don't really, but Marko and this girl spend a lot of time together."

"She's his girlfriend?"

"Well, she's quite taken with him. Obsessed, I would venture to say. But I don't think Marko confines himself to one girl. When he was a child, he learned not to get attached to anyone, because he might lose them at any moment."

"Is Marko usually late getting in?"

"Sometimes he doesn't get in at all, to be honest. Sometimes he stays at Alicia's house."

"Alicia Reynolds?" I ask, thinking of a troubled girl in the senior class.

"That's right."

I turn onto the bypass and drive in the direction of Paul's subdivision. "Paul, do you mind if I ask you a few questions about Marko?"

"Not at all. I know you've spoken up for him at least once on the school board, and I appreciate it. But before you ask me anything, let me say this. I know a lot of people think I just bury my head in the sand when it comes to that boy. But that's not the case at all. Nobody around here has any idea what Marko went through in Bosnia. He was in Sarajevo during the worst of it, Penn. He was ten years old, and he saw unspeakable things there. Nobody who experiences those kinds of things comes out whole on the other side—especially a child. Marko doesn't talk about it, but I know some."

"Would you feel comfortable sharing any of it with me? It might be relevant to the current situation."

"Well . . . Marko reminds me of that kid in *Empire of the Sun*, the Spielberg film about World War Two. Christian Bale plays the kid. He's in a prison camp, and conditions are abominable. John Malkovich teaches Bale to survive, and Bale becomes the consummate hustler. That's Marko. And if that's what you are, you don't change overnight just because you've been dropped into the land of milk and honey."

"Have you ever seen Marko get violent?"

"Never."

"The kids at school think he carries a gun."

Silence. "I've certainly never seen him with a gun. I'm not saying it's impossible, considering his level of paranoia. But I've never seen one. I'd be very disappointed if I did."

You might be disappointed. Someone else might be dead. "Do you keep guns in the house, Paul?"

"Not one. I'm a firm advocate of gun control."

"Hm."

"Penn, I heard a rumor that the board is thinking of expelling Marko. Maybe even trying to get him deported."

Wonderful. As I told Holden Smith, nothing in those meetings stays secret. "Just between you and me, Paul, that's true. I told them they couldn't do it without proof that he's broken the rules."

"I see. Penn . . . I know it's late, but I think perhaps you and I should have a face-to-face conversation about Marko. If he's in serious trouble, I need to know the extent of it. And I know some things about his experiences in Sarajevo that you should probably be aware of."

I look at my watch. 11:25 p.m. Mia is probably getting antsy by now. But on the other hand, Marko is the biggest question mark in this whole bloody mess. And after having Sonny Cross's gun stuck into his mouth this afternoon, there's no telling what he might decide to do tonight.

"I think that's a good idea, Paul. I'll be there in ten minutes."

"I'll pour you a glass of wine."

I dial home, and Mia answers, her voice alert.

"How you doing, girl?"

"I'm good. Annie's sound asleep."

"Why aren't you?"

"I finished Bowles's book, and I started *The Secret History.* I meant to read just one chapter, but it hooked me. I can't believe this was written by a girl from Mississippi."

"In longhand, no less. Don't you ever just have fun?"

"This is my idea of fun, believe it or not."

As I ask Mia if she can stay another hour, a crackle of static fills my ear. Then the felt wall of silence that heralds a failing connection greets me. I accelerate up the hill in front of me until my phone shows three bars, then pull over to the curb and dial Mia again.

"Can you hear me now?" she asks.

"Yeah, I had to pull over. Can you stay another hour?"

"Sure."

"What will your mom say?"

"I already called her and told her I might have to stay over."

This takes me aback. "Meredith was okay with that?"

"Yeah. She knows you're working on Drew's case."

"How does she feel about Drew after all she's heard?"

"She's reserving judgment. Mom doesn't put much stock in gossip. She's always respected Drew, and she told me she has a really hard time believing he could have killed Kate."

"But she believes he slept with her?"

"Oh, yeah. I mean . . . he's a guy, right?"

I laugh softly. "Well, I don't think you'll have to stay over. I'm going by Paul Wilson's house, but it shouldn't take long."

A sudden tension enters her voice. "Are you going to talk to Marko?"

"I'd like to, but he's not there. He's out with his girlfriend."

Mia makes a derogatory noise.

"What is it?"

"Marko doesn't have a girlfriend."

"Then what was Paul talking about? What about Alicia Reynolds?"

"*God.* Alicia worships Marko. She's kind of . . . I don't know, Goth, I guess. For about a year she had black fingernails. Now all she talks about is Third World debt. I think she's kind of a sex slave for him, actually."

"But not his girlfriend."

"Marko's not into boundaries. He takes whatever he can get."

"Does that make him different from most of the guys you know?"

"Well . . . I guess when it comes down to it, no."

"Okay, thanks. I'd better get going."

"Hey, wait," Mia says. "I heard a cop got killed tonight. Is that true?"

The cellular jungle drums are beating overtime tonight. "Yes."

"Do you know who did it?"

"Sort of."

"Was the killer local?"

"Why do you ask that?"

"I didn't figure you'd tell me who it actually was. So I asked for what you could tell me."

"You seem to realize the drug business extends outside of Natchez."

"Well, sure. They don't grow the stuff here. Except for some shitty pot out in Jefferson County."

"Mia, I think you should consider a career in law enforcement."

"I might. But I don't think they teach that at Brown."

I laugh again. "I'll see you in less than an hour."

"If I fall asleep, wake me up."

"I will," I tell her, realizing as I do that we sound like nothing so much as a married couple.

The Wilsons live on Espero Drive, part of a large subdivision built in the 1970s, one that I once thought of as the "new" part of Natchez. Now Espero and its parallel street, Mansfield Drive, are shaded by mature oaks and house many retired couples who keep perfectly manicured lawns. The Wilson house is a one-story ranch set well back from the road. Behind it and to the right stands a two-story garage, the upper story containing the apartment where Marko lives.

I park on the street and walk up a flower-lined sidewalk, trying to recall what I can about Paul Wilson. His wife is a Natchez native, but Paul hails from Ohio. He taught political science for years at the University of Southern Mississippi at Hattiesburg, about three hours by car from Natchez. I once attended a lecture he gave on race relations, at the Natchez Literary Festival, and I was impressed. Paul seemed to have a better grasp of his subject than most Yankees ever get, and I credited his wife for that. He probably knows more about the former Yugoslav republics than I could learn in a year, and I suspect that his choice of Marko Bakic as an exchange student was rooted in that knowledge. On the other hand, he might simply have been assigned Marko at random.

The doorbell rings loudly enough for me to hear it through the door, but no one answers. I wait about thirty seconds, then ring it again.

Nothing.

Maybe Marko got home, and they went out to his room to talk to him. I step over some shrubs and walk around the right side of the house, where the driveway runs back to the garage. Rather than interrupt a family conference, I decide to check the rear of the house proper. If I remember right, the Wilsons added a large sunroom to the main house a couple of years back.

They did. The glass enclosure juts out unnaturally from the original brick, but I imagine the Wilsons were more than willing to trade symmetry for a nice place to drink wine and admire their garden without mosquitoes eating them alive.

As I move closer, I see Janet Wilson sitting in a wicker chair in the sunroom. I don't see Paul. I'm walking up to the glass door to knock when something stops me cold. From this distance, what I thought was a floral print on Janet Wilson's blouse looks more like spattered blood. With my own blood roaring in my ears, I scan the yard behind me for intruders.

Nothing.

I lean against the door and search the rest of the room with my eyes. Two chairs lie on their sides, possible signs of a struggle. Then I see Paul. He's lying facedown on a pale blue sofa, and this, too, is splashed with blood. I pull out my cell phone and dial 911, not quite believing that I'm reporting murder for the second time in one night.

"911 emergency," says the dispatcher.

"This is Penn Cage again," I whisper. "I'm at 508 Espero Drive, and I have two probable homicide victims. Paul and Janet Wilson. I need paramedics and cops. The killer could still be on the property."

"Could you speak up, sir?"

"*No.* Double homicide, 508 Espero. Get two squad cars and an ambulance here, and tell them to come with sirens screaming."

I hang up and try the door handle. It's open.

I'd give ten grand for my lost Springfield right now, but there's no use wishing. The smart thing would be to wait in the bushes for the cops. This isn't rural Adams County, like Sonny Cross's property. There should be a squad car here inside two minutes. But there's also a chance that Paul or Janet could still be alive, and for them every second could be critical.

I open the door and go to Janet first, pressing my finger underneath her jawbone while I survey her wounds. She's been stabbed more than a dozen times, with most of the wounds concentrated in her chest and abdomen. Both hands show the multiple slashes of defensive wounds. There's no pulse in her throat.

Moving to the sofa, I see that Paul, too, has suffered multiple stab wounds, a half dozen on his back alone. I kneel, squeeze his shoulder, and speak close to his ear. "Paul? Paul, it's Penn Cage."

A low rasp comes from his throat. As gently as I can, I roll him over.

Paul's eyes are open, but his throat has been slashed from his trachea to his left ear. It was a clumsy effort, a butcher's job. A small amount of bubbly red fluid pulses from the wound, but I sense that the bulk of Paul's lifeblood is soaking into the sofa and the rug beneath it. His eyes are glassy, and his face is so gray that I can't believe he's alive.

"Paul? Can you hear me?"

The rasp comes again. Not from his mouth, though. It's coming from the laceration in his windpipe. The contents of my stomach come up in a rush, and it's all I can do to keep from vomiting on Paul. When I recover myself, I realize that the dying professor is trying to turn his head to look at his dead wife. All I can think of is Sonny Cross's dying concern for the safety of his sons.

"Janet's fine," I assure Paul, hoping he didn't see her stabbed, but certain that he'll be dead soon in any case.

Air continues to bubble through the slash in his throat, and he struggles harder to turn.

I take him by the shoulders and stop him. "The paramedics said Janet's fine, Paul. It's you they're worried about. Hang on, okay? You have to hang on for Janet. Another ambulance is on the way."

His eyes close.

A crazy thought comes to me, and before I can stop myself, I voice it. "Did Marko do this, Paul? Did Marko stab you?"

His eyes open again, wide this time, and with a remarkable feat of will, he shakes his head.

"Did Marko do this?" I repeat, wanting to be sure.

Paul shakes his head once again, then closes his eyes and sags backward.

"Can you hear me, Paul?"

Nothing.

I take his hand and squeeze it. "I'm here, Paul. You're not alone. Can you hear me?"

Nothing.

I reach across him with my left hand and grasp two of his fingers. "That's Janet holding your hand. She wants you to hold on. Can you hear me?"

The fingers move, and for an instant I feel hope. But then a seemingly endless rasp issues from the throat wound, slowly diminishing to a fluid rattle. Paul Wilson is still in the way that only dead men are still.

I drop his hands and get to my feet, suddenly aware of how foolish I've been to focus on these two while their killer could still be near. I dart back outside and move into the shadows at the side of the house.

In the distance, I hear a siren.

As it grows louder and higher in pitch, I find myself looking up at the apartment over the garage. Suddenly I realize the obvious, that the Wilsons weren't the target of whoever killed them: Marko was. Sprinting across the driveway, I bound up the steps to Marko's apartment.

The door stands ajar.

While I try to decide whether or not to enter, I hear the scream of burning rubber out on the street. Someone is fleeing the scene right now. *Jesus.* The killer was probably still in Marko's apartment while I was checking on Paul and Janet. Praying I won't find Marko's corpse inside, I enter the apartment.

It's a single room, with a bed, a kitchenette, and a toilet behind a partition. The floor is a sea of bedclothes, books, and drawers jerked from the dresser against the wall. An armoire lies facedown on a table, its front shattered by the force with which it fell. Only a computer screen glowing against the far wall seems to have escaped the damage.

The siren is closer now.

I pick my way through the debris and go to the computer. It's a Windows platform system. I go to the *My Documents* folder and check its contents. The files look innocuous: school reports and letters from junior colleges regarding a possible football scholarship. I scan the rest of the hard drive, but nothing jumps out at me. Marko seems to be a serious gamer, with numerous combat-oriented games residing on his drive.

The wail of an ambulance joins the police siren, and the cacophony sounds as though it's coming from the Wilsons' front yard. Knowing I'm pressing my luck, I go to the Windows control area and click "Show Hidden Files." When I recheck the hard drive, several new folders have appeared, each with a semitransparent icon indicating that it was designated by the computer's primary user to be concealed from a casual user. I try to open one folder, but I'm immediately prompted for a password. Another folder gives the same result. Desperate for some clue to Marko's inner psyche, I look down at the floor, into some drawers that were ripped from the computer desk. Between the drawers, lying amid cracked CDs and DVDs, is a USB flash drive similar to the ones in Kate Townsend's shoe box. This one is a Sony, about a half inch wide and three inches long.

As the sirens fade into silence out front, I plug the flash drive into the USB port and copy the formerly hidden folders onto it.

Then I dismount the drive, shove it into the instep of my shoe, and run downstairs to the driveway.

"Stop!" yells a male voice. *"Police! Put up your hands."*

I can't see the face of the officer in the driveway because a floodlight on the side of the Wilsons' house is backlighting him. But I see the gun in his outstretched hands.

"I'm Penn Cage! I made the 911 call."

"Reach slowly into your pocket and take out some ID."

As I obey the command, I speak in the calmest voice I can muster. "The bodies are in the sunroom out back. Paul and Janet Wilson. They have an exchange student living with them, but he's not here. He's involved in the drug trade, and the killer tore his room apart. He lives over the garage."

The officer moves toward me and checks my ID, then follows me back to the sunroom. He's Natchez PD, not a sheriff's deputy, and I'm glad for that. While he surveys the crime scene, two paramedics with a gurney arrive, followed by more uniformed cops and a plain-clothes detective named John Ruff. I've talked to Ruff five or six times, but never in a professional capacity. Usually I see him at the softball field. Like me, he has a daughter who plays.

"This is something, huh?" he says in a soft voice.

"I can't believe it, John. After what's already happened?"

Ruff nods and steers me away from the patrolmen to question me. I answer his questions as fully as I'm able, but the shock of seeing three murder victims in one day is taking its toll on my concentration. The vagaries of fate and chance are hitting home as well. Paul and Janet Wilson must have been attacked only seconds after I hung up with Paul. If I hadn't pulled over to maintain good cellular reception with Mia, the couple might still be alive. *Or I might be dead . . .*

While Ruff questions me about the immediate past, a memory from my more distant history intrudes. It was here, on Espero Drive, that the first homicide that ever touched me personally occurred. A divorced young schoolteacher was raped and brutally murdered one night while her four- and seven-year-old daughters slept in the house. Her killer wasn't a depraved stranger passing through Natchez, but a fifteen-year-old boy with whom I had played often. I was seventeen at the time, and while I understood both rape and murder, I'd never heard of the two being united in the way I would come to know so well later, when serial murder became an American obsession. But what shocked me most deeply—and likewise the town—was that such a crime could intrude upon our placid little universe at all. Even now, twenty-six years and infinite blows of disillusionment later, the spectacle of Paul and Janet Wilson cut to pieces in their own home seems more like a stunt mounted for *Punk'd* rather than reality. As I recite my narrative to Detective Ruff, I keep expecting Paul and Janet to get to their feet, wipe the fake blood from their clothes, and burst out laughing. But they just lie there, bad sports about the whole thing.

At last Ruff runs out of questions and tells me I'm free to go. As I rise to leave, I hear a commotion in the front of the house. Angry voices, all male, the volume steadily increasing. I hear what sounds like a scuffle, and then a red-faced deputy charges into the sunroom. My fists tighten involuntarily. It's the black-haired deputy who stole the fingerprints from Drew's private bathroom while Drew gave his blood for the DNA test. *Deputy Burns*, I remember, or so Chief Logan guessed after I described the guy.

"You better straighten out those boys at the door!" Burns yells at Detective Ruff. "Or they'll wind up in the county jail!"

Ruff squares his shoulders at the shorter man. "What the hell are you talking about, Burnsie?"

"Sheriff Byrd is commandeering this crime scene. That's what I'm talking about."

Ruff glances at me, at his men, then back at the deputy. "You been smoking something from your evidence room, Burnsie? Didn't you notice this house is in the middle of Natchez? That makes it our jurisdiction."

Before Deputy Burns can reply, two more deputies appear behind him. This makes it a fair fight: three county officers versus three from the city. The paramedics are staring in amazement and anticipation. They've already declared the Wilsons dead, and are only waiting for the police photographer to complete her work.

Emboldened by the appearance of his comrades, Deputy Burns continues. "Sheriff Byrd's the chief law enforcement officer of Adams County. The city's part of the county. That makes *every-thing* his jurisdiction. He can take over any crime scene he deems necessary for public safety, and he already told me that these murders will be investigated by the sheriff's department. End of story."

John Ruff draws himself to his full height and puts his hands on his hips. "Burnsie, if you or your buddies touch anything in this room, you're gonna find yourself in a world of shit. You've already contaminated the crime scene by tromping three men through it without any need. Now get your ass outside and wait for the sheriff and the chief to work this mess out."

Unbelievably, Deputy Burns lays his right hand on the butt of the automatic in his gun belt. "If you want me to arrest you, I will," he says in a bellicose tone, nodding as though to convince himself.

The paramedics blanch.

John Ruff is clearly outraged, but he's also reluctant to escalate this argument into an armed confrontation. After fifteen years working with seasoned professional cops in Houston, I have no patience for this kind of crap. I step in front of Ruff and address the deputy in a strong voice.

"Look over there," I say, pointing at the Wilsons' bloody corpses. "Do you see those people?"

"You stay out of this, Cage," he snarls.

"Look at them!" I shout. "They were murdered less than ten minutes ago. Are you investigating the crime? No. You're standing here obstructing the investigation, bowing up for a fight like some junior high redneck. There's an enemy in this town, Deputy Burns, but it's not the police department. You and Ruff are after the same thing—or you should be—and your boss's small-town political bullshit shouldn't have a thing to do with this crime."

The deputy's chin is quivering, but whether from shock or anger, I can't tell.

"You're not looking at them!" I yell, unable to control my frustration. "How many murders have you seen like that in your career, Burns? One? None? You think a single person in this town gives a damn about Billy Byrd's feud with Chief Logan? You leave that crap back at the station and do your work!"

The deputy's gun is out of its holster now. He's not pointing it at me, but it's plain that he'd like to. "I'm puttin' your ass under arrest!" he yells, spittle flying from his mouth. "Goddamn big-city lawyer!"

I hold out both hands. "Go ahead, Deputy. Arrest me. Arrest me, and in thirty days I will *have your ass.*"

"Penn?" Ruff says, gripping my shoulder from behind. "Take it easy, now. Seeing these bodies got you upset. But don't be stupid."

I know Ruff is right, but under the gaze of the Wilsons' dead eyes, I cannot rein in my anger. "You think these bodies upset me?" I take a step toward Deputy Burns. "I was an assistant district attorney in Houston for fifteen years. I've seen more murder victims than you will in your whole career. I've sent twelve men and women to death row. You want to arrest me? Clap 'em on. You just be ready to take the heat for it."

The deputy's face has gone from scarlet to gray, but he still gets out his handcuffs. He's trying to fit one around my wrist when Sheriff Billy Byrd swaggers into the room.

"Whoa there, Tommy boy," he says in the voice of a poor man's John Wayne.

"Sheriff Byrd?" sputters Burns. "This crazy sumbitch—"

"I heard him," says the sheriff. "You just leave him be for now." Byrd glances at Detective Ruff. "Did you get a statement from Mr. Cage, John?"

The detective nods warily.

"Okay." Byrd shifts his gaze to me. "You're free to go."

I start to ask him about the jurisdictional dispute, but then I remember the flash drive concealed in my shoe. With a last look at Paul and Janet Wilson, I exit the house through the door no one answered when I arrived and walk down the sidewalk to my Saab.

Closing myself into the little space, I start the engine, but I don't pull into the street. My hands are cold and shaking, and my chest feels full of something besides air. "What's happening?" I ask aloud. "I mean what the fuck?"

One thing I know for sure: the murders of Paul and Janet Wilson will stun this town in a way that the attack on Cyrus White's safe house never could, and possibly even more deeply than the murder of Kate Townsend. The reason is simple. When drug dealers get killed—black or white—the public perception is that the victims simply got what was coming to them. When a young girl is raped and murdered—black or white—our knowledge of the primitive laws of attraction and male sexual dominance informs our response. But when middle-aged white people minding their own business are murdered in their home in the safest part of town, the fundamental order of Southern life is thrown out of balance. And the repercussions of such a severe anomaly are inevitably dire. By noon tomorrow, the full resources of law enforcement will be mobilized to a degree only surpassed by the response to a kidnapping or to the murder of a cop. A multiagency task force will almost certainly be formed. The DEA and FBI will be part of it. But as I sit in my idling car on Espero Drive, images of Paul and Janet's butchered bodies running through my mind, one question comes to me: *What are all those agencies going to do?* Because despite having been embroiled in this mess from the start, I have absolutely no idea what is going on.

CHAPTER
24

"Dad, it's Penn. You awake?"

"You know me," my father says in his deep voice. "I'm dictating and smoking a cigar."

Dad was doing exactly the same thing thirty years ago, while I tried to stay awake to watch the late movie, back in the dark ages before HBO. Eternally behind with his hospital charts, he would dictate late into the night and then reward himself with three hours of reading on the Civil War or the history of the Crusades.

"I heard the ER's been pretty busy tonight," he says with understated curiosity.

"Yeah."

"What do you need, son?"

"A gun."

"What kind?"

Not a moment's hesitation. My father has collected guns for most of his life. The bulk of his collection consists of Civil War muskets, with a few pieces dating back to the Revolutionary War. But he also has a nice collection of modern pistols.

"I need an automatic with a big magazine."

"I've got a nice Browning you can use. You on your way over?"

"Yep."

"You in a hurry?"

"I need to get some sleep."

"I'll meet you outside."

Five years ago, my parents' house—my childhood home—was burned to the ground by a man trying to stop me from working on a thirty-year-old race murder. Five years, yet I still find myself turning into our old neighborhood, as though the house I grew up in is still standing. It's not. My father had the wreckage cleared but built a new house elsewhere. Now our old lot holds only flowers and a small granite monument to Ruby Flowers, the black maid who raised me and my older sister. Ruby died as a result of the fire that took the house, and part of me died with her. The new house is south of town, where most new construction in Natchez goes up.

True to his word, Dad is standing in his carport when I arrive. In the glow of my headlights, I see the Browning automatic hanging from his right hand. I leave my engine running and walk up to him. Seventy-two years old, half crippled by diabetes, arthritis, and coronary artery disease, he still manages to practice medicine more hours per week than most internists fresh out of medical school.

"Thanks," I say, taking the gun.

"Is Annie in danger?" he asks.

This is no idle question. The man who burned our house five years ago also targeted my daughter for kidnapping and death. "Not yet. But I try to learn from past mistakes."

Dad nods. "By the time most people realize they're in danger, it's too late to do anything about it."

"I may give Daniel Kelly a call."

"Sounds like a good idea. I thought he was working in Afghanistan."

Daniel Kelly is a former Delta Force operator who worked with me during the Del Payton case. Now an operative for a prestigious corporate security firm based in Houston, Kelly has truly frightening skills, but more important, he knows and loves my family.

Dad probes my eyes with a gaze that has searched out illness and deception for more than forty years. "What happened tonight? You look shell-shocked."

"Somebody tried to kill a drug dealer. Three black guys got killed—teenagers, probably."

Dad shakes his head. "That's not all of it, is it?"

"Paul and Janet Wilson were just murdered in their home."

Now it's my father who looks shell-shocked. "Professor Wilson?"

"And his wife. Cut to pieces."

"Who the hell would do that?"

"I'm not sure yet. I think the killer was after an exchange student who lives with them."

"Why? Is this a drug thing, too?"

"I think so."

"Are you involved in that case?"

"In a way. I'm afraid it might be connected to Drew's case."

"How?"

"This is you and me, right?"

Dad gives me a look that makes me embarrassed to have asked the question.

"Ellen Elliott was addicted to Lorcet," I tell him. "Drew had the DEA on his back for keeping her supplied, so his girlfriend started getting it for Ellen to make life easier on Drew. She got it from this black dealer."

Dad closes his eyes. "Damn it. I suspected something like that."

"What?"

"Drew called me once and asked if I'd write Ellen a scrip for fifty Lorcet."

"Did you?"

"Sure. But I knew if he was asking me to do it, he was already at the limit himself."

"Do a lot of local people abuse that drug?"

"Patients ask for it by name every day. I take it myself for arthritis. Couldn't get by without it. But it's addictive as hell. You don't hear about it much. Oxycontin gets all the headlines, but Lorcet is an opium derivative, too, and it makes you feel pretty good."

I look down at the Browning and familiarize myself with the safety mechanisms.

Dad grips my wrist in his hand. "You're shaking, Penn."

"That crime scene was pretty bad."

"What can I do to help?"

This is no idle offer. At nineteen my father was part of the infamous retreat from the Chosin Reservoir in Korea. He also had occasion to use violence a couple of times in civilian life after that. But I would never put him in harm's way now, despite his willingness to put himself there. "Nothing right now, but I appreciate the offer."

"You know my number."

As I start to go, an idea hits me. "Do you have a pistol with one of those lights on it? Sonny Cross had one, and it looked pretty useful."

"A laser sight?"

"No, it was more like a powerful flashlight."

"A tactical light," Dad says. "Sure, I've got one I can mount on that Browning. Be right back."

He disappears into the house, then returns with a small black object. "Look here. You flip this catch, then slide the light onto these grooves cut into the gun stock. When you let go of the catches, it's locked on." He demonstrates the move for me twice. "To flick on the light, just push up this lever with your trigger finger."

I test the light by shining it toward Dad's backyard fence. An armadillo rooting in the yard freezes, then scuttles away.

"Take him out," Dad says. "Those bastards tear this yard to pieces."

"I'll leave him to you. I'd better get moving. I've got a babysitter keeping Annie."

Dad frowns. "Caitlin's still out of town?"

"Yeah."

He shakes his head but says nothing. He doesn't have to.

"I'll see you, Dad."

"Remember," he calls, "there's more where that came from."

The gun or Caitlin? I wonder. But of course he meant both.

By the time I reach Washington Street, my hands have steadied a bit. I park in front of my house and look over at the town house to the right of mine—Caitlin's house when she's in town, which is less and less of late. Some nights when she's gone, I look that way with an infantile wish that I'll see lights on inside, signifying a surprise return, but that's never happened. And tonight I don't even feel the wish. It's just an empty house.

I walk up the three steps to my familiar blue door, unlock it, and walk inside. For a brief moment I'm suffused with terror, an irrational fear that I'll find Annie and Mia slashed and bleeding on the floor. But of course they're not. Mia is asleep on the couch in my study, balled up beneath the comforter from my bed. Her cell phone sits on the back of the couch beside a paperback copy of Donna Tartt's *The Secret History*. Annie is undoubtedly asleep in her room upstairs.

I don't know whether to wake Mia or to let her sleep through the night. I don't even know what to do about myself. I'm exhausted, but I don't think I could sleep without a strong sedative. I should have asked Dad for something. Maybe a Lorcet.

Sensory overload, says a voice in my head. I told Deputy Burns the truth about my past in Houston, but that was a long time ago. Another life ago. The grotesque scenes I saw tonight hit me with the same impact they would a layman, or perhaps even harder. I think human beings can endure only so much carnage and waste; beyond a certain limit, one either breaks down or becomes utterly desensitized. That break point differs from person to person, but I sense that I'm close to mine. I've seen dozens of murder victims in person, and hundreds in crime scene photographs. I've watched nine of the twelve men and women I sent to death row be executed. I watched my wife die a horrific death from cancer. And I watched the maid who practically raised me die from third-degree burns despite my best efforts to save her. Spread among those dead are the people I've watched suffer but live to tell about it. If this tally continues to grow, I'm not sure which side of the equation I'll tip over on—breakdown or numbness.

"Hey," says Mia, blinking and smiling up from the sofa. "What time is it?"

"Around midnight," I reply, setting my father's Browning on top of a glass-fronted bookcase behind me.

Mia squints at me. "Are you okay? You don't look good."

"I'm not sure."

She rises from the couch and walks past me to the hall. "Stay there. I'll make some tea."

I obey, grateful to be told what to do. When Mia returns with the tea, I'm still standing in the spot where she left me, staring at the rows of hardcover books on my shelves.

"Come sit," she says, setting two china cups on the coffee table before the sofa.

"Sarah chose those cups," I say softly.

Mia watches me closely. "Your wife?"

"Yes."

"I've seen pictures of her in the photo albums. Annie showed them to me."

I nod distantly.

"I think Annie still misses her a lot." Mia sucks her lips between her teeth as if reluctant to continue. "Do you?"

"Sometimes."

"I thought you'd have a family picture out. With the three of you, you know?"

"I used to. I think it started to bother Caitlin after a while. She never said anything, but I took it down when I repainted and then pretended to forget to put it back up."

Mia nestles herself into the corner of the sofa and tucks her legs beneath her. "I think the tea's ready to drink."

I walk to the coffee table and drain half my cup in one swallow. The tea is almost scalding, but I welcome the pain.

"Can you tell me what happened tonight?" Mia asks.

"You don't already know?"

"Nobody called me with anything new. Is it bad?"

"Yes."

"Can you tell me?"

"I guess. It'll be all over town by tomorrow. I just . . . I'm really wiped out."

"Thirty words or less?"

"Somebody tried to kill a black drug dealer. He got three of the dealer's friends instead. And the Wilsons are dead."

Mia's eyes go wide. "The Wilsons Marko lives with?"

"That's right."

"Did Marko do it?"

This brings me partly from my trance. "You obviously think he's capable of it."

"I don't know why I said that. Maybe I do. Or maybe I'm retarded. Like I told you, Marko's different from the rest of us. He liked the Wilsons, though. No, I don't think he would do that."

I sit on the end of the sofa opposite Mia. She's still staring at me with wide eyes.

"Penn, what the hell is going on?"

"I don't know. I really don't."

"I mean, it's been, what . . . three days? Three days, and how many people dead?" She counts off the casualties on her fingers: "Kate, Chris, the narc . . . three black guys. And now the Wilsons."

"And that Catholic kid is still in intensive care."

"Right, Mike Pinella. I mean, does anybody have any idea what's going on?"

I shrug.

"What do *you* think? Seriously."

"I think it's a drug war. That's the only explanation I can come up with."

She nods slowly. "Can Natchez cops handle a drug war?"

"That question's moot. Tomorrow we'll see federal involvement. At least the DEA, and maybe a task force. That's what needs to happen. Some of the violence is coming from the Asian gangs on the Gulf Coast. The rest of it . . . I don't know."

Mia processes this in silence.

I lay my elbows on my knees, then turn and look hard into her eyes. "You've seen Marko selling drugs to St. Stephen's kids, haven't you?"

She doesn't move. She doesn't even blink. But then, very softly, she says, "I feel so bad about that now. Like maybe I could have stopped some of this."

"You couldn't have. But you need to tell me the truth now. Have you seen Marko sell drugs on school property?"

She nods.

"Have you seen him hurt anybody? Physically, I mean."

A deep breath, held in. "No. I haven't seen that."

"Why the hesitation?"

"I was thinking about something else."

"What?"

"Private stuff."

I decide to leave this alone. "Was Marko in school today?"

"No."

"What about Steve Sayers?"

"Steve was there. He was trash-talking Dr. Elliott when I saw him."

An image of Kate's ex-boyfriend rises in my mind. A Matthew McConaughey look-alike with a more redneck bent. "Have you ever seen Steve do drugs?"

Mia rolls her eyes. "I've seen him smoke weed. But most of the guys do that on occasion, even the jocks."

"Nothing harder than pot?"

"No."

"Do you think Steve could have killed Kate?"

She picks at a thread in the fabric of a pillow beside her. "Only in a fit of rage. He'd be screaming and crying as soon as he realized what he'd done."

"Maybe that's exactly what happened."

"If Kate insulted his masculinity or something, I can see him hitting her."

"What about choking her?"

She tilts a hand from side to side. "Yeah, I can see that."

"Steve still has a weak alibi. And he assaulted Drew before word about the affair with Kate was really out in the community. Will you see if you can find out how he first learned about Kate and Drew?"

"I'll ask him."

"Be careful."

"Don't worry. Steve's pretty much a brick." Mia hugs the pillow to her chest. "You know, I've been sitting here trying to figure out what's behind all this violence."

"Have you?"

"I think people's motivations are pretty basic, you know? Primitive."

"Go on."

"It's like sex."

"How do you mean?"

She shrugs as though her point is self-evident. "Sex is always there, you know? People act civilized, they go through the motions of public life, but these secret attractions and affairs are always going on. Look at St. Stephen's—the parents, I mean. How many of them are having affairs with other people's husbands and wives? Quite a few that I know about. How do those affairs start? With a glance that lingered too long? Bumping into each other in the grocery store? My point is that sexual energy is always there. That desire to be loved and wanted is always looking for a connection. And that's the secret motivation of a lot of what we see."

"You're right. So?"

"That's what's missing from history, I think."

"History? What do you mean?"

Mia is hugging the pillow hard, but she seems unaware that she's doing it. "In school we learn about all these events, historical trends, stuff like that. But what we don't learn—and probably can't ever know—is the true nature of personalities. I mean we can read biographies—and if we're lucky, personal letters—but the real interplay between individuals, the chemistry of aggression and submissiveness, pride and shame, sexual attraction—we can't ever know that. That's why it was so shocking to the country when they proved that Thomas Jefferson had children by his black slave. Suddenly he was no longer a granite figure on Mount Rushmore. He was just like us, you know? Feet of clay. We tell ourselves that we know everyone is human, but then we act as if we expect something else. We expect our heroes to be immortal. *That's* the real problem Drew has now."

Mia's words are almost tumbling over themselves, but her command of the language amazes me. Did I speak this way as a high school senior? I don't think so. I have a feeling Mia goes through life holding herself in, praying for someone who might be receptive to her thoughts. It strikes me as even stranger that this vocabulary is pouring from the mouth of a beautiful girl. That's only my prejudice, of course, but I wouldn't be half so surprised if Mia were a plain girl who sat at home all the time. But she's the head cheerleader, with a body to make the shallowest high school jock drop his jaw in lust. Kate Townsend shared this quality with her, though Kate was not so conventionally beautiful. It's not hard to see why Drew was drawn to this unusual combination of qualities.

"Most people in Natchez thought Drew was the greatest guy they'd ever met," Mia says. "Now it turns out he was having sex with his babysitter, and they're so pissed off they're about to pop. But their anger's not really about Kate, you know? It's about *them*. They feel betrayed. They put him up on a pedestal, and then he committed the crime of being human. So fuck him, right? Never mind that Kate was two weeks shy of eighteen, and on the make for exactly the kind of affair she had with Drew."

"So you think Kate was the aggressor?"

"I'd bet all the money I have on it." She grins, exposing perfect teeth. "Which isn't much."

"If only Drew could get jurors with your mind-set. But go on. You said you've been trying to figure out what's behind this violence."

Mia looks startled. "Oh! Sorry, I went off on a tangent, as

usual. Okay, I know this sounds obvious, but I think you should start with the people and move forward, rather than the way cops work."

"Which is?"

"They start with the murder and work backward. Right?"

"Some of them. Go on."

"We're not just looking for a killer. We're trying to understand the secret reality of this town. Like Kate and Drew. *That* was the reality, not Drew and Ellen. You see? If you figure out the true connections, the killer will be obvious."

Mia is right. Of course, the best homicide detectives use the exact methodology she's describing. They're experts on human psychology, even if they've never taken a single psychology course. But I doubt they developed their methods by the age of eighteen.

"Mia, I think you should think long and hard before you choose a career. Because you need to find something that's going to make use of all of your gifts."

She stares at me without speaking. Then she blinks as though suddenly coming awake. "It's time for me to go, isn't it?"

I give her an apologetic smile. "I think so."

She forces herself to release the pillow, then speaks without looking at me. "Are you in for the night?"

"Absolutely. I don't think I can move from this spot."

Now her eyes find mine. "You don't need me to stay and take Annie to school?"

"No, my eyes will pop open at seven."

A skeptical smile. "I left my backpack in the kitchen. I'll get that, and then I'm gone."

"Okay. I can't thank you enough for staying late. You just did something I didn't think anyone could do."

"What's that?" she asks, standing.

"Took my mind off of the Wilsons' bodies."

"Well, I'm glad for that. See you tomorrow."

She picks up her paperback and her cell phone, then leaves me alone in the study. I take a deep breath and settle back against the soft cushion. Mia's theories of history and detective work acted like a tranquilizer on my frayed nerves. Driving home, I feared I would have trouble sleeping tonight, but my only trouble is going to be making it upstairs to my bedroom. The couch is plenty soft enough to sleep on.

I must have dozed off, because the next thing I feel is strong hands massaging my shoulders. I wouldn't have allowed Mia to do this if I'd been awake, no matter how good it feels, which—frankly—is pretty damned good. Her fingertips dig expertly into the muscle fibers of my neck, then climb to the base of my skull, slowly easing the pressure on the disks between my cervical vertebrae. I groan involuntarily, and the sound of my pleasure brings me to full alertness.

"Mia, that feels great, but I can't let you do that."

"Why not?"

I jerk my head around to find Caitlin staring down at me, looking half amused and half angry. She raises her eyebrows and says, "You were a little slow to tell the babysitter she shouldn't be rubbing your neck."

"I was asleep!" I protest, getting to my feet.

Caitlin gives me a look of mock suspicion. "Were you?"

"How the hell did you get here?"

"Hug first, then talk."

I walk around the sofa and crush her body against mine. Only after I sense her having difficulty breathing do I pull back and look at her. No matter how much time I spend with Caitlin, I can't get accustomed to the luminous green of her eyes. They seem almost incongruous in her face, which is porcelain pale, while her hair is jet black and very fine.

"Where's Mia?" I ask.

"She's gone home, where she belongs. I slipped through the back door and saw her in the kitchen. She left that way."

"That's some timing."

A little color comes into Caitlin's cheeks. "I watched the two of you from the porch for a little bit."

"Spying?"

"A girl has to protect her investment."

I maintain my smile, but the thought that came into my head was, *You haven't invested much in me lately—or in Annie, either.*

"Are you all right?" Caitlin asks. "I know you were at the Wilson scene."

"How do you know that?"

"I've been in touch with my reporters all the way down."

I pull her over to the couch and sit beside her. "Down from where? Explain yourself."

She laughs at my puzzlement. "I was flying down to Wilmington to see my father. He wanted to talk to me about an acquisition for the chain. Face time, not phone time."

Wilmington, North Carolina, is the home base of Caitlin's father, the owner of one of the fastest-growing and most successful newspaper chains in the South. They're at eighteen papers and counting. Daddy's company owns the Cessna jet that allows Caitlin to change her flight destination on a whim.

"Ann Denny called me after Sonny Cross was shot," Caitlin goes on. Denny is the editor of the *Natchez Examiner,* which means she reports directly to Caitlin, who is still technically the publisher, despite her long absences. "I figured you were probably in the middle of whatever was going on here, so I decided, 'Screw it, let's turn this plane southwest and go to Mississippi.' "

"Well . . . I'm glad you did."

Her lovely eyes narrow. "Are you?"

"Of course."

She gives me a long and searching look. "Then why aren't you raping me?"

Her eyes flash invitingly, but I feel no reaction other than anxiety. If I make love with Caitlin now, and then tomorrow vent the feelings that have been building up while she's gone, she will feel betrayed. Besides, the truth is, I don't feel like having sex right now. What I most want now is sedation. General anesthesia.

"You're upset, aren't you?"

"Yes," I concede.

"I heard the Wilson scene was bad. Was it?"

Even this simple question causes resentment in me. Is she asking me out of curiosity, or out of professional interest? "It was a murder scene."

"You don't want to talk about it?"

"Not tonight."

"What do you want to do?"

"I know this sounds bad, but I think I need sleep more than anything else."

Caitlin shakes her head and smiles. "No, I understand completely. Do you want me to stay here?"

"Can you stay all night?"

She seems to steel herself, then says, "I promised Ann I would go over to the paper at two-thirty for a strategy meeting. She's working through the night."

I shake my head. "Don't worry about it."

"Penn, that still gives us almost two hours. I can tuck you in and watch you sleep."

A year ago I would have loved hearing this. Not now. "I don't think I'm very good company tonight. I'll have my resources back in the morning. We can start over then."

Caitlin stands. "Okay. I need to air my house out anyway. I'm going to open all the doors and windows and drink a gimlet. Maybe two."

"I wish I was up to joining you. Sorry."

She looks down at me, silently imploring me for some explanation, but she must already know the truth of the situation.

"Caitlin . . . you wouldn't even be in Natchez if it weren't for these murders, would you?"

She bites her lip and thinks this over. "That's probably true. But I was coming back in two weeks no matter what, and staying for a whole week."

"Were you?"

"Yes. Penn, what's wrong? Please talk to me."

"We should talk before we slip back into our old routine."

"Let's talk now."

"No. I'm too exhausted. I've seen too much tonight. I'm happy to see you, and Annie will be ecstatic. Let's leave it at that for now."

Caitlin starts to reply, then thinks better of it. She steps forward and gives me a soft kiss on the lips, then turns and walks out of the study. She's never been slow on the uptake.

One way or another, change is coming.

CHAPTER

25

The St. Stephen's high school gymnasium sounds like a Broadway theater before the lights go down. Four hundred students ranging from fifth-graders to the senior classmates of Kate Townsend and Chris Vogel have been crowded into the bleachers on both sides of the gleaming basketball court. Most teachers are sitting with their classes, trying in vain to keep the anticipatory energy under control. About fifty adults from the community—many of them St. Stephen's parents, but some teachers and coaches from other schools—stand against the wall by the large double entrance doors. Coach Wade Anders, our athletic director, stands by the smaller door to his office, glaring at the loudest of the students to quiet them down.

A podium has been placed at the center of the tip-off circle, with chairs on both sides of it. In the chairs sit Jan Chancellor; Holden Smith; Dean Herrick, minister of the Presbyterian church Kate attended; Roger Mills, minister of the Methodist church Chris Vogel attended; and Charles Martin, the school chaplain. There's no chair for Jenny Townsend, Kate's mother, but she must be here somewhere. Likewise, the Vogel family.

Jan Chancellor stands and walks to the microphone, a folded

piece of paper in her hand. On any other occasion, it would require some effort to obtain quiet, but not today. Today the room
goes still as though everyone has suddenly held his breath. Death
retains its power to awe.

"We have gathered here," Jan says in a strong voice, "to remember two of the most distinguished students ever to attend this
school: Kate Townsend and Chris Vogel. Because St. Stephen's is
such a small institution, we are truly a family. And today we all
grieve the loss of two family members."

As Jan goes on, I realize she is an even better speaker than I
thought. She doesn't distance herself from the kids by being too
formal; neither does she condescend to them. She paints a brief
picture of each dead student that brings home their special qualities and avoids all mention of the manner in which they died. I
suppose that subject will be handled by the ministers winging the
podium.

As Jan introduces Reverend Mills, I find my thoughts drifting
away from the proceeding. This gymnasium served as a backdrop
for some of the most seminal moments of my life. Several of the
royal blue banners hanging from the far wall have my name in-
scribed in gold upon them, along with the names of boys I knew
from the age of four until today. From this tiny town, we sallied
forth in a creaking old school bus and claimed state titles in basketball, baseball, football, and track. If I close my eyes, I can still
hear the sound of rain thundering on the tin roof as we run line
drills during P.E. and basketball practice. We even practiced football on this floor when it rained, barefoot to protect the wood,
wearing shorts, shoulder pads, and helmets. On this floor I stole
kisses under the eyes of watchful chaperones during school dances,
devoured barbecue chicken at athletic banquets, received ribbons
on academic awards days, watched school plays, and ran endless
sprints as punishments for various infractions. But this is the first
time I have come here for a funeral.

It's not a funeral really, but a memorial service. The real funerals
will begin in less than an hour, in churches downtown. Students
from the tenth grade and above will be excused from school to at-

tend them, if they so choose. The rest will sit in class and pretend to work while they wonder what is happening at the funerals.

Reverend Mills is speaking now, trying his best to deal with one of the thorniest issues any believer must face: why an innocent young person should be cut down for no apparent reason just as his life is about to begin. By my measure, Mills isn't doing a very good job. He seems to be following the "God has a plan inscrutable to us mortals" line. I stopped buying this rationalization at age fourteen, and I doubt it's resonating with the students sitting in the bleachers today.

Scanning the faces in the crowd, I realize I'm searching for Marko Bakic. I don't see him anywhere. I suppose the incipient drug war has changed his opinion of the relative value of an American high school education.

Reverend Mills segues into the evangelical section of his eulogy. He has no more intent than Jan Chancellor of delving into the issues of sexual homicide or drug abuse. As his deep bass voice drones on, I wonder who will finally articulate the feelings of these students, and of the town proper. After the unprecedented losses of Kate, Chris, and Sonny, news of last night's deaths hit Natchez with the force of a tornado. I've never seen the city in such a state, not even during the race riot of 1968. Then, at least, the threat was understood. But now all sense of control has been shattered. Driving through downtown this morning, it felt as though the air had been sucked from the streets. People hurried along the sidewalks with their heads down, like medieval villagers awaiting the onslaught of some unknown calamity. So many deaths in so few days almost begs the question of divine retribution, and I'm sure that theory has been raised in some local households.

Mills's somnolent drone makes me want to get up and phone Quentin Avery, who is setting up his offices at the Eola Hotel right now. But Reverend Mills suddenly yields the floor to his "Presbyterian colleague," Reverend Dean Herrick. Herrick is about my age, and I've met him a couple of times. He's from Tennessee, and he seems to have more liberal ideas than any of his predecessors or peers. He's about twenty pounds overweight, and he's starting to use the dreaded combover to combat his receding hairline. He stands at the podium in silence, surveying the assembled students with dark eyes

"Boys and girls," he says finally, "I'm not going to take much of your time today. And I'm not going to lie to you. I'm not going to spout a bunch of platitudes that sound good in a preacher's guide but give no comfort to a grieving soul or a troubled mind."

Reverend Herrick did not look at Reverend Mills as he said this, but he might as well have. I sense that he has the full attention of the assembly.

"The premature death of someone like Kate Townsend or Chris Vogel is the toughest test a Christian ever faces. As a minister, I have no special powers of understanding. Like you, I'm rendered speechless by these tragedies. My heart is broken. And in the face of deaths like this, the Bible is strangely silent. We search its pages for comfort, but we find little. Death, like birth, is a mystery. We feel that we understand birth because we know what comes after it. But do we know what comes *before* birth? No. We believe that souls originate from God, but more than this we do not know. So, what of death? For Christians, death is the time when we shuffle off this mortal coil and return to God. But as for details, we know none."

Reverend Herrick pauses. The air in the gym is still; not one student shifts in his seat.

"As I lay in bed last night," he goes on, "one question filled my mind. *Why?* Why was this beautiful girl taken so young? Does God have a plan that requires her death? The Bible doesn't tell us so. What *does* the Bible say? Jesus said, 'No one can come to me unless the father who sent me draws him.' In other words, only through death can we return to God. Well, all right. But does that answer my question? Why, after eighteen years of rigorous and joyous preparation for life, were Kate and Chris taken from us? If they were not to be granted a full life, why were they born at all?"

Some of the parents stir at these words, as if Reverend Herrick has trespassed on territory best left unexplored in the presence of children. But he's got the kids; I can feel it.

"But here we may find some comfort," Herrick says. "Because you and I would not be the people we are, the souls that we are, had we not known Kate and Chris. Both those young people brought joy into my heart and yours. Simply watching Chris perform on the fields and courts of this state was a revelation. Seeing Kate work with children on mission trips made me think of Audrey Hepburn working with the starving children of Africa. But Kate didn't think of herself that way. Like the rest of us, she spent much of her time worrying whether she was living up to the ideals her mother and this community had bred into her."

Herrick spreads his arms as if to take in the whole school. "People, this institution would not be what it is today had Kate and Chris not walked its halls. Their lives had *purpose*. And their deaths have purpose, too. Because in the dark hours of the last three days, all of us have been forced to face one inescapable truth: *In the midst of life, we are in death.* You hear that a lot, but what does it really mean? I'll tell you. 'Live each day as though it's your last, for one day you're sure to be right.' For a Christian, that means living out the meaning of our creed. It means following the example of Jesus' life."

Just when I think Herrick is going to repeat Mills's error by proselytizing, he veers into still more surprising territory. "What is the purpose of this memorial service?" he asks. "What's the purpose of the funerals you will attend in a few minutes? The answer will probably surprise you. For though the words of these rituals are gentle, our intent is *fierce*. In a Christian funeral, we raise our fists at death and *shake* them! We remember Jesus Christ, who suffered death, battled death, and ultimately triumphed over it."

Reverend Herrick takes out a handkerchief and wipes his forehead. He seems overwhelmed by his own passion. "The Bible tells us it was through sin that death entered into the world. And some people draw unwarranted conclusions from that language. There's been a lot of talk about Kate's private life, a secret life that none of us was privy to. There's been a lot of talk about Chris Vogel, too."

The parents against the wall are shifting uncomfortably again.

"Yes, Kate had secrets," Herrick says. "Chris had secrets, too.

Kate needed love and affirmation, and she found it in her own way. Chris needed help to face the stress of this world, and he found it where he could. But I don't condemn these children for that. How can I? Because I need love and affirmation, too. I need help facing the stress of this world, just like every one of you out there. And what tortures me today is not anything Kate or Chris did in life, but what they did *not* do. They did not come to me with their fear and confusion. And the fault for that lies with me. With us. Somehow, we did not make Kate feel safe enough or loved enough to come to us with her pain and loneliness. And I know this: Kate and Chris weren't the only ones among us with secrets. We all carry private burdens. We all carry guilt. We *all* sin. That's why death comes to all men and women. But premature death is not a punishment sent from God. To those of you who may be suffering in silence, I say, please do not suffer alone. And to those people who speak ill of Kate, I repeat the words of Jesus of Nazareth: 'Let him who is without sin among you cast the first stone.' "

Reverend Herrick's words echo through the gym with unexpected power. The children appear dumbstruck by his honesty. I sense that some in the room want to stand and applaud. As Herrick walks to his seat, the only sound is his heels clicking on the floor. Jan Chancellor rises again, probably to introduce the school chaplain, but Reverend Herrick's words are the last I need to hear on the subject of Kate's death. I'm seated at the far end of the bleachers, close enough to the door to make a discreet exit, and I do.

Walking down the familiar halls, I decide to drive straight to the Eola Hotel for a conversation with Quentin Avery. As wise as the famous lawyer is, his primary motive is to torpedo Shad Johnson, not to get Drew acquitted. But I have to finish with Quentin in time to ride out to the cemetery for Kate's interment. My interest in the burial isn't personal, but professional. Murderers often attend the funerals of their victims, particularly in cases of sexual homicide. I brought my digital camera in my car to shoot pictures of those who will gather at the grave, just in case the local cops neglect to do it. In a town that averages only one or two murders a year, such an error wouldn't surprise me.

As I reach the main atrium of the high school, I pass the back door of Coach Anders's office. On impulse I walk in, meaning to have a word with the athletic director when the service is done. But like me, Anders has left the gym early. He's sitting at his desk, staring blankly at a poster of Peyton Manning on his wall. Wade Anders is thirty, with close-cropped black hair and the body of an aging athlete past his prime. There's a growing spare tire around his middle, but his legs and forearms still ripple with muscle. Anders is fast with a grin and smooth when dealing with the school board, but during basketball games out of town I've seen him lose control of his temper and be ejected from the gymnasium. The students seem to like him, but then he is all they have ever known. Anders makes me long for the coach I had at St. Stephen's, a gentleman athlete with a paternal manner and a steely eye, a natural leader who took Kipling's advice and treated both victory and defeat as impostors, yet still managed to bring home state titles. One raised eyebrow from him was the equivalent of a violent outburst from Wade Anders. But though my coach's name is painted over the gym door, it's Anders sitting in his chair now—one more sign of the way the world has changed.

"Wade?" I say softly.

Anders starts from his trance, then comes quickly to his feet. "Hey, Penn. What can I do for you?"

"I wanted to ask you about Marko."

Anders shakes his head. "That boy . . . what can I tell you?"

"Have you seen him at all in the past two days?"

"Not hide nor hair. He's gone. And I'd just about sewed up a scholarship for him at Delta State. They need a new kicker, and one thing that boy can do is kick. Tell the truth, it's about the only thing he can do on a football field."

I give Wade the laugh he expects.

"I heard Marko was with you on the afternoon Kate died. Is that right?"

"Yessir, it is. He rode home from school with me. I worked on his kicking with him, then worked the phones for a while, talking to college coaches on his behalf. I was trying to do what I could for the damn fool. I knew he was into drugs, and I thought a college football program might get that out of his system. Even a junior college program."

"And now?"

"Hell, Penn, if Marko doesn't come back to school soon, he's not even going to graduate. I already talked to his teachers. He's practically a washout now."

"Sit down, Wade. This isn't a formal meeting. This is just two guys shooting the shit, okay?"

"Sure, yeah." Anders sits, but he doesn't look comfortable. The fact that I'm a member of the school board as well as a lawyer is probably enough to make him nervous. But still, something seems wrong beyond simple anxiety.

"Did you give Marko a ride to the Wilsons' house after you were done with your phone calls?"

"No, some other kids picked him up."

"Did you know them?"

Wade shakes his head. "They were black kids. Homeboys. Looked like druggies to me."

"What time was that?"

"A little after six. Marko said they were going to Baton Rouge to watch a movie."

"Did he tell you what movie?"

"Adam Sandler, I think. Don't remember the title."

I watch Wade in silence for a while, trying to figure out what I might be able to learn from him. He has the athlete's discomfort with stillness. "Has Marko ever talked to you about what he experienced back in Europe?" I ask.

"He told me he saw his family killed. Happened in a place called Srebece—something like that, anyway. The place where he's from. He's got a hell of a scar on his belly, and when I asked about that, he told me about his folks. The scar came from a bayonet. He didn't tell me any details, though."

"Did you ask?"

"Once, yeah. Late one night on the team bus, on the way back from an away game. He didn't want to talk about it, though."

"Some people think Marko's dangerous, Wade. Capable of serious violence."

Anders shrugs as though this is unlikely. "I don't think so. He hates the Serbs now. That's who killed his folks. If you asked me would Marko kill a Serb, I'd say don't get between them."

"How did Marko feel about the Wilsons?"

Wade laughs. "He liked them. Hell, they let him do whatever he wanted most of the time. Why wouldn't he like them? Professor Wilson's in another world half the time, anyway. Was, I mean."

"Absentminded, you mean? Head in the clouds?"

"That, too, I guess. But I meant drunk."

A new thought hits me. "Paul Wilson didn't do drugs, did he?"

Wade shrugs again. "Never thought about it. But I wouldn't reject the idea out of hand. He spent his whole life teaching college. He's bound to have smoked some reefer, at least."

"Hm. What did you think of Kate Townsend?"

Wade swallows hard, shakes his head, and looks at the floor. "Jesus, Penn. You see a kid like that maybe once every ten years. Gifted on the field and a genius in the classroom. I've really never had one like her myself. Tell the truth, I can't really believe she's dead."

"Do you have any idea who killed her?"

Shock blanks Anders's face. "Hell, no. Do you?"

"No."

"I mean, people are saying Dr. Elliott did it. But I don't really hold with that."

"Why not?"

"Drew's not the type. I mean, I'm sure he was in love with her. Hell, you can't help but love a girl like that. But he wouldn't have killed her. I mean, not unless he's got a different side, you know? A jealous side. Some guys are like that. Seem like great guys on the outside, but at home they're real control freaks. Paranoid, you know?"

"Yeah."

"You're his friend, right? Is Drew like that?"

"No."

"I didn't think so. You can tell from how a guy deals with his kids. Drew never pressures his son in football practices. He comes out to watch, you know, but he never gets onto Timmy, not even when he makes a mistake. Which surprised me, since Drew played college ball and all. Look, man, what do I know? I'm just a coach."

"You've made some good points, Wade. What do you think about Drew having sex with Kate?"

Anders blinks as though confused. "What do you mean?"

"Do you condemn him for it?"

Wade looks at his office door, which I realize is open about a half inch. He closes it with his foot. "You want the party line or the real answer?"

"You know what I want."

His eyes shine as he shakes his head. "Penn, these girls . . . they're not the girls we went to school with, okay? There's a group of girls here who have a club called the Bald Eagles. Know why?"

"Do I want to know?"

"They all shave their pussies."

"Is that a big deal?"

Wade raises his eyebrows. "They're in the eighth grade."

"Jesus." Even in our frankest discussions, Mia and I have not gotten to this level of detail.

"And the juniors and seniors? Man, they put it right in your face. Day in and day out. Sex is no big deal to them. I'll be honest with you, Penn, the hardest thing I've ever done is said no to the girls who've come on to me in this office. I've had 'em start changing clothes right in front of me, like they forgot I was here, then ask if I want to see more."

Wade's honesty surprises me. But is he playing me as well? "Do you always say no, Wade?"

His jaw tightens. "Yessir, I do. Know why?"

"Why?"

"My mama taught me one lesson. Don't shit where you eat."

He glances at the door again. "I need this job, Penn. And screwing a seventeen- or eighteen-year-old would eventually lose it for me. Because these girls can't handle what they're playing with. They have sex, but they don't understand what it really is, you know? Hell, adults don't either, half the time. Maybe that's what happened to Drew. The truth is, we'll probably never know what happened to Kate."

"Yes, we will," I promise. "Because I'm going to find out."

Wade Anders stands and offers me his hand. "More power to you, brother. Anything I can do to help, you let me know."

I shake his hand and turn to leave the office.

"Oh, hey," he says. "I had my baseball team go over the football field and track with a fine-toothed comb, but they never found that pistol you told me you lost."

I stop and look back at him, searching for hidden meaning in his face. "Did the crew I sent over get your light control box fixed?"

"Yep, good as new." Wade leans back in his chair and puts his feet up on his desk. "Man, those bullets tore up the inside of that box. Good thing you didn't hit anybody with them."

I freeze. "I never told you it was me who shot the box."

He looks blank. "I guess you didn't. I just assumed . . ."

"What?"

"That you were down here spotlighting deer or something. That you crossed over from the hunting camp. I didn't mean nothing by it."

I keep studying his face, looking for cracks in his composure. "That's pretty much what happened. Thanks for the effort, Wade."

"No problem. You be careful. Lots of crazy shit happening in this town."

"I will."

CHAPTER

26

At seven stories the Eola Hotel is the tallest building in Natchez. Built in 1927, the year of the great flood, the Eola has weathered boom and bust to find itself in the National Register of Historic Places. When I was a boy in the 1960s, the lobby of the Eola was a seedy place where old men played chess and smoked cigars while families fresh from church walked through the stale air to eat their Sunday dinners in the hotel restaurant. In that era, uniformed black men operated the elevator and attended the restroom while Yankees like Dan Rather, his CBS news crew, and New York print journalists stood in the café watching robed Klansmen on horseback march down Main Street outside. Quentin Avery remembers that era a lot better than I do. And now he will run Drew Elliott's legal defense from the penthouse suite of a hotel that wouldn't have given him a reservation when he was a thirty-year-old lawyer.

Today I operate the elevator myself as I ride up to the seventh floor. When the door opens, I see two young white men carrying computer equipment between rooms. They have the harried look of young lawyers. I nod at them and make my way up the hall to Quentin's suite. The door is propped open with a heavy law book. I knock and walk inside.

The suite is huge: three separate rooms and two baths, all decorated with obsessive attention to detail. Quentin is standing on the
long balcony, which gives a panoramic view of Natchez, the Mississippi River, and the Louisiana delta stretching away for miles to
the west. He's wearing jeans and a white button-down shirt. From
the rear, his grayish-white Afro gives him the look of a much
younger man.

"Quentin?" I call. "It's Penn Cage."

Avery turns and smiles, and though I see every one of his sev-
enty-plus years in his face, the light in his eyes tells me he's excited
to be back in the game again.

"What do you know?" he asks. "Anything new?"

"I talked to Chief Logan this morning. Marko Bakic has vanished. Ditto Cyrus White."

Quentin's smile broadens. "Good, good. That's just how we like it."

"Why's that?"

"You need to ask me that? Come out here into the sun. Maybe
it'll prod your brain."

I walk out onto the balcony. There's a cool breeze blowing off
the rust-colored river, which is high for this early in the spring.
"Tell me."

"This is a murder case, Penn. Our goal is acquittal. To get that,
we need one thing: reasonable doubt."

"And?"

"Cyrus White is our reasonable doubt. Just as he is. If I could
stop time right now and go to trial, I would. Because no sane jury
can convict Drew Elliott of murder with unidentified sperm in that
dead girl and Cyrus White on the loose. Not with proof that Kate
and Cyrus knew each other."

"I'm not sure we can prove that."

Quentin's smile vanishes. "You told me the police had video of
the dead girl going into Cyrus's apartment."

"Sonny Cross told me that. He's dead now. And, well . . . he
worked for the sheriff's department."

"So the sheriff's department will have the video. We'll get that
during discovery."

"I hope so."

"What do you mean?"

"When I talked to Sonny, I got the feeling he kept a lot from the sheriff. I don't think they got along too well."

Quentin's face hardens. "I need that video, Penn. You've got to get it for me."

"I'll do my best."

"Is there any other proof that Kate Townsend and Cyrus knew each other?"

An image of Kate's secret journal fills my mind, but I'm not ready to tell Quentin about that yet. There's no way we could use that diary in the trial without causing Drew further damage. Besides, Jenny Townsend gave me Kate's private things specifically so that they wouldn't be seen by prying eyes. Even if I wanted to make the diary public, I'm not sure I could bring myself to violate Jenny's trust. If it meant saving Drew's life, I would, of course. But right now, that journal is as likely to hurt him as help him. There might be digital proof somewhere that Cyrus was tracking Kate's cell phone, but I'll find that out on my own.

"I don't know," I murmur. "I'll try to find out."

"You'll have to talk to Cyrus's crew," Quentin says, "see if they remember her coming around."

"You think they'll talk to me?"

Quentin shrugs. "You're my investigator. We'll subpoena them if we have to, but that's never the best way to get information."

It's time for me to come clean with Quentin about Kate's relationship with Cyrus. As succinctly as possible I explain Ellen Elliot's Lorcet addiction, and Kate's reason for visiting Cyrus once a month. He listens like a man who has heard it all in his time. He can't be shocked, only disappointed.

"This ain't good," Quentin says when I finish. "I can make the jury feel sorry for a good doctor who happened to fall in love with a beautiful young girl. Even an underage girl. But I can't make them feel sorry for a manipulator who used a high school girl in a sleazy scheme to get drugs."

"I'll be very surprised if Shad makes that connection."

Quentin raises one eyebrow. "I've learned something in my long years of practicing law, Penn. What holds true of adultery holds true for most other sins. Sooner or later, *people find out.* For us the important question is, how long does this particular sin stay secret?"

"In other words, how soon will Drew be indicted and go to trial?"

Quentin nods. "I look for sooner rather than later. As soon as Shad gets a DNA match on the semen taken from the girl's rectum, he's likely to ask for an indictment."

"That's usually three weeks, minimum, although Shad hinted to me that it might not take that long. If he really wants Drew bad—and we know he does—he could use a private lab to do the analysis. That could knock ten days off the wait, maybe more. The irony is that Shad will be helping us if he rushes to trial."

"Only as it relates to that single issue," Quentin points out. "Connecting the Lorcet to Ellen Elliott. Maybe you shouldn't talk to Cyrus's crew after all. We don't want to jog anybody's memory too hard."

"We're at the beginning of a court term now," I think aloud. "Even if Shad gets an indictment, the trial will be scheduled for the next term, which gives us two months to prepare."

"I wouldn't count on that," Quentin says.

"Why not?"

"Shad's thinking about the special mayoral election, not the trial. That's the whole point of the trial. If he gets the indictment, he'll try to have the trial scheduled for the current term."

"Judge Minor and Shad are thick as thieves. All Shad will have to do is steer the case to Minor's court, and Minor will schedule the trial for this term."

"We're likely to be trying the case in less than a month," Quentin says.

"That's unethical!"

Quentin laughs heartily. "Try convincing the Supreme Court of that. The founding fathers specifically guaranteed the right of the accused to a speedy trial. If we protest against Shad rushing this trial, he can argue that he's only trying to provide what the Constitution demands, the right of an innocent man to prove his innocence as soon as possible. Hell, that was the way it worked all the time in the old days. In some rural counties, they still indict the accused and try him within a week. The system has gotten so ass backwards over the past three decades that we routinely expect capital cases to take years. But that's not how it's supposed to be. If Judge Minor is on Shad's side, there's no way we'll slow this trial down."

"Great."

Quentin nods thoughtfully. "It is great. Because we want the trial over before anyone can figure out just what a sleazy character our defendant really is. And we want Cyrus White to stay lost."

Quentin's description of Drew offends me, but I hold my tongue.

"Out with it," says the lawyer. "Am I pissing you off?"

"A little bit."

A tight smile. "I understand human frailty, Penn, believe me. I'm only talking the way the jury will behind closed doors. I don't care if your buddy was Albert Schweitzer right up until he met Kate Townsend. His behavior since then is going to make him scum in the eyes of most potential jury members. Now, a lot of jurors will understand the psychological dynamics of extramarital affairs. And *some* of them will even forgive that. But this drug angle . . . they'll fry his ass for that."

"The sheriff's men will be questioning Cyrus's crew about Kate's visits to Cyrus. I hope to hell Kate never said anything about Ellen to Cyrus or his men."

"Yeah, it would be a lot better if you hadn't told Byrd about that video."

"I didn't tell him there was video."

"You told him there was documented evidence. That's video or still photos."

I squeeze my hands into fists, wishing I could change the past.

"Stop beating yourself up," says Quentin. "Cyrus's homeys won't say shit to those cracker cops. The cops *may* find out Kate was going there to buy drugs, but they'll assume she was getting them for herself. At first, anyway."

"But the toxicology on her body will be clean."

"Are you sure? Have you seen the report yourself?"

"No. But Sonny Cross said it was clean."

Quentin chides me with a smile. "We'll request that in discovery. If we're lucky, our prom queen popped a few Lorcet herself to ease the pain of waiting for her lover to get divorced."

"I'm glad I never came up against you in court, Quentin. You're a pragmatic son of a bitch."

His eyes twinkle. "That I am, my boy. You are, too. You just have this romantic haze over your eyes. You want the world to be better than it is. But I know your record. You're as hard as I am when it comes down to it. You just get there by a different route."

"I'm not sure about that."

Quentin snorts. "As many people as you got executed, I hope you're sure."

Images of desperate men fill my mind, some of them glaring at me from death row cages, others staring through bulletproof glass as a technician injects paralyzing drugs into their veins. In some of those eyes I see a plea for forgiveness, in others unalloyed hatred. But one thing is common to them all: the animal fear of death.

"Stop it," Quentin says. "Let the dead bury the dead."

"Sometimes I can't stop it."

The old lawyer looks out over the rooftops toward the river and speaks in a low voice. "Fifteen years ago, I was asked to review the case of a young man sitting on death row in Huntsville, Texas. He was black, and his family told me he'd been railroaded by the state. The facts sounded promising as presented, so I flew down to Texas and reviewed the file." Quentin glances at me. "You were the lawyer who convicted him."

A chill goes through me. "What was his name?"

"Doesn't matter." Quentin looks back at the river. "The point is, I spent three days and nights going over that case. I had two associates helping me. And we couldn't find one chink in the wall of evidence that had convicted that boy. There wasn't a glimmer of hope. I gave the family back their files and flew home." He spits over the brick wall of the balcony, then turns to me. "I don't believe in the death penalty, Penn, not in this mortal world. It's applied unfairly, and innocent men are executed. But I will say this: according to the law of the land, that boy in Huntsville got exactly what he deserved. And you have nothing to be ashamed of. I've reviewed a lot of death penalty cases, and that was the best work I've ever seen."

"Why are you telling me this?"

"Because that's the reason the two of us are standing here now, working together. We're about to go through some shit, you and I. And I want you to know *I* know you've got what it takes to do it. Now, if you want to do your friend any good, you're going to have to start looking at the facts as coldly as you would if you were dealing with some dead-eyed killer in Texas."

"It's hard for me to look at Drew like that."

"That's because he's white."

I feel my back stiffen. "That's not true. I sent five white men to death row. I killed a white supremacist myself."

Quentin shakes his head like a patient tutor. "I said he's white, not white trash. When you look at Drew Elliott, you see yourself. When you look at Kate Townsend, you see your sister, or your daughter, or your mother. How do you think I got so many black men off of death row? When I looked at them, I saw myself. Or what could have been me, with just a tiny push at the wrong time."

"I see what you mean. So, you're telling me not to try to find Cyrus?"

"Damned straight. As long as Cyrus White stays a mystery, he's our acquittal on the hoof. The last thing we want is that depraved hoodlum on the witness stand telling a jury how Kate was scoring dope for Drew's wife. You get me?"

"Yes. Only . . ."

"What?"

"I tried a lot of murder cases, Quentin. If you don't really know what happened at a crime scene, you can get your ass handed to you in court."

"Stop thinking like a prosecutor. We're the defense, boy! We don't *care* what really happened at the crime scene. We don't even want to know. All we care about is *reasonable doubt*. That's your mantra from now on. I want you saying it in your sleep: *reasonable doubt*. Say it, man! It's like, 'Show me the money!' " Quentin grins. "Come on . . . *reasonable doubt*."

I'd like to humor him, but at bottom I just don't believe in his strategy.

He puts his hand on my shoulder and squeezes. "It's human nature to want to know the truth, Penn. But what if the truth is that your best friend flew into a jealous rage, raped that girl in the ass, and strangled her to death?"

Quentin's frank tone tells me that he fully believes in this possibility. I know what he's trying to do, but I simply can't abandon my faith in my friend. If I do that, I abandon my faith in myself. "I don't think that's what happened."

"But you don't *know*. And at least until this trial is over, that's the way I want it. Because if you find out that is what happened, you won't be any earthly good to me or Drew Elliott. And I need your help. Just remember, you're the foot soldier here, not the general."

"I got it."

"Make sure you do."

CHAPTER

27

Cemetery Road runs through the old black section of town, past the Little Theater and up along the two-hundred-foot bluff that stretches along the Mississippi River north of town. The road is narrow, bordered on the right by a low stone wall and on the left by a tangle of kudzu that festoons the bluff from top to bottom. As I pass the second wrought-iron gate in the cemetery wall, I realize that my plan to photograph the mourners at Kate's interment is impractical. The turnout for burials is usually much smaller than that for funeral services, but the faded green tent over Kate's open grave is surrounded by more than a hundred people.

I drive past the third gate in the wall, pass a row of shacks on my left, then turn right into the fourth gate, which lets me drive up the back side of Jewish Hill, the highest point in the cemetery. Jewish Hill holds the remains of Natchez's second-generation Jewish settlers, and it has the best view of the Mississippi River anywhere in the nation. I take my camera and walk past the stones of the Rothstein and Schwarz families, then stop behind a wall in the Cohen plot. From here I can see the whole sweep of the ninety-acre cemetery.

This ground was consecrated in 1822, but some of the coffins

were moved here from an even older graveyard, where Natchez settlers were buried in the early 1700s. Kate Townsend's grave has been
dug in an area near the bluff called the Zurhellen Addition. It lies between the steep rise of Jewish Hill and the long row of majestic oak
trees that borders the next section of graves to the south. About forty
yards in front of Kate's grave, near the stone wall at the edge of the
cemetery, stands the most famous monument in this city of the dead:
the Turning Angel. Erected in 1932 to commemorate five girls who
died in a fire, this marble statue has become an object of both legend
and ritual in Natchez. The life-size angel stands on its pedestal in an
attitude of purposeful repose, writing names into the Book of Life.
The angel possesses a face of Madonna-like serenity, but its musculature and powerful wings make it appear almost masculine. When
you drive down Cemetery Road, the angel appears to be looking directly at you. Yet once you pass the monument and look back over
your shoulder, the angel is *still* looking at you. Thus the appellation:
the Turning Angel. For me, the effect is much more dramatic at
night, and it's probably caused by a trick of light as the beams of
headlights create ever-changing shadows on the monument. In daylight—from up close—you can clearly see the angel standing with its
back to the bluff and the river. Yet so famous is this legend that every
Natchez teenager at some point in his life drives or is driven down
the dark stretch of road to watch the angel turn. Thus has legend
spawned a rite of passage for all the children in the town.

The faded green tent at the center of the funeral crowd reads,
"McDonough's Funeral Home," and it's been the centerpiece of
almost every white funeral in town for as long as I can remember.
The crowd is pressing so close to the tent that I have no hope of
photographing anyone. My only hope is to walk down and join
the throng.

A concrete staircase leads down Jewish Hill to the flat rectangle
of the Zurhellen Addition. As I walk down it, I hear the chime of
an acoustic guitar. Then a young male voice floats over the tops of
the mourners' heads, cracking with grief but also communicating
defiance. It's singing about unpredictability and fate and the brevity
of youth.

I guess Kate Townsend was a Green Day fan.

Very slowly, I weave my way through the crowd, nodding to those mourners who meet my eye. I know most of the people here, but some I don't. As I near the tent, the crowd becomes too thick for me to negotiate further. Thanks to my height, though, I can survey the gathering from here.

Jenny Townsend is sitting beneath the burial tent with her ex-husband, the Englishman. Reverend Herrick is performing the graveside service, a much more traditional one than he gave in the school gymnasium. There are other people beneath the tent, but they don't interest me. The people gathered around the tent do. I see most of the St. Stephen's school board, with Holden Smith at their head. Jan Chancellor is wearing a silk pants suit. Steve Sayers stands in the front row to my right, one eye swollen and purple. Not far down the line from him stands Mia Burke with her mother, a paralegal for the city's largest law firm. To my surprise, Mia is wearing a black dress and makeup; with her dark hair pulled up in a bun, she looks twenty-five. She catches my eye and vouchsafes a demure smile. Coach Wade Anders is standing with his back to me, but I recognize his head and shoulders, even in a suit. I have to do a double-take to confirm that one of the women on the far side of the tent is Ellen Elliot, but I'm right. I guess Ellen felt she needed to show the town that she mourns Kate as much as anyone, despite whatever her soon-to-be-ex-husband might have done to her.

As Reverend Herrick prays, I turn my head and scan the grave-stones on Jewish Hill, then the mausoleums on the high ground above the superintendent's office. I have a feeling that someone else is here today. But who? Cyrus White, maybe? Marko Bakic? Or could Drew be here? Some part of me can't quite accept that Drew will not see his paramour lowered into the ground. How difficult would it be for him to slip out of the fence behind the city jail and make his way here? Prisoners with half his intelligence and strength have done it. But I see no one hiding among the stones. Of course, that doesn't mean there's no one there.

Reverend Herrick is reminiscing about Kate. As I look around the cemetery, I recall many memories of this place: sneaking into it as a twelve-year-old with friends to ride madly through the dark lanes on our banana bikes; walking through the stones in the heat of summer with a lovely girl, then lying on the soft grass beneath a wall to explore each other; meeting the love of my life on Jewish Hill in the dead of night, twenty years after I lost her, hoping to learn the secret truth of our lost lives—

"Excuse me."

A woman I don't know brushes past me. The crowd is dispersing. Car engines start in the lanes and idle softly, while figures in black recede from my vision. I recede with them. I see Mia looking for me, but I turn away and walk toward the concrete steps in the wake of some people who parked where they could avoid the long funeral cortege.

Breaking away, I climb to the top of Jewish Hill and turn back toward the river, watching the last of the living depart. Kate's gleaming casket lies suspended above her open grave. Soon all evidence that she lived will be buried forever. Jenny Townsend still stands beside the tent, alone with Reverend Herrick. The minister reaches out and lays a comforting arm on her shoulder. As they speak, a lone figure appears from beneath the tent. Ellen Elliott. Reverend Herrick hesitates, then moves away from the two women. What can Ellen be saying? And how is Jenny responding? Jenny knew about the affair between her daughter and Drew for some time, yet she didn't try to stop it, nor did she inform Ellen about it. Thank God, Ellen doesn't know any of that.

Watching Ellen offer her condolences, I realize that she's adhering to a code of Southern womanhood that demands precisely what she is doing now: maintaining composure and grace through all trials, however difficult. The women do not embrace, but they do shake hands. Then Ellen walks toward the last two cars in the lane with quiet dignity.

"You fucked up, Drew," I say softly. "You couldn't see what you had."

Of course, I've never known Ellen as a wife. The gracious figure that gave her sympathy to Jenny Townsend is a far cry from the drug-crazed addict Drew has probably faced more nights than I would have been able to endure. Conjuring that image, it's not hard to see how appealing Kate Townsend must have looked to him.

Christ, what do I really think about Drew? Quentin Avery is willing to believe that he committed brutal rape and murder. But the mother of the victim is not. Of course, Jenny doesn't have all the facts of the case. I do. Most of them, anyway. Is there a dark corner of my heart where I admit that Drew might have blown a gasket and murdered the teenager he'd fallen in love with? That he got her pregnant, panicked, and then—terrified of losing the family he'd worked so hard to build and sustain—erased her from the world?

No. The boy I grew up with, had he committed such a heinous act, would have owned up to it and taken his punishment like a man, as the archaic phrase goes. That may be a quaint and sexist notion these days, but some of what is best about the South is archaic. The tragedy is that it should be so.

If Drew didn't kill her, says a voice in my head, *then why didn't he call for help when he found Kate's body?*

"He's a doctor," I say aloud. "He knew she was already dead. All he would have accomplished by reporting the body was the destruction of his family."

But what if he didn't mean to kill her? What if they were playing a sex game, and it simply got out of hand?

"He would have told me that," I mutter. "He would have."

When you start talking to yourself in a graveyard, it's time to go home.

As I turn toward my car, my cell phone vibrates in my pocket. It's Caitlin, calling from the newspaper. I haven't spoken to her since last night. My phone showed a missed call from her when I woke up this morning, but she'd called from the paper and hadn't left a message, so I didn't call her back. She must be desperate to question me about all the murders, but she's trying hard to preserve the illusion that she won't exploit our relationship in order to write a better story.

"Hey," I answer, looking down the hill toward Jenny Townsend and Reverend Herrick.

"Where are you?" Caitlin asks.

"The cemetery."

"Oh. Can you talk?"

"Yeah. Go ahead."

"I've got bad news and bad news."

No mention of last night, just straight into our old banter. "Give me the bad first."

"The cops just located the spot where Kate Townsend died. The actual crime scene."

"Where?" I ask, almost afraid to hear the answer.

"They've been searching St. Catherine's Creek ever since they found Kate's cell phone. About two hours ago, they found human blood and hair on the edge of a wheel rim that was half buried in the sand. They say it's where the edge of the creek would have been on the day she was killed. It was flooded, apparently."

"Yes. I think the rain slacked up about an hour before Kate died."

"The blood they found is the same type as Kate's. They're going to send it for a DNA test, of course. But the hair is a perfect match."

My shoulders sag. "Was this anywhere close to where they found Kate's cell phone?"

"About fifty yards away. Right between Pinehaven and Sherwood Estates."

Right between Drew's house and Kate's house, and exactly where he told me he discovered her body. If Kate bled heavily there, she probably died there—which means she did not *die far upstream at Brightside Manor. Cyrus White suddenly looks a lot less guilty than he did thirty seconds ago. And the chances that the police will tie Drew to the actual murder scene with physical evidence just went up astronomically.*

"I know that's bad for Drew," Caitlin says in a careful tone.

"He'll be okay. Who found the blood? The sheriff's department or the police?"

"The police."

Thank God for small favors. "Hm."

"The FBI is in town now, though. DEA, too. They're setting up a multi-jurisdictional task force in the old Sears store at Tracetown Shopping Center."

"Good."

"So maybe all the evidence will be shared from now on."

"I wouldn't assume that."

Caitlin is silent. She wants more information about Drew, but she's not going to push for it.

"What's the other bad news?" I ask.

"Ten minutes ago, Mayor Jones officially resigned. He's no longer the mayor of Natchez."

I close my eyes and reach behind me for somewhere to sit down.

"Jones issued his statement to me personally. The Wilson murders were the last straw. This poor guy was trying to do chemotherapy and run the city at the same time. It might have been possible during normal times, but now . . . it's sad, really."

I can't quite get my mind around this. A decision I'd thought I had at least a month to ponder will now have to be made within days, and maybe within hours.

"Are you there, Penn?"

"Here."

"Are you picking up Annie today?"

"Mia's bringing her home."

"Oh." *A little coldness in the voice?* "Penn, now that Jones has stepped down, there's going to be a special election in less than forty-five days. That's the law."

"I know."

"Well, you've made some oblique comments about pursuing that job yourself in the past month."

"I know."

"Well . . . if you're going to run, you'll have to announce in a matter of days."

"I know that, too, Caitlin."

I hear her breathing, slow and steady. "Are you going to do that?"

This isn't the time or place to reveal anything, but I can't deceive her. "I'm not sure. But right now, I'm leaning in that direction."

More silence. Then she speaks in a falsely chipper voice. "If Mia's keeping Annie after school, let's try to get some early dinner. We can spend some time with Annie later at your house."

"That sounds good."

"Good. Planet Thailand?"

"Ah . . . no privacy. How about the Castle?"

"Okay. Call me."

"I will."

I put the phone back in my pocket, then turn and sit on the brick wall behind me. I've come to the proverbial fork in the road. I began my adult life as a private practice lawyer. Then I became a prosecutor. When I could tolerate that life no longer, I started writing about it instead of living it. That career has been good to me. But has the time come to leave it behind and take up yet another profession? Or would I necessarily have to leave writing behind? Would running this city require every waking hour of my days and nights? *Of course it would,* says my inner censor. *You're not talking about taking on a new job. You're talking about a cause, a mission, a crusade—trying to save the town that bore you, to lift it out of a paralysis caused by economic stagnation and persistent racism. And no one's going to thank you for the effort. You're going to pay a price, and losing Caitlin may be part of it. And the biggest joke of all? You could spend every ounce of time and energy you have and not make a bit of difference—*

A slamming car door snaps me back to reality. Down in the Zurhellen Addition, Jenny Townsend and Reverend Herrick are finally leaving. It's time for me to go, too. But something holds me here. For the first time, Kate Townsend and I are completely alone. I wish she could speak to me. If she could describe her last minutes, a lot of people's lives would be simplified, and justice might actually be served. But she can't speak, and in her muteness she will become the center of a political storm that will be a trial only in name.

After a silent prayer for Kate, I jog down the hill to my car, then pull onto Cemetery Road. An overloaded log truck is rumbling toward me. Last week I might have tried to squeeze around it, but after Chief Logan's tale of drivers who drink beer in the cab all day, I pull onto the grass beside the cemetery wall to let it pass. The ground shudders as the big truck roars by me, but after it does, I pull back onto the road and head toward town.

On my right, the Mississippi River cuts inexorably through the continent, rolling down toward Baton Rouge and New Orleans like Time Incarnate. As I clear the steep slope of Jewish Hill on my left, the Turning Angel comes into sight. The serene face watches my approach, as though waiting only for me. Of course, the angel only *seems* to be watching me; I know it's actually facing away from the road and the river. Nevertheless, I drive slowly as I pass the monument, trying absurdly to catch the angel in the act of turning.

I can't do it. Only when I pass and look back over my shoulder do I see the ageless visage staring after me again. Stepping on the brake, I make a three-point turn and pull alongside the cemetery wall. The Turning Angel is trying to tell me something. Not with words, perhaps, but there's a message here. *What?* What is the message of the marble angel? *What you see isn't always the reality.* We look at one thing but see another. Why? With a marble statue, because of a change in perspective or a trick of light. But with human beings, the reasons are more complex. People project only what they want others to see, or at least they try to. And even when unintended clues to the being behind the mask are exposed, we often refuse to see them. Our perception of others is always distorted by our own prejudices, hopes, and fears. And sometimes, as Quentin Avery suggested, we look at others and see ourselves.

"Appearance versus reality," I say softly. That sounds like the title of an essay I was forced to write in high school English class.

As I stare over the gravestones at the angel's androgynous features, several faces seem to project themselves onto the white stone, slowly morphing from one into another like the faces in the classic Sinéad O'Connor video. Mia first. The angel most resembles her, with its oval face and Madonna-like serenity. Yet as I stare, Mia somehow becomes Drew—not Drew as I know him now, but as the beautiful boy he was when he scorched across the

firmament at St. Stephen's more than twenty years ago. I blink my
eyes and Drew becomes Ellen, and then Ellen, Kate, until I lose my
sense of balance though I'm sitting in my own car on terra firma.
Throwing the Saab into gear, I spin onto Cemetery Road and race
toward town. But one glance in the rearview mirror tells me what
I already know: the Turning Angel is watching me go.

CHAPTER

28

Caitlin and I are sitting in a small private dining room in the Castle, the finest restaurant in Natchez. The building is a restored carriage house behind Dunleith, the city's premier antebellum mansion. One of more than eighty such mansions, Dunleith is a colossal Greek Revival palace that dwarfs even the mythic mansions from *Gone With the Wind*. Sited on forty pristine acres in the middle of the city, Dunleith functions as a high-end bed-and-breakfast, while the Castle, named for two Gothic outbuildings on the grounds, exists to feed the guests and, incidentally, the people of the town.

Caitlin and I didn't drive over together; we met here. She came from the newspaper office, while I left Annie with Mia at my house. We still haven't spoken face-to-face since she left my house last night.

I was surprised to find the main room of the restaurant crowded when we arrived, so I asked the maître'd to seat us in the private dining room. The owner of Dunleith is a fan of my novels, so my request was granted.

"Do you get that kind of treatment in New York?" Caitlin asks with a smile.

"Not a chance. They'd seat me by the bathroom."

We order crab cakes as an appetizer, then set aside our menus and simply look at each other for a while. Just as they did last night, her luminous green eyes exert a hypnotic effect on me. Set in her pale face framed by night black hair, they seem almost independently alive.

"Small talk or big issues?" she asks.

"I think we owe it to ourselves and Annie to go ahead and deal with some things."

Caitlin nods in agreement. "Annie called me when she got out of school today. She asked if I'd watch a movie with her tonight."

"She told me you said yes."

"I've missed her."

Then why haven't you called her? "Why don't we lay some ground rules for this conversation?"

Caitlin looks puzzled.

"Absolute honesty," I tell her. "No sugarcoating anything."

"We've always been good at that."

"Have we?"

"I think so."

The waiter appears and pours two glasses of chilled white wine. I wait for him to depart. "We've been together for five years now," I reflect. "It seems unbelievable, but we have."

"It seems more like two."

"I know. It's easy to let time slip past. Too easy. I guess the question I want to ask you first is, do you still want to spend the rest of your life with me?"

She looks incredulous. "Of course I do. I can't imagine being with anyone else."

"If that's true, it's hard for me to understand why you've been spending so much time away."

"Is it?"

"Well, you've basically been like a mother to Annie for the past five years—when you're here, at least. But she's getting older now, Caitlin. She's *nine*. She needs more than you've been giving her. And I honestly don't know if you're ready to give her more."

I see traces of moisture in Caitlin's eyes, but she doesn't speak.

"I'm not saying it's your duty to give more. I know you *want* to. But there's a difference between wanting to do something and actually committing the time and effort to do it." *God, I sound like my parents.* Caitlin is watching me intently, but still she doesn't speak. "I mean, you're actually getting to the age where if you want to have kids of your own, it's time to get started."

She closes her eyes, and a tear slides down her left cheek.

"Am I crazy?" I ask her. "Tell me. How do you feel about all this?"

She opens her eyes, then reaches across the table and takes my hand. "I love you, Penn. And I love Annie." She looks as though she's about to continue, but then she stops. I've never known Caitlin to be at a loss for words.

"I know you love us," I say softly. "But you're gone for very long periods. I mean, you're the publisher of the *Examiner,* but you're working as a *reporter* fifteen hundred miles away. And not even for your father's chain. I don't understand it."

"I'm not sure I do either. I never really thought about it, but maybe it's *because* I'm not working for my father that I enjoy these assignments so much."

The waiter sets an exquisitely browned crab cake before her, and another before me.

Caitlin looks up at him. "Thank you."

"Are you ready to order?" he asks.

We haven't even glanced at the menus.

"I'll have the blackened catfish," Caitlin says, withdrawing her hand from mine.

"The duck," I tell him.

"Very good. Anything special on the side?"

"Surprise us," Caitlin says with a smile.

"Yes, ma'am."

When the waiter leaves, she says, "Penn, I'm taking these assignments because it's what I love to do. It's the rush, it's where it's happening. It's a big story and they want me. And I like it that they want me."

"I understand that need. When I worked as a prosecutor, even though I was in a big city, only a few people really knew what I did. What I was accomplishing. But after I became an author, I started getting feedback from hundreds of people, then thousands. That kind of affirmation is a powerful thing."

She nods as though I'm getting it.

"But you won your Pulitzer for a series of stories you wrote right here in Natchez, about events that happened right here."

"I know. During weeks like this one, Natchez is a great place to do what I do, as cold as that may sound. But fifty weeks out of the year, it's Little League games and aldermen meetings that are mired in racial crap that got solved elsewhere twenty years ago."

The resentment in her voice is palpable. "I don't think that's true," I reply. "Race is a problem everywhere. It's just more in the open here."

"Let's don't even go there," Caitlin says with surprising irritation. "Let's talk about Annie. You said no sugarcoating, right?"

"Right."

"The schools here are atrocious, Penn. The public schools, I mean. They have the lowest ACT scores in the nation. And thirty-five percent of their seniors don't even take the ACT."

"Actually, the ACTs in Washington, D.C., are lower," I correct her. "The only ones."

"You want to guess why that is?"

"I know why."

Caitlin taps the table to emphasize her points. "This is the most illiterate state in the union. It's number one in single-mother homes. And Natchez is number two in the state in those rankings. Forget the political implications of that. What does it mean for Annie?"

I start to point out that Annie doesn't attend a public school— and that she has a single *father*—but Caitlin pushes ahead before I can say anything. "St. Stephen's does a decent job, I know. Smart kids like Mia and Kate still go on to the Ivy League. But for most kids, St. Stephen's doesn't compare to what's available elsewhere."

"Like Boston?"

She shrugs. "Sure, Boston. Or New York, or even Wilmington. *Any* major city, you know that. And I'm not talking about elite private schools. Here you pay through the nose to get an average education. I'm talking about cities where the public school systems actually function, where there's not racial segregation accomplished by high tuition."

"And that would be where, exactly?"

She closes her eyes and sighs. "It's not just the schools. It's extracurricular opportunities. And what about diversity? I mean, kids here are either white or black. There's no other major demographic group. A couple of Indian kids, a few Mexicans. One or two Asians."

"You want to be honest?" I ask. "All right. Is Annie's education really your main concern here?"

Two pink moons appear high on Caitlin's cheeks. "I'm concerned about it, yes. But I have my own issues, too, I'll admit. I love this town, Penn, but I also see what we're missing by being here. There are no real art galleries or museums, no—"

"Is that what you spend your time in Boston doing? Going to museums and art galleries? Or are we really talking about restaurants and clubs?"

"That's not fair," she says, looking genuinely hurt. "But now that you bring it up, there isn't even an Olive Garden or an Appleby's here, for God's sake. Forget truly exotic cuisine. There's one cineplex with four screens, and I don't think they've *ever* booked an art film."

She's right, but that doesn't make me glad to hear it. "Caitlin, you talk about Boston like it's the best of everything, beyond the reach of people here. Well, Drew Elliott, our murder defendant and small-town doctor, just passed the Massachusetts state medical boards, and he scored in the top five percent. So don't act like you're coming down to Hicksville, USA, to preach the gospel of urban enlightenment."

Caitlin looks stunned. She's realized that Drew taking those boards means he was planning to move north with Kate when she went to Harvard. But she doesn't comment on that. "Drew is an exception," she says. "And so are you."

"Am I?"

"You know you are. You're not like the other people here. Not anymore, anyway. The irony is, you can do your work here and still stay connected to the larger world. But *I* can't. To work at the highest level in my business, I have to be in a city. Not Boston, necessarily, but some major city. Penn, the simple truth is that you don't have to give up what I would to live here full-time."

At last we come to the truth. "You're right," I admit. "I know that."

"Do you want me to give up my work?" There's a note of challenge in her voice.

"No. Not when I think about it intellectually. But if you ask me what I want in my heart, I want you to be with us more. All the time, actually."

Caitlin smiles, but I see pain in her eyes. "I do, too. And that's the crux of our problem."

"How so?"

She lays her hands flat on the table and looks deep into my eyes. "I know you're seriously considering running for mayor. Penn, if you do that—and you win—you'll be tying us to this town for a minimum of four years."

"Tell me how you feel about that possibility."

She takes a slow sip of wine, her eyes on the candle at the center of the table. "I'm afraid you're about to make this town your personal crusade. You may disagree—you may believe you're simply running for mayor. But what that job really means is playing referee in a race conflict. I've covered Natchez for nearly five years. Every single vote by the board of aldermen is decided along racial lines. *Every one.* And if Shad Johnson gets in, they'll be decided on the black side, regardless of what's right, ethical, or even legal."

"But if I get in, they'll be decided fairly."

"Don't kid yourself. No good deed goes unpunished. What makes you think you can get elected, anyway? You'll have to get black votes to do it. A lot of them."

I've given this a lot of thought. "I think my record in Houston speaks for itself. I convicted black murderers, but I also convicted whites. I put away a notorious white supremacist, and I killed his brother myself. When I got here, I solved the murder of Del Payton. I think there's gratitude in the black community for that." I take a quick sip of wine. "And then there's my father."

Caitlin smiles in spite of herself.

"Dad's treated the black community in this town for forty years—as equals, with kindness and respect. He's built up a lot of goodwill. I'm my father's son in most ways, and I think the voters would see that. Finally, the alternative to me is Shad Johnson. I think enough black people in this town have recognized Shad's true nature to take a gamble on me."

"What scares me," Caitlin murmurs, "is that I think you're right. I think if you run, you'll probably be elected."

"Would that be such a disaster?"

A soft sigh escapes her lips. "For the town? Or for us?"

"Caitlin, this city is at the watershed point of its history. That's saying a lot, when your history stretches back to 1716. The cotton economy is gone. The oil is all but gone. Industry won't be coming back here until we fix the public school system. That leaves tourism. To make tourism work takes someone with vision, someone who can unify whites and blacks to sell a history in which blacks were *slaves* to whites. That's a tall order, but if someone doesn't do it, this town will wither from twenty thousand souls to ten. It'll be another black shell surrounded by a white ring of suburban homes, and it will cease to be a real community. I don't want that to happen. More than that, I feel an obligation to try to stop it."

She reaches across the table and squeezes my hand. "I know you do. You grew up here, and you know what this town once was."

"And what it can be again," I say quietly. "Natchez has become a place where we have to raise our children to live elsewhere. Our kids can't come back here and make a living. And that's a tragedy. A lot of people I went to school with would love to come back here to raise their kids. They just can't afford to do it. I want to change that."

Caitlin picks at her crab cake with her fork. "What does your father think about this idea?"

"He's not convinced that saving the town is possible. He's also said that the Del Payton case proved I'm a crusader at heart."

She smiles at some private thought. "You're a romantic, Penn. It's one thing I've always loved about you. But sometimes . . ." She shakes her head again. "Do you want to know what I see?"

"Yes."

"It's going to shock you."

"Fire away."

"I see a town that doesn't want to be saved. Black and white both, but mostly black."

"Really?"

"Absolutely. When I came here five years ago, I lectured you on white racism."

I laugh softly. "You sure did."

"But now that I've seen the reality up close, I understand white frustration. Black people here are just *different*. Not all of them, but so many. I don't know why. Maybe it's because this was one of the biggest slaveholding cotton counties along the river. I don't know. I used to think it was ignorance, but I'm starting to see it as willful ignorance, and maybe worse. Their belligerence in public places, their rudeness . . . there's almost a pride in ignorance here. Black employees refuse to wait on white customers in stores. They treat incompetence as though it's some kind of act of civil disobedience. I'm sick of it, Penn. And the black politicians . . . my God. I've watched black aldermen do patently illegal things and then brag about it. They don't care whether something is legal or not."

"White politicians abused the system for years, Caitlin. They just did it in a more subtle way."

"I know that. But is that an excuse for blacks to repeat the abuses of the old system? The system Martin Luther King and Malcolm X died to dismantle?"

"No, but—"

"We talked about the schools before. You want to know the hard truth? The public high school here is ninety-eight percent black. Its budget is five times higher than St. Stephen's—*per stu-*

dent—yet it turns out the second-lowest ACT scores in the nation. Most St. Stephen's graduates score well above the national average, and nearly all of them go on to four-year colleges. The same is true of Immaculate Heart."

"There are black students in both those schools."

"Very few, and they're the exceptions that prove the rule. We talked about the single-mother statistics. You want to guess what color the huge percentage of those mothers are?"

"Caitlin, listen—"

"I know, I know, you're going to give me your great analogy between African-Americans and the American Indian. Well, I don't want to hear it. Too much water's gone under the bridge. I'm tired of hearing about slavery and Reconstruction. *Brown v. Board of Education* was almost fifty years ago, Penn. What's wrong with this picture? How obvious does it have to get before people admit the truth?"

"Which is?"

"The system is broken! And one of the reasons it's broken down here is that it's largely run by and for black people. They simply do not place a high cultural value on education, and I'm not going to pretend otherwise any longer."

I can't believe it. Like so many Yankee transplants, Caitlin has had a dramatic change of heart on the issue of race. But though I've seen it before, I would never have expected it from her. "That's a pretty racist view, Caitlin."

"I'm not a racist," she asserts. "I'm a realist."

"If I said those things, I'd be labeled a racist. Does being from Boston make it all right for you to espouse those views?"

Her fork jangles on her plate "I'm not some spoiled dilettante, okay? That's what I was five years ago, when I got here. Now I have a personal stake in this issue." She takes my hand again and squeezes with urgency. "Let them have this town, Penn. They want their turn on top? Give it to them. Let Shad Johnson turn this beautiful little city into another Fayette. You can't stop it anyway. Not even if you're mayor. Maybe after they run it down to nothing, they'll learn something about running things."

"What's that?"

"That you have to give a damn. You have to sacrifice. You have to work."

"This from the child of a multimillionaire?"

Her eyes flash with anger. "You think my father didn't work to build what he has? You think I haven't worked?"

"Calm down. Of course he did. But he did it in a different context. He did it with certain advantages of law, capital, and . . . frankly, the old-boy network."

Caitlin shakes her head in exasperation as the waiter delivers our entrées. Her blackened catfish smokes on the plate, and my duck looks perfectly seared. The only problem is that I'm no longer hungry. After the waiter leaves, I say, "Well, at least I know where you stand now."

She puts her hands together as though praying. "Don't do this, Penn. Let us have a life somewhere else. Someplace where this conflict doesn't have to be at the center of our daily lives."

I point at her plate. "Are you going to eat?"

She looks down at her catfish and grimaces. "I know you hate everything I've said. If I were the person I was five years ago, I'd be screaming invective at the person I am now. To someone with no experience of this place, I sound like a native redneck. But there's no teacher like experience."

"Why don't we change the subject while we eat?"

Caitlin nods, then lifts her fork and breaks off a piece of fish.

"We can talk about anything but race, politics, or Drew's murder case," I say.

Her eyes flick up at my last words.

"Don't," I warn her.

"Penn, what's going on? We worked together all through the Del Payton case. I helped you with your investigation, and you fed me parts of the story."

"That was a different situation."

"Was it? Or was it just that in that case you could exploit me in return?"

I hate to admit it, but she might be right.

"Just tell me this," she says. "Is the possibility that you might run for mayor what kept you from representing Drew?"

I sigh heavily. "Probably so."

A deep sadness fills her eyes. "You're becoming a politician already."

"No. A realist."

"I was afraid you didn't represent him because you thought he'd killed Kate."

"No."

"Good. I'm glad." She forks a small piece of catfish into her mouth. "The seasoning is perfect on this. Wow."

"You can't get it like that in Boston."

Caitlin rolls her eyes.

"What do you think about Drew and Kate?" I ask. "Not the case—their relationship."

She takes a long drink of wine. "I understand it. They both got something they wanted—maybe even needed—from the relationship."

"What did Drew get?"

"The adoration of a beautiful and brilliant young girl. He got to break Thomas Wolfe's rule and go home again. And he got the possibility of a whole new life with a person a lot like himself. That's probably a more powerful rush than heroin to a guy like Drew." Caitlin smiles strangely. "Can you imagine the ecstasy he must have felt making love to Kate? I mean, that's like *evolutionary nirvana*. You know?"

No, I don't, I think, as an image of Mia flashes behind my eyes. "What did Kate get out of it?"

"Apart from the obvious? The Freudian thing?"

"You mean Drew as father figure?"

"Sure," Caitlin says, laughing. "Kate's dad left the family when she was six—something she shares with Mia Burke, by the way. I don't think Mia ever even knew her father."

"No. He left when Mia was two."

"All love is transactional by nature," Caitlin says, chewing thoughtfully. "The boost to Kate's self-image must have been enormous. Being wanted by Drew didn't just make her feel loved—it made her feel *worth* being loved. You can't overestimate the value of that to an adolescent girl. And of course she got other benefits. Her intimacy with Drew probably gave her a five-year jump on her classmates in real-world relationships."

"It sounds like you don't really have a problem with what happened."

Caitlin shrugs. "I know people get all bent out of shape about this kind of affair, but what do they expect? Half the models we see in magazines are sixteen or seventeen years old. Ad agencies dress them up like twenty- and thirty-year-olds, but that's just costume. The truth is, no woman over twenty-three can look like those models. That kind of perfection is the province of late adolescence. So we hold up these perfect little girls to the world as the zenith of desirability, and what happens? Duh. Men desire them, and women get depressed because they can't attain their perfection. It's pathetic. It says so much about who we are as a society."

I finally take my first bite of duck.

"The thing is," Caitlin goes on, "men like Drew—men who are rich or famous or still handsome and charismatic—they can actually possess girls like that. I give Kate credit, too—she wasn't some bimbo who couldn't balance a checkbook. She was accepted to Harvard, for God's sake. But still, she would have paid a price in the end. Even if she wasn't murdered. And so would Drew."

"Isn't there a price to be paid in every relationship?"

She gives me a wry look. "Point taken."

"I didn't mean us."

"But it's true." Caitlin wags her finger at me. "No sugarcoating."

She's silent for a bit, but I can tell she's thinking. "You know," she says, "one thing you might bring up in Drew's defense is the fact that he had very little choice of partners."

"What do you mean?"

"I'm talking about his affair with Kate, not the murder. After the economic downturn here, the middle class *vanished*. There simply aren't any single women between thirty and forty here. Not the kind Drew would be interested in. The bright women in this town of that age are married or divorced. And if you're looking for brilliant ones, forget it. To start fresh, he almost had to go with someone as young as Kate, because girls like that leave here at eighteen and never come back."

Caitlin is right, although her argument would probably offend every woman on the jury.

"I mean," she goes on, "who the hell would you be dating if I hadn't shown up here?"

I don't even want to think about that. I put down my fork and look into her eyes. "Earlier you said that you couldn't imagine being with anyone else but me."

"That's right."

"*Are* you with anyone else? When you're away, I mean."

She looks at me with disbelief. "Absolutely not. I'd never do that to you." She starts to take a sip of wine, then stops with her glass poised in midair. "Are *you?*"

"No. Not even close."

She watches me a little longer, then drinks her wine. After she swallows, she takes a bite of stuffed potato and says, "Mia's in love with you, by the way."

A lump of duck sticks in my throat. "What?"

"You haven't realized that yet? I saw it through your window in five minutes. I'm not saying she knows what love is, just that she *thinks* she's in love. So, for all practical purposes, she is."

"And I should do what about this?"

Caitlin looks up at me, her eyes inscrutable. "Be careful. We were just discussing the lack of available partners. Drew is a handy object lesson."

"Jesus."

"No evolutionary nirvana for you, buster."

I take her hand and smile. "*You're* evolutionary nirvana for me."

She smiles with genuine pleasure. "I am ten years younger than you, old man."

I laugh so loudly that the waiter sticks his head into the room. I motion for him to leave us alone.

"So, are we sleeping together or not?" Caitlin asks in a casual voice. "I miss it."

"Do you?"

Her voice drops in pitch but becomes richer somehow. "This is the longest I've gone without sex in years. So anytime you're ready, you let me know, okay?"

"Okay."

She gives me one of her feline smiles. "Couldn't we declare détente and return to hostilities in the morning?"

I reach out and take her hand.

"Finish your duck," she says. "Annie's waiting for us, and I don't want the movie to take all night."

Two hours later, I'm sitting in the glow of the flat-panel television in my home theater, a converted guest room on the first floor. Annie has nestled between Caitlin and me, her eyes glued to the television as Nemo swims brightly across the screen. Above Annie's head, my fingers are threaded into the soft hair at the base of Caitlin's neck. The last few minutes of our dinner at the Castle seemed so natural, they could have happened before any of our tensions came into being. But despite the promise of sex in the air, something seems wrong.

It's been too long since Caitlin and I made love. I miss it at least as much as she, and yet . . . something is short-circuiting the desire I should feel for her. The pessimism in her dinner speech really hit me wrong, and some of what she said actually offended me. Caitlin truly was a liberal when she arrived in Natchez, and she routinely chastised me for being too conservative. But now it seems that her liberal "convictions" weren't convictions at all, but rather easy opinions based on the lectures of Ivy League professors. After a few years in the South, she's ready to give up on racial harmony and flee to more "enlightened"—read homogenous—environs.

As for my sexual desire, that's been running in overdrive for weeks now. Like Drew, I have consciously turned away from many women willing to ease that tension. Opportunity is always present in a town like this, where wives easily become bored with their limited routines. Every day those women present to the world a perfectly coiffed and manicured lady, but inside they're like captive panthers pacing their cages. I haven't yet sought solace there during Caitlin's absences, but tonight, with Caitlin actually lying beside me in anticipation of sex, I don't want solace here either. It's a predicament, but my solution is simple and time tested—though never by me.

I'll simply fall asleep.

I don't even think Caitlin will mind that much. She's checked her cell phone for text messages a half dozen times during the movie. And no matter how understanding I want to be, that irritates me. But these are small issues. My real dilemma is simple, my choice a stark one: love or duty.

A woman or a town?

CHAPTER
29

Sonny Cross's funeral is very different from those of Kate Townsend and Chris Vogel. It's held not in a church, but downtown at McDonough's Funeral Home. The benches reserved for the family are filled, but there are several empty rows at the back of the funeral parlor. Many mourners in the pews are cops, most of them in uniform. Sonny's flag-draped casket stands at the head of the center aisle, and a picture of him as a much younger man stands on an easel to the right of it.

The service is conducted by the elderly Baptist pastor of the Second Creek Baptist Church, one of the most rural white churches in the county, a strong Klan area in the bad old days. He preaches a sermon of anger, not love, venting "righteous outrage" at the loss of a man who gave his life so that the rest of us might live in peace. I don't care for the pastor's tone, but I can't argue with his sentiments. When he begins the eulogy, I discover something I didn't know: Sonny Cross served as an infantryman in Vietnam, and was decorated for battlefield gallantry. I knew the man for four years, but he never once mentioned this. I never would have guessed it, either. He must have been drafted right out of high school.

As I ponder Sonny's life and death, it strikes me that, whatever his prejudices, he was one of the quiet heroes of this country. He never made much money; he rarely if ever got his picture in the paper; he never asked for special recognition. He simply worked hard to protect the ideals he was raised to believe in, and in the end, when called upon by fate, he gave the last full measure of devotion. When a plain woman with waist-length hair rises from the front pew and begins to sing "Amazing Grace" without accompaniment, I realize there are tears in my eyes.

The singer is wearing a cotton dress that looks hand-sewn from a Simplicity pattern. As she sings about toils and snares, I relive the moments when the Asian face was illuminated in the window of the Lexus, when the holes appeared in the door below that face, and then me turning and seeing Sonny standing in his combat stance with his pistol, returning fire in the face of an automatic weapon. Sonny Cross was no movie actor with nothing to fear, but a man of flesh and blood facing his last seconds on earth with remarkable courage. That brave last stand was what sent the Lexus fleeing down the road. In retrospect, it almost certainly saved my life.

And what did Sonny Cross say as he lay dying on the ground? Did he scream, "Call an ambulance!" Did he beg me not to let him die? No. He told me to check on his sons, to make sure they hadn't been hit. Then he told me to make sure that the wife he'd divorced knew that he was sorry, that he was thinking of her at the end. Today those boys and that ex-wife sit in the wooden "family box" at the side of the funeral parlor, their faces rigid with the stoic resignation of Appalachian hill people. Only the youngest boy has the glitter of tears in his eyes. There's a man in the box, too, elderly but big, with the rawboned hands and red skin of a day laborer. His face is a more weathered likeness of Sonny's. The father, I'll bet.

When the hymn is done, the pastor motions for the pallbearers to come forward. Eight deputies rise as one and lift the casket from its bier. Sheriff Billy Byrd stands at their head, his rigid jaw making plain that he's more than ready to deliver the righteous retribution that the pastor demanded during his service. As the casket leaves the parlor by a side door, I rise with the rest of the mourners and walk out into the sunlight.

Unlike the City Cemetery, Greenlawn Memorial Park has existed for only fifty years. It's a more conventional graveyard, sited on rolling hills in the blue-collar area of Morgantown Road. People of all denominations may be buried here, so long as they're white. There are probably more Baptist "residents" here than anything else, originating from the staggering aggregation of Baptist churches in the state. It always struck me as telling that Mississippi has the highest per capita number of churches in the nation but the lowest literacy rate. Yet somehow, out of this strange marriage of extremes, we produce some of the greatest artists in the world.

About thirty people have gathered around Sonny's open grave: family members, cops, an honor guard from Camp Shelby. There's no pretense here. The pastor quotes some scripture; the honor guard fires its salute—seven rifles, three shattering volleys; then, as the echoes fade, a strange new sound floats across the hills.

Bagpipes.

I turn toward the sound and squint. Standing on a hill about sixty yards away is a lone piper wearing a tartan kilt and a black beret. Again the tune is "Amazing Grace," but this time it carries a stark and lonely beauty that accomplishes what words and gunfire cannot: it pierces our veil of denial and makes us one with the departed, even as we find comfort in the sound. When the piper finishes, the honor guard folds the flag and delivers it to the mother of Sonny Cross's children. She may be his ex-wife, but no one is arguing legalities today. True widowhood has little to do with the law.

The crowd breaks up swiftly, and soon only the family is left by the grave. The big, red-faced man stands talking to Sonny's widow. He's wearing an ill-fitting suit, almost certainly the only one he owns. Cross's sons stand a few yards away, looking awkward and uncomfortable as they watch the cars in the lane drive away. As I study them, the oldest of the two seems to recognize me. He lifts his hand in a little wave, then walks toward me. I meet him halfway and offer my hand.

"You were there when my dad died," he says.

"That's right, Sonny," I say.

"They call me Junior."

"Probably not after today. I think you're going to be Sonny from now on."

A look of utter seriousness takes possession of his face. Then, slowly, pride replaces it.

"I know this is tough," I tell him. "My wife died of cancer, and she was a lot younger than your dad."

This gets the boy's attention. "Really?"

"Yeah. It takes a long time to get over something like this. In some ways you never really do. But it gets better."

The boy bites his lip and kicks at a stick on the ground.

"If you guys need any help, I want you to call me. My name is Penn Cage. I'll be glad to help you out. That's what your dad would have wanted."

"Okay."

"Has the sheriff asked after you boys? Is the department doing anything for your mother?"

Anger tightens little Sonny's face. "The sheriff's a son of a bitch. He's making out like my dad did something wrong. Not in public, you know, but with us. He said my dad took things from work he wasn't supposed to take."

I swallow hard and try to hide my interest. "I don't think your dad respected the sheriff much when it came to police work."

Sonny nods firmly. "That's why he worked alone so much. He told me that."

My pulse quickens. This eleven-year-old knows much more than I would have expected. "Sonny, did you know I was working with your dad?"

He nods again.

"He told me it was up to me to finish the job. To catch the guys he was trying to get. Do you understand?"

"Yes, sir."

"I know the sheriff has probably asked you what I'm about to ask. But I'm not the sheriff, you know what I mean?"

"I think I do."

"I figure your dad must have had a special place where he kept his work stuff."

The barest hint of a smile lights the boy's eyes. "They been searching our place for two whole days."

"But they didn't find anything?"

"Nope."

I start to speak again, but a deep voice overwhelms my own. It's the red-faced man from the funeral. "You boys get back to your mama," he orders.

Sonny and his brother instantly scamper toward their mother. This man is obviously accustomed to being obeyed. He walks toward me with a slow gait, his blue eyes focused on mine. I hold out my hand as he reaches me, and he shakes it carefully, like a man who knows he could hurt someone by simply closing his hand.

"Hello, Mr. Cage," he says.

"Are you Sonny's father?"

"That's right. Your daddy was my doctor back when I worked for Triton Battery."

I'm thankful for this. I've yet to meet a former patient who doesn't have fond memories of my father. "I can't tell you how sorry I am about what happened to Sonny."

Mr. Cross takes a slow breath, then lets out a deep sigh. "You were with him when he died, they said. That right?"

"Yes, sir. I was."

"Did it really happen the way you told the sheriff?"

"Yes."

"Sonny done his duty?"

"Mr. Cross, I never saw anything like it."

The big man grimaces, then nods twice as though settling something in his own mind. He's shown no more emotion than a man making sure his son finished cutting someone's grass as promised, but I sense that inside he is boiling with emotions that will never be outwardly expressed.

"I saw you talking to Sonny, Junior," he says.

"He was saying that his father didn't like the sheriff much."

Mr. Cross pokes at the dirt with his booted foot. "Billy Byrd's a showboat. He cares more about newspaper headlines than he does about enforcing the law. That's one way to be, I reckon. It's not my way. Sonny's neither."

"I think you're right."

"Sonny told me you was working with him."

"That's right."

"He said you put a lot of bad outlaws away in Texas."

"I did my best."

"And now you write books?"

"Yes, sir."

The big man sniffs but asks no more questions.

"Mr. Cross, as Sonny lay dying in his driveway, he asked me to finish the job for him. I mean to do that, if I can."

"Go on."

"I think Sonny kept a lot hidden from Sheriff Byrd. I think he did that because he knew the sheriff was likely to damage his investigations. But if I'm going to do what Sonny asked me to do, I need whatever evidence he had. Now, I know there were some surveillance videotapes, and I imagine he had notebooks, still photographs, and maybe even a computer. I'm also sure that Sheriff Byrd has been pressing you about this. I just want you to know the sheriff is no friend of mine. In fact, to be frank, I consider him an enemy."

Mr. Cross stares at me in silence for some time. Then he says, "You know where I live?"

"No, sir."

"Way out Kingston Road. Almost where you turn to cut through to Liberty Road. I got thirty acres out there."

I wait for him to continue.

"We're having some family out there. Some food, some whiskey, you know the drill. You ought to ride out there."

"Now?"

"It's up to you. But Sonny spent quite a bit of time out there of an evening. I'd take the boys fishing or riding the four-wheeler, and he'd work. Might be worth your time to ride out."

My heart thumps in my chest. "I'll do that."

"Just past Second Creek Baptist Church. Mailbox has a wrought-iron bronco on it. You can't miss it."

"I'll be there."

The bucking bronco mailbox marks a dirt driveway that leads back into the thick woods that border Kingston Road. On the way in, I pass two ponds and a baseball backstop. Then I see several pickup trucks parked before a simple frame house. I hate to interrupt a family gathering after a funeral, but Mr. Cross did invite me to come. Thankfully, as I park my Saab behind a massive Dodge truck, the big man opens a screen door and lumbers out to meet me.

"Have any trouble finding it?"

"No, it was just like you said."

Mr. Cross changes direction and walks toward a green Ford pickup. "Let's take a little ride. My knees are too bad to do much walking these days."

I walk around his pickup and climb into the passenger seat.

Mr. Cross drives onto the lawn and circles behind his house. The backyard looks about as I expected. There's a Kubota tractor under a tin shed with some fig trees growing beside it, a glitter-painted bass boat on a trailer half covered by a blue tarp, and plastic hummingbird feeders hanging from almost every tree. Mr. Cross steers the truck into a couple of ruts and begins climbing a grassy hill. He obviously doesn't feel talkative, so I say nothing. As we crest the hill, I spy a stand of trees beside yet another pond. Descending toward it, I make out a small camper trailer parked under the trees.

"Sonny liked it out here," Mr. Cross says. "I bought this place after Triton downsized me in 'eighty-six. Cost me my severance pay and all my stock options, but it was worth it." He pulls the truck up beside the trailer but leaves the engine running. "This is where Sonny did most of his work."

"Is there electricity down here?"

"Yes, indeed. Put it in myself. There's a satellite dish on the south side of the trailer. Sonny had to have that damn Internet out here. You'd know more about that than I would."

The trailer looks like it should be sold for scrap, but maybe it's nicer on the inside.

"I need to get back to the folks," says Mr. Cross. "You take as long as you need."

"Is it locked?"

"Never has been. No need out here. Protected by Smith and Wesson."

Of course. "What if I find something I need?"

"Take it. Take anything you want. This was Sonny's business, and now it's yours. I reckon I ought to give this stuff to the sheriff, but I just don't believe he'd do the right thing with it. You're welcome to come and go as you please. Just honk your horn as you pass the house driving down here." Mr. Cross offers me his hand. "Good luck to you, Mr. Cage. And keep your eyes open for those bastards who shot Sonny."

"I will." I shake the giant hand, then climb out of the truck.

Mr. Cross immediately drives away, leaving me in the shadow of the trailer. It's an ugly thing, the kind of rig you tow behind a pickup truck. It was probably built to sleep two people, but there's only one way to know.

The trailer's door has almost no weight. I pull it open and step up into the unit.

I expected a bad smell, but a little mildew is the only odor that greets me. The interior of the trailer is a remarkable sight. The camper's beds have been converted into worktables. A metal filing cabinet stands against one wall, and a computer glows on a Formica countertop that apparently served as Sonny's desk. The yellow kitchen cabinets have had their doors removed and now function as bookshelves. Most of the books are criminal justice texts, but there are a couple of loose-leaf binders on the right side of the bottom shelf. Two cameras rest on the top shelf: a digital still camera with a telephoto lens, and a small Sony video camera. When I check the drawers in the kitchenette, I catch my breath. Rows of MiniDV tapes line the drawer bottoms, and they seem to be organized by date.

Surveillance tapes.

I can hardly contain myself. Probably the best thing to do is pack the tapes, the computer, and the binders into my car and take them home to study. If I stay here, I risk Mr. Cross changing his mind, or some other family member challenging my presence. I've seen enough families fight over property after a death to spend more time here than necessary.

Two steps out of the trailer, my cell phone rings. It's Caitlin.

I almost don't answer. I don't want to lie about being here, but Caitlin wouldn't be calling if it wasn't important.

"Hey," I answer.

"Steel yourself, Penn."

My first thought is Annie, then my father's weak coronary vessels. "Tell me."

"The grand jury just indicted Drew for capital murder."

There's a roaring in my ears that sounds like breaking surf. It's only blood, of course, pumping under the enormous pressure generated by my clenching heart. Why the intense reaction? I knew this was coming. And I've heard much more devastating news in my life: verdicts rendered in death penalty cases, my father telling me that my wife died during the night. Yet somehow I sense that this indictment will set in motion unprecedented pain and suffering. Why, I don't know. Maybe because Shad is trying Drew for the wrong reasons. Or maybe—

"Penn? Are you there?"

"Yes."

"You sound out of breath. What are you doing?"

"That took me by surprise. I didn't think it would happen this soon."

"Me, either. Where are you?"

I close my eyes. Caitlin cannot know about the trailer or Sonny's private stash of evidence. "Talking to the Cross family. I'm going home soon, though."

She says nothing. She senses something wrong, but she hasn't enough facts to work out what it is. "Penn—"

"Don't worry, babe. We'll talk later, when we have some time. I need to finish with these people now."

"Okay, but call me back."

"I will." I pocket my phone and start jogging up the hill toward my car. I need to pack Sonny's things and stash them in my floor safe as soon as possible.

Then I need to talk to Quentin Avery.

CHAPTER

30

For the first time since I met Quentin Avery, his face is taut with anxiety. The lawyer is sitting across from me in the main room of his penthouse suite at the Eola, his artificial foot resting on the floor, the bare stump of his lower leg crossed over his left knee.

"This is fast," Quentin ruminates, "really fast. You say Shad hand-carried the indictment over to the circuit clerk?"

"That's what Caitlin told me." I spoke to Caitlin by phone again on my way from my house to the Eola, and she filled me in on the most recent developments of the case. "There are two circuit judges in this town. The system ensures randomness by simple rotation, assigning each judge every other case that's filed. The problem is, every lawyer in town knows that. If a lawyer wants a particular judge for a case, he carries three cases to the clerk's office. The first case he files is a stalking horse. If that case is assigned to the judge he doesn't want, the lawyer immediately files the case he wants to steer, and it goes to the judge he does want. But if the stalking horse goes to the judge that the lawyer *does* want, he has to file all three cases to steer the one he cares about to the right judge."

"The true bills returned by a grand jury are normally filed as a group," Quentin says. "But that's more a matter of convenience than anything."

"If Shad carried Drew's indictment over personally, he carried two other cases with him. You can bet your good foot that he's already steered Drew's case to Judge Arthel Minor."

"Then you can bet your ass that Arthel will schedule Drew's case in the docket for the current term. The only question is how soon will it be."

"Four weeks or less," I reckon. "And now that Mayor Jones has stepped down, I look for it sooner rather than later."

"Any sooner than two weeks," says Quentin, "and even the man in the street will know Drew's trial has nothing to do with justice."

"I'm not sure Shad's worried about that. You said it yourself, his concern is the special election. That means making good on his promise to make the system equal, i.e., to nail a rich white man. That's what will get Shad a unified black vote. I expect Judge Minor to move as fast as legally possible."

Quentin nods slowly. "Why is the white sheriff lined up with Shad and Judge Minor? Did Shad promise him the black vote in the next election?"

"I don't think Shad can guarantee that. I'm not sure what Billy Byrd hopes to get out of this, but it's something. You can bank on that."

"We should try to find out. It might give us an advantage."

"I will."

"When will we know about the trial date?"

"Caitlin has reporters at the circuit clerk's office and Judge Minor's chambers. If Arthel sets a trial date today, we'll know about it."

A trace of a smile touches Quentin's lips. "Kind of handy having the publisher of the newspaper on your side, isn't it?"

"It's a two-edged sword."

He nods thoughtfully. "What the hell is Shad thinking? I know he has a hard-on to indict Dr. Elliott, but it's not enough for him to want it bad. Something happened today that persuaded the grand jury to indict."

"The DNA must be back," I conclude. "That's the only explanation."

Quentin's eyes narrow, and then he nods slowly. "If you pay a hefty rush fee, a private lab with a good sample can do the analysis in seventy-two hours."

"You're right."

"Would Shad pay for that?"

"Hell, yes. And the timing just works."

"That's it, then," says Quentin. "One of the samples matched Dr. Elliott, and that convinced the grand jury to indict."

"I think there's more. If Shad paid a private lab for a rush job, he would have had both samples analyzed, the vaginal and the rectal." I close my eyes and try not to focus on any particular line of reasoning. "That means he's got the data on our mystery man as well. The vaginal sample."

"What could Shad learn from that?" Quentin asks. "They couldn't ID that sperm without someone to compare it to. Do you think it matched the Sayers boy? Or the fishermen maybe?"

A small epiphany sends a tingle along my forearms. I open my eyes. "No. What Shad could learn from that second semen sample is that our mystery man *wasn't black*. Ergo, that semen was *not* deposited by Cyrus White."

"Son of a bitch," Quentin breathes. "Son of a *bitch!*"

"There goes your reasonable doubt." I take a sip of coffee from the room service tray on the table between us.

Quentin closes his eyes and rubs the stump of his ankle. "Maybe . . . but maybe not."

"Quentin, yesterday you told me DNA was subtle science. I know juries can get bored with technical testimony. But if I'm right, this science is pretty simple and compelling. *A black man didn't rape Kate Townsend.* That's a message that black jury members will love to hear. And the location of the crime scene away from Brightside Manor already screwed your chance to paint a scenario in which Kate was murdered there by Cyrus."

"Goddamn it," Quentin mutters. "What *do* we have that links Kate Townsend to Cyrus?"

"I can testify that Sonny Cross told me he saw her visit Cyrus at Brightside Manor while he was conducting surveillance operations."

"That's hearsay, unless you have videotape."

"We may have the actual surveillance tape in our possession, but I'm not sure yet. I haven't had time to go through the tapes."

"That's your first priority. Do we have anything else?"

An image of Kate's journal rises in my mind, but I'm still not prepared to reveal its existence. "Not at this time." I stand and walk over to the window. "Given what we've deduced here, does the second semen sample still look like reasonable doubt to you?"

"Shad's case is still circumstantial," Quentin says firmly. "Even Dr. Elliott's semen in the girl's rectum doesn't place him at the crime scene."

"But his car parked in that vacant lot damn near does. Shad's case may be circumstantial, but it just might be strong enough for a conviction. I would have gone to court with it in Houston."

Quentin takes a sip of coffee and makes a face. "There are only two possibilities for disaster. One, the police find physical evidence that links Dr. Elliott to the crime scene. Two, they find out that Dr. Elliott had the victim scoring dope for his wife."

"Which brings up an even thornier question. Do you plan to put Drew on the stand?"

Quentin closes his eyes like a man experiencing deep internal pain.

"If they tie him to that crime scene, and he hasn't admitted that he was there, the jury won't believe a thing he says after that."

"That's a chance I'm going to have to take," says Quentin. "I'm not putting him on the stand to tell the jury he found that girl dead and didn't report it to anybody."

"Have you discussed this with Drew?"

"We haven't gotten that far."

"I'll bet you any amount of money that Drew will demand to tell the jury his side of the story."

Quentin goes absolutely still. "Tell me he's not that stupid."

"If he's innocent, that's what he'll do."

"If the police somehow tie him to the murder scene, Shad will have to let us know that before the trial. He has to, according to the rules of discovery. If that happens, I'll still have time to put Drew on the stand and let him tell his story. At least that's a margin of safety."

"Is it? You said yourself that Shad would break the rules."

"If he withholds evidence, it's grounds for a mistrial."

I mull this over. "You're forgetting that Sheriff Byrd is on Shad's side. What if Byrd were to pretend that his men found such evidence *during* the trial, and you hadn't admitted Drew was at the scene? You'd be screwed. Quentin, you're going to have to tell the truth. Drew is an innocent man whose adultery made him too afraid to report a murder. You've got to admit he was at the scene from the start."

Quentin gives me a hard look. "That's not the road I want to take."

"Your client may not give you any choice."

The lawyer laughs bitterly. "*Now* I see why you brought me into this case. You know what a knucklehead your friend is."

I'm about to bring up another problem when my cell phone rings. It's Caitlin.

"What's up?"

"Judge Minor just set the trial date," she says. "Next Wednesday."

My blood pressure plummets. "Did he make any official statement to the media?"

"No. I got this from a guy in the circuit clerk's office."

"Did you have to flirt to get it?"

"A little." She laughs. "This is bad for Drew, isn't it?"

"Not necessarily. Call me if you get anything else." I hang up and set my phone on the coffee table.

Quentin watches me expectantly.

"Next Wednesday."

His mouth falls open. "You're shitting me."

"Wednesday, baby."

"I'll give Shad credit. That little son of a bitch plays hardball."

"I'm afraid we've got another problem. As soon as Drew was

indicted by the grand jury, that put him into the state system. That means he has to be transferred from police custody to the sheriff's department. The county jail. My guess is, Sheriff Byrd will move him today. He hasn't yet, because Chief Logan promised to warn me about any problems. But we need to warn Drew."

"Worst-case scenario," Quentin says.

"Billy Byrd locks Drew into an interrogation room without either of us there and sweats him under the lights."

"Drew doesn't strike me as the type who would crack under that kind of pressure."

"He won't crack, but his desire to explain his innocence might cause him to make statements against his interest."

Quentin shakes his head. "Do you really think he'd talk to the sheriff at this point without me present?"

"In a word? Yes."

"Goddamn it." Quentin reaches down and begins strapping on his artificial foot. "I thought doctors were supposed to save lives, not put you in an early grave."

"I appreciate you doing this, Quentin."

The old lawyer looks up at me, his eyes curious. "Tell me this. Now that Doug Jones has stepped down, are you going to announce for mayor?"

I can't help but laugh. "My significant other is not in favor of the idea."

Quentin finishes with the limb and sits up. "Who wears the pants in your family, man?"

"That depends on the issue."

"Well, no matter what you do, Shad has to wait until the end of the trial to announce. That's why he's rushing this circus, and why I've got less than a week to prepare for trial."

"Yep."

Quentin grins. "Ain't politics something?"

"Do you still feel the same about Cyrus White?"

"What do you mean?"

"You want me not to find him?"

Quentin folds his arms and fixes his eyes on me with unsettling intensity. "Do you really think Drew is innocent?"

"I do."

"Then I'll tell you what I want." He picks up his car keys and jabs them at me. "I want you to find me that girl's killer. Fast."

CHAPTER

31

At just after 9 p.m., I reenter Quentin's suite, this time with Mia and a male friend of hers in tow. Quentin and Doris are sleeping in a smaller room down the hall, so that this one can be used for business at all hours. Caitlin is spending the night at my house with Annie. I feel guilty about asking her, but it was the only way I could free Mia to work with me and also be sure that Caitlin wouldn't discover what we were doing.

Mia's friend is a high school sophomore who dresses like a New York investment banker. The only openly gay student at St. Stephen's, Lucien Morse is as slender as a sword and has short, glistening black hair. I met him only ten minutes ago, but I know one thing already—his eyes don't remain still for longer than three seconds.

Lucien is here to hack Kate Townsend's USB flash drives.

I'd planned to overnight the drives to a computer security firm in Houston, but when Mia heard me making the arrangements, she told me I could save at least a day by having a friend of hers hack them. I was skeptical at first, but she assured me that this particular tenth-grader was capable of doing the job. Mia's price for arranging this service? That she be allowed to see what's on the drives after they're hacked. Desperate to see the contents as quickly as possible, I agreed. Computer hackers aren't thick on the ground in Natchez, Mississippi.

Lucien Morse isn't short on confidence. When I opened my leather portfolio downstairs and showed him what I had, he rolled his eyes and asked me where the nearest computer was. Now that we're in the suite, I point to the Dell that one of Quentin's young lawyers installed here yesterday. Lucien walks to the machine and plugs one of the flash drives into a USB port.

"The thing about these little wankers," he says, "is that the security isn't fundamental. It's basically obfuscation. I ought to have it open in less than five minutes."

"Remember," I tell him, "the second you break in, you get up from the monitor and walk away. You don't look at the files. Even if a full-screen picture pops up, you shut your eyes and walk away."

"Touchy, touchy."

"Your payment is dependent on that condition."

"Five hundred dollars?" Lucien says, rapidly tapping at the keyboard. "Right?"

"Five hundred."

"Easy money."

I set my portfolio on the coffee table. It still contains Kate's private journal and Marko Bakic's flash drive. My plan is to have Mia try to put a time line to the list of men and boys in Kate's "hook-ups" lists, but only after Lucien leaves.

"Can we order tea or something?" Mia asks.

"Order whatever you want. Drew's paying for it."

She picks up the hotel phone and dials room service. She starts to order, then stops in midsentence and pulls her cell phone from her jeans pocket. It must have vibrated. She asks the room service clerk to hold on, then checks a text message. Her mouth opens in surprise.

"What?" I ask.

She puts her finger to her lips, then she pulls me into the next room.

"No arguing in front of the children?" Lucien calls.

Mia holds up her phone and shows me the blue LCD screen. It reads: *Rave 2nite. Square 1 tracetown movie theater. Heard marko coming with KAs from ole miss and killer d.j. from memphis. Leaving now with stacey.*

"What's Square 1?"

"That's where the first clue will be."

I recall Sonny's description of the complicated security precautions that precede a rave. Kids are prompted by various riddles or poems to drive from place to place until they're sure no one is following them. Then they're told the location of the drug party.

"What do you think?" Mia asks, her eyes sparkling. "You want to go?"

I glance back toward the other room, but what I see in my mind is the LCD screen. *Heard marko coming . . .* "Yes. I want to go."

Mia grins. "Yeah!"

"What about Lucien?"

"He sleeps at school, not at home. For five hundred bucks, he'll come back later."

"I *heard* that," Lucien croons.

"Well?" I ask, walking back into the main room of the suite. "Can you come back later?"

Lucien slaps the Enter key, then stands and steps away from the keyboard. "No need. Job's done."

"You're kidding."

He smiles, revealing small white teeth. "I don't kid about work."

"I gave you two drives."

"That was the second one. View them at your leisure. No password, no problems, and yes, I take cash."

I take out my wallet and remove five one-hundred-dollar bills. "I'd like you to look at one other drive, Lucien."

"No problem. It'll cost extra, though."

"I pay for results." I open the portfolio on the coffee table and remove the flash drive I stole from Marko's garage apartment. This one's a Sony, not a Lexar, but Lucien seems unconcerned.

"We really need to go," Mia says.

"What's the hurry?" asks Lucien.

I give Mia a pointed look. "This is important."

Lucien takes the drive and slides it into the USB port. Mia stands on tiptoe and whispers in my ear, "The clue won't be there long. If we're late, we'll miss the party. And Marko."

"We really need this. And Lucien's fast."

"Not this time," he says. "There's a separate encryption program hiding whatever's on this drive. It looks like military-grade stuff. Where did you get this?"

I should have known Marko would take precautions. What did Paul tell me? In Sarajevo, Marko became the consummate survivor. "You don't need to know that. Can you hack it or not?"

"Maybe."

"How long?"

"Maybe an hour, maybe a year. If I took it home—"

"You can't take it home."

"Then I guess I'll see what I can do."

"We'll be back in a couple of hours."

"Can I order room service?" Lucien asks with a smile. "I missed supper."

"Get whatever you want."

The smile turns beatific. "I hope they have a wine list."

Riding north on Highway 61 in the passenger seat of Mia's Honda Accord, I'm scrunched underneath a St. Stephen's letter blanket that Mia pulled from her trunk—to facilitate my "being shady," as she calls it. For the past forty-five minutes, I've been living a scene out of a screwball comedy from the 1960s, updated with touches from 1970s car-chase movies. After Mia read the doggerel verse taped to the ticket window of the old theater, we joined a convoy of jacked-up pickup trucks, handed-down family sedans, and high-end foreign sports coupes. These vehicles charged from place to place to find and unravel successive clues, dodging in and out of traffic and smashing beer bottles against road signs. My heart nearly stopped when I saw one high school boy leap from the bed of one pickup truck to another at seventy miles per hour.

Dave Matthews is playing softly on Mia's CD player. She drives with one hand, while the other sends and receives text messages on her cell phone in an Olympic-caliber display of manual dexterity. Using the LED penlight on my key ring, I've been reviewing Kate's "hook-ups" lists in her journal, and asking Mia to give me a time line on the names. Mia has laughed at some names and dropped her jaw at others. One made her curse and tense in her seat. The story behind this was simple enough.

"Kate stole my boyfriend in ninth grade," she told me. "Chris Anthony. It was just after she got back from England. It wouldn't have been so bad, but she did it behind my back. They saw each other for like six weeks before someone told me. When I confronted Kate, she wouldn't even discuss it. She acted like I was a total loser. Beneath her notice. I know that sounds trivial, but it hurt. We didn't speak for over a year."

"Is that the root of your competitiveness?" I asked.

Mia kept her eyes doggedly on the road. "Part of it, I guess. Doesn't matter now, does it?"

Mia knew almost every name on Kate's hook-ups lists, and the picture that emerged from her time analysis was that Kate had been promiscuous during junior high and the early part of high school—before she began having intercourse—but beginning in the summer before the eleventh grade, she'd dated Steve Sayers exclusively. Two of the names Mia didn't know had notations beside them indicating they had occurred while Kate was living in England. Only two names seemed remotely worth checking out as people Kate might have "cheated on" Drew to see, and thereby become the object of jealousy that led to murder.

Mia got her shocks from Kate's "rejected" and "rejected by" lists. The fact that Kate had tried to seduce a girl named Laurel Goodrich made Mia gasp. The adults on Kate's list didn't surprise her, though. She agreed with Kate's assessment of Mr. Dawson, the religion teacher, as a "perv." The rejected "Dr. Davenport" turned out to be a psychologist who had commuted to Natchez for part of one year. The "Dr. Lewis" who had apparently rebuffed Kate's advances was her longtime psychiatrist, who practiced in New Orleans. "Mr. Marbury" was a gymnastics coach who had worked with the cheerleaders for two summers. Mia seemed quite happy that he'd refused Kate's attentions. When I read Wade Anders's name from the list, Mia wrinkled her brow and turned to me.

"Kate says Coach Anders came on to her? Not the other way around?"

"Well, he's under the 'rejected' column."

"Huh."

"What do you think about Coach Anders?"

"Wade's okay. He's never hit on me."

"He told me a lot of girls have come on to him in his office."

Mia nodded. "Some girls think he's hot—or they did before he gained that weight, anyway." She laughed softly. "He did say something about my butt once."

"What?"

"No way."

"Come on."

"*God.*" She bowed her head as though mortified. "He said I had a ghetto bootie."

I grabbed the wheel to keep us on the road. "Meaning?"

"You know . . . a butt like a black chick."

I laughed at Mia's expression of mixed embarrassment and amusement. "*Do* you have one?"

"You tell me."

"Yeah, you kind of do."

She burst out laughing.

"It is a good one, though, I'll admit that."

"It better be," she said. "I work on it enough."

Now that we've covered the hook-ups lists, I'm reviewing the other entries in the journal, looking for things Mia might be able to clarify. Her cell phone has chirped a hundred times with text messages, but this time when she checks the phone, she pumps her hand in triumph. "Got it!"

"What?"

"The last square. The party."

"Where is it?"

"Oakfield."

I can't believe it. I figured the rave would happen in the middle of nowhere. Oakfield is an eighty-acre antebellum estate north of town, the site of one of the most beautiful Italianate mansions in the Natchez area. "That's a three-million-dollar house."

Mia glances at me. "Is it?"

"Easily."

"Janie Moffitt's grandparents own it. They're out of town."

"How many kids do you think will be there?" I figure I've already seen forty to fifty en route to the party.

"There were a couple of hundred at the lake party. And with the terrible stuff that's been happening, I have a feeling everybody will come to this one. X gives you that sense of total empathy, you know? Oneness with everybody. I think that's what everyone's looking for right now. Some way to share what they're feeling."

"If I weren't here, would you take Ecstasy tonight?"

Mia glances over at me. "I might take some anyway."

The convoy turns left on Airport Road, which leads into the northwest part of the county. When I was in high school, we held a lot of informal parties under a tin-roofed pavilion near the airport. There was little danger of discovery, since the Natchez airport didn't have commercial service (and still doesn't). But Oakfield is truly high cotton. In California the estate would cost forty million dollars. The convoy slows, then turns onto the narrow lane that leads to the mansion.

"Get down," Mia says. "I see the gate."

The Accord slows to a stop, then creeps forward. From my nearly fetal position, I spy the head of a lion mounted on a tall stone gatepost. Mia jerks the blanket over my head and shoves me toward the floor with surprising strength.

"*Mia!*" yells a male voice. "S'up?"

"You're up, Jamie."

"You all by yourself?"

"As always."

"It's a crime, man."

"Do I get in?"

"Hell, yeah. I want to dance with you. Be careful, though. It's wild down there."

Mia starts to drive off, but Jamie calls, "Hold up!"

She skids to a stop on gravel.

"I almost forgot," Jamie says, giggling. "Don't forget this."

It sounds as though something is changing hands at the window.

"Thanks, Dad," Mia says, and then she drives on.

"What was that?" I ask.

She shoves something under the blanket. "There you go, baby."

I click on my penlight and see a yellow-and-white pacifier in her hand. From my years in Houston, I know the significance of the pacifier. MDMA—or "X"—makes abusers grind their teeth. Ravers use pacifiers to prevent sore jaws the morning after, and also to prevent damage to their teeth.

"*Wow,*" Mia says almost reverently.

"What is it?"

"Look outside. But be careful."

I raise my head above the door frame. The rolling hills of Oakfield are flickering under multicolored spotlights. Tents of various sizes have been set up around the estate, and pounding techno rock rolls down from the mansion atop the hill on our left. Sixty yards ahead, a huge crowd of teenagers dances in front of a lighted stage. Pickup trucks and four-wheelers race over the hills in all directions, ramping into the air while kids in the beds behind scream and laugh.

"Is this how these things usually go?" I ask.

Raucous male laughter followed by a female screech pierces my right ear. As I turn, three naked girls sprint toward Mia's car, chased by two shirtless boys in blue jeans. One of the boys is spraying beer at the girls from a large bottle, while the other shoots at them with a battery-powered water gun. The first girl slams headlong into Mia's right fender, then spins and darts across her headlight beams into the darkness on the other side of the road. A second girl follows, but the third falls laughing to the ground. The two boys fall beside or on top of her.

"No," Mia says softly. "This is not the usual thing." She starts forward again, bringing us closer to the dancing throng. "What do you want me to do?"

"I want to talk to Marko. Will the kids freak out if I get out and walk around this party?"

"They won't freak, but it'll get around that there's somebody old here. They'll probably ask you to leave."

"Park in the dark, then. But put me where I can see the main action."

She turns off the long driveway into a pit of blackness on the left. The Accord bumps up and down, then stops. "You want me to hunt for Marko?" she asks.

"If you're up for it."

"What if I find him? Do I just tell him you want to talk to him?"

Actually, I haven't thought that far ahead. "I don't know."

"Does he know you?"

"He knows me. But if you can get him over this way without letting him know what's up, that would be good."

Mia studies me in the dashboard lights. "You mean pretend that I want to hook up with him."

"If that's not too scary, I guess so. I'll take over as soon as I see you. You could ring my cell to give me a heads-up. One ring and I'll see your ID."

"Okay," she says finally. "But I wouldn't get my hopes up. No-body's seen Marko for two days." She reaches for her door handle.

I take her right wrist and squeeze it. "Thanks, Mia."

"No problem," she says, but she's not smiling.

And then she is gone.

Someone is knocking on my door. I grab for the Browning in my jacket pocket, trying to remember where I am.

"Are you going to shoot me?" Mia asks, sliding into the driver's seat. The smell of alcohol wafts through the car. "You fell asleep, didn't you?"

"I guess so. Sorry."

I didn't tell her I was carrying a gun tonight, but she did give my coat a second look back at the hotel. It's close to seventy degrees outside. "What about Marko?"

"I couldn't find him."

"Has anyone seen him?"

"A lot of people saw him earlier. He was apparently up onstage with the DJ, dancing and talking to the crowd. He dedicated a song to Kate and Chris."

"But nobody knows where he is?"

"No. He might be in one of the tents, but I'm not going in there for you."

"Why not?"

"I'm just not."

"What's going on inside them? Drugs? What?"

Mia gives me a hard look. "The kind of sex I'm not into, probably."

"I wasn't asking you to go. I just wanted to know."

She leans back in her seat and closes her eyes. She sounds a little out of breath.

"Did you take any Ecstasy?" I ask.

"No. I was kidding before. I don't do drugs. I had a couple of vodka shots, just talking to people."

"What's the general state of the crowd?"

"Up by the stage it's mellow. Everybody's hugging and holding hands. Out on the edges it's out of control. The rednecks in the trucks are doing crystal meth. I saw a fight down by one of the ponds. Some of the girls are really drunk. Incomprehensible. That's who winds up in the tents."

I roll down my window to let the breeze blow across my face. "Do anybody's parents have any idea what's going on out here?"

"I don't think so. But they might by next week. I saw flashbulbs going off in one tent. You get naked out here, you'll wind up on the Internet for sure."

"Shit."

Mia leans forward and pulls her hair into a ponytail, then puts an elastic band around it. "What do you want to do now?"

"Let's get back to the hotel and see what's on Kate's flash drives. We're not doing Drew any good out here."

She nods and starts the car.

"Hang on," I tell her, opening my door.

"Where are you going?"

"It's a long ride back."

"Oh. Don't wander off."

I walk a few yards down the hill, away from the car. As I unzip my pants, a truck rolls slowly up the drive. To escape its beams, I walk farther down the hill, toward a tall oak with low, spreading branches. After the truck's headlights sweep past, I open my fly and begin urinating. I'm nearly done when a strangely musical voice seems to fall from the sky.

"My little bird likes what she sees."

I jump backward and nearly piss on my leg. High-pitched laughter echoes through the dark.

"Who's there?" I ask anxiously.

"Up here," says the voice.

I look up. Lying in the bow of a horizontal oak limb is a shirtless teenager who looks a lot like Marko Bakic. Seated beside him, her bare legs hanging down in the air, is a girl who looks no older than fifteen. *Alicia Reynolds.* She's shirtless, too, her breasts barely covered by a push-up bra. The white ring of a pacifier dangles from her puckered mouth.

"You can finish," she says, giggling around the pacifier. "I've already seen it, anyway."

The shirtless boy grins like the Cheshire Cat. "Mr. Cage, right?"

The East European accent is unmistakable. It's Marko, all right. I take a step forward and look up at him. "Hello, Marko."

"What brings you out here tonight, man? You looking to get high?"

"I came to see you, actually."

The smile doesn't waver. "Yeah?"

"How can he just stop peeing like that?" asks the girl. "I couldn't do that."

"Go get yourself another drink," Marko tells her, never taking his eyes off me.

"I don't want another drink."

"Get lost, then. You can take this with you."

He passes something small to her. Pills, no doubt. "The rest of you go with her, okay?"

As though materializing out of thin air, three more young men drop to the ground from other limbs and start walking up to the road. Alicia goes with them. The back of one boy's T-shirt reads, "KA OLE MISS."

After they disappear, Marko swings down from his perch. He's about an inch taller than I, with lanky, muscular arms and a scrawny chest. His mouth is smiling, but it seems separated from his eyes somehow, which are watching me like the eyes of an animal uncertain whether to fight or flee. *Maybe it's the drugs,* I think.

"What can I do for you, Mr. Cage?"

"Do you know about the Wilsons?"

The smile disappears. "Sure. Terrible, yeah?"

"Were you home when the killers got there?"

Marko's eyes narrow. "No way. I'd have killed them right back."

"I found the bodies."

"I read that in the newspaper."

I watch him for a while without speaking. The silence doesn't seem to make him nervous. It's making me nervous.

"Why are you carrying a gun?" he asks. "You scared?"

I guess in Sarajevo you learn to spot weapons pretty quick. "Things are a little crazy in town just now. I like to know I have options."

This earns a smile. "Options . . . I like that. I like options, too."

"Who killed the Wilsons, Marko? Who tried to hit you?"

He shrugs. "Who knows, man? America's a crazy country."

Marko's accent combined with his lanky physique makes me think of Goran Ivanisevic, the Croatian tennis star. Marko is actually handsomer than Ivanisevic, but not quite as wholesome looking.

"Listen, Marko," I say in a friendly voice, "I'm not here to try to hurt you. In fact, if you let me, I can almost certainly help you. I know you've opened up some new drug markets with the white

fraternities at Ole Miss and LSU. Some other places, too. But now
that you've done that, you're expendable."

"Cyrus seems to think so."

Honesty. A good start. "Was it Cyrus who hit the Wilsons?"

"Don't know, man."

"Or was it the Asians?"

All the levity leaves Marko's face. "You know a lot, Mr. Cage.
Maybe too much, yeah?"

"I'm not the only one who knows this stuff." Low down on
Marko's belly is a mass of white scar tissue shot through with purple. Wade Anders told me Marko had been bayoneted as a child.

Marko sniffs like a fox and looks up toward the road. "That
cop with the mullet knew it. Look what happened to him."

"I saw the Asians kill him."

"Maybe the Asians think I'm expendable, too, eh? If they do,
I'm dead. If I went back to Croatia, I might get away from them.
But I don't want to go back."

"Are you coming back to St. Stephen's?"

"Can't do it."

"Don't you want to graduate?"

Tiny points of light dance in his eyes. "I want to live more."

"How can you stay in the U.S. if you don't graduate and go to
college?"

He shrugs. "I can live anywhere. I'll just become someone else."

"Is that how you want to spend your life? As someone else?"

"Might be nice for a while."

I hold out empty hands and step closer to him. We're no more
than five feet apart. "I don't care about the drugs, Marko. I'm here
because I want to save my friend. You know who I'm talking
about?"

"The doctor. The guy who raped Kate."

"Why do you say that?"

Marko shrugs again. "That's what everybody says. The doctor
raped her and then he killed her."

"Drew wouldn't do that. He was in love with her."

This seems to amuse Marko. "Men kill women they love all the time, no? And vice versa. What you call it here? Crime of passion?"

"Yes. But that's not what happened to Kate."

"No?" He looks confused. "What happened to her then?"

"I'm trying to find out. I think somebody else raped and killed her. Someone who might not even have meant to kill her. He might only have been trying to keep her quiet. That happens a lot."

"Why are you telling me this?"

"Before he died, Sonny Cross told me you thought Cyrus had murdered Kate."

Marko scowls. "I told that *kopile* whatever would get his gun out of my mouth. He was bad news, man."

I feel my hope deflating. "You lied to Cross?"

"Some lies, some truth."

"Did you lie about Cyrus being obsessed with Kate?"

"Ha! No way. That nigger wanted that girl bad."

Marko says "nigger" with such an unfamiliar pronunciation that I almost misunderstand the word. "How do you know that?"

"Every time I saw him, he wanted to know every little thing about her. He tracked her cell phone. All he thought about was her coming to get those pills. It made him forget every other chick, you know? He'd wait the whole fucking month to see her. He thought she was some kind of goddess."

"And you? Didn't you want to use the Lorcet to get into Kate's pants?"

"Sure." He laughs. "Why not? Kate was hot, no doubt about it. No goddess, though. No woman is a goddess. They shit and fart just like we do, even the pretty ones. And they all want the same thing."

"What's that?"

"Same thing a man wants! Money and power. And a little sex— maybe." He laughs again. "If sex gets them more money and power!"

Now that I'm face-to-face with Marko, I wonder if he can really help me at all. "Do you know where Cyrus is now?"

"Hiding out. Like me."

"What does Cyrus have to be afraid of?"

Marko bares his teeth. "The yellow men."

"Do you think he's close by?"

"He can't be too far. You can't leave this business very long. Somebody else come along and take it from you."

"Did you ever sleep with Kate?"

"I don't sleep much." A smirk.

"Did you fuck her?"

His teeth show again. "Now you're into what I like."

I can see how Kate might be drawn to Marko Bakic. He's the ultimate bad boy. She already had Drew, the ultimate "good guy," but maybe she felt the need to privately balance the scales. Maybe Marko was the answer to that craving. "So? Did you screw Kate?"

Marko shakes his head. "Never got the chance."

"Will you put your money where your mouth is?"

"What you mean?"

"Will you give me a hair off your head? One hair?"

Instant suspicion. "What for?"

"A DNA test. You know what that is?"

"Sure. I watch TV."

"If your DNA doesn't match the sperm that was found inside Kate, then a lot of your problems with the law will vanish."

"The cops think *I* killed Kate?"

"The possibility has been raised," I lie.

"I was with Coach Anders, man. You tell them! I got enough problems without this bullshit."

"One hair from your head would solve this particular problem. If you're innocent, what do you have to lose?"

Marko shakes his head. "You just want to save your friend. You can make a test say anything you want."

I didn't expect him to give me the hair. There's no upside for him. I just wanted to read his reaction. He's watching me with what looks like curiosity. Then suddenly he steps forward, sending my hand into my pocket.

Marko's pistol is out before I even touch mine, its barrel pointed straight at my chest. Fear turns my bowels liquid.

"*Careful,*" he says, stepping closer. Then he pulls at his dark hair with his free hand and holds something out to me. "There you go. Get the police off my back, okay? At least on that shit."

I take the hair and squeeze it tight in my fist.

"Now, maybe you better go home, Mr. Cage."

"Maybe you're right."

He puts his gun away. "I think this is the last time we're going to see each other. Thank you for talking for me at the school board meeting a while back. That was a big help."

"No problem," I say, wishing I'd joined the campaign to have him expelled three months ago. "Are you leaving town or something?"

Marko sucks at his bottom lip, apparently weighing the issue. "I've got some moves to make first."

"Moves?"

"Unfinished business."

"Cyrus?"

An easy laugh. "Maybe. Or maybe the Asians. Maybe I decide *they're* expendable, yeah?"

"I can see that point of view. But where would you get your inventory then?"

This buys the biggest laugh of all. "Afghanistan, man! Where else? It's better than that Colombian shit, anyway."

"Ecstasy and LSD from Afghanistan?"

"Hell, no! *Heroin,* man. Black Pearl. You know what keeps these whitebread kids from doing heroin? The *needle.* That's the line they won't cross. They're afraid of AIDS and hepatitis, or just plain scared of the fucking needle. But now the purity's so high that you can snort and smoke heroin just like coke. You don't *need* the needle. It's the future, man. I'm going to give those frat boys the ride of their lives! And I'm going to be *rich.*"

"Why are you telling me all this?"

An indifferent shrug. "Because it doesn't matter. In a day or two, Marko Bakic will exist no more. I'm going to reinvent myself, like Madonna. You like Madonna?"

This exchange has become surreal. All I want to know now is how to get back to Mia's car without turning my back on Marko.

"It's okay, Mr. Cage," he says, reading my thoughts. "I'm not going to shoot you."

As I back away from him, one last question occurs to me. "Do you think Steve Sayers could have killed Kate?"

"Steve? Sure, why not? He's crazy guy."

"I thought he was pretty straight. A jock."

Marko snickers. "Those pickup trucks driving around scaring everybody to death?"

"Yeah."

"Steve's driving one of them. He'll probably kill somebody before morning, and he won't even know it. Just another bump in the grass."

"Steve's semen didn't match what they found in Kate's corpse."

"So what? Maybe he wore a raincoat. Or maybe he pulled out, you know? In my country, ten Serbs rape a woman, maybe half of them come in her. Maybe that's what happened to Kate, you know? Ten guys could have raped her. Why not?"

"Gang rape?"

"Who knows? America's crazier than Bosnia when it comes to sex. It's all they think about."

"What do *you* think about?"

A broad grin. "Business!"

"Is that why you blew five grand on fireworks the other night?"

"Sure! Promotional expense. I'm an entrepreneur, like Bill Gates."

I stop backing away. I've dealt with a lot of criminals, but Marko Bakic is a new experience for me. He's like a Russian mobster, convinced that he's in the vanguard of capitalism even as he leaves a trail of carnage behind him. Of course, American capitalism left quite a wake of destruction during its infancy as well. Maybe Marko isn't completely wrong about himself.

"Will you give me your cell number?" I ask. "I may need to reach you."

He smiles lazily. "You know better than that, Mr. Cage. You give me yours. Maybe I'll check in with you before I go."

Why not? Better to have some chance of talking to Marko again than none. I give him my number. As he punches it into his cell phone, I'm suddenly terrified that Mia will walk down the hill in search of me. I don't want Marko to know it was she who brought me here.

"Well, good luck," I tell him, backing farther up the hill.

Marko knows how scared I am; he sees it in my face. But I don't care. Fear is infinitely more powerful than pride, and I have so much to lose. I hope I never see Marko Bakic again.

When I reach the road, I cross it and sprint toward Mia's car.

"*Go!*" I shout as I jump into my seat. "Get out of here now!"

"What happened?" she asks. "You were gone forever."

"I talked to Marko. Go! I don't want him to know you brought me."

Mia throws the car into reverse, backs onto the road, and guns it for the gate.

"Drive normally," I tell her, digging in the glove box for an envelope.

"Fuck that," she says. "I want out of here."

Very carefully, I slip Marko's hair into the envelope containing the title to Mia's car.

"Don't worry," she says. "Everybody's too wasted to remember anything."

Yeah, I think. *Everybody but Marko.*

CHAPTER

32

Quentin Avery's suite is empty. Lucien has apparently gone home, but from the dirty dishes littering the coffee table, he ate a full meal and several desserts before giving up on the Sony flash drive I took from Marko's apartment. The flash drive itself is sitting on the keyboard in front of the flat-panel monitor on the desk. Though it's long after midnight, Mia looks wide awake. The rave is forgotten. Her excitement at seeing what Kate kept hidden from the world is plain to see.

"Why are you so excited about seeing what's on Kate's drives?" I ask, taking a seat before the computer and slipping the Sony drive into my pocket.

Mia pulls up a chair and sits beside me. "I just want to understand where she really was in her head. Maybe then I'll know why she died."

When I insert the first Lexar flash drive, Windows offers to open a folder to view the files. "Thank you, Lucien." I click the mouse, and a group of folders and individual files pops up. Some are .jpeg image files, others are WordPerfect documents, and still others appear to be hypertext documents saved from the World-wide Web.

"What do we look at first?" Mia asks.

"The pictures, I guess. I have a feeling some of this stuff is going to be explicit."

She gives me a look that says, *Give me a break*.

I click a .jpeg file, and a picture of two men having sex fills the screen.

"Whoa," I say, feeling my face color.

I try to click the image away, but Mia grabs my hand. "That's no big deal," she says. "This isn't 1980, okay? I've seen women doing it with horses on the Internet. Everybody in my class has."

It's not her revelation about bestiality that shocks me, but the way she refers to 1980 as if it's the Dark Ages. I was twenty years old in 1980. For me, 1984 still carries the dread of an Orwellian future; for Mia it's the name of a bad Van Halen album released two years before she was born.

"It's just gay sex," she says. "And the guys are hot."

"Do you think that's why Kate has this?"

She shrugs. "I don't know. Open some more files."

More images of gay sexual action appear.

"I think Kate was into anal," Mia says in a matter-of-fact voice.

"That's what Drew told me. That's why they found his semen in her . . . in . . ."

"Her butt?" Mia finishes, looking at me like I'm being ridiculous.

"Yeah. Shad's going to use that fact to make it look like Drew raped Kate. He's relying on the jury being unwilling to believe a girl that young would do that voluntarily."

"He might be right, if the jury's old enough. But you never know. They might surprise you."

"I wouldn't mind being surprised like that."

Mia is still watching the screen. "Keep clicking."

I open some more files, moving quickly down the directory. A few heterosexual images appear, but the collection is still heavily weighted toward gay porn. As the images flash up and vanish, I realize that I'm simply not young enough to judge how normal or abnormal it is for a girl to possess this kind of material today.

"Mia, I don't want to embarrass you, but I need to know something."

"What?"

"Do you have stuff like this on your computer? I don't mean gay porn, but . . . you know."

At last Mia blushes. "Do *you?*"

"Well . . . some. But I'm a guy."

She laughs nervously. "Yeah, I've got a few pictures."

"I wouldn't have thought that."

She gives me a strange smile. "Am I ruining your perfect image of me?"

"Maybe."

"Everybody's human, Penn. Even girls like me."

"I guess I keep hoping that's not true."

She points at the screen. "Try this folder at the bottom. It has a D and a K in the file name."

Her instinct is dead-on. When I click the folder she's pointing to, a host of file icons appears, all coded "DK" with a number. And when I click the first icon, an image of Kate and Drew having intercourse fills the screen.

"Jesus," I whisper.

Mia whistles softly.

Drew and Kate are in the missionary position, but there's no hokey mugging for the camera or anything like that. It looks as though someone hiding in the bedroom caught them in the act of tenderly making love. Not many people look good having sex, but Drew seems frozen above Kate like a statue by Michelangelo, his muscles flexed in stark relief. He's looking down into Kate's eyes, and she appears awestruck, her mouth partly open, her eyes filled with indescribable emotion. This single image brings home the reality of their relationship in a more visceral way than all Drew's explanations of it, or even my imagined reality. They don't look like two porn actors, but two people deeply in love.

"It's so sad," Mia says. "Isn't it?"

"Yes."

"Open another one."

I sigh, then move to the next file. When this image fills the screen, Mia gasps. It takes me a minute to process what I'm seeing. Drew stands facing the camera, holding Kate against him as they make love. But she is not facing him; she's facing the camera, her long legs bowed at the knee, her feet hooked behind Drew's powerful legs. Drew's hands are clutching Kate's inner thighs, while her lithe arms disappear beneath his muscular ones, presumably to grip his lower back. Somehow these few points of contact manage to support Kate's full weight. The position spreads her chest to the limit, pushing her modest but shapely breasts up and outward through her long blond hair. And though her eyes are closed, her face communicates utter bliss. Drew's jaw is clenched with effort, but he looks as though he could hold Kate suspended for eternity.

"I've never done that," Mia says softly. "Have you?"

"No."

"Is he in her front or back?"

I study the picture. Kate's pubic area is trimmed to a barely visible shadow. What must be a third of the shaft of Drew's penis is visible below her vaginal lips, but the slight downward angle of the shot makes it difficult to see the point of entry.

"Front, I think."

Mia shakes her head again. Her breathing has gone shallow, and there's a tension in her body that wasn't there before. The photo is shockingly erotic, and it makes me wonder whether Drew and Kate shot this photograph, or whether someone else was indeed in the room. It's hard to believe they staged this shot with a timer.

Mia leans closer to the screen. At some level, I know that viewing this material with her is inappropriate, but I also know that I'm not about to stop.

"What do you think about that?" I ask.

"It's beautiful."

"Is it?"

"He's hot."

I can't help but feel a pang of jealousy. "And Kate?"

"She's so *long*. I'll never look like that."

"Why would you want to look like that?"

Mia shakes her head. She doesn't want to answer. But neither does she take her eyes from the picture. As she stares, I decide to ask something I've wondered about ever since the murder—and especially after last night's conversation with Caitlin.

"Would you do something like that, Mia?"

"What? The sex?"

"No. Would you do what Kate did? Get involved with an older man. Like Drew."

She takes a deep breath and closes her eyes. Then she turns to me and opens them. "Do you want me to be honest?"

"Of course."

"Will you be honest?"

"Yes."

"Have you ever thought about kissing me?"

In one moment my face is burning. I can't be honest with her about that. Maybe not even with myself.

"That wasn't a discussion question," she says. "It's yes or no. True or false."

"Mia . . ."

She looks down. "It's all right. I already know."

"Do you?"

"I think so."

"Well?"

She shakes her head and looks up again. "You asked if I would do what Kate did. My answer is yes. With the right man."

"Why would you?"

She looks back at the screen and covers her mouth with her hand. Then she closes the file and turns to face me, her eyes bright with intensity. "Because I'm ready to experience more than I have up to this point. I want to know the essence of life, and of myself. I want to learn what I'm capable of. And the boys I know can't help me do that."

She pauses, but she seems to have more to say.

"I realize that I could be hurt by an older man," she goes on.

"But that's what you do when you're my age, isn't it? You get your heart broken, and you learn. You try to figure out who you're supposed to be with."

"I suppose you're right."

"I'm not Kate. I'm not even *like* Kate. I'm my own person. I'm eighteen, and I understand what that kind of choice means. It's a risk, but it's one I would take. It's something I'd like to experience before I leave for Brown. And my feeling is that the consequences of that kind of relationship don't have to be negative." She gives me a tight smile. "I'm not a *Fatal Attraction* kind of girl. No dramatic scenes, no pregnancy, no suicide attempts, no diseases. Just intimacy."

Her dark eyes are only inches from mine, and they seem almost bottomless.

"Mia—"

"I'm not the angel you think I am, Penn."

"You're more of one than you think."

She raises an eyebrow in answer, then lays her right hand over my left. "Will you answer *my* question?"

"Which one?"

"You know which one."

As blood suffuses my cheeks again, it strikes me that only truth will resolve this situation. "Yes, I've thought about what it would be like to kiss you."

She acknowledges my words with a nod, but she already knew the answer.

"But that doesn't mean it's all right for me to do it," I add.

Mia's smile is as serene as the face of the Turning Angel. "I've thought about it, too," she says. "I thought about it during the drive out to Oakfield. And during the drive back."

"I don't know what to say."

"Don't say anything. Just kiss me."

"I can't do that."

She smiles as though we share some intimate secret. "Did you know that Humphrey Bogart married Lauren Bacall when she was twenty?"

"No."

"He was forty-six. That's more of an age difference than we have."

"Not by much."

She laughs softly. "Just giving you a little history. I wasn't saying we have to be together forever. You already have a life, and I'm going to Brown in the fall."

Before I can speak again, she takes my other hand in her free one and squeezes. "Look at me, Penn. Not your idea of me, but *me,* the mortal girl. The flesh-and-blood Mia. And don't say anything—please."

I can't obey her. Because to look into Mia's eyes for too long would send me straight down the road Drew has already traveled. The reality of a stunningly beautiful and intelligent young woman explaining why it's all right for you to make love to her is enough to make any male lose all capacity for rational thought. In my mind I hear Wade Anders telling me that the hardest thing he ever did was turn down the girls who've come on to him in his office. Those girls, I am certain, were not even in Mia's league. But what refuses to leave my mind is the image of Drew and Kate making love before the camera. Mia viewed that photograph with me and felt no embarrassment at all. On the contrary, she wants to experience the same intensity she saw there with me. More than that, she's telling me beforehand that I'll have no obligation to her.

Evolutionary nirvana, Caitlin called it. *God, was she right.*

I close my eyes, slip my hands from beneath Mia's, and grip her upper arms. "Listen to me, Mia. Do you have any idea of the power you possess? You sitting there saying that—the way you said it—makes me believe in witchcraft. It's like a spell. And I know you're telling the truth. You *have* outgrown this town and its people. You *are* ready to taste a deeper level of life. You're ready to explore yourself, and you probably do need a man for some parts of that journey."

"But you're not that man?" she says.

I nod slowly. "We both have to tell the truth here, okay? That's the only way to be fair to each other. Do I want you in this moment? Yes, I do. Do I have any idea of what it would be like to experience with you what we saw in that picture? I think I do. Do I have any inkling of the connection you and I could have, despite our age difference? Of course I do. Because we *already have it.* I've been forcing myself to ignore it for weeks. It's a cliché, I know, but I feel as though I've known you all my life. But the thing is . . . I haven't. I couldn't have. Because you're half my age. You are literally young enough to be my daughter."

"But I'm *not* your daughter," she says, laying her hands over mine again.

I breathe slowly, trying to stay focused. "In some ways, I feel you are."

Mia shakes her head, her eyes anxious now. "Don't say that. Because it's not true. I've seen things in your eyes that a father doesn't feel for a daughter."

"Of course you have. I'm a man, and I respond to all that you are. But I also feel things that a father feels for a daughter. Mainly, I feel very protective of you. And my first duty is to protect you from me."

She stares at me in silence, trying to process what I've said. In this strange lacuna of time, I feel the shattering intensity of the moment that Drew stepped over the line with Kate. He looked into a face this beautiful; he gazed into eyes like twin pools in some mythic grove; he touched skin this flawless; he listened to the siren song of eternal youth falling from bloodred lips, and then he leaned forward—not back. And from that moment forward he was lost.

Mia reads my eyes with the precision of a clairvoyant. Sadness touches her lips for a moment; then she blinks three times and looks back at the computer screen.

"Forget I said anything," she says, clicking the mouse to open a WordPerfect document. "I was being retarded."

"No, you weren't. You were just . . ." I stop talking. I've lost her. The walls have gone up, and nothing is going to bring them down any time soon.

"Look at this," she says. "It looks like e-mail from that guy you talked about."

"Who?"

"The drug dealer. Cyrus?"

The name shocks me back to the present. Mia's right. The letter is three paragraphs long, and incredibly enough, it's signed: *Peace+, Cyrus.* I read it aloud, searching for a sense of Cyrus White in the way his words feel in my mouth.

Dear Kate, I've been thinking about you a lot. I don't want to freak you out, but I don't think you're the kind of girl who freaks out too easy. I've been looking at that picture, the one Jaderious took. You look so fine in that, girl. You look like a movie star in a magazine, when they catch them coming out of a theater or something. I mean it. I saw a girl on the cover of "US" magazine that made me think of you. I looked inside to find out who she was. Her name is Katie Holmes. Y'all even have the same name, so I rented two of her flicks. You're kind of like her, only with blond hair and blue eyes, and more to-gether. Not silly or flighty or anything.

I hope what I gave you did you right. I can't see you doing that myself, but I don't really know you yet. Every-body carries some pain around, and I'm sure you've been through your share. You told me your old man was never around, and I can relate to that. I didn't even know who my father was. The guy I thought it was, turned out he was just some guy, you know? My mama's boyfriend. But that was a long time ago.

I just want you to know I'm thinking about you. That I see you're different from everybody else. I know you already know that, but I want you to know I know it too. I know it cause I'm the same way. I live in a different world, of course. But I always knew I was different. That's how I got where I am now. When the plants closed down around here, a lot of guys just gave up. Some took shit jobs, but others just sit at home with their head in a bottle, or smoke weed, whatever. I guess that's all right for them. But not me. I got screwed out of my living, so I give it right back to the bas-

tards who did it. I'm not letting them take me down. I'm getting enough money to do anything I might ever want to do. I got big plans, I want you to know that. I know you got plans too. If you ever want to talk, like you said, just mail me back, or call me, whatever. I'm open to it, you know? That's all I want to say. You be cool. Peace+, Cyrus.

"Let's look for the picture he's talking about," Mia says.

"Look for 'CW' in the file name," I think aloud. "Or 'CK.' "

"Snap!" says Mia. "There it is."

She clicks on another .jpeg file, and a new photo fills the screen. A large, sullen-faced black man stands before a gray wall with his arm around Kate, almost crushing her against him. Kate has a smile of sorts on her face, but it's the smile of someone making the best of a bad situation. She looks like a girl being molested by a customs official while trying to get out of a hostile country; she has to play along to get out of the situation, but she's not okay with it. But then again, maybe that's just prejudice coloring my view of the photograph.

"Does she look happy to you?" I ask.

Mia shakes her head. "That's one of Kate's fake smiles. Everybody has one, of course. Kate has about five, and that's one of them. She looks scared to me."

"I agree."

I lean closer to the screen and try to read Cyrus's eyes, but the flat-panel model doesn't have the fine resolution of a CRT. Still, his whole appearance and posture radiate a sense of threat. Sonny Cross told me that Cyrus was thirty-four, but the drug dealer looks about twenty-eight in this photo. He's built like an NFL cornerback: his bullet head is shaved clean, his neck is corded with muscle, and his biceps are thicker than Kate's thighs. His skin is the color of café au lait—I'm guessing a quarter of his blood could be Caucasian. He's wearing a black wife-beater tank top and tight white painter's pants. A solitary gold chain hangs around his neck, but the links are thick enough to pull a truck out of a mudhole. I wonder if the chain is meant to symbolize the chains of slavery.

"Look for more letters," I murmur.

"Definitely," says Mia.

She begins opening WordPerfect files. Most of them seem like diary pages that didn't make Kate's handwritten journal. Ironically, these entries are of the more casual sort:

> *Ate crawfish pasta at Pearl Street Pasta . . .*

> *Got an acceptance letter from Colgate—too late, people . . .*

> *Grandma sent me a check for $10. What does she think I can buy with that? . . .*

> *Steve almost cracked his skull today on his 4-wheeler. He made a huge deal out of it, but I couldn't pretend to be too worried. It's not like there was much risk of brain damage . . .*

For some reason, Kate chronicled the most sensitive events of her life by hand, where they could easily be discovered, while her quotidian record was saved to a password-protected disk. Why? *The password was to protect the pictures,* I realize. The person most likely to discover Kate's journal was her mother, and Kate wasn't worried about that. She simply wanted to spare her mother from the explicit visual evidence of her sexual life.

"That looks like the only letter from Cyrus," Mia says.

"I'm going to have to find a way to get a look at Kate's actual computer."

"Would Mrs. Townsend let you do that? She gave you the journal."

"I think she would. But the police probably have it by now. I'll get Quentin to request access to it."

"Wait! Here's another letter!"

As I read the next e-mail from Cyrus, my face grows hot. The chatty tone of the first letter is gone, replaced by seething anger. This time Mia reads aloud:

What the fuck, huh? You said you were going to write me back, talk to me, but you just leave me sitting here like I don't exist. And that's the truth, isn't it? In your world, I don't *exist. I only pop into your head when the dope gets low. Yeah, I know how it is. I know more junkies than I can count, and they're all the same. You just look better than the rest. But the beautiful people got the monkey on their back too, baby. You'll see that when you get to Harvard. You can bet your ass those rich kids are snorting and main-lining and everything else. The only difference is, they got better dope. If you ever come down off that high horse, write me back.*

"Cyrus thought Kate was getting the pills for herself," Mia says. "She was protecting Drew."

Mia shakes her head. "I don't like Drew too much right now. He was really taking advantage of her."

I'm disgusted myself, but I'm also excited. If Cyrus White didn't know Kate was buying the Lorcet for Ellen Elliott, then Shad Johnson can't possibly learn the truth behind Kate's visits from any members of Cyrus's crew. Quentin will be ecstatic over this.

"Look," says Mia, reading another note from Cyrus. "You see what Kate was doing? She was playing Cyrus to keep the pills coming. He wanted her, so he held the dope over her head, and she played the game. I wonder how far she went?"

"Too far, I'm afraid," I reply, reading farther down.

You played me, didn't you, bitch? You made me feel like you saw past my skin and my trade. But you don't. You made me believe you see me the way you see yourself. But you don't. To you I'm just another nigger. After you get to Harvard, I'm going to be that big bad black dope dealer you tell colorful stories about, while your spoiled-ass friends laugh. Well, fuck you, bitch! You knew I wanted you, and you held out that pussy like bait to get what you wanted. Just like every other bitch tries to do. But women don't play *that shit with Cyrus. Hear? I got some bitches you ought to talk to about that. They learned quick. You will too. You can hide all you want. You can ignore my e-mail, not answer my calls. But when that dope gets low, you'll be back. And don't be trying to get it from Marko. I <u>own</u> that mother-fucker. Your best bet is to fake a toothache and go to a horny dentist. You can probably play him for some of what you need. But you won't make it through the summer, baby. You'll be back to me. And this time you're going to pay like all the other bitches. With pussy.*

"Holy shit," Mia says softly. "This is scary."

"This is dynamite is what it is. Are there any more like this?"

"Let's see." She opens another folder containing WordPerfect documents. Most are to-do lists relating to admission to colleges. There are five drafts of essays written for applications.

"Look at this hypertext document," Mia says.

The saved Web page is a visual encyclopedia of medications containing hydrocodone. There's a picture of each brand of pill, and beside each the pharmacological information about it—how much hydrocodone it contains, how much acetaminophen, etc.

"Kate was a comparison shopper," I comment.

"She wanted to make sure Cyrus didn't screw her."

"In the drug-dealing sense."

"In both senses," says Mia. "I feel so sorry for her."

"What's that?" I ask, pointing to a Microsoft Notepad document.

Mia opens the file. "It looks like she copied the text from an e-mail and posted it into Notepad. Holy shit. Look at that."

I saw you today, it begins.

You were talking to that doctor I see running all the time. Y'all were being shady as shit, too. You found a new source, didn't you? You didn't go to a dentist, you went to a doctor. I saw how you were with him. You're giving your shit to him, all right. He wouldn't give you the dope without some kind of payment, and what else do you got that he'd want? Of course you won't see it that way. You probably think you're in love. Well, I got something for you, Cinderella. You don't shit on Cyrus and walk away clean. You ain't clean. And don't think your doctor man can help you. He may look big, but I'll take that motherfucker down. How did you get this way, anyway? Does your mama know you do this shit? Or did she TEACH you this shit? I bet that's it. Have a nice day, okay? Enjoy your ride in that boxy-ass Volvo. It ain't gonna last long.

"What's the date of that e-mail?" I ask.

"There's no date. It's just copied text."

"What's the date of the Notepad file?"

Mia checks it. "The twenty-eighth."

"Three days before Kate was murdered."

I pull the flash drive from the computer and get to my feet. My neck and back are stiff from staring so intently at the computer.

"What are you going to do?" Mia asks.

"Get to work. That letter is going to save Drew's life."

"Will it, really?"

"This letter alone will create reasonable doubt in the mind of the jury."

Mia nods, but she doesn't look convinced.

"What is it?"

"A lot of people get upset when they're rejected," she says. "You know? A lot of people say they want to kill the person who hurt them. Or at least they think it."

"Have you ever thought that?"

She looks straight into my eyes. "Yes."

"Who was the person?"

She shakes her head. "I told you I'm not the angel you think I am."

I want to know more, but right now I can't make myself concentrate on the love life of my babysitter. It's late—probably too late to wake Quentin—but I need to get Mia home and start working on Drew's defense. It's hard to get my mind around the fact, but his trial begins *next Wednesday*. At least now we'll have a big surprise for Shad Johnson.

"You want me to go, don't you?" Mia says.

"Well, I'm going to be working all night on subpoenas and things like that. Drew doesn't have much time."

"I understand. I'll go." She picks up her backpack and starts toward the door.

"Mia, it's really late. Let me run you home."

She stops. "You don't have to. I've got my car."

"I'll follow you then. And tomorrow I'll let you know everything that happens related to this. I know you want to know about it."

"I do. Thanks. And to tell you the truth, I don't feel like driving. I can pick up my car tomorrow."

"Good." I open the leather portfolio I brought Kate's journal in and zip Kate's flash drives into one of its inside pockets. Then I slip the envelope containing Marko's hair into another. "I'm not letting this stuff out of my sight." As I reach for Marko's flash drive, which is still in my pants pocket, it hits me that Mia is seriously upset. I walk to her and put my hands on her shoulders.

"Mia, I can't tell you how much help you've been tonight. Helping me find Marko, getting these disks hacked. You've been critical throughout this investigation. When Drew is acquitted, it's going to be due to your efforts more than anyone else's."

A smile touches the corners of her mouth. "You really think so?"

"Absolutely. Drew's going to have to make a large contribution to your college fund."

She laughs, her eyes sparkling. "How large?"

"Five figures for sure. Hell, I think it ought to equal Quentin's fee."

"You're kidding, right?"

"I'm not. If Drew doesn't take care of you, I will. That's a promise. But he will. I know him. Now, let's get you home."

Mia shoulders her backpack and leads the way through the door. As we enter the elevator, though, I realize that her smile is gone again. *Wake up, stupid,* says a voice in my head. *It's not pay-ing for college that she's worried about. It's what happened in front of the computer ten minutes ago.*

We're standing about two feet apart, facing the elevator door. Our reflections are staring at us from the brass plating. Mia looks tiny and vulnerable with her backpack slung over her shoulder. I'm so glad I didn't cross the line with her upstairs.

"Mia . . ."

She gives the slightest shake of her head. She can't bear to dis-cuss what happened between us. As I stare at her reflection, I real-ize there are tears on her face. After a moment's hesitation, I reach out and take her hand in mine. It's very small and soft, not so dif-ferent from my daughter's hand. After a moment, she squeezes my hand in return, then steps close to me and lays her head on my chest.

Putting my arm around her, I feel ineffable sadness at the plight of this girl. Her father abandoned her when she was two, yet she and her mother somehow struggled through, not just to the point that they're okay—which would have been triumph enough—but to the point that Mia has become a self-possessed young lady accepted into one of the finest universities in the country. If Drew really is acquit-ted, I'm going to *make* him set up a college account for Mia. And the first deposit is going to be a hundred thousand dollars.

The elevator dings, and the doors open onto the empty lobby. To our left, a clerk behind the desk stands and gives us a sleepy wave.

"Do you need anything, sir?"

"No, thanks."

"My car's in the back lot," I tell Mia, stopping by a large sofa. "Stay here until I bring it around."

She slips her heavy pack off her shoulder and drops into the soft cushion of the sofa.

"Don't fall asleep."

"I might."

I point to a side door that leads to the hotel's check-in lanes. "That's where I'll be. You'll be able to see me pull up."

"Can you bring a pizza with you? I'm hungry."

"We can grab something on the way home."

I walk past the desk and out the back door.

The Eola parking lot occupies the hollow center of a large city block. It's mostly empty, so I jog straight to my Saab. Laying the portfolio on the passenger seat, I crank the engine, back out of my space, and pull around to the check-in lanes. With six stories of hotel sitting on top of them, they're effectively in a tunnel, and for some reason the arrows painted on the ground go against the normal American traffic flow. The right lane—which would put me in front of the hotel door—is painted with an arrow coming straight toward me, as it would in the UK.

"Screw it," I mutter, pulling into the right lane.

As I come abreast of the glass doors, I see Mia waiting just inside them. Then I see a man standing behind her. Not a man, really, but a boy. A boy with an Asian face. He's pressing a gun against Mia's right temple.

And he's smiling.

CHAPTER

33

The Asian boy kicks open the glass door and shoves Mia through it, the gun still hard against her head. Mia's face is drained of blood, her eyes blank with terror. I want to reach for the gun in my jacket pocket, but that would probably get Mia a bullet in the head. As I stare, I realize I'm looking at the guy who shot Sonny Cross from the black Lexus on Beau Pré Road. He'll have no qualms about blowing Mia's brains out.

What does this guy want?

I start violently at the crack of metal against my window. I look to my left. A second Asian boy is aiming a stubby submachine gun at me. It looks like a Heckler and Koch MP5, a favorite of law enforcement. He motions for me to roll down my window. I do.

"Keep your hands where I can see 'em," he says in a Southern accent.

For some reason I expected him to speak Vietnamese, but why should he? He's from the Mississippi Gulf Coast.

"Keys!" he snaps. "Give 'em here!"

If Mia weren't part of this equation, I'd hit the gas and peel out of this tunnel. But she is part of it. I shut off the Saab and hand the boy my keys.

"That, too," he says, jabbing the gun at the portfolio on the seat.

I brought the portfolio with me because I knew other people had access to Quentin's suite, and I didn't want to take a chance on losing it. I glance at Mia as I reach into the passenger seat and pass the portfolio across my chest. Her mouth is hanging slack.

"Get his gun!" yells the boy holding Mia. "We'll take his car."

As the boy at my window reaches inside, a shadow appears behind the one holding Mia. I assume it's another member of his gang, but then the right side of his forehead explodes, and he drops like a sandbag.

Mia screams and looks down.

The hand at my chest jerks out of the window.

"*Run, Mia!*" I shout, ramming my door into the gunman's midsection. Then I yank out my father's pistol, fire three times through the window, and scramble over the passenger seat for the opposite door.

Whoever shot the guy holding Mia is firing to give me cover. I shove open the passenger door and dive onto the cement, wondering who the hell it could be.

"*Get in here, Penn!*" shouts a male voice. "*Move!*"

As my unknown savior fires, I crab-walk across the cement and dive through the glass door. It's swinging shut behind me when a burst of machine-gun fire blasts plate glass all over my back.

"*Over here!*" shouts Mia. "*Hurry!*"

Mia is hiding behind a gigantic Oriental vase. I crawl to her and take cover, searching for whoever saved us. Gunfire from the tunnel sends glass spraying through the lobby. Thank God it's two in the morning.

"Get her clear!" screams a voice from my right.

"Who are you?"

"Logan! Don Logan!"

The chief of police . . .

"Get her out of here, Penn! There's probably more of them!"

He's right. "We've got to run for it, Mia." I look out into the seemingly empty lobby. "Call for backup, Don!"

"On the way! Get moving!"

As I pull Mia to her feet, Chief Logan rises from behind a club chair and begins firing his handgun through the shattered windows.

Where do we run? The door to the parking lot is beside the check-in desk, but the lot offers no guarantee of safety. There's another exit on Main Street, but that's a long run from here, and something tells me the Asians will be covering the main doors. I sprint across the lobby toward the hall that leads to Main Street, pulling Mia alongside me.

"Don't go outside!" Logan yells.

I'm not headed outside. There's a staircase in the hall that leads to the mezzanine, which has sheltered access to the elevators. When we reach the stairs, I start to send Mia up first, then change my mind. As I lead the way, I try to do what my father often preaches: *realize the danger before you're in it.*

"Don't hesitate," I say as I run. "If something happens, shoot first, sort it out lat—"

Mia screams so sharply that it hurts my ears.

I whirl, figuring someone is chasing us, but Mia is pointing past me, *up* the stairs. I half pull my trigger as I spin, then depress it the final distance as a blurry figure comes flying down toward me. I don't know if he's armed or not, but I keep pulling the trigger until a hundred and fifty pounds of muscle slams into me, knocking me back onto Mia.

"Is he dead?" she grunts, trying to scramble out from under me.

There's an Asian boy lying half on top of me. I don't know if he's dead or not, but he's still clutching a pistol in his hand. I slam my father's Browning against his elbow. Nothing happens. Not even a reflex jerk.

With great effort, I roll the kid off us and pull Mia to her feet.

"What do we do?" she asks, her chin quivering. "Where do we go?"

"Up. Back to the suite."

We race up to the mezzanine elevators. The wait is almost intolerable. When the door opens, I'm so nervous that I nearly fire a slug into the empty car, but we board, and before long I'm opening the door to Quentin's master suite. I thought the gunfire would have awakened half the hotel, but no one on the seventh floor seems to have noticed anything.

Inside the suite, I go straight to the window. Flashing red and blue lights bounce off the buildings on Pearl Street. The cavalry has arrived. Blue lights mean police, red lights the sheriff's department. It seems everyone has responded to Chief Logan's distress call.

Mia walks up beside me, panting. "Who was that? Why did they do that?"

"Those kids killed Sonny Cross. I guess they never left town after all."

The phone beside the sofa rings. I pick it up. "Hello?"

"Mr. Avery?" says the desk clerk.

"No, this is Mr. Cage."

"Hold, please. I have someone who wants to speak with you."

A ragged voice says, "Penn? Are you okay?"

"Don?"

"Yeah."

"We're okay. Is it secure down there?"

"Yes. We've got the PD and the sheriff's department here now."

"What the hell were you doing here?"

"I'll explain in a minute."

"Is my car still down there?" I ask, desperately wondering about my leather portfolio.

"No. The guy who had the drop on you stole it and made a run for it."

"Did you catch him?"

"Not yet."

"Don . . . I shot a guy on the mezzanine staircase."

"We found him. He's dead. Why don't you two come back down? It's completely safe, and we're going to need you to answer some questions."

"We'll be down in a minute." I hang up and look at Mia. "Are you up to talking to the police?"

She nods slowly. "I guess. God, my mother's going to *freak*."

My laughter starts as a chuckle, then blossoms into full-throated hysteria. Mia soon joins me. After we calm down and walk into the hallway, I consider waking Quentin. There's really nothing he can do tonight. And since Chief Logan, the hero of the hour, can't stand to be in the room with Quentin, it's probably best to let Drew's lawyer sleep. Especially since it looks like I lost Cyrus's threatening e-mails.

Quentin can cuss me out in the morning.

The lobby of the Eola looks like the site of a terrorist attack. More than a dozen uniformed cops and deputies move through the capacious room with their guns at the ready, eyeing each other suspiciously. Chief Logan is standing by the doors he was shooting through only minutes ago. At his feet lies the body of the boy who murdered Sonny Cross. I seat Mia in one of the club chairs and walk over to him.

"Hey, Penn," Don says, his voice muted. "The girl okay?"

"Yeah. I need to get her home, though."

"Who is she?"

"Mia Burke. She was a friend of Kate Townsend."

"I see," says Logan, but his eyes tell me he doesn't see at all.

"It's a long story."

"I've got time. Why do you think they attacked you?"

I point at the corpse. "Probably because I saw this punk kill Sonny Cross. They were wiping out the only witness against them."

Don looks down at the boy's shattered skull. "He doesn't even look human anymore. Are you sure that's the same kid?"

"Positive. I knew it the second I saw his face."

Logan looks relieved. "Good."

"What were *you* doing here? I mean, if you hadn't been . . . we'd be dead."

"An off-duty cop called in a report that he'd seen a black Lexus near the hotel this afternoon. I knew this was Avery's command center for Drew's defense, and I knew you'd seen the Asians hit

Sonny. I haven't been sleeping too well the past couple of nights, so I took a ride downtown. I saw you go into the hotel with the girl. I decided to hang around and see what was gonna happen after that."

I clap him on the shoulder and squeeze hard. "I owe you, buddy."

He shakes his head. "Just doing my job. Sonny Cross may have worked for the sheriff's department, but I knew him for most of my life. He was a good cop. He shouldn't have died the way he did."

"No." I look around at the deputies prowling the lobby. "Who called the sheriff's department?"

"I did. They were closer." Logan laughs quietly. "When the chief of police calls the sheriff's department for help in this town, you know he's desperate."

As I chuckle, Chief Logan turns to make sure no one is within earshot. "Did they take anything from you, Penn?"

I think about the evidence lost in the car. "No. Just the car."

He watches me carefully. "I imagine we'll find that soon enough. You sure there's nothing in there I need to look for, if we find it?"

The chief must have seen the portfolio in my hand when I walked across the lobby with Mia. "Spell it out, Don."

He looks over at two deputies talking a few yards away "I'm talking about something you wouldn't want to accidentally get lost before it could be returned to you."

Christ. If things have come to the point where the police chief can ask me this, this town is truly in bad shape. I look deep into Logan's eyes. I don't know him well—we've talked a few times at our daughters' softball games—but what I see in his face now convinces me that the time has come to take a chance. I hate to rely on anyone but myself—especially with a friend's life at stake—but sometimes you have to have a little faith. I lean toward Don and speak in a whisper.

"There was a leather portfolio in the car. There were two computer flash drives in it, and one envelope. I need that stuff bad, Don. Drew's life depends on it."

Logan nods. "What's in the envelope?"

"A hair from the head of Marko Bakic."

The chief's head snaps up, his eyes questioning.

"Find that car, Don."

"We will. *You* just make sure I know everything I need to know."

"I will. Can I take Mia home now? I have a feeling she's barely keeping it together."

Logan blows out a stream of air and looks back at the men moving through the lobby. "I guess we can take a statement from her tomorrow."

The crunch of glass heralds the approach of someone from the tunnel. My relief at being released evaporates at the sight of Sheriff Billy Byrd. The sheriff stops before the body on the ground and leans forward to look down past his gut. Then he surveys the lobby through the shattered doors.

"Christ on a crutch," he says in his heavy drawl. "They told me it looked like a war zone. I never thought I'd see something like this in my town."

Chief Logan offers Byrd his hand. The sheriff takes his time about shaking it.

"Who killed this one here?" Byrd asks, gesturing at the body on the ground.

"I did," says the chief.

"Contact wound, looks like."

"It was a hostage situation."

Byrd nods, then turns to me, his eyes boring into mine. "You got one, too?"

"That's right."

"Lucky, huh?"

"I don't feel too lucky, Sheriff. And I'm about to go home. Do you need me for anything?"

"Got a couple questions for you."

"I can pretty much fill you in," Logan says, tacitly claiming the crime scene for his department.

Byrd ignores him. "It's pretty late, Mr. Cage. What were you doing here with Mia Burke at this hour? She's still in high school, isn't she?"

"That's right."

"Does her mother know she's here with you?"

"My mother knows I'm with Mr. Cage," Mia says, stepping up to us.

Byrd smirks. "So what were you two doing here? Is this like Dr. Elliott and the Townsend girl?"

Hot blood rushes to my face. "You've got no right to say that to us."

The sheriff snorts and looks over at his men, who are gathering to watch our exchange. "It's my job to get to the bottom of this mess, ain't it?"

"Actually, I believe that's Chief Logan's job. And since he just saved our lives while you were sleeping at home, I'm not too well disposed toward you and your bullshit just now."

Sheriff Byrd pales. "You don't talk to me that way, smartass."

"I didn't hear anything," Chief Logan says quietly. "Why don't we let these two be on their way and concentrate on the work at hand?"

Sheriff Byrd hikes up his trousers and leans in close to me. "This is where Avery's staying, ain't it?"

"That's right."

"Is the girl helping you with the case?"

"She's working for us, yes. As a runner, basically. A gopher."

"Is that right, Miss Burke?"

Mia nods uncertainly.

"Are they paying you anything?"

Mia looks worriedly at me. "No. I'm doing it because I believe Dr. Elliott is innocent."

The sheriff snickers. "You're one of the few."

"All right, that's it," I say. "You want to ask more questions, you arrest us."

Byrd looks as though he's considering it.

Chief Logan takes a single step, but it's a big one. He places himself directly between me and the sheriff. "Get going, Penn," he says. "Call me tomorrow morning."

"Thanks again, Chief." I take Mia by the arm and lead her toward the corridor that runs out to Main Street. Then I stop and turn back to Logan. "I don't have a car."

Logan motions to one of his patrolmen. "Lee will drop you off."

"Thanks."

A young black patrolman detaches himself from a group of cops and walks toward us. Sheriff Byrd stares at me with open fury, but I ignore him. Too much has happened tonight to give a damn about a redneck sheriff and his agenda.

"Follow me, Mr. Cage," says the patrolman.

"Thank you."

The ride to Mia's house is mostly silent. The young patrolman driving us asks a couple of questions, but his only intent is to learn more about the kind of gun battle he is unlikely to see in this town again.

"How'd you get the guy on the stairs before he shot you?" he asks. "He was carrying a Glock, and there was a round in the chamber."

"I'm not sure. I killed a man like that once before. When I lived in Houston."

"A burglar?"

Mia is staring at me from her corner of the backseat.

"No," I reply, watching her. "He was the brother of a white supremacist I'd sent to death row. He broke into my house to kidnap my daughter. She was an infant then, and he was actually holding her when I shot him. I was so scared to shoot, I almost let him get out of the house."

"But you didn't."

"No. I was lucky then, too."

"Sho' was," says Lee, looking at me in his rearview mirror. "Man alive."

The squad car slows, then stops before Mia's house, a thirty-year-old home in a middle-income subdivision off Liberty Road.

"This it?" asks Lee.

"Yeah. Thanks."

He releases the locking mechanism on the rear doors, and we get out.

"I'll walk you up," I tell Mia.

She nods gratefully. After thanking Lee at his window, she starts up the sidewalk.

"I'll come by tomorrow morning," I promise, walking beside her. "I'll talk to Meredith and explain what happened."

"Or try to," Mia says, laughing nervously.

"Yeah. I think your Nancy Drew days are over."

She makes a sound I can't interpret. "You lost Kate's flash drives, didn't you?"

I nod. "And her journal."

"I'm sorry. How badly will that hurt Drew?"

"I was never going to use the journal. But we needed those drives."

"What about Marko's flash drive?"

I tap my pants pocket. "I still have that. Let's just hope it has something useful on it."

"And that Lucien can crack it."

"If he can't, someone can."

Mia unlocks her front door and steps through it. She looks into the depths of the house, then back at me. "Mom's asleep, thank God. I hope no one hears about everything tonight and decides to wake her up."

"I think you'll be okay on that."

Mia reaches out and pulls my hand until I'm standing inside with her. All I can see clearly are her wide eyes shining in the dark.

"What is it?" I ask.

"I almost died, didn't I?"

"You could have," I admit. "And it would have been my fault. If Chief Logan hadn't been there—"

"Look at me, Penn."

"I am."

"I've never felt more alive than I do at this moment."

My palms are still tingling from the aftereffects of the fight at the hotel. But there's something else happening within me, too. "I think that's pretty common in these kinds of situations."

"I want to kiss you," Mia says.

"We talked about this before."

"I know. I know we can't have a relationship. I even respect that. I just want this moment, okay?"

Before I can think of a response, she stands on tiptoe, takes my face in her hands, and kisses me full on the mouth. I don't kiss her back, but neither do I pull away. The truth is, I feel exactly as she does about our brush with death—phenomenally alive to every molecule of existence. And I can't imagine anything more alive than the swelling mouth pressing against mine. Mia's lips part slightly, and I feel her tongue brush against my lips. For one moment, I open my mouth and taste her, and in that moment I feel a rush of overwhelming desire, the first few feet of a plunge into bliss that Caitlin dubbed evolutionary nirvana. Mia gives my lower lip a soft bite, then pulls away.

"There," she says, her eyes shining. "See? No harm, no foul. Tomorrow I'll act like it never happened. I promise."

"Try to sleep, Mia."

"Not a chance. But don't worry about me. And don't feel guilty. Promise me."

"I'll try."

Her teeth flash in the darkness. Then she gently pushes me out the door.

As I walk down the sidewalk, the chatter of a police radio brings me back to the present. I've got a lot of work to do tonight. I might have lost Kate's flash drives, but I still have Sonny Cross's computer and case notes. If I'm lucky, something in them will lead me to the dark soul who has brought so much death to this town. *My* town.

Cyrus White.

CHAPTER
34

News of the shooting at the Eola Hotel sent the town into shock. Caitlin published a detailed account of the attack, based on the account I gave her after waking her from a deep sleep in my bedroom early that morning. There was no point in trying to keep it from her. Besides, I figured the more people who knew about my stolen Saab, the better the odds it would be found. Caitlin seemed particularly interested in what I'd been doing at the hotel with Mia at 2 a.m. I explained that Mia was helping Quentin and me investigate Kate Townsend's life, and that beyond that I couldn't say more. This didn't satisfy Caitlin, but she was so glad to get the inside story of the attack that she let it go, at least for a while. After she exhausted my memory of the night's events—the ones I could tell her about, anyway—I pretended to get ready for bed. Caitlin got dressed, called her editor, and drove down to the *Examiner* offices to begin working the story.

As soon as she left, I brewed a pot of coffee and retrieved Sonny Cross's private case materials from my safe. Then I scanned twelve of Sonny's MiniDV surveillance tapes using fast forward. It was a tedious process, but by the end of it, I'd found two that showed Kate Townsend walking into and out of Cyrus White's building at the Brightside Manor Apartments. These tapes were what Quentin had asked me to get for him, but they didn't satisfy me. I wanted Cyrus in the flesh.

I began sifting through Sonny's case notebooks, line by line. They contained copious notes on the drug activity at Brightside Manor—and elsewhere in Natchez—but nothing that would help me locate Cyrus, unless he's staying at one of his known safe houses. And Chief Logan assured me that all those are being checked on a regular basis. Sonny's notes made it plain that he got most of his information from drug users or couriers he'd busted and then forced to work for him in exchange for their continuing freedom. My problem was that Sonny only referred to these snitches by code names. The code names seemed oddly chosen until I realized that they were all characters played by John Wayne on the big screen. "Rooster." "Chance." "Ethan." "Cahill." "Big Jake." "Chisum." "McQ." Almost all the information Sonny had on Cyrus White had been provided by "Ethan," but nowhere in the notebooks could I find a key to the identity of these snitches.

Setting aside the notebooks, I began scouring the files on Sonny's laptop computer. After nearly an hour, I hit pay dirt. An encrypted file. I couldn't open it, but what excited me was that this file seemed to be the only encrypted one on the computer. As soon as I was sure of this, I called Lucien Morse's cell phone. Lucien happily agreed to meet me at the Eola the next morning to hack Sonny's file. All he required was another five hundred dollars.

Then I called Quentin at the Eola and briefed him on the battle he'd slept through last night. He told me that Doris had awakened at one point, thinking she'd heard a shot, but no sound followed, so they went back to sleep. Quentin cared little about the deaths of the Asians, but the loss of Cyrus's threatening e-mails left him sputtering with rage. He'd enjoyed about thirty seconds of euphoria after I told him about the existence of the e-mails—then disaster. When I tried to mollify him by telling him I'd draw up a subpoena for Cyrus's e-mail records, Quentin just laughed.

"He uses that e-mail address for dope trafficking, man. You're never gonna find that. He's got that shit under somebody else's name."

"Then we somehow have to convince Cyrus's crew that giving us that address is for Cyrus's own good," I argued.

Quentin laughed harder. "They'll never buy that. The e-mails for that account could probably put Cyrus in Parchman for five hundred years on drug charges. The chances that he'll be convicted of Kate Townsend's murder are practically zero. Cyrus can read the newspaper and see that for himself. Drew looks like a slam dunk right now. You leave the defense strategy to me. I've been here before."

After this conversation, Quentin left the Eola to visit Drew at the county jail. I called my father and asked him to take Annie out of town for a few days. He agreed without hesitation. He and my mother plan to leave for Jackson tonight.

Those arrangements made, I drove to the Eola Hotel and found Lucien Morse waiting for me in the lobby. The St. Stephen's sophomore was dressed to the nines, just as he was last night. Plastic sheets had been tacked up over the shattered hotel doors, and a construction crew was already working to repair the bullet damage. In the elevator, Lucien asked some morbid questions about the attack. The only answer I gave him was Sonny Cross's notebook computer.

While Lucien tried to break Sonny's encryption program, I sat at the coffee table and drafted a letter for the *Top of the Morning* column of the *Natchez Examiner,* a feature that usually contains editorials on the local political scene or articles on community events. The purpose of the letter was to announce my intent to enter the special mayoral election as a candidate. I'm not sure how the community will respond to it, but I know two people who will be profoundly affected. Shad Johnson will be enraged, and Quentin Avery will be ecstatic to have Shad distracted from Drew's upcoming trial. A third person will be more deeply affected, of course. When I deliver that letter to the *Examiner* offices, Caitlin will know I mean to run for mayor. What will happen after that, I don't know. But I have more important business to take care of before delivering the letter—business that Lucien made possible twenty minutes ago.

I am holding in my hand a printout of the contents of Sonny Cross's encrypted computer file: a key to the true identities of Sonny's snitches. Along with their names, Sonny recorded in this file the addresses and telephone numbers of each informant, and also details of the offenses they had committed—in effect the swords that he dangled over their heads.

Trying not to hope for too much, I lift the hotel phone and dial one of the two numbers given for code name "Ethan"—a drug courier whose real name is Jaderious Huntley. "Jaderious," I recall, was the name of the person who shot the photo of Cyrus and Kate that was stored on Kate's flash drive. The "597" prefix tells me the number I'm calling is a Natchez cell phone. After five rings, I get the familiar automated voice-mail greeting of Cingular Wireless. I hang up without leaving a message, then try the next number beside Huntley's name.

This one looks like a residential phone. After seven rings, a young male voice says, "Jaderious."

"Hello, Ethan."

Jaderious gasps, and then the phone goes dead.

I dial the number again.

No answer.

I dial again and let it ring twenty times. No answer. I hang up and dial again. I can almost see a young black man staring at his telephone in horror, wondering if he's hallucinating. I have no doubt that the only man in the world who knew the real identity of "Ethan" was Sonny Cross. And everyone knows that Sonny is dead. On my eighth try, someone picks up the phone but says nothing.

"This is Sonny Cross," I say in a calm voice.

The silence stretches to infinity.

"You might as well talk, Ethan. I'm not going away."

A tense voice says, "Sonny be dead."

"That's right. But I'm not."

"Who are you?"

"A friend of Sonny's."

"Oh, man, don't be telling me that. That shit be over with now."

"It's not over, Jaderious. But it can be. I need one thing from you. Just one thing. After that, I'll burn your file. It'll be like you never knew Sonny at all."

"Don't play that shit, man. You guys don't never stop. You think I'm a slave or something."

"You put yourself in this spot, Ethan. Not me."

"Don't say that name, man. Just tell me what you want."

"I want to see you face-to-face."

"No way! Shit gone crazy in the street. That task force be on everybody's ass. Everybody's uptight. I can't be seen with you."

"You don't even know who I am."

"I know you white, that's enough. Just tell me what you want!"

"I need to know where Cyrus is."

Jaderious sucks in his breath like a monk hearing the voice of Satan. "You *crazy*," he hisses. "You stone crazy, man."

"You're going to have to talk to me, Jaderious. One way or another."

"No, I ain't. If you know my number, you know where I stay at. And you ain't coming up in here, I know that. Especially right now."

"Tell me where he is, Ethan. Nobody will ever know it was you."

Jaderious laughs openly. "Not even if I *knew*, dog, which I *don't*."

"If I have to come talk to you at home, people will see."

"You come talk to me in person, you won't make it out of here. So it don't matter. You bluffing anyway, dog. I gots to go. Don't call back."

He hangs up before I can respond.

I sit quietly on the sofa for a while. Then I call Quentin Avery's cell phone.

"What is it?" Quentin asks in a taut voice.

"Are you still at the jail?"

"Yes. And I'm not happy."

"I need to get into the Brightside Manor Apartments."

"So?"

"I need to get in there safely."

"And?"

"Shit, Quentin, don't play stupid. Can you get me in and out?"

Silence. "I suppose so. But I'm not sure I want to do that."

"Why not? Drew's acquittal could depend on it."

"I'm not sure that's a good enough reason, considering the price I'll pay for doing it. Besides, this deluded ass you call your friend is ready to move to death row right now. He won't listen to me."

"What do you mean?"

"Are you at the Eola?"

"Yes."

"Stay there. I'm on my way."

Twenty minutes later, Quentin storms into the suite with as much violence as a man with one foot can muster. His eyes are almost wild.

"What did Drew do?" I ask.

"Just what you said! He's demanding to take the stand!"

I nod but keep silent. There's no point in saying I told you so.

"This fucking guy," Quentin mutters, "he's the worst kind of chump, you know that?"

I still don't respond. The best thing to do with this kind of anger is let it be vented as quickly as possible.

Quentin opens the minibar, takes out a small bottle of bourbon, unscrews the top, and swallows half the contents. "*Hell*, yeah," he says, wiping his mouth on his sleeve. "Doris would fry my ass if she saw that."

"Why is Drew the worst kind of chump, Quentin?"

The lawyer walks to the plush sofa, ponders it for a moment, then turns and lets himself fall into it. "Because that fool has decided he wants to tell the truth, the whole truth, and nothing but the truth."

"And that surprised you?"

"He's a fucking Boy Scout!"

"An Eagle Scout, actually."

Quentin drains the rest of the bourbon. "Drew Elliott is a chump because he thinks the rules are different for him. Because he's done the right thing for ninety-nine percent of his life, he thinks all he has to do now is get up on the stand to explain to everybody how it really was. And what I can*not* make that boy understand is that if he does that, he's going to destroy himself. I mean, this guy has been lying to his wife every day for almost a year. He's been fucking his babysitter! And now the girl is dead! Dead and *pregnant!* So why the hell should a jury believe anything he has to say now?"

"You're preaching to the choir, Quentin."

"There's no way in hell I'm letting this guy get up and tell the jury he found Kate's body and didn't report it."

"How can you stop him?"

"I can't. But maybe you can."

I don't want to have this discussion right now. "What about getting me into Brightside Manor?"

"What's in there that's so all-fired important?"

"A snitch who knows where Cyrus White is."

Something tugs at the corner of Quentin's mouth, something disagreeable. "How about another bottle of bourbon?"

I go to the minibar and retrieve another bottle. Quentin sips slowly from it, his eyes still smoldering. "I can get you in and out, all right. But if I do, every black man and woman in that complex is going to know I did it. And that's going to cost me down the road. You understand? That may not be the noble thing to say, but it's the truth."

"What's it going to cost you?"

"Cases. Business. Reputation."

The question I left unasked on the day I met Quentin at my father's office returns to haunt me now. Why did he stop taking civil rights cases to pursue personal injury and class action suits? But at this point, I feel the answer is self-evident.

"What the hell am I supposed to do?"

"I'm not saying I won't do it. I'm just saying it would be better if you could find another way."

"Such as?"

"Lure the guy you need out of there."

"With what? He's scared shitless."

"Then find somebody else to get you in."

"Such as?"

As Quentin ruminates over his whiskey, anger rises into my throat. Drew's life is on the line, and his lawyer is worried about some personal injury case five years down the road? I get up without a word and walk to the door of the suite.

"Where are you going?" Quentin asks.

"To do my job. You need to start thinking about whether you've got what it takes to do yours."

"Hey, don't—"

I slam the door and hurry down the hall.

The Brightside Manor Apartments stand like a visual reprimand to every liberal fantasy of government-subsidized housing. The dilapidated buildings look like sets built for a Blaxploitation flick from the seventies, like you could walk up and push them down with your foot. Thirteen big saltboxes grouped on the edge of St. Catherine's Creek, all centered around a massive square of asphalt crowded with one of the strangest collections of motor transportation in the nation.

At least fifty people are sitting or standing within sight of me. The oldest ones sit on their stoops beneath dented metal awnings. The middle-aged stand in little knots, the men sharing bottles wrapped in paper sacks, the women holding babies. I don't see any teenagers—it's as though they've been drafted for some special war—but several toddlers walk unsupervised through the parking lot. Three of them are naked.

"How long has he been gone?" asks my father.

Dad is referring to James Ervin, a retired black police officer he has treated since the 1960s, when he was the doctor for the

Natchez police department. After Dad agreed to help me get into Brightside Manor, he recruited Ervin to make the initial foray into Jaderious Huntley's building. Ervin graciously agreed, and also volunteered his beat-up pickup truck for the mission.

"Eleven minutes," I answer.

Dad clicks his tongue against his teeth. "I don't like it."

"Let's give it a little longer. Ervin sounded calm before he went in."

Dad nods thoughtfully.

When I called him from the lobby of the Eola, he and my mother were only minutes from leaving for Jackson with Annie. He told me he'd visited Brightside Manor many times in the old days, which to him means the era when he made frequent house calls. Back then, he carried a spotlight and a pistol in his black medical bag. He rarely makes house calls these days, but he still has patients who live at Brightside Manor. He understood my anxiety about visiting the place uninvited, but he felt confident that with him along for the ride, we could do it. I was inclined to believe him. No white doctor in this town has treated more black patients than Tom Cage. More important, he's treated them exactly as he treats his white patients, and the black community knows that.

Today could be the acid test of that goodwill.

Our plan was to send James Ervin up to Jaderious's apartment to verify that the informant was inside. Then we would go up ourselves, pretending to make an emergency medical call at number 28. This subterfuge was primarily designed to protect us, not Jaderious; that it might also give the snitch some cover is incidental.

The ring of my cell phone makes us both jump in the seat.

"Hello?" I say, putting my cell on speakerphone.

"Your boy's up here," says James Ervin. "He tried to rabbit. I'm holding a gun on him now."

"Damn," says Dad. "I didn't know James took a gun up there."

"Bring your black bag," Ervin says. "He's more likely to talk if we give him an out with Cyrus's people."

"We're on our way," I promise.

Any hopes that we might make a covert approach to Jaderious's building were dashed when we arrived. Our white faces began to draw attention as soon as James Ervin left the truck. A lot of people have pointed at our truck, but no one has yet confronted us. If we weren't sitting in such a junky vehicle, they'd probably think we were cops. They may think that anyway.

Dad and I are both armed, but something tells me we should leave our guns behind. Dad doesn't agree, so we compromise. I leave the Browning behind, but he brings his small Smith & Wesson .38—the "Lady Smith"—in his bag. We cross the parking lot with purposeful strides, but not too fast. People sense fear the same way animals do. We're just two guys with a job to do.

Two white guys.

I'm glad one of us is over seventy. The people milling around the buildings don't know what to make of that.

Like most apartments in the South, the staircases at Brightside Manor are outside the buildings. We climb to the door that James Ervin entered fifteen minutes ago, give a perfunctory knock, and walk inside.

The stink of burnt grease and garbage hits me like a sucker punch. Jaderious Huntley is sitting on his hands in a wooden chair at the center of the front room. James Ervin stands eight feet away, a nickel-plated pistol in his hand. Sonny's notes said Huntley is twenty-eight years old, but he looks forty. He's wearing nothing but a pair of gym shorts, and his torso is so gaunt that I wonder if he's eaten in weeks. His face is hollow, his eyes set deep in their sockets. If he's a drug courier, he's been using the product he carries for a long time.

I walk to the chair and kneel in front of him. "Let's make this quick and painless, Jaderious."

Refusing to meet my eye, he shakes his head as though he's being addressed by a moron. "You don't get it, dog. You done killed me already."

"I tried to do this long distance. You wouldn't play."

Huntley leans back and folds his arms. He seems to equate this gesture with donning a suit of armor. "I ain't saying *shit* about what you asked me on the phone. You ain't cops!" He points at James Ervin. "'Cept this useless motherfucker, and he too old to do shit now. Too old to fuck his old lady no more."

Ervin's face remains as unmoved as the face of a cliff.

"You're right," I say patiently. "We're not cops. That's why you're looking at this the wrong way. You're thinking that if you don't tell me what I need to know, I'm going to have you busted for that old drug charge."

Jaderious sniffs with the arrogance of an exiled dictator. Then he begins picking his fingernails.

"But I'm not going to do that," I go on. "Because it doesn't help me any. No, if you don't tell me what I need to know, I'm going to put it out on the street that you've been Sonny Cross's snitch on Cyrus for the past year and a half."

The informant's whole body jerks.

"Then I'm going to give your name to the task force. They'll haul you over to Tracetown and question you for about six hours. And all your homeys will know about it."

"You can't do that, man!" he cries, shaking his head violently.

"I don't want to. Because if I do, you won't see the end of the week. Maybe not even the end of the day. And I really don't have anything against you personally."

Jaderious's eyes watch me as they might an angry rattlesnake. "You don't know Cyrus," he says softly. "You don't know the things he do."

"I have an idea."

"No, you don't. I'm talkin' 'bout mutilating people, man. Cutting off *parts* and shit! Drilling holes in their bones. While they still *alive,* dog."

Spittle flies from Jaderious's mouth, and the whites of his eyes betray true panic. His tale of torture has taken me by surprise. I would have expected such tactics from an Asian drug gang, but not from a Natchez drug dealer. If Jaderious were to suffer such a fate because of my visit here today, what would I do? If I were still a prosecutor, I could offer him police protection. But as a private citizen, I can offer nothing. Yet when I think of Sonny Cross dying in his front yard, afraid for his sons' lives, and Kate Townsend jammed half-naked into the waterlogged limbs of a tree, my concern for Jaderious Huntley quickly bleeds away.

"You've got one way out of this," I tell him. "This man over here"—I jerk my hand at my father—"that's Dr. Tom Cage. He can give you something to make you puke like you're going cold turkey. And when people ask what we were doing up here, you can say he made a house call as a favor to your mama. You got a mama, Jaderious?"

He nods suspiciously.

"The story may be thin, but it's all you've got. And you're not getting *that* unless you give me what I need. If you don't give me what I need, you get a neon billboard screaming, 'Jaderious Huntley is a punk for the cops.' And then you get some personal quality time with Cyrus White."

Huntley blinks with jittery speed, as though his eyelids are a meter for brain activity. I look over at James Ervin. The retired cop has the eyes of a beagle, perpetually sad. What does he think about me interrogating a fellow black man? Does he see Jaderious as a brother? Or does he see a lost soul who long ago gave himself over to evil?

"If he's that scared," Ervin says quietly, "Cyrus must be close by."

Jaderious turns to Ervin. "Close enough to cut your motherfucking head off, old man. You Tom-ass mother*fucker.*"

Ervin stares at the drug courier for a bit, then takes three deliberate steps toward him and looks down into his face. "Boy, you nothing," he says. "You know that? You worse than nothing. You dragging your whole people backwards, and you don't even know it. And you ain't got nobody but yourself to blame."

Jaderious turns his head and looks at the wall, as though pulling a curtain around himself.

James Ervin walks to the door. "I say feed him to his boss."

I join Ervin at the door. "Come on, Dad. He's too stupid to save himself."

My hand is on the doorknob when Huntley says, "Hold up, now."

I open the door.

The snitch jumps up from his chair. "I said hold up, dog!"

"Your mouth is moving, but I don't hear anything."

Fresh panic twists his face. Even this desperate to live, he can't wring the information out of himself. "I don't know where Cyrus be, man! But I know somebody who might."

I step outside the apartment.

"I ain't playing, man! That's all I got! *Please,* dog. It's Cyrus's cousin!"

This stops me. "What's his name?"

"Stoney Washington."

I look at James Ervin. He nods and says, "He's a truck driver. Couple of possession busts."

"That's him!" says Jaderious. "Cyrus fucked up his sister. Quenisha was a ho' over in Ferriday, and she got crossed up with Cyrus over some coke."

"And?"

Jaderious's eyes close, then open slowly. "Cyrus fucked her up, man."

"How?"

The snitch shakes his head again.

"Tell us."

"He cut her up, man. He messed up her insides and shit. I don't want to think about it. Cyrus be *bad,* man. He's like the devil when he's mad. Why you think I been talking to Sonny?"

"Because he could send you to Parchman."

Jaderious stops twitching and stands before us, like a starving soldier in the act of surrender. "No, man. Cyrus makes Parchman look like Christmas. I knew that girl. I loved her. She was a ho', but I don't care 'bout that. Now she just be fucked up. Stays home all the time. Takes medicine to keep her from killing herself."

I force myself to focus on the problem at hand. "What about her cousin?"

"Stoney still be tight with Cyrus. Moves shit for him in his truck. After the thing with Quenisha, Cyrus made him choose, see? Stoney swore he wouldn't try to do nothing 'bout what Cyrus had done. Said Nisha deserved that shit. What else could he say?"

"Go on."

"If Stoney believes you can really take Cyrus down, he might talk to you. You give me your number, and I'll call you."

"You think I'm stupid, Jaderious?"

"What choice you got, dog? You wouldn't be here if you had something else. And I'll probably be dead tomorrow anyway."

From behind me, my father says, "Give him your number, Penn."

I pick a pizza box off the floor and write my cellular number on it. Then I walk back to the door.

"Wait!" Jaderious cries.

"What?"

"You forgot to give me the stuff. The shit to make me puke."

I'd already forgotten.

Dad opens his bag and digs in it for a few seconds. Then he takes out the bottle of syrup of ipecac we purchased at Walgreen's an hour ago.

"Open your mouth," he tells Jaderious.

Huntley obeys. "Will this get me high, Doc?"

"No, low. In a few minutes, you're going to make a beeline for the john."

Dad pours a stream of the syrup down Jaderious's throat. The snitch gags, then swallows three times. When he straightens up, he grimaces. Without a word he walks swiftly out of the room.

"Throw an opened syringe in his trash," I tell Dad.

He does, and then we depart.

There's a reception committee waiting at the foot of the stairs. Two large black men in their thirties block our passage, with a woman who looks about sixty standing to the side of them.

"What y'all doing up there?" asks one of the men. "You cops or what?"

Before I can answer, Dad says, "I was making a house call. That boy was near death. He was trying to go cold turkey, and it almost killed him."

"What you mean 'house call'?" asks the woman. "Doctors don't make house calls no more."

"I do," Dad says, walking to the bottom of the stairs without the slightest hint of anxiety. "You ought to know that, Iola Johnson."

The woman's eyes go wide. "Dr. Cage!"

Dad smiles. "In the flesh."

"What you doing up in here? Lord, I ain't seen you in twenty years. I should have known you, though."

"That boy's sick, Iola. Dope sick. His mama called me, and then James Ervin called me, and I thought I'd better get on out here."

The woman shakes her head in wonder. "That boy ain't no good, Dr. Cage. He's all up *in* that dope, just like most of these young no-goods." She nods at the men with her. "We didn't know who you was, that's all. Me and my boys try to stay up with who comes and goes round here. Now and then we get some bad white men."

"Who have you been seeing for medical care?" Dad asks. "Dr. Jeffers?"

Iola cackles. "Ain't been seeing nobody! Ain't had to, thank God. Ain't got no money to see one. I tell you, though, old Arthur starting to get me now that I'm getting up in years."

Dad gives the woman advice about her arthritis, and then we walk out to James Ervin's truck. As the engine rumbles to life, Jaderious's terror comes back to me, and with it his description of Cyrus's acts of retribution: *I'm talkin' 'bout mutilating people, man. Cutting off parts and shit! Drilling holes in their bones. While they still* alive, *dog*

"It's time to get Annie out of town," I say softly.

"Past time," Dad agrees. He turns to Ervin. "Thank you, James."

The retired cop shakes his head, his beagle eyes filled with pain. "This world be goin' down, Dr. Cage. I never seen it this bad. It's like the end times or something."

Dad squeezes Ervin's knee but says nothing. Then he turns to me and says, "I read that Mayor Jones finally stepped down."

Perfect timing, as ever. "I heard that, too."

"You heard what James just said. Do you still think you want that job?"

"I'm considering it. Caitlin seems to think this town doesn't want to be saved. I recall you expressing that sentiment not long ago."

"Not precisely that sentiment." Dad reaches into his pocket, takes out a cigar, and begins unwrapping it. "There's a quote I remember—I don't recall where it's from. It may be the Torah."

"What is it?" I ask, ready to hear a proverb about the wisdom of knowing when to walk away from something.

" 'Just because you will not see the work completed, does not mean you are free not to take it up.' " Dad smiles and takes out his lighter. "Or something to that effect."

"Like Moses," intones James Ervin. "He never saw the promised land, but he sho' led his people there. Sho' did."

Dad's eyes twinkle with mischief.

An hour after we left Brightside Manor, Annie and my parents were on Highway 61 South, bound for the relative safety of Jackson. When I got home, I found Caitlin sitting on my front steps. It was odd to see her at rest, without even a cell phone in her hand. I started to ask if she wanted to cook dinner together, but before I got five words out, she stood and put her finger to my lips. Then she took my hand and led me through the blue door. She didn't stop in the kitchen, but walked me down the hall to the door of my bedroom. There she stood on tiptoe and gave me a long, gentle kiss. The resentment that kept me from making love with her two nights ago still simmered somewhere within me, but I'd been through too much in the intervening time to worry about who was right or wrong about anything. Desire rose in me with primal intensity, and Caitlin responded with passion bordering on violence. As our clothes fell around us, she turned and splayed both hands against the wall, then thrust her hips back against me. I stood back for a moment, enthralled by the black mane of hair falling over her shoulder blades.

"*Hurry,*" she said roughly.

CHAPTER

35

I'm sitting in the Center City Grill, a microcosm of New Orleans located at the geographical center of downtown Natchez. Center City has a brick courtyard, wrought-iron tables, lush ferns, a fountain, a good bar, and well-traveled owners of some cultivation, as the local euphemism goes. Seated across the table from me is Jaderious Huntley. The snitch is wearing black sweatpants and a dirty T-shirt, and he looks about as twitchy as a junkie waiting for his next fix.

This morning, Jaderious called me to say that Stoney Washington was willing to talk to me about Cyrus, but only face-to-face. That smelled like a trap to me, so I said the meeting would have to happen at a public place of my choosing. Jaderious put this to Stoney, who reluctantly agreed. I chose Center City Grill because it's always busy at lunch, and also because Jaderious and Stoney are unlikely to run into anyone who would recognize them here.

"Why didn't Stoney come with you?" I ask.

Jaderious looks anxiously at the nearby tables. They're filled, but nobody's paying attention to us. "Stoney don't want to be seen with me. Bad for his health. Don't worry, he'll be here."

My cell phone vibrates. It's Caitlin, calling from the newspaper office. I'll call her back after the meeting. I can't relax my vigilance with Jaderious for even a moment. He looks like he'd bolt if a waitress dropped a tray.

"What you gonna do if you find Cyrus?" he asks.

"Talk to him."

Jaderious shakes his head. "You crazy. You want to stay *far* away from that cat. You ought to just walk away now. Both of us. There's still time to call Stoney and—"

"Forget it. After this, you might be free of me, but you're staying for this meeting. You have to make sure I'm talking to the right guy."

Jaderious freezes, his eyes fixed on something behind me.

I turn and glance at the main entrance of the restaurant. To get in or out of Center City, patrons walk through a long courtyard lined with wrought-iron tables, then pass through a door with windows set in it. Right now, a black man of about twenty with a red rag tied on his head is standing outside that door, surveying the tables inside.

"Is that Stoney?" I ask.

Jaderious's chair screeches on the floor.

I whirl and grab his arm before he can run. Jaderious is half out of his seat with terror. I grab his arm and hold him tight. "Who is that?"

"One of Cyrus's guys! I gotta get out of here!"

"Okay. Just stay calm. He won't do anything while we're sitting with all these people. I can have cops here in two minutes."

Jaderious looks at me like I'm insane. "Man, he'll shoot *all* these motherfuckers to get me. We gots to go *now*."

I look toward the kitchen. There's probably an exit there, but I've never seen it. There is, however, a small door in the back wall of the main dining room that leads to an alley. On busy days, I've sometimes parked in that alley and entered the restaurant that way.

"What's he doing now?" I ask.

"Looking straight at me," Jaderious whispers. "I'm dead, man. Aw, *shit*."

"There's a back way out. A door in the wall almost directly be-hind you, about thirty feet away."

"He's coming in, man!"

I rise and pull Jaderious to his feet. As I lead him between the tables toward the door, I reach into my jacket pocket for my cell phone.

"You got a gun?" Jaderious asks.

"Yes. Tell me if he pulls his." I pull out my cell phone and dial 911.

A female voice says, "911 emergency."

"This is Penn Cage," I say quietly. "There's about to be a shoot-ing at the Center City Grill. Get some squad cars here as fast as possible. Call Chief Logan and tell him what I said."

We're almost at the door. I pocket the phone and grip the butt of Dad's Browning. "You open it," I tell Jaderious.

He does.

"Penn Cage!" warbles a woman from the table nearest the door.

It's one of my mother's friends. I smile at her, then slip through the door and pull it shut after me.

Jaderious is already sprinting toward Main Street.

"Wait!" I yell.

"Fuck that shit!"

I charge after him. He's younger than I am, but I'm betting a junkie's wind won't last long. Jaderious slows down to slip around a work van blocking the alley. I speed up, hoping to finesse the gap between the van and the wall at high speed. As I twist my body, someone leans out of the van's side door and slams a fist into my chest.

The breath explodes from my lungs. As I tumble forward, the man who hit me catches me under the arms and drags me inside the van. He throws me onto the metal floor, steps on my chest, and jerks my gun from my jacket. While he slides the side door shut, the engine roars to life, and the van races up the alley—away from Jaderious.

When the foot leaves my chest, I see that I'm lying in an open space with power tools all around me. My assailant, an enormous black man wearing a purple Alcorn Braves football jersey, is sitting on a homemade bench that runs the length of the van's cargo area. The van lurches to the right, onto Franklin Street, then left again.

"Hello, Mr. Cage," says a deep voice from behind my head.

I tilt my head back.

A heavily muscled black man is sitting against the bulkhead of the van. He has a bald head and dark, penetrating eyes. A solitary gold chain adorns his neck.

"Cyrus?" I ask.

The bald man grins. "Oh, yeah." He looks back at his compatriot. "Hold him down, Blue."

The mountain of a man who hit me rises into a crouch and plants what must be a size-16 Nike running shoe in the center of my chest again.

"I stomp on your heart," he says, "you'll be dead. So don't do nothing."

"I won't."

A strange and powerful hissing sound comes from behind my head. Filled with unreasoning panic, I jerk my head back again. Cyrus is holding a small blowtorch in his hand.

"*Wait!*" I scream, recalling Jaderious's tales of torture. "*What do you want to know?*"

Cyrus belly-laughs at my terror. The man called Blue just shakes his head. I'm trying to think of a way to bribe Cyrus when he picks up a stainless-steel spoon from the bench and holds the flame of the blowtorch to its bottom. He smiles as he watches the spoon, then kills the flame and sets the spoon on the bench. A white blister pack like those in my father's medical bag appears in his hand. Cyrus rips it open and removes a syringe. Then he draws whatever is in the spoon into the syringe.

"What are you doing?" I ask. "Are you going to give me an overdose?"

Cyrus holds up the syringe and taps it a couple of times. "Naw, man. Gonna give you *just* the right amount. Give you a nice little ride."

I try to twist away from the needle, but Blue puts more weight behind his Nike. It feels like a tree trunk pinning me to the floor.

"Get his vein up," says Cyrus.

Blue cocks Dad's Browning, presses the barrel against my forehead, then closes his free hand around my left biceps with an iron grip. "He got good veins, man."

Cyrus squats beside me, his black eyes gleaming. Then he slips the needle into my antecubital vein with the casual expertise of a phlebotomist. I don't feel the prick, but when he depresses the plunger of the syringe, I feel absolute terror.

"*What was it?*" I scream.

Blue releases my biceps. Cyrus pats my inner elbow, then gets back up on the bench. "You'll find out," he says, his eyes shining. "Here it comes."

The first thing I feel is a rush of warmth to my stomach, just below my heart. Then it spreads outward, suffusing my limbs with a wholly unfamiliar numbness. Panic balloons in my chest, but just as suddenly the pressure evaporates, and my muscles go limp.

"Don't fight it," urges Cyrus. "Let it find the place."

"What . . . ?"

"Jesus Dust," says Cyrus.

"Look at his eyes," says Blue. "Shit, dog, he gone now."

Cyrus laughs deep in his chest.

"Where we going?" asks an unfamiliar voice.

The driver? I can't make my head turn to look. My muscles refuse to obey my nerves.

"You know where," says Cyrus. "You still with us, Mr. Cage?"

I try to answer, but what emerges from my mouth is one long, meaningless syllable.

"*Yeah,*" says Cyrus, infinitely amused by my behavior.

Blue leans over me and laughs like a father watching his baby trying to speak his first words.

I come awake on a sleeping bag on a hard floor. A metal floor. I roll over and squint against bright fluorescent lights.

"Here he is," says a deep voice. "Here he comes."

Cyrus is sitting in an office chair about eight feet away from me, his elbows on his knees, his dark eyes on me. The huge man called Blue leans against the wall behind him.

"How you feel?" asks Cyrus.

"I don't know. Weird."

"That's the dust. You never done heroin?"

A ripple of shock courses through me, but the reaction is strangely muted. "No."

Cyrus nods happily. "Sweet, ain't it?"

My watch is gone. So is my cell phone. "What time is it?"

"Party time!" laughs Cyrus.

"Oh, yeah," says Blue. His voice can't be much higher than Barry White's.

"Where are we?"

"Look around," suggests Cyrus. "You don't know?"

The room appears to be a laboratory of some sort. Thirty feet wide by forty feet long, it contains several pieces of what appears to be industrial electrical equipment. In the far corner, a Naugahyde recliner sits before a small television on a counter. A sleeper sofa stands against another wall. Against the wall to my right is some sort of mechanical cart. Emblazoned on its steel side is a blue trident with the letters "TBC" beneath it.

"Triton Battery?" I ask.

Cyrus nods. "My old employer. They helping me out now in ways they never dreamed."

"I used to work here, too. The summer after my freshman year in college."

"Yeah? Most everybody worked here at one time or other. Here or IP."

The Triton Battery Company came to Natchez in 1936 to build batteries for Pullman railcars. In 1940 they retooled the line to manufacture batteries for diesel submarines. After the war it was truck batteries, marine batteries, whatever fit the changing market. When the plant shut down three years ago, Triton was using its ancient equipment to produce motorcycle batteries for European and Asian manufacturers.

"What part of the plant are we in?"

"Testing area. It's the only part where the air-conditioning still works. This and the guardhouse. This is my temporary crib."

If I'm not dead, it's because Cyrus needs me alive for something. Probably information. Again Jaderious's stories of torture zing through my head. How should I play it? Tell everything I know right away? Or hold something back so that I'll have something to "give up" later? A predator like Cyrus won't believe I've revealed everything until he sweats something out of me. But what does he want to know?

"What am I doing here?"

"You on ice, man. That's what they call it in the gangster movies."

"Why am I on ice?"

"'Cause I can't have you running around town stirring up shit and causing aggravation. Old Shad's got the right idea, and we need to let him get his business done."

"Are you talking about the trial? Or the election?"

Cyrus looks puzzled. "The mayor's election?"

I nod.

"What you got to do with that?"

"Nothing."

"I'm talking about the *trial,* man."

Of course. "You don't want me investigating Kate's murder?"

At the mention of her name, the humor vanishes from Cyrus's eyes. "Like I said, I can't have you stirring up any shit. And you been stirring up a lot of it this past week."

With drug-induced stupidity, I say, "Did you kill her, Cyrus?"

His bullet head draws back on his neck. "You think I did that?"

"I don't know. I know you wanted to sleep with her."

A slow, almost reptilian blink. "Yeah, I wanted her."

"But she didn't want you."

He looks over at Blue, then studies me in silence.

"I read your e-mails," I say softly. "You threatened her."

The drug dealer's black eyes flash with anger. He gets up from his chair, closes the distance between us, and squats beside me. "That wasn't any of your business, you know?"

"You're right. I just . . . it's the dope talking."

Cyrus flexes his right forearm as though doing imaginary curls. "Everybody know who killed that bitch anyway, right?"

"Who?"

"Dr. Elliott."

An image of Cyrus tracking Kate's cell phone by computer comes into my head. But arguing with him about Kate's murder under these circumstances could be suicidal. "How long am I going to be here?"

"That depends. How long you think the trial will take?"

"A week, maybe?"

"That's how long you gonna be here, then."

When Blue first dragged me into the van and I saw Cyrus's face, I was certain I would die. When that fear lessened, the horror of torture rose in me. But now the reality is settling in: I'm going to be held prisoner until Drew's trial is over. I won't be able to investigate further for Quentin. He'll be facing the trial in two days with little or no good information. A private detective hired at this point won't be able to learn anything meaningful. And that's why I'm here—to ensure Drew's conviction.

The side effects of my kidnapping will be more personal. Unless Cyrus demands some sort of ransom, my family will believe I've been murdered. My father and mother. Annie . . .

"You gonna be on the nod most of the time," Cyrus says. "That week's gonna go by like a day for you. Maybe two. You ain't gonna get hungry, you ain't gonna get horny . . . you just gonna get happy. *Numb*, baby. The weight of the world gonna be lifted off your shoulders. You gonna be thanking me."

"And when the trial's over?"

He shrugs. "That's up to you."

"You're going to let me go?"

"If I wanted you dead, you'd be lying in that alley behind the restaurant."

"I don't get it. From what I hear, you're not a half measures kind of guy."

Cyrus begins cracking his knuckles, starting with his left forefinger. He maintains his squat as effortlessly as a Major League catcher during this operation.

"I tell you how it is," he says. "I'm thorough, all right. I checked you out. You ain't no civilian. You sent a lot of people to Huntsville Prison. Bangers, killers, Klan, everything. And about five years ago, you damn near got the head of the FBI sent to jail."

It's true. Of course, the crime committed by the FBI director was not committed as director, but as a field agent assigned to Mississippi in 1968.

"I kill you," Cyrus says, "there'd be consequences."

This is a nice idea, but probably untrue. My father would likely commit the rest of his life to finding out who had murdered me, but no nationwide quest for vengeance by a cabal of powerful cops would result. There's an ex–Delta Force operator who might get upset about my demise, but he has a living to make. Although now that I think about it, Daniel Kelly might just take it into his head to get some payback if I were murdered. And anybody with Kelly on his ass truly has a problem.

"Did Jaderious set me up?" I ask.

Cyrus stands and walks over to the counter where the TV and microwave stand. "We got Lean Cuisine and Dr Pepper. Got some Dannon in that fridge over there. You take what you need. But don't be getting up in my Pringles. Got it?"

"Leave your Pringles alone."

Cyrus looks at Blue and says, "He's smart, ain't he?"

Blue's big belly rolls with laughter.

"You just bide your time," says Cyrus. "Enjoy the ride. When the trial's over, if you've been a good boy, you can leave here the way you come."

"Good as new?"

"A little rehab, maybe. Or you can become a customer. I wouldn't blame you. Not many people can chase the dragon and walk away. It's too good. Like classy white pussy gone bad."

"Why do you want to keep me high?" I ask, genuinely puzzled. "Why not just lock me in here?"

"'Cause this is where *I'm* staying part of the time. And I don't need you bugging me, trying head games and shit. You on the nod, it's less stress on you and me both. For me it'll be like you ain't even here. You'll be like a pet dog or something. You okay with that?"

"Fine." *If I'm still alive, I'm okay with just about anything.*

"I thought so. But you listen, right?" Cyrus points at me "I don't want to kill you. But I *will*. Understand? You cause me any kind of shit, you become even a minor inconvenience, and I'll send you right back to the void. Clear?"

"Clear."

"And don't even think about not taking the dust. 'Cause I *know* how to hurt a motherfucker. So does my crew."

I don't reply.

Cyrus takes a cup of yogurt from the fridge and rips off the foil top. "After two or three days, you gonna be begging for the shit anyway. Wait and see. You won't want to live without it."

"How do you come and go from here?" I ask. "Don't they have security?"

Cyrus spoons yogurt into his mouth. "Triton's got an old nigger manning the guardhouse at night. He works for me, though, not those motherfuckers."

How much more perfect could it get? Cyrus can live in relative luxury two miles from town, and keep tabs on his drug business without any fear of discovery by the police.

"Me and Blue gotta make a couple runs tonight," he says, setting down his yogurt. "So it's time to hit you up again. Don't make us hold you down. You do that, you gonna pay a price."

I tell myself not to resist the injection, but when Cyrus starts cooking the heroin, my adrenaline begins to pump. When he picks up a loose syringe off the counter, I can't help but back away.

"Fuck!" Cyrus mutters. "Blue?"

Blue pulls a small revolver from his pocket and points it at me. He forces me into the nearest corner, then cracks the gun against my left shoulder with deceptive speed. My arm goes numb from shoulder to wrist.

"Lay down, now," he says in a surprisingly mild voice. "Ain't no use fighting. Just gon' make it worse on you self."

"Has anybody else used that needle?"

Cyrus shakes his head. "It's the same one I used on you in the van. Come on. We're running late. Don't make me hurt you."

Fighting all my natural instincts, I lie on the sleeping bag and let Blue squeeze my biceps to pump up my antecubital vein. Cyrus slips in the needle again, no pain whatever. As a test, I begin counting softly. When I hit seven, the rush begins. Again it starts in my belly, then spreads outward through my limbs. A heat like the warmth of plunging into a woman envelops my entire body.

"Is it good?" asks Blue. "How you feel?"

"Like a jellyfish," I murmur. "But I'm part of the water."

"Most people say it's like their mama's womb."

I nod in vague agreement. "Could be . . . don't remember."

Blue giggles like a little boy.

"I get back to the womb another way," Cyrus says. "Right, Blue?"

"Oh, yeah. Best way there is."

"Maybe I *can* remember," I think aloud. "Go back in time, you know?"

"No," Cyrus intones. "Don't work that way." He kneels beside the sleeping bag and lifts my sagging chin until I'm looking into his deep black eyes. "Let me tell you 'bout time, brother. I done some reading on that shit. People say time be like a river. That's bullshit. You can swim upstream and downstream in a river. Can you do that with time? Hell, no. Time ain't no river. Time is a big fucking razor blade scraping across the universe. And the edge of that razor is *now*. See? That's all there is, man. No upstream or down, no past or future—just *now*. And all the stuff we feel, like hoping and feeling sorry for shit, that's nothing. Useless. Nothing matters in this world but now."

"I . . . understand your metaphor," I manage to slur. "But things we do in *this* now can change our reality in the *later* now. See? That's why . . . why what we do matters."

Cyrus stares at me, working out my logic. Then he shakes his head. "You missing the point, dog. It's 'cause you're on the dust. That's the only thing that can take away the now. Dust *blurs* it, like. Stretches it out into this big warm blanket. That's why people kill to get it."

"No," I whisper, but my grip on reason is fading fast. "This stuff *is* the now. It takes away the past and future. It's the only thing that can."

Cyrus laughs. "Oh, yeah. You *way* up in the good now."

"Am I?" I ask, wondering if I'm speaking at all.

Cyrus stands. "Sleep tight, brother. Enjoy the ride."

He walks toward the door, but before he opens it, my eyelids fall, and I snuggle under the warm blanket that heroin has thrown over my soul.

Cyrus was right about the passage of time. Soon I had no idea whether it was day or night, whether five minutes had passed or five hours. The heroin came and went like a warm tide, and my consciousness waxed and waned with it. People came and went, too, but I paid scant attention. An elderly black man in a uniform. A white girl. Jaderious Huntley. A teenager. And always Blue, who administered my heroin as lovingly as a gifted nurse. If Cyrus looked like an NFL cornerback, Blue was a nose tackle. Blue was Refrigerator Perry with a kind face. Blue was my nurturing angel.

Heroin was something else.

Heroin was an epiphany.

Suddenly all the disjointed images I'd never understood made sense: the generations of Englishmen who gave up everything to lie in opium dens in India; the ragged junkies in the Houston court system; the Scottish fuckups in *Trainspotting*; Tuesday Weld in *Dog Soldiers*; even Frank Sinatra shooting up in *The Man With the Golden Arm*, back in my father's day. This was why those people did what they did. *This* was what they were after. You go your whole life without understanding something. You know people who do it—who are even obsessed with it—but you feel no pull yourself. And then you experience it.

And the earth shifts on its axis.

I think the fact that I'd tried other drugs in college created my misconception of heroin. Marijuana took away anxiety, made my head thick and mellow. Powdered cocaine—the three times I tried it—sent me into a euphorically controlled high, during which I felt capable of anything. But heroin short-circuits pain right at its source. It bathed me in a primitive bliss that must indeed be the closest thing to the womb. Hour after hour, I lay half comatose on the floor of the lab, trying to get my conscious mind around what was happening in the base of my brain.

I couldn't do it.

Eventually I realized that time was indeed passing. Drew's trial had begun. Cyrus showed me copies of the *Examiner*. The changing front pages showed photos of Shad, Drew, Quentin, even me. But it was all so far away, like something happening on the other side of the world. I knew I should fight what was happening to me, but how could I? Blue outweighed me by a hundred pounds, and Cyrus wore his pistol all the time. He even wore it while watching DVDs in his recliner.

He watched them on the little thirteen-inch Sony on the counter against the wall. Even when he wasn't watching movies, he played them. His taste surprised me. He watched a lot of science fiction: the original versions of *The Thing* and *The Planet of the Apes*; Kubrick's *2001: A Space Odyssey*. He watched conspiracy films from the seventies: *The Conversation, The Parallax View*. War films: *The Bridge on the River Kwai* and *The Great Escape*. Perhaps most surprising of all, Cyrus watched westerns. He seemed to choose his westerns by their stars: Steve McQueen, Robert Mitchum, Henry Fonda. And he watched *The Godfather*—over and over again. I figured his cinematic tastes might have developed during his service in the Gulf War.

Most of the time Cyrus ignored me, but he would talk to me about movies. He was stunned and pleased to learn that *The Bridge on the River Kwai* and *The Planet of the Apes* had been written by the same man. I remarked that he seemed young to be a fan of such old movies, and he laughed. "Mama had a boyfriend," he said. "All that guy did was watch HBO and TNT Classics. He never worked, man. He had a job as a bag man for a guy who ran numbers, but that was it. He'd just watch movies and drink. I'd sit there with him all day long, eating fish sticks and watching movies. I got to liking them. Like meditation, you know? That's why I run them all the time, the way most people listen to music. Movies are my drug, man."

He showed me a newspaper article with a picture of my father above it. He said Dad had hired private experts to mount a search for me. I asked if I could read the article, but Cyrus refused.

"You just keep cool," he said. "Pretty soon the jury's gonna convict the doc, and you can go home to your little girl."

I peered into his eyes, searching for deception. "Why wouldn't I be a fool to believe that?"

Cyrus grinned. "Good question. But you got people on your side you don't even know about."

"What do you mean?"

"Let's just say the word's out in the community that I might have you. And I'm hearing things about making sure you don't get hurt. Del Payton's widow's making some noise, for one."

Althea Payton is the widow of the factory worker whose murder I solved five years ago. In the matrix of Natchez society, she's the equivalent of Coretta Scott King.

"Then there's the preacher of Mandamus Baptist," Cyrus goes on, "where your maid went to church. Quentin Avery's put in his two cents' worth. And then there's your daddy's patients, which seems to be about half the black people in this town."

This gave me some real hope. "What about Shad Johnson?"

Cyrus laughed hard at that. "I think he'd be fine if you didn't make it."

I laughed with him, trying to foster some sense of comradeship. Cyrus might be a monster when it came to his business, but he seemed sincere about letting me go. If he wasn't, why hadn't he killed me the first day? My best strategy was to wait out Drew's trial and do nothing to upset my captor. Drew and Quentin would have to make it on their own.

As always, when the effects of the heroin began to fade, manic anxiety began building in my mind. But Blue returned and injected me again, and again I felt content to wait out my term in the wilderness.

Soon, Cyrus and Blue left to "make a run somewhere," as they often did when I was on the nod, so I decided to make a trip to the restroom. I threw off the top half of my sleeping bag and forced myself to get up. I told my feet to walk, but they refused. They were asleep. I stood there for a while, waiting for my circulation to normalize. Then I tried to walk again. No progress. I looked down at my feet. They looked strange. They were the wrong color. Almost blue, really—especially the toes. I reached out for the wall to stabilize myself, then slowly rose up and down on my toes. After about a minute of this, the feeling slowly returned to my feet. As my toes woke up, the blue faded away.

I figured it was no big deal.

CHAPTER
36

I'm going to die here.

I'm going to die because Cyrus White has no real knowledge about the human body, and because in the end—as he told me in the beginning—he doesn't really care if I survive or not.

Three days ago, as best I can remember, my feet began to burn. Around the same time, my hands and face began to tingle. I wrote this off to the heroin, but the symptoms didn't abate between fixes. They got steadily worse. Two days ago, when I sat on the commode, the underside of my thighs began to burn. I tried to ignore the stinging pain, but after thirty seconds I had to stand up. A half hour later, I tried again. Same result. My skin couldn't tolerate the pressure of the toilet seat without intense pain. That's when the paradox hit me: I was mainlining a powerful painkiller, yet I was feeling pain.

That night, my chin went numb and stayed that way. Then the hair on my head began standing up in different places, like a fear reaction—only I wasn't afraid. This erection of small groups of hairs coincided with the onset of shooting sensations in my face, much like electrical shocks. They weren't acutely painful, but they were icy cold and they left numbness in their wake. By morning I had to sit on the commode to urinate, because I got dizzy trying to stand. I couldn't stay seated long enough to finish, so I squatted over the bowl like a girl in a nasty bathroom.

What the hell was happening to me?

If I stood erect for any length of time, my hands would grow painfully heavy, as though overfilling with blood. When I held them up to my face, I was shocked to see that my palms were dark red with a bluish cast. Only by holding my hands above my head could I get the blood to drain out of them.

Cyrus and Blue thought I was crazy to be afraid, that I was freaking out over normal drug effects. I prayed they were right, but the next time I sat on the john, the tip of my penis began to sting so badly that I had to roll onto the floor. It took several minutes for the pain to ease. When I examined myself, I saw that the tip of my penis was blue. Though the skin eventually pinked again, two tiny black pinpoints remained.

Dead tissue.

My extremities weren't getting enough blood. As the symptoms worsened, I began to experiment. Every time I stood erect, blood gathered in my feet and hands until they ached and pounded. The veins around my ankles bulged with pressure. Sitting on the john caused the blood in my torso to collect in my abdomen, and also in the only extremity attached to my abdomen. After a few hours of experimenting, I realized what was happening. My extremities were getting adequate arterial flow; the problem was my *veins*. They weren't carrying away the deoxygenated blood fast enough.

Something was interfering with my venous circulation.

Cyrus quickly tired of hearing me catalog my symptoms. When I showed him my red hands and bulging veins, he shrugged and returned his attention to *Das Boot*. He muttered that he'd never seen heroin cause problems like that, or at least not so quickly. Plus, he assured me, the batch he was using on me was exceptionally pure.

I told him I was probably having an allergic reaction of some kind. An immune reaction, possibly. Something in the heroin was causing inflammation in my blood vessels—probably an adulter-

ant used to cut the drug. Cyrus told me to shut up and let him
watch his movie. It was usually best to let him alone, but panic
had begun gnawing at my brain. When your skin starts to die before your eyes, your common sense gets a little out of whack.

My plea to be spared further doses of heroin produced exactly
the opposite result. When the sound of Cyrus's little blowtorch
filled the room, I scrambled into the corner and put up my fists.
Cyrus called in Blue and another guy and ordered them to hold me
down, then began prepping the dose. I marshaled my fear and
tried to channel it into strength. Something in the heroin was
killing me, and one more dose might finish the job. But I was no
match for Blue and his companion. Cyrus was still laughing when
he popped the needle into my vein.

I screamed in rage and terror, but within ten seconds the Jesus
Dust performed its magic. A rush of warmth bathed my soul, and
my health concerns suddenly seemed rather academic in nature.
The shooting pains in my face became interesting events, like lightning bolts across a summer sky. The black pinpoints of flesh on
my penis became decorative tattoos, aboriginal art that some unknown artist had added to my manhood during my sleep. But
hours later, as I began to come down, I knew I'd been right about
having a reaction to something in the powder.

Whenever I changed position, I felt tidal shifts of blood in my
body. When I laid down, my stomach would pound for two or
three minutes—not my heart, but my abdominal aorta. When I
tried to stand, consciousness flickered, my face went numb, and
the inside of my left thigh would throb. My femoral artery was
trying desperately to shunt adequate blood through a system crippled by clogged veins. Cyrus laughed as I wavered on my feet, assuming I was still stoned.

I knew then that if I didn't get out of the factory, I would die in
it. I had to find a way out. That, or a way to kill Cyrus and Blue.

I curled into my sleeping bag and waited for them to leave.

Hours later, after Cyrus and Blue disappeared on a run, I struggled
to my feet and began to inventory the lab. Despite my pain and

fear, I quickly discovered a reason for hope. I didn't know much about battery production, but I knew a lot more than Cyrus and his crew. The lab contained quite a few leftover parts and other materials—materials that knowledgeable men would not have left lying around. There were boxes of lead plates stacked against one wall, and also rolls of electrical wire. The cart I'd seen when I first awakened in the lab had a trickle-type battery charger sitting on it.

I forced myself to stay calm and proceed methodically.

Ten minutes later, I found two glass bottles among some plastic ones containing floor cleaner. When I removed their cork stoppers, I smelled nothing, but I had a feeling that the cloudy liquid in the bottom of one of the bottles wasn't water. To test it, I dropped a bit of wire I found on the floor into the bottle.

The wire began to steam. Five minutes later, it was gone.

Sulfuric acid.

The presence of acid in the lab was no big surprise. It's one of the two main components of lead-acid batteries—the main product of the Triton Battery Company. But how could the acid help me? If I flung it into Cyrus's eyes, it would cause intense pain, but it wouldn't stop him from shooting me. Strong acid could burn through the metal lock on the door, but a cursory examination revealed dead bolts in addition to the lock in the doorknob. To eat through those bolts, I'd have to slosh acid through the narrow crack again and again. I didn't have enough acid to do that, and even if I did, someone outside might notice what I was doing. In the end I used the acid to further my exploration of the lab.

The bank of cabinets that Cyrus used for a TV stand had padlocks on its doors. If the cabinets were locked, I reasoned, there must be something worth protecting inside them. The question was, did they contain something Triton Battery wanted to protect? Or something Cyrus had stashed here? I held the glass bottle over the padlock and carefully dripped sulfuric acid on the curved metal shackle of the lock. The metal hissed and bubbled. It took eight minutes to eat through the shackle. When it was done, I pried the lock from the doors and pulled the cabinet open.

Inside were several lead-acid batteries stacked in a metal frame.

The batteries appeared to be wired together in series. Their presence in this room was a violation of federal environmental law on the storage of hazardous materials, but as Quentin Avery would know, such laws are honored more in the breach than the observance. Even the thought of law made me laugh, so comically irrelevant was it to my quest for survival. But what about the batteries? Could they be of use? At first, I thought not. After all, they would be dead after two years in storage. But then I remembered the battery charger on the cart. If the batteries still contained their lead plates and acid, they could be charged. I popped the cell caps off two batteries on top of the array and found fluid inside.

Trying not to get ahead of myself, I sat on the edge of Cyrus's recliner and stared at the batteries. I felt like I'd gone to sleep and awakened in an episode of *MacGyver*. Only I didn't have Mac-Gyver's knowledge of all things mechanical. I had, however, spent a summer working in this plant. On the loading dock, it's true, but I'd talked to a lot of people in other jobs. Something tickled the back of my brain. *What?* Batteries could be dangerous, of course. Everyone who worked at Triton Battery knew that. But it wasn't the acid that was dangerous, as most people thought. Acid could burn you, but it couldn't explode. It wasn't even flammable. No, the explosive danger came from . . . *hydrogen.*

Every rechargeable battery in the world produces hydrogen gas. Usually it's produced in small amounts that remain sealed in the battery case. But because of its light molecular weight, hydrogen is more prone to leak than any other gas. Hydrogen is what kills people who get careless when jumping off the dead battery in their car. If they connect the negative jumper cable to the dead battery rather than elsewhere on their car, they create a spark above the battery. And if hydrogen is present—*boom*—it's lead plates through the skull and a corrosive acid bath.

There were warning signs all over the Triton plant when I worked here. BEWARE! HYDROGEN GAS IS INVISIBLE. I remember a safety guy walking slowly through the loading dock with a straw broom, trying to detect a hydrogen fire. In open air, hydrogen burns almost invisibly, giving off only a faint blue light. The old black guys on the dock called that straw broom the Witches' Broom.

As I stared at the batteries, the excitement in my chest grew swiftly, but with it came fear. I'd wanted a weapon, and I'd found one. But that weapon was not controllable. It was the kind of weapon that could only be used by someone with nothing to lose. *Someone who was going to die anyway.* As I searched for some other way out of the lab, a realization hit me with nauseating certainty: *You have no alternative. You can wait to die here, or you can kill yourself trying to get out.*

That was twelve hours ago.

For the past eleven hours, I've lain on my sleeping bag in a worsening state of heroin withdrawal. Cyrus and Blue left the works for me this time—substituting a book of matches for the blowtorch—a merciful gesture in their minds, a salve for the burgeoning junkie. But I can't use that white powder to ease the aching hunger in my jaw muscles and back. The blood pounding like a second heart in my abdomen tells me that. If my veins continue to become inflamed, I could stroke out or go into cardiac arrest. A more immediate risk might be kidney failure. That's a common cause of death in people with malignant high blood pressure, which is what my condition resembles.

My plan is simple—simple and insanely dangerous. It was Cyrus's TV sitting on the cabinets that inspired it. I perched on Cyrus's recliner and worked it out in my head. The heavy battery array could remain inside the cabinet. I would take the trickle charger from the cart and put it inside the cabinet with the batteries, then connect it to the first battery in the series. Then I would remove the cell caps from the batteries. As the batteries charged, hydrogen gas released by the lead plates would bubble steadily upward through the acid in the cells. The closed cabinet would serve to confine the gas. And confined hydrogen gas is basically a bomb.

All I needed was a fuse.

I found my fuse in less than a minute. Near the back of the soapstone countertop was a hole for electrical cords to pass through. Farther down the counter, above the next cabinet, was another hole. Both were sealed with rubber gaskets, but the gaskets popped out easily. The hole nearest the TV would be my fuse. Lighting it at the proper time would be the hard part, but I resolved to deal with one problem at a time.

In my weakened physical state, it took me half an hour to manhandle the charger off its cart and into the cabinet. I shivered as I connected the leads to the first battery, fearing that the cabinet might already contain free hydrogen. When the leads were connected successfully, I popped the caps off the battery cells and shut the cabinet doors.

The last step was to prep the TV for Cyrus. This trick I learned in seventh grade, by watching a friend of mine blow the school's fuses from our study hall. His technique was simple. He'd take a paper clip, straighten it out, then wrap the wire around both prongs of the electrical plug on the box fan at the back of the classroom. Then he'd shut his eyes and jam the plug into the socket. Blue sparks would shoot from the wall, and the lights would go out all over St. Stephen's.

If I'm lucky, Cyrus will do the same thing for me.

I've spent eleven hours pondering everything that could possibly go wrong. Hydrogen is invisible, as the Triton signs warned me long ago. If Cyrus stays gone too long, the gas will build to a lethal concentration, and I'll suffocate in here. For that reason, I can't let myself fall asleep. Then there's the paper clip. I found a whole box of them in one of the lab drawers. They looked like they were made of metal, but what if they're made of some nonconducting material? A research lab might use something like that.

And then of course there's Cyrus himself: an unpredictable factor if ever there was one. The moment I hear him unlocking the dead bolts, I'll have to jump up and pull the rubber gasket out of the hole in the countertop. That will allow the trapped hydrogen to vent through the hole. But to ignite that gas, Cyrus will have to insert the jerry-rigged TV plug into the outlet above the countertop. What if he finds the unplugged TV cord suspicious? What if he simply gives me a once-over and leaves again, as he's done a couple of times before? What if, what if, what if?

The wait is killing me. Literally.

Time is a big fucking razor blade scraping across the universe, Cyrus told me. *No past or future—just now.* Maybe he's right—I think I actually read something like that somewhere. But right now I feel like he's wrong. Time *is* a river, and I can swim backward in it as effortlessly as I please. Sometimes, even when I don't want to think about the past, it floods over me anyway, a liquid wall of memory and emotion that sweeps away everything in its path. Lying on this sleeping bag, my skin itching, my muscles aching, my mouth dry as sand, I try not to let sadness overwhelm me as pictures of my wife float through my head, my wife before the cancer got her. I see her giving birth to Annie, screaming in agony and then smiling in exhaustion. Sarah is gone now, of course, but Annie remains. For a while I wonder if Sarah has appeared to me because I will soon join her. *That's just fear,* I conclude. *Think about Annie. Annie's still alive. Annie still needs you . . .*

As I repeat this mantra over and over, a new emotion is born within me—strangely enough, for the first time. It's hatred. Not a generalized hatred, but a highly specific animus directed at one man: Cyrus White. Because of Cyrus, I lie helpless in a locked room, drifting slowly but steadily toward death. Because of Cyrus, my daughter might have to grow up without her father. And she has already done without her mother for too long.

Up until now, I have excused Cyrus in my head. He hasn't tortured me as he has supposedly done to others; he has promised me life. Did Cyrus create himself? *No,* said my guilt. *Cyrus is a product of the town we created.* But lying here now, I reject that idea utterly. Cyrus had choices—more than a lot of people less fortunate than he. He made it out of this town. He served in the military. Yet despite this chance to rise above his disadvantages, he chose evil over good. And not once, but again and again. Images of the dead and injured fill my mind. *Kate Townsend. Sonny Cross. Chris Vogel. The Catholic kid in the hospital, Mike Pinella. Paul and Janet Wilson.* Cyrus may not be directly responsible for all of them, but he happily feeds the beast that took their lives.

And the next time he walks through that door, I will devote every atom of my being to killing him.

I'm nearly asleep when I hear the click.

I tell my body to move, but it doesn't respond. I'm lying on the surface of Jupiter, with twice the gravity of Earth sucking at my bones.

As the first dead bolt clicks open, I roll over and struggle to my feet. My belly pounds with terrifying pressure as I stagger over to the counter and pull the rubber gasket out of the countertop.

I'm only halfway back to my bag when Cyrus opens the door.

"What the fuck?" he says. "Look at this junkie motherfucker!"

Trying to turn toward him, I collapse on my sleeping bag.

"What the hell are you doing?" he asks me. "You mainline that whole bag or something?"

I groan in mock agony, but I don't have to fake it much. The pains shooting across my face feel like someone's pinching me with pliers.

Anger twists Cyrus's face when he looks at the countertop. "What the fuck? This place is a mess!"

"I'm sick," I grunt, twisting my sleeping bag around me. "I'm sorry."

"You sorry, all right." He walks into the room and stops. "Motherfucker! You been up in my *Pringles?*"

"I was hungry."

"Junkie motherfucker! I shoulda killed yo' ass in the beginning."

I writhe on the sleeping bag, then straighten out on my stomach. "I'll be all right soon. I just . . . I don't know." I close my eyes and lie still. Right now hydrogen gas is rising through the hole in the counter in an invisible column.

"I got to get out of this place," Cyrus mutters. "Got that old nigger in the guardhouse talking my ear off, and back here I got your nasty ass. I'm gonna lock you in a broom closet in the plant or something. *Shit.*"

"*Witches' Broom*," I whisper.

"What?"

I don't reply.

"Hey, Blue!" Cyrus yells. "Shoot this motherfucker up. Shut him up for a while."

Heavy footsteps sound in the lab, then soft creaks as Cyrus sits in the Naugahyde recliner.

"*Shit*," he curses. "My TV don't work!"

"Probably the remote," says Blue, moving toward me with the blowtorch.

Cyrus gets up and walks somewhere. I want to look, but I don't.

"No," he says, slapping plastic. "It's broken, man."

"Plugged in?" asks Blue.

The big man kneels beside me and picks up the baggie and the spoon.

"That's it! This stoned motherfucker done got into my Pringles *and* unplugged my TV. If it was me on that syringe, I'd waste his ass."

Blue starts cooking the heroin. "You ain't gonna fight me this time?"

"No." The tiny roar of the blowtorch floods my system with adrenaline. If the hydrogen escaping from the cabinet fills this room fast enough, we'll all die before Cyrus even picks up the TV plug. I groan and roll onto my side so I can watch Cyrus.

He has the plug in his hand. He's holding it near the electrical socket, but he's stopped to say something to Blue.

"You know why he ain't fighting you? 'Cause the rush is worth the pain."

Cyrus grins, then pushes the plug into the socket.

There's no flame, not even a flash, but that side of the testing lab moves to this side without visibly traveling the space between. My plan was to shelter under my sleeping bag, but everything happened too fast. Now Blue's elephantine body lies across my head and torso, and it's not moving. Someone is screaming, but it's not Blue. I touch my mouth to see if it's me.

It's not.

With colossal effort, I roll Blue off me and look to my right.

Cyrus is writhing on the floor, screaming gibberish and clawing at his eyes. His entire body is peppered with bloody wounds. *Shrapnel wounds,* I realize, *fragments of the lead plates in the batteries. They exploded out of the cabinet at supersonic speed and sliced through everything in their path.*

That's what killed Blue. The top of his head is gone, as though someone put it partway into a guillotine. When I glance at his lower body, I see that my own legs are bleeding from several wounds. I retch, but there's nothing in my stomach.

The shrill ring of a fire alarm sounds over Cyrus's shrieks. There's no fire that I can see, but the explosion obviously triggered something. The custodian in the guardhouse is bound to investigate. Unsure of my legs, I flatten my palms on the floor and struggle to my feet. My legs are shaking badly, but they seem able to support my weight.

The lab door is standing open, but it may not be the only one between me and freedom. I try not to look at Cyrus's face as I bend and take his keys from the ring on his belt loop. His jerking torso is almost too much to take. The acid blown out of the batteries has vaporized the cotton of his T-shirt and is now eating into his skin. Cyrus claws at my wrist as I lift the keys, but I yank my hand away and hurry to the door.

His screams follow me down the tiled corridor outside. I'm not familiar with this part of the plant. I have no idea where to go. Pausing by the door at the far end of the corridor, I try to recall anything I can.

"Hey!" someone yells. "Cyrus? Blue? What happened in there?"

Wavering on my feet, I move to the side of the door and flatten my back against the wall. The door bursts open, and a black man in a blue uniform runs through it, making for the lab. As he enters it, I leave by the door he just came through.

Now I'm in a much larger room; the ceiling is thirty feet over my head. *The production line.* The fire alarm is louder here. I see light, a streetlight shining through a high window. Low down on that wall is another door, and it's standing open. I walk toward it, stumbling the last few yards. My pants are soaked with blood; I'm leaving a trail of it behind me.

When I clear the door, new sirens cut through the shrill scream of the fire alarm. I fall to my knees, but I keep moving. I have to get clear of the factory. The custodian could shoot me just to cover his ass, then blame my death on Cyrus.

I smell the river now—it's only five hundred yards to the west— and kudzu, too, the greenest smell in the world. As I crawl forward, red light flashes crazily on the walls of the buildings around me. I force myself to my feet and hold my hands high in the air. A fire truck careens around a huge building on my left and bears down on me. I wave my arms frantically, but I don't have the energy to maintain my balance, and I fall.

I hear a door slam, then nothing.

CHAPTER

37

Four hours after the fire department rescued me—maybe twenty hours after Blue last injected me—I was lying in a bed in an intensive care unit, cold sweat bursting from my pores. By the twenty-four-hour mark, my skeletal muscles were cramping, twisting me into a fetal position. After thirty hours, every cell in my body was screaming for heroin. My father had to send a nurse to Jackson for methadone; there was none available in Natchez. An addiction expert he consulted by phone attributed my severe withdrawal after such a short experience with heroin to the likelihood that I'd received a steady flow of extremely pure product for six and a half days.

But it wasn't completely pure.

When I arrived in the ER, Dad immediately diagnosed me with a dangerous vascular condition called hypersensitivity vasculitis. My guess had been right. Whatever had been used to cut the heroin had triggered my immune system to attack my own body, particularly my veins. My bone marrow had begun churning out proteins called immune complexes, which immediately began clogging my smallest veins—the venules. This silting process started in my extremities and steadily moved toward my core organs. A blood-pressure reading taken on my arm in the ER was 140/95, but a reading taken from a cuff on my finger was 145/180. I had an irregular heartbeat, and tiny patches of skin on my toes and penis had died. I assumed that stopping the injections of contaminated heroin would short-circuit this immune reaction, but Dad soberly informed me that as long as the adulterant remained in my system—and he feared that some of it was embedded in the walls of my veins—the potentially deadly immune reaction would continue. He was considering a treatment called chelation, but after he described it to me, I felt more inclined to wait it out and hope for the best.

My legs had been peppered with shrapnel from the exploding batteries. The wounds themselves weren't severe—my bones had escaped damage—but since the shrapnel was mostly lead fragments from the battery plates, poisoning was a serious concern. A surgeon spent two hours under a fluoroscope digging every fragment out of my body.

Before Dad admitted any visitors into my glass-walled cubicle in the ICU, he drew the curtains and stood close beside my bed. The white hair and beard gave him the look of a doctor who had seen everything, but I could tell that he'd never dreamed of seeing his son like this.

"Annie's had a tough time these past few days," he said. "We all have, but she had it the worst. She thought you were dead. And nothing we said to her would change her mind. I guess losing her mother so young proved to her that the worst nightmares *do* come true. You need to spend a lot of time with her, Penn."

"You can count on it. How's Mom?"

Dad shook his head. "She's a tough old girl, but this just about did her in. She sat by the telephone day and night, waiting for word. I don't believe she slept more than three consecutive hours the whole time you were gone. She was afraid they were going to find you in a ditch somewhere."

"I'm sorry. I'm sorry I got myself into this mess."

A small smile touched my father's lips. "That's your nature, son. I understand it. But you've got a family to think about."

I nodded.

Dad looked through a crack in the curtains at the nurse's station. "When they brought you into the ER, they put you on the same treatment table they put Kate Townsend on two weeks ago. I saw Jenny Townsend that night. And I felt just like her when I saw you." Dad's jaw muscles flexed with the effort of holding in his emotion. "I'm not burying my son," he said in a shaky voice. "I won't do it."

I reached up and gripped his wrist, squeezing as hard as I could.

"I couldn't just sit and wait," he said. "I knew if there was a way to stay alive, you'd manage it. After meeting with Sheriff Byrd and Chief Logan, I called your old assistant and got the names of every FBI agent you'd ever worked with. I called them all, and they lit a fire under the task force here. I still wasn't convinced that was enough, so I called Dan Kelly's security company in Houston."

Daniel Kelly is the former Delta operator I considered bringing in to protect Annie. My father got to know him well during the Del Payton case.

"Kelly was still in Afghanistan, but twelve hours later, he returned my call. When he heard you were missing, he promised to get back to the U.S. by hook or by crook. It took three days for a replacement to arrive in Kabul, but forty-eight hours ago Kelly arrived in Natchez and started searching for you. He even brought a buddy with him to protect Annie. You may not believe it, but Kelly was planning to search the Triton Battery plant the day after you escaped. I saw it in his daybook."

"He has good instincts. But I probably would have been dead when he found me."

Dad shook his head slowly. "No doubt about it."

"Is he still in town?"

"Yes. He said to tell you he's waiting for instructions."

For some reason, Kelly's continued presence brings me a blessed feeling of relief.

"Now," Dad said, "there are some people waiting to see you."

He turned to go, but I said, "Wait."

"What is it?"

"What about Cyrus White? Did they bring him into the ER?"

Dad nodded but said nothing.

"Did he make it?"

"No. He died. Bad."

Dad left me in silence with my memories of Cyrus and Blue. I felt no satisfaction at having killed them. New predators would soon take their places in the local drug hierarchy, and probably already had. Cyrus and Blue had never meant to kill me, but they *had* been content to watch me die by a process they didn't understand. Now they are dead, and I am alive, and that is all that matters.

Two minutes after Dad left the ICU, Caitlin led Annie into my room. When Annie stared at me as if unsure I was real, I told her to climb up into my bed. I hugged her tight, and Caitlin hugged us both from behind Annie. We watched an episode of *Leave It to Beaver* on TV Land, hardly speaking as we did, but words didn't matter at that point. My mother came into the room during the show. She sat on the edge of my bed for a while with her hand on my knee. She had aged visibly since I last saw her, but I sensed that she was still far from broken. When *Leave It to Beaver* ended, she kissed me on the forehead, then lifted a sleeping Annie into her arms and left for home.

Finally alone, Caitlin and I simply held each other, both shivering from an emotion we could not name. After a while, she asked to see the damage done to my body by the vasculitis. She cried then, but she knew the outcome could have been much worse. Though I was still suffering from the reaction, at least no more skin had died.

As for Drew's trial, the news was almost all bad. A few hours before Caitlin's visit, Shad had stunned the court by providing proof that Kate had been visiting Cyrus to procure drugs for Drew, who had then given them to his addicted wife. To prove this, Shad produced four different witnesses, each of whom knew only part of the story. The most powerful of those witnesses, Caitlin said, was Ellen Elliott herself. Because Ellen was testifying about her drug habit, and not giving direct testimony against her husband, her testimony was allowed. I figured Ellen would be glad to give testimony that might convict Drew, but Caitlin said Ellen had been very hostile to Shad during direct examination, and as she left the witness box, she appeared to have been shattered by the ordeal. This testimony had fulfilled Quentin Avery's worst fear, and it left me deeply troubled. Cyrus himself had not known whom Kate was buying the Lorcet for, so how had Shad Johnson divined that the hydrocodone was for Ellen? I resolved to discover this as soon as possible.

According to Caitlin, Quentin had been playing catch-up throughout the trial. He had little inside information to work with, and he was saddled with a client who seemed bent on self-destruction. Drew remained firm in his belief that he should tell the whole truth about everything, and he was still demanding to take the stand in his own defense. That might happen as soon as tomorrow.

After Caitlin returned to the newspaper office, I settled back in my bed and tried to rest, but my withdrawal symptoms made it impossible. I was shaking like an epileptic when Daniel Kelly walked into my room.

I hadn't seen him for five years, but he looked the same: curly blond hair, sea blue eyes, an Irish smile, and a reserved manner. Kelly also sported a desert tan, which somehow added to the aura of centeredness he always projected. Kelly knows how to go unnoticed in a crowd, but when he reveals himself, you know you're in the presence of a man of supreme competence.

I asked him what he'd been doing in Afghanistan, and he gave me a typical one-word answer: "Babysitting." I thanked him for dumping his contract and playing seventh cavalry on my behalf, but then I told him I was fine and that he could go back to Asia. Kelly gave a small shake of his head and said, "I've been checking things out for a couple of days. Been to the trial, been out in the street. This thing isn't over, Penn."

"It is for me."

Kelly raised his eyebrows. "That may not be your choice. I went out to Triton Battery and looked at the lab where they held you—

what was left of it. And I found two pounds of ninety-eight per-cent pure heroin."

"*You* found it? Not the cops?"

"They took drug dogs out there, but Cyrus had figured a way to beat the dogs. Probably learned it in the air force. I've seen most of those tricks in my time, so I knew where to look."

I've learned to expect Kelly to amaze me. "Two pounds of pure heroin. What's the street value of that?"

"You could buy a small island. And the people who lost that dope are going to be mighty angry."

He gave me his cell number and told me he would stay within reach for the next couple of days, at least. Then he squeezed my right hand in both of his and walked to the glass door. "By the way," he said, turning back to me, "that was a neat trick you pulled. Couldn't have done better myself."

I blew out a stream of air, fighting a memory of Blue's massive body crushing mine. "Necessity's the mother of invention, right?"

Kelly smiled. Then his eyes twinkled and he was gone.

Not long afterward, Quentin Avery called me. He apologized for not coming to the hospital, but I understood. A lawyer defend-ing a client on a capital murder charge is one of the busiest people on earth. Quentin let me know he was glad that I'd survived, but then he quickly asked if I had any rabbits I could pull out of my hat for him. Had I learned anything during my captivity that might help Drew in the courtroom? I had to tell him no. When I asked for a summary of Shad Johnson's strategy, Quentin told a depressing tale.

Though Shad's case remained circumstantial, he had painted a compelling picture of Marko Bakic as the "mystery man" who'd had consensual sex with Kate within seventy-two hours of her death, and then of Drew as the older man who'd discovered this infidelity and killed his underage paramour in a jealous rage. DNA analysis of the fetus in Kate's womb had proved it to be Drew's child. But Drew, Shad told the jury, had no way of knowing that. He might have believed the child belonged to Marko (or any other man). Shad's hypothesis was helped greatly by the fact that no one had seen Marko since the night of the X-rave at Oakfield. Shad had even suggested that Drew had paid to have Marko killed, which would explain the Croatian's disappearance.

While Don Logan's police department had been searching frantically for Marko, Sheriff Byrd had taken a more leisurely approach. I wanted to laugh at the irony when Quentin griped about this; he himself had ordered me not to hunt down Cyrus for the same reason. It suited both lawyers' purposes to work with a myth in court, rather than a flesh-and-blood person who could contradict their theories. I offered to put Daniel Kelly at Quentin's disposal, but Quentin demurred. He didn't seem to grasp the value of Kelly's help—probably because Kelly has no inside knowledge of Natchez.

Late on my second night in the hospital, Mia called. She told me she had wanted to visit earlier, but that Caitlin had told her it was best that I have as few visitors as possible. This surprised and even angered me, but on reflection I understood. It took me a while to realize that Mia was crying softly. To raise her spirits, I asked her to update me on the progress of her investigation. I knew better than to believe my absence would end her Nancy Drew efforts.

Mia had deduced that I'd been kidnapped or killed by either Cyrus White or the Asians, since I had provoked both parties. Because she had no way to work the Asian angle, she had focused on Cyrus. The only possible line Mia had into Cyrus's organization was Marko, so for the past week, she had talked to every high school student in town, trying to find some clue to Marko's whereabouts. She'd badgered Alicia Reynolds, Marko's girlfriend, but Alicia had blown her off. When Mia tried to follow Alicia in her car, she quickly discovered that the police were doing the same thing. After being warned off, she went home and fell into a mild depression. I thanked her profusely for everything she'd done, but this didn't bring her out of her mood. She'd cut school twice to attend Drew's trial, she said, and she had a bad feeling about the way it was going.

I wanted to see for myself, but my withdrawal symptoms grew worse, not better. The methadone helped, but it didn't stop the pain that bored like rusty nails into my bones. I still had an irregular heartbeat, as well, but Dad told me that was caused by the vasculitis, not the withdrawal.

This morning I learned that Shad and Quentin were scheduled to give their closing statements, but as badly as I wanted to hear them, I simply couldn't function well enough to go to the courthouse. It was all I could do to stand beside my bed for five minutes, or sit in the visitors' chair watching television. I got so agitated at my failure that Dad finally sedated me. I lay in the bed half conscious, waiting for an update from Caitlin, who was in the courtroom.

I waited in vain. Caitlin wasn't about to give up her seat in the packed courtroom to call someone who couldn't do anything about what was happening anyway. I switched on the TV and tried to think about something else, but it was no use. I'd never felt so impotent in my life. I lay shaking under the blanket, troubled by thoughts of Blue, almost wishing the big man would appear at my bedside with his blessed syringe. But he couldn't do that, of course. He was dead. I'd cut the top of his head off with a battery plate. When the sedative finally overwhelmed me, I almost wept with relief.

"Penn? Penn, wake up."

I blink my eyes in confusion. My mother is standing beside my bed.

"What's the matter?"

"Caitlin's on the phone. The jury's back."

A bolus of adrenaline shoots through my body. "Give it to me!"

Mom passes me the phone. "Caitlin?"

"The jury's coming back in," she whispers. "They deliberated ninety-four minutes."

My face goes cold.

"What do you think?"

"Guilty."

"If they see me on this phone, they'll kick me out," Caitlin says. "I'm going to leave the connection open. If you can't hear the verdict, I'll tell you as soon as I can."

My phone begins hissing like a link to outer space. I've never listened to a jury verdict this way before. A friend of mine once called me and held up his cell phone at a Paul McCartney concert: "Eleanor Rigby," I think.

"Who is the foreperson?" asks Judge Arthel Minor, his voice replacing the hiss with amazing clarity.

For some reason, I don't hear the reply. Probably because the judge has a microphone while the jury box doesn't.

"Have you reached a verdict?" Judge Minor asks.

Again nothing.

"Please pass the verdict to the clerk."

Silence now, but I know what's happening. The clerk is giving the verdict to Judge Minor, who will check to see if the jury has worded it correctly. Minor will then pass it to the clerk, who will read the verdict aloud. At least three deputies will surround Drew to keep him from bolting in panic in the event of a guilty verdict, or to protect him from angry relatives of the victim in the opposite event.

"Ladies and gentlemen," says Judge Minor, "I'm warning you. There will be no outbursts when the verdict is read, or afterward. There will be quiet and order. Do not test me, or you will find yourself in the custody of the sheriff."

After a brief silence, Minor says, "Read the verdict."

A female voice says, "In the matter of the *State of Mississippi versus Drew Elliott,* we find the accused guilty on two counts of the charge of first-degree murder during commission of a felony."

I sag against my pillow.

"Did you hear that?" Caitlin whispers.

"I heard."

"I can't believe it."

"Believe it."

"Are you okay?"

"Yes. Go. I know you need to work."

"Wait. Judge Minor's going to poll the jury."

"They always do that in capital cases. It's over, Caitlin."

"I'll call you as soon as I can," she promises.

I let the phone drop and reach for my water glass.

I wish there were some way I could talk to Drew. Right now he's standing at his table in shock, Quentin Avery beside him, watching Judge Minor excuse the family of the victim—Jenny Townsend and perhaps her ex-husband. Next Drew's family will be excused. I wonder who was there for him. His parents are dead. Ellen? Probably not. Timmy is certainly not there. But after whoever is there for him has left the courtroom, Drew will be escorted straight back to the county jail. What can he be thinking? An innocent man convicted of capital murder. The realization that twelve citizens believed him capable of brutally raping and murdering a young girl will stun Drew into shock. If it wasn't for Tim, I'd be afraid he might try to kill himself.

"Penn, are you all right?" asks my mother.

"Yes."

"What happened?"

"Guilty. They found Drew guilty."

"Oh, my God. Oh, no."

Peggy Cage takes several steps around the room, then stops, shaking her head. "I just don't believe it. I watched that boy grow up. He ate tuna fish sandwiches in my house every day, every summer, for years. That boy was *raised right*. There's no way on earth he hurt that poor girl like that. No *way*. This world has turned upside down."

"I agree with you. But twelve other people don't."

"Fools," she says conclusively. "Poor protoplasm."

"It was a solid case, Mom. But it doesn't matter now. Now Drew has to look toward the appeal."

"Did he get the death penalty?"

"That's a separate phase of the trial. They may do that today, or they might wait until tomorrow."

Mom walks back to my bed, her eyes worried. "You look bad, Penn. Worse than you did two minutes ago."

"I don't feel too good," I admit.

"I'm going to get your father to give you something. Something to help you sleep."

"I don't need anything, Mom."

"You let me worry about that."

Ten minutes later, my father appears, a syringe in his hand. If only he had what Blue used to bring me . . .

But soon enough, I'm gone again.

"Penn?"

I groan and force myself to open my eyes.

"Who is it?" I croak, squinting against the light.

"Me."

"Who?"

"Ellen. Ellen Elliott. My God . . . are you all right?"

"It's not as bad as it looks."

"It's probably worse."

I can see her now, her skin greenish under the fluorescent lights. Ellen doesn't look too good herself. She's lost weight over the past two weeks. A lot of weight. Her color job is fading, the Nordic blond hair now rooted with brown and gray.

"What time is it, Ellen? Did you hear the verdict?"

She nods. "That was two hours ago, Penn."

"Oh. Were you in court?"

"No. I couldn't watch. I wanted to be with Timmy." Ellen tries to force a smile, but the effort goes in vain. "It's very difficult to go out in public now. People just stare and point like I'm some circus animal. They don't spare Timmy, either. The kids at school . . . they're awful."

"That's what happens in these trials. I don't blame you, Ellen. I know Drew missed you being in there for him, though."

She gives me a mistrustful glance. "Do you really think so?"

"I know it, no matter what's happened between you. Today could mean the end of Drew's life. And he's spent most of that life with you."

She blinks several times, and then tears begin streaming down her cheeks. "How could they do that to him?" She raises a shaking hand to wipe her face. "He's given so much to this town, to so many of those people. How could they believe Drew could do that?"

"I thought you believed it, too."

Ellen seems not to have heard me. "What am I supposed to do now? I have a son, Penn. What do I tell Timmy?"

"Try to explain things, I guess. Tim's old enough to understand some of it."

She shakes her head violently. "No. He's younger than you think. Emotionally, I mean."

Ellen sits beside my bed, then stands again immediately. I can't get a handle on her emotional state. Maybe she can't either. As I study her face, her lips smeared with too much lipstick, it hits me that she might be deep into drug withdrawal, just like me. With Drew in jail and Kate dead, her sources for Lorcet have dried up.

"Did you come just to visit me?" I ask. "Or is there something I can do for you?"

She sucks in her lips and knits her brow. Then she shakes her head several times, as though having a silent conversation with herself.

"Ellen?"

"I want you to know something, Penn. I don't . . . don't know who else to tell."

"You can tell me. Whatever it is, I'm sure it's all right."

"No, it's not." Her red eyes burn into mine. "I killed Kate, Penn."

It takes a moment for the words to register. It's as though Ellen said, "I just arrived from the planet Tralfamadore." But she didn't say that. She said, *I killed Kate.* And she meant it.

"Tell me what you're talking about, Ellen. Are you speaking figuratively?"

"I'm afraid not. No, I killed her." She holds up her hands. "I killed her with these . . . my own two hands."

For a moment I wonder if I'm hallucinating. But Dad is giving me sedatives, not LSD. Then it hits me: *Ellen is lying. She's trying to save Drew's life.*

"How did you kill her, Ellen?"

"I choked her."

"I thought you were with your sister when Kate died."

She shakes her head again.

"Your sister lied to protect you?"

"Yes. Don't blame Jackie, though."

My pulse is returning to normal. Overcome with guilt about her past behavior in the marriage, Ellen is trying to save Drew by sacrificing herself. "Why don't you tell me what happened? Just sit down in that chair and let it out."

She looks at the chair with disdain. "I don't need to sit. It's simple really. The day it happened, I was supposed to be shopping with Jackie. But before I met her, I stopped by Drew's office. I wanted to show him some paint samples I'd gotten from Sherwin-Williams, for the living room."

"Did Drew know you were coming?"

"No. Anyway, when I got to his office, I happened to walk past his car. The Volvo. I saw a piece of paper taped to his window, and something made me stop. Probably because it didn't look like an advertisement. It looked like a note. Like, 'I backed into your car by accident, here's my phone number'—that kind of thing." Confusion enters Ellen's face. "But it wasn't. It was a note from Kate."

Fresh anxiety wakes in my gut. "What did it say?"

"'I need to see you. Meet me at the creek.'"

"That's it?"

"Yes."

"Did she sign it?"

"No."

"How did you know it was from Kate?"

Ellen's eyes crinkle at the corners. "I didn't really. Not for sure. But Kate worked for us two summers. I'd seen her handwriting lots of times. So when I saw the note, I think . . . on some level I recognized it."

"Keep going. Tell me sequentially."

"I drove back home and walked down to the creek."

"Did you leave the note on Drew's car?"

"No. I took it with me."

"Why?"

Ellen touches her forefinger to her chin and taps it softly. "I don't know."

"Go on."

"I took the path I used to take when I walked Henry." Henry was their black Lab, now dead. "There's only a couple down there anyway. I wasn't sure I was headed to the right spot, and yet . . . it was like the handwriting. I had the same instinct. If Kate had written the note, then I was going the right way."

"I understand."

"I walked down to this place about halfway between our two neighborhoods." Ellen's gaze drops, and she speaks like someone under hypnosis. "She was sitting on a log when I saw her. She looked upset. When I was about thirty feet away, she looked up. She didn't see me, because I was under the trees. Then I stepped into the sunlight. The look on her face . . . I can't describe it."

My fists are tight under the covers. "Tell me."

"She was afraid, of course. But there was something else."

"What?"

"Relief. That the truth was finally out, I guess. She must have been holding in so much for so long."

Ellen actually sounds sympathetic. But her feelings had to be much different on the day these events transpired. "What happened then?"

"I called out her name. Like a question. 'Kate?' She stood up then, as though my words had brought her to life. God, she was a beautiful girl." Ellen suddenly fixes me with a furious glare. "I hate Drew for what he did. Not to me—though it's almost destroyed me—but to *her*. He had no right to alter Kate's life like that. He disrupted the natural order of things. She had so much to offer, she was so fresh, and he *stole* that from her. Her whole future."

"Please go on, Ellen. What happened next?"

"I showed her the note."

I close my eyes briefly. "And?"

"I asked her to explain it to me. I think at that point I was still hoping for some sort of innocent explanation. I know that sounds pathetic, but it's true. Kate got very upset, but she didn't even try to lie. She told me she was in love with Drew, and that he loved her back. It was a wife's worst nightmare, really. I just . . . I couldn't process it, you know? But when I finally got what she was trying to tell me, I saw red. I couldn't believe she'd deceived me that way. I couldn't believe that this *child* had made such a fool of me. How stupid I'd been! And she wasn't talking about sex, oh, no. She was talking about *love*. She lost her embarrassment very quickly. She was almost crowing, really. Or I felt that she was."

"What did you do, Ellen?"

"I told Kate she was a fool, that Drew was lost in a midlife crisis, that she was giving up her youth for an affair that would come to nothing. I told her Drew would never leave Tim. And—that's when it happened."

"What?"

"Kate got this serene smile on her face. She told me they were running away together." Ellen is staring at the wall as though she can still see Kate before her. "I told her she was crazy. Nuts. But she just kept smiling. Then she said, 'I'm pregnant, Ellen. Drew and I are going to have a baby.' " Ellen's mouth hangs slack for a few moments, as though she's still in shock. "I don't think I was functioning normally from that point on."

"Go on."

"I screamed at her. I called her a slut and a liar. She just laughed. That made me so furious. I couldn't stand it! I got right up in her face and slapped her. *Hard*. She started screaming then. Cruel things . . . terrible things. She told me I could never make Drew happy, that he was miserable, that I was killing him. Then she told me why. And . . . she was right about a lot of it."

"Ellen, you don't have to go there. Just—"

"Let me finish. I have to tell it all. Kate knew all about my drug problem. That hurt me so badly, that he'd told her about that. She said she'd been getting me my Lorcet to keep Drew from losing his medical license. She acted like I was some kind of pathetic monster. And she was *right*. But that only made me angrier. I wanted her to shut up, Penn. I had to make her shut up. I slapped her five or six times, yelling, '*Shut up! Shut up!*' But she wouldn't. She just laughed like a maniac. That's when I grabbed her. I got my hands around her throat and squeezed as hard as I could. She knew then how angry I was. Her eyes almost bugged out of her head. She tried to push me off, but she didn't have a chance. Kate could beat me at tennis, but that was touch, not strength." Ellen shakes her head slowly, remembering. "She went out so quickly, I couldn't believe it."

I nod. "It only takes seven seconds without direct blood flow to the brain to cause unconsciousness. Did she fall?"

"Into the water," Ellen says distantly. "But her head hit something. A rusty wheel rim, half buried in the sand. The sound was awful, like hearing a kid's ACL pop on the basketball court. The sound did something to me. It snapped me out of whatever trance I was in. I dragged Kate's head and shoulders onto the bank and started trying to revive her. I couldn't believe what I'd done. Thirty seconds before, I'd looked at her like a ruthless home wrecker. Now all I could see was the little girl who'd sold me lemonade on the corner when she was six. I was crying, hyperventilating . . . I was losing it, Penn."

"Did you have a cell phone?"

"No. It was in my purse, back up at the house."

Watching Ellen now—telling her story with almost the same stunned detachment that Drew exhibited when describing his discovery of Kate's body—I realize that she's telling the truth. Ellen *did* kill Kate. Only she did it without meaning to. With this realization comes a memory of Ellen lingering behind at Kate's burial to offer her condolences to Jenny Townsend. My God, the torment she must have been going through. *What the hell am I going to do now?* I wonder. *What will Quentin say about this? And what about Drew?*

"What did you do then?" I ask.

"I couldn't wake her up. There was no respiration. I realized then that she was probably dead."

"Why didn't you report it, Ellen?"

Her eyes lock onto mine, silently begging for understanding.

"As terrible as it was, I just can't imagine you not reporting what happened."

"I know. I feel exactly the same way. It's like it wasn't me, Penn. Kate and Drew had turned me into a different person. But more than that . . . I just didn't have time to think."

"What do you mean?"

"While I was kneeling there, staring at her in disbelief, I heard something. At first I thought it was my mind playing tricks on me. But then I heard it for real—someone coming through the woods. And instinct just took over. I couldn't sit there and wait to be caught. I can't explain it. It was a primitive reaction—fight or flight."

"Who was in the woods?"

"Well, Drew, I guess. I mean, I know that now. But in my mind he was still at his office. I'd taken the note off his car, so why would he show up there? Anyway, the louder the noise got, the more I panicked. I just couldn't wait around to see. I'm not even sure why I was so afraid, except . . . God, I've been wondering if part of me—and I hate to admit this, Penn—if even then part of me was afraid it *was* Drew. You know? I was afraid that if Drew knew I'd killed Kate, he might kill *me* in a rage."

"Has Drew ever been violent to you?"

"Never. Oh, he slapped me once, but I was in withdrawal. I was slugging him like some redneck bitch. He should have hit me with a hammer."

The pitch of Ellen's voice is rising, and her words are coming faster. Though she appears to be in control, I sense that she's headed for some sort of breakdown.

"Where's the note now? Kate's note?"

"I burned it."

Damn. "Listen to me, Ellen. I want you to be very calm, all right?"

"I am calm."

"Now that you've told me all this, what do you want me to do?"

She looks at me as though I've asked the world's stupidest question. "I want you to tell the district attorney," she says in a brittle voice. "I want you to get Drew out of jail. I mean, you have to tell the D.A., don't you? Now that I've confessed?"

If only it were that simple. "Was there anyone in my room when you walked in?"

"Your mother was reading by the bed. I asked her to leave me alone with you."

"All right. She's probably still outside. I'm going to talk to her, and then I want you to wait outside with her. Go to the cafeteria and have some coffee."

"That's all right. Jackie's here with me."

"Tell Jackie to go home."

Ellen looks confused again, but then she seems to get it. "All right. I'll tell her."

"Don't tell my mother anything you just told me. Okay?"

"What are you going to do, Penn?"

"Try to get Drew out of jail."

Relief smooths the lines of Ellen's face. "Thank you. My God . . . it's finally out. I couldn't go one more minute carrying that around."

I force a smile and pick up my bedside phone.

Quentin Avery is staring at me like he would an insane person. He has just listened to Ellen Elliot repeat her tale of murder—or manslaughter, in my book—and Ellen has just walked out to rejoin my mother in the hospital cafeteria.

"You believe that story?" Quentin asks.

"Every word."

He nods slowly. "I do, too. But it doesn't make a damn bit of difference."

"What?"

"It doesn't change anything."

"*What?*"

Quentin runs both hands through his gray Afro, then looks down at me like a patient law professor. "Drew Elliot was just convicted of capital murder. That woman is his *wife*. Nobody's going to see this as anything but a last-ditch effort to save her husband from the death penalty."

"By risking prison herself?"

"Hell, yes." Quentin snorts in frustration. "I've seen this a half dozen times, at least. Mothers try it all the time. And you can bet Judge Minor has seen it, too."

"But it's the truth, Quentin."

He looks at me with something like pity. "Are you a lawyer or a philosopher? The person you'd have to take this story to is Shad Johnson, who at this moment is celebrating the biggest triumph of his career. Shad thinks this conviction's going to propel him straight into the mayor's office. Do you think he's going to bend over backwards to overturn that conviction? Throw away Drew and capital murder to nail the wife for *manslaughter?* You think he's even gonna *listen?*"

"We'll go to Judge Minor, then."

Quentin throws up his hands. "You told me yourself that he's on Shad's side, and you were right. Judge Minor so blatantly favored the state that I have no doubt about the outcome of the appeal." Quentin lays a hand on my shoulder. "Forget this craziness, Penn. Drew's best bet is the appeals process."

"He's innocent, Quentin. And they're about to enter the death phase of the trial. At the least, Ellen's story could introduce enough doubt to keep the jury from voting for execution."

Quentin looks down at a vase of wilted flowers. After about a minute, he looks up, his eyes filled with resolve. "All my experience and instinct tell me that would be a mistake. With this D.A. and judge, it's the wrong way to play it. We should save the impact of Ellen's story for the appeal."

"Fuck the appeal," I mutter. "I want a new trial."

Quentin's eyes darken. "I'm chief counsel, Penn."

"This isn't your call. It's Drew's."

The old lawyer sighs angrily. "If you really want to upset him like that, I'll go down to the jail and put this to him."

I shake my head. "I'm going with you."

"You can barely make it to the bathroom."

I raise myself onto my hands and sit up. "I'm going with you, Quentin."

He picks up his coat and walks to the door.

"Go back to the hotel," I tell him. "If I haven't called you in a half hour, go talk to Drew alone. Fair enough?"

He nods once. I expect him to offer an olive branch—or fire a parting shot—before he goes, but he does neither.

After he's gone, I pick up the plastic device that connects me to the nurses' station and punch the Call button.

"Yes, Mr. Cage?"

"Is my father still in the hospital?"

"His light's on."

"Would you page him and ask him to come to my room?"

"Yes, sir."

"Thank you."

Ten minutes later, my father walks into my room and closes the door.

"What's the matter?" he asks.

"I need to get out of here, Dad. You've got to help me."

"What's going on? I heard they convicted Drew."

"Ellen Elliott just confessed to Kate's murder. Right here in this room."

Dad's mouth opens, but no sound emerges. Then he says, "You believe her?"

"I do."

"Jesus Christ."

"You've got to get me out of this bed. I've got to see Drew face-to-face, and that means going to the jail. I want to overturn his conviction, but Quentin doesn't see eye to eye with me on that. I've got to make sure Drew has a chance to save himself. If nothing changes between now and the sentencing phase, I'm afraid he'll be sentenced to death. His son shouldn't have to go through that, even if the decision is reversed six months from now."

Dad sits on the side of my bed and surveys me from head to toe. "You're in bad shape, Penn."

"How bad?"

He sighs deeply. "Your heart's sounding better, but the vasculitis is still a serious problem. If you start moving around, you're going to have hydrostatic problems with your blood pressure. You could faint very easily."

"It's not my blood vessels that are keeping me in this bed. It's the withdrawal. I get horrible muscle cramps when I move. If I stand for ten minutes, I fall down and twist into a ball of agony. *That's* what I need help with."

"The methadone's not helping?"

"Not enough."

Dad makes a clucking sound with his tongue.

"Drew saved my life," I say quietly. "You remember."

"I remember, all right." Dad taps his right fist into his open palm. "There's one thing I could try. It's unethical as hell, but . . . Hang on, I'll be back in a minute."

"Where are you going?"

"Hospital pharmacy."

He's back in less than five minutes. In his left hand is a bottle of pills, in his right, a mortar and pestle.

"What's that?"

"Oxycontin."

"Will that help me?"

His eyes glint beneath raised brows. "We're about to find out."

He takes out two yellow tablets, drops them into the china vessel, and crushes them to powder. "Abusers crush the tablets because they're time-release formulas," he says. "Crushing them gives you the full dose almost instantaneously. It's a lot more like mainlining heroin." He takes a white card from the flowers by my bed and carefully brushes three quarters of the powder into the glass of water on my bedside table.

"Drink it down."

I swallow the bitter mixture.

"That ought to give you some relief."

"How long will it last?"

"I don't know. But don't do that yourself. When the pain comes back, just take one pill by mouth."

Dad dons his stethoscope and lays its cold bell against the skin beneath my left nipple, over the apex of my heart.

"What are you listening for?" I ask. "My heart slowing down?"

"No. With a narcotic dose like this, your respiration will slow down, but your heart may race to try to provide more oxygen. It's called reflex tachycardia."

The rush doesn't come as quickly as the one from Blue's syringe, but come it does. After five minutes, I feel the warmth spreading from beneath my heart. "Jesus," I murmur. "That's it. The pain is *gone*." I flex my arms, then stretch gloriously in the bed. "Talk about a miracle drug."

"There's a reason opium has hung around since Alexander the Great." After a while, Dad removes his stethoscope and says, "Your heartbeat's within normal limits."

I take several deep breaths, then sit up and hang my feet over the edge of the bed. Dad takes hold of my arms and helps me stand.

"I feel like a new man. Literally."

"Only while the drug lasts," he says. "Remember that. You're like Cinderella at the ball."

"Right."

"Your mother would boil me in oil if she knew about this."

"Don't tell her." I suddenly feel light-headed, but I mask my difficulty by sitting on the bed again.

"Are you going to the jail now?" Dad asks.

"Yes."

"I'll drive you."

"That's all right. Kelly will take me."

"Even better." Dad looks me from head to toe again. "Let's get some clothes on you."

CHAPTER

38

"Where's Ellen now?" Drew asks in a voice I can barely hear.

"At the hospital with my mother."

Drew blinks rapidly, then looks down. Even through the bullet-proof glass of the visiting window, I can see he's close to breaking. His skin is so pale that he looks like he's suffering from severe anemia. With Quentin standing behind my chair, I've just re-counted what happened between Ellen and Kate at St. Catherine's Creek. To his credit, Quentin did not interrupt once.

"Drew, you've got a big decision to make," I say. "And it's yours alone."

He closes his eyes. Quentin lays a hand on my shoulder, but before I can turn, a single, racking sob bursts from Drew's throat. His mouth makes it appear that he's laughing, but I've seen that effect in many distraught people. I wish I could shatter the glass separating us and hug him, but there's no way to do that. As I watch helplessly, he starts banging his forehead against the window like an autistic child.

"Drew? Drew!"

He doesn't seem to hear me.

I rise and put my mouth up to the metal vent in the window.

"Drew!"

"Dr. Elliot!" Quentin barks from behind me. "We've got to make a decision about this matter!"

Drew stops banging the glass and stares at Quentin. "Decision?"

"Your wife wants us to take her confession to the district attorney."

He blinks in shock. "Take Ellen to Shad Johnson?"

"That's what she wants," Quentin says. "She's ready to confess to Shad that she killed your lover."

I glare at him, but Drew is already shaking his head. "No," he says. "Absolutely not. She can't do that."

Quentin looks at me in triumph. "Those are exactly my feelings, Doctor. The D.A. wouldn't believe her anyway. Neither would Judge Minor. We have to focus on your appeal now."

"Drew, listen to me," I implore. "Right now, Tim is at risk of losing his father. At the very least, you're about to be sentenced to spend the rest of your life in prison. At worst, you'll get death by lethal injection. And *Timmy will know that.* All the time you're waiting for your appeal, Timmy will be suffering. If you had killed Kate, that would be one thing. But you didn't. I believed you before, but now I *know.* All through your trial, you told Quentin that you wanted the jury to know the truth. Well, now we know the real truth. And the jury should know it, too. Don't you see?"

Drew is staring at me as though paying close attention, so I press on.

"If we can prove Ellen's story, your conviction will be overturned. You'll be a *free man.* Free to be the father Tim needs."

"What would happen to Ellen?"

"She'd probably serve a brief sentence for manslaughter."

"He can't guarantee that," Quentin says. "Your wife could get life for murder."

"Manslaughter," I insist. "No jury's going to convict Ellen of murder for fighting with a girl who was pregnant by her husband. We could plea-bargain it ahead of time. There wouldn't even have to be a trial. I'd represent Ellen."

Drew stirs at this, but then Quentin says, "You're forgetting Ellen's drug habit, Penn. How Kate was used to feed that habit. No jury is going to buy Ellen as a noble wife who lost control just once."

"It doesn't matter," Drew says in a monotone.

Quentin and I fall silent, waiting for him to explain.

"If I hadn't gotten involved with Kate, none of this would have happened. Ellen did what she did because I put her in an impossible position. I won't have her punished in my place. Not for my weakness." Drew stares out of the little cubicle with absolute conviction. "I carry my own water, guys."

"Drew—"

"Let it go, Penn. I'll take my chances on appeal." He stands and holds his cuffed hands up to the window. "I appreciate you trying. But I want you to forget what Ellen told you. Every word of it."

I bow my head, marshaling my strength for further effort. Then I flatten my hands against the window like starfish and lean close to the vent. "You want to punish yourself? Fine. But don't cheat Timmy out of a father. You owe it to him to be there for him."

Drew lifts his eyes to mine, but all I see in them now is resignation. "Tim will be okay with Ellen. Go home and hug Annie. Don't worry about me anymore. Let it go."

He turns away and knocks for a deputy.

I search for the right words to make Drew reconsider, but he's gone before I find them. I turn to Quentin in anger and confusion.

The old lawyer is looking at the glass where Drew stood just a moment ago. "That's a man, right there," he says. "Haven't met any like him in at least twenty years."

I clutch Quentin's upper arm. "You'd better get him off on appeal. You hear me? He doesn't belong in a cell."

"If it can be done, I'll do it."

"That's what you said about the last trial."

Quentin pats his coat flat, then shoots his cuffs. "Nobody could have got him acquitted for that girl's murder. Not in this town. Not this week. The deck was stacked, and Elliot's too goddamn noble to play the game the way he would have had to for us to win. Even with his life at stake."

I say nothing. It's time for me to get back to the hospital, as much as I hate the idea. My jaw muscles are already aching, and the bone pain won't be far behind.

Quentin and I take the elevator down together. Doris Avery is sitting with Daniel Kelly on a bench in the lobby, talking quietly. As Quentin and I walk toward them, my cell phone rings. The caller ID says, MIA.

"Hello? Mia?"

"Yes! I've got to talk to you." She's breathing as though she's just run a hundred-yard dash. "Face-to-face. Where are you?"

"The county jail. Where are you?"

"Your hospital room. I thought you'd be here." Her voice is crackling with energy, but I can't tell whether that energy is the result of excitement or panic.

"Hang on." I shake Quentin's hand, then motion him onward. "It's my kid's babysitter. I'll call you later at the hotel."

Quentin says, "We may head back out to the country tonight. Call me there if you don't get me at the hotel."

I wave to Doris as Quentin makes his way to the bench. Then I turn away and walk back toward the elevators. "These are digital phones, Mia. No one's going to hear you. Tell me what's happened."

"I can't. It's too dangerous."

My patience has worn down to nothing. "Mia, stop the melodrama and just tell me what's going on."

The silence that follows tells me I've hurt her feelings. I'm sorry for that, but there's too much at stake now for high school detective games. "Mia . . ."

"It's okay," she says.

"What's this about?"

"Coach Anders."

"Wade? What about him?"

"He's been sleeping with a student."

My stomach goes hollow. "Who?"

"Jenny Jenkins. She's a *junior.*"

"How did you find this out?"

"She told me herself, not fifteen minutes ago. I was up at the school, in a meeting about the senior trip. When I came out, Jenny was waiting for me."

"Are you two friends?"

"Not really. She told me because I've been bugging everybody all week about Marko. You know, trying to find you."

"I don't get it."

"That's what I'm trying to tell you. This isn't really about Coach Anders—it's about *Marko*."

I can hardly contain my frustration. "What about Marko?"

"His alibi is bullshit."

I feel a wave of disorientation, but I'm not sure if it's Oxycontin or the first hint of true knowledge. "His alibi for which day? The Wilsons or Kate?"

"Kate!"

"Wade Anders was Marko's alibi."

"*That's* what I'm telling you! Coach Anders's story was bull-shit!"

I blink in disbelief. "Don't say another word."

Mia laughs. "Told you."

I think quickly. "Do you know where Jewish Hill is?"

"The City Cemetery?"

"Meet me there as soon as you can."

"I'm on my way."

Daniel Kelly and I stand on the edge of Jewish Hill, waiting for Mia in a softly falling rain. Beyond the twin bridges over the Mississippi, the sun is sliding down the last of its arc; soon it will slip silently into the great river. I turn and look out over the cemetery. Kate's grave is only a low mound of mud now. The faded green tent that protected it is gone, and there's been no time to carve a gravestone. That takes weeks in this town.

Looking down the road that runs along the bluff, I spy a solitary figure in the rain. The Turning Angel. She's not turning now, but merely standing with her head bowed, trying to weather the coming storm. As I stare, a hundred thoughts sweep through my mind. Ellen told me she killed Kate, and I believed her. But if Ellen killed Kate, why did Marko Bakic get Coach Anders to lie about his where-abouts that day? Could he have been doing a drug deal? If so, and Kate happened to get killed at the same time, then Marko must have improvised the alibi to cover his dope deal, not a murder.

It's a plausible theory. But something has been bothering me ever since I heard Ellen's confession. It's the sequence of events as she described them. Ellen told me that after she began choking Kate, Kate quickly "went out"—or became unconscious—and then fell and hit her head on the buried wheel rim. But the pathol-ogist who autopsied Kate determined the cause of death to be strangulation, not head trauma. I believe Ellen choked Kate long enough to make her unconscious, but probably not long enough to kill her. In fact, my impression during Ellen's confession was that she believed Kate died from the blow to her head. Ellen must have read otherwise in the newspaper, but she probably figured Kate was dead before her head hit the wheel.

But what if Ellen didn't kill Kate at all? What if Marko—un-known to Kate—was at the crime scene, too? What if the person Ellen heard walking through the woods after Kate fell was not Drew, but Marko Bakic? That would have put Marko with Kate after Ellen left her, but before Drew arrived and discovered her corpse. The more I think about that scenario, the more convinced I become that it might be true.

But why would Marko have been there?

The answer comes to me so fast that it leaves me breathless. Marko met Kate there to sell her—or more likely, give her—Lorcet Plus. Cyrus had cut off Kate's supply of pills; Cyrus's e-mails to her told me that. Cyrus had warned Kate not to go to Marko in search of Lorcet, but what alternative did she have?

Because Marko gave me his hair so willingly at the X-rave, I discounted the possibility that he'd raped Kate. But maybe he gave me that hair because he knew he would be long gone before the police could arrest him. No . . . that would have been stupid. He would only have given me the hair if he was positive it could never come back and bite him on the ass.

"Oh, God," I say softly. Marko gave me that hair because he knew I would be dead in a matter of hours—long before I could deliver his DNA to anyone who mattered.

"What is it?" Kelly asks.

"Wait a minute."

The events of the past two weeks are realigning themselves in my head with nauseating speed. Why is the chain of cause and effect so hard to see sometimes? Sonny Cross sticks his gun into Marko's mouth to interrogate him. Five hours later, Sonny is dead. Murdered by the Asians. Three days later, I track Marko down at the X-rave and question him about Kate's murder. Four hours later, the Asians try to kill me in the lobby of the Eola Hotel. Coincidence?

Not likely.

Marko and the Asians have been working together all along—probably against Cyrus. That's why Cyrus didn't kill me when he had the chance. Cyrus never saw me as a threat. I was after Kate's killer, and Cyrus knew he was innocent of that crime. But to Marko . . . I was a genuine threat. *Jesus.*

At Drew's trial, Shad painted the jury a picture of Marko as the "mystery man" who'd left the other semen sample in Kate's vagina. Shad chose Marko not based on evidence, but because Marko was conveniently missing, and thus offered the most possibilities for exploitation in court. But Shad painted Marko as Kate's consensual partner—and Drew as the jealous killer. But what if those roles were reversed in reality? The rightness of this logic settles into my soul with the weight of gospel.

"That's it," I whisper. If Marko discovered Kate's prone body just after Ellen fled, he might well have killed her, and then witnessed Drew finding her body. If so, Marko could have been the blackmailer who extorted money and drugs from Drew on the night of the crime. Was Marko the man on the motorcycle that we chased through the woods behind St. Stephen's? Or was he the rifleman by the press box, shooting as we tried to get through the fence?

Another rush of images fills my brain. The lone killer dressed in black who shot so many of Cyrus's men . . . who was that but Marko Bakic? What makes me sure is that it was the same night—just hours later—that the Wilsons were brutally murdered. And they weren't gunned down in the style of the Asian gang, but stabbed dozens of times, as though in uncontrolled fury. What was that attack but retaliation by Cyrus's crew against the man they believed responsible for the attack on their safe house?

Marko . . .

"There's your girl," Kelly says. "Blue Honda Accord?"

Mia's car is racing up Cemetery Road. She slows by the second gate, turns in, and speeds along the narrow lane toward the superintendent's office. I watch her turn and climb the road to Jewish Hill.

"What do you want me to do?" Kelly asks.

"Give us some space, but watch us. I have no idea where Marko is, but I have a feeling that kid's a lot more dangerous than I thought."

"You're covered."

As Kelly walks down through the stones on the back side of Jewish Hill, Mia's car noses onto the grass and drives along beside the wall shielding the graves. When I motion for her to stop, she opens her passenger door and waves me inside. I shake my head and beckon her out.

"It's raining!" she calls.

"That's what's keeping me awake!"

She nods and gets out of the car. She's wearing old jeans and a royal blue St. Stephen's sweatshirt. When she reaches me, she looks me up and down. "You look really sick. Are you all right?"

"I've definitely been better."

Mia tries to smile, but it doesn't work. She buries her head in my chest and hugs me hard. I hold her for a minute, then gently separate us and lead her to the far edge of the hill, where the view of the river is unobstructed.

"Why did Coach Anders lie for Marko?" I ask.

"Because Marko knew about Wade and Jenny."

"What else did Jenny say?"

"Coach Anders has been really stressed out for the past week and a half. *Really* stressed, like talking to himself and stuff. Jenny didn't know what that was about, but today at school she was worried he might have a heart attack or something."

"Go on."

"Jenny went into Wade's office after fifth period, and he was crying. She begged him to tell her what the matter was, and he finally did. It was Drew's conviction. Apparently Wade had suspected for some time that Marko had something to do with Kate's death. He told Jenny all about Marko and the fake alibi. But he was afraid to tell the police, because he knew Marko would blab about Jenny, and he'd lose his job. Maybe even his career as a coach."

"It's worse than that," I tell her. "Wade's in a position of trust as defined by statute. He'd be facing the same kind of sexual battery charges as Drew. Thirty years in the pen. He might even be charged as an accessory-after-the-fact in Kate's murder."

Mia looks at me in shock. "Well, Wade told Jenny he'd been praying all week that Drew would be acquitted. When he heard it had gone the other way, he lost it."

"What did Jenny do?"

"Freaked out. She knew she couldn't keep quiet about the Marko thing. She'd already been going crazy herself because of the affair. She's been late for her period a couple of times, and she was worried that Wade was sleeping with somebody else. It's a mess."

"God, this town has gone crazy."

"No rules anymore," Mia says, pulling up the hood of her sweatshirt against the rain. "It's definitely Wade's fault, but you can bet Jenny pushed hard to make that affair happen. She's been with seven other guys that I know about, and she's only sixteen. She's got a messed-up home life."

I'm not thinking about Jenny Jenkins, but Wade Anders.

"What are you going to do, Penn?"

"Call our esteemed athletic director."

"Is that the best thing?"

"I need to know if he's willing to admit the affair."

Mia nods, but she looks unsure. "Why should he, though? I mean, if he thinks Marko murdered Kate, and if he knows how crazy Marko is—which he does—he'd be crazy to tell on Marko. Forget keeping his job—he'll be worried about his *life*. He only told Jenny what happened because he thought she'd keep quiet."

"Will Jenny repeat her story to the police?"

"I have no idea. My gut says no."

"I have to know, Mia. Call Information and get me Wade's home number."

"I already have it, from being head cheerleader." She calls the number and hands me her cell phone. "Wade drives the bus to all the games. I had to deal with him a lot this year."

The phone rings twice. "And he never came on to you?"

Mia shakes her head. "I guess he had Jenny taking care of him."

"Mia?" Wade Anders says in my ear.

He's looking at his caller ID. "No, Wade, this is Penn Cage."

"Oh. What can I do for you, Penn?"

"I know about you and Jenny Jenkins."

The silence on the phone makes the silence of the cemetery seem a roar.

"Wade? Are you there?"

"Yeah, but I don't know what you're talking about."

"I don't have time for lies, buddy. I don't even care about your affair. I'm trying to solve a murder here. There are lives at stake."

"What lies are you talking about, Penn?"

I look at Mia and shake my head. "You've been having sex with Jenny Jenkins. That's bad enough, okay? But you lied about where Marko Bakic was on the day Kate Townsend died, and that's unacceptable."

"I don't know where you heard that, but it's bullshit."

"*Wade,*" I say in a locker-room voice, "this is me, man. It's gone too far already. You can't get out of it now. Don't even try. Drew's already been convicted of murder because of you, and he could get the death penalty."

"Listen, goddamn it!" Anders says, anger hardening his voice. "I know you were helping defend Drew, and I know you guys lost today. But don't try to blame your failure on me. That's bullshit, what you said. Jenny Jenkins has problems at home, real problems. I've tried to help her out. She may have made some advances toward me, but I never touched her. Not inappropriately, anyway. And I don't know what the fuck you're talking about with this Marko stuff. And . . . and that's all I have to say about it. You want to talk to me again, call my lawyer."

"Do you have a lawyer, Wade?"

"I guess I better get one, if you're talking this kind of shit."

I start to press him further, but there's no point. I hang up and give Mia back her phone.

"He denied it?" she asks.

"All the way, the chickenshit."

"What are you going to do?"

"I don't know." I reach into my pants pocket and take out the bottle of Oxycontin. Mia watches as I open it and dry-swallow one of the tablets.

"What's that?"

"It helps with the withdrawal."

"Withdrawal?"

I forgot that she has no idea what I went through during the kidnapping. "Cyrus shot me up with heroin. It really wiped me out."

"Once? Or the whole time?"

"The whole time."

"Wow." She walks over and sits on the low wall bordering the Jewish graves. "That's the Turning Angel down there, huh?"

"Yes."

"I never really saw it turn, you know? It always looked the same to me, no matter which way I came from. I figure it's like those paintings where if some people stare long enough, they see another painting hidden inside the first one. I never saw those things either. I'm too much of a realist, I guess."

"That's not necessarily a bad thing."

She shrugs and looks up at me. "So do you want to hear my great idea?"

"What idea?"

"I think I can get Marko to tell me what happened on the day Kate died."

"How? No one even knows where he is."

Mia smiles wickedly. "His girlfriend does."

"Alicia Reynolds? The cops have been following her for days, and they haven't seen anything suspicious."

"Twenty-four hours a day?"

"I assume so. I don't know."

Mia's eyes gleam with certainty. "Alicia knows where he is, I'm telling you. If she didn't, she'd be a basket case. But she's happy as a clam."

"You think Marko's close by?"

She nods.

"At the rave, he told me he was leaving town."

"I think he waited around to be sure Dr. Elliot got convicted. If he is leaving, he's told Alicia he's taking her with him."

"Would she go with him?"

Mia snorts. "What else is she going to do? Work at the Piggly Wiggly? She hasn't even applied to college."

"Okay, let's say Marko is hiding in town somewhere. Why would Alicia tell you that? You've already bugged her for a week without results."

"Because this time I'm going to scare her. And when she talks to Marko, *he'll* be scared. And he'll ask to see me."

"What could possibly scare Marko at this point?"

"The truth."

"Meaning?"

"Coach Anders recanted Marko's alibi. That should knock Marko's legs right out from under him, even as cocky as he is."

"You might be right. But even if Marko's scared, why should he risk seeing you in person? He'll already know what the threat is."

"No, he won't. I'll only tell Alicia that it has to do with Coach Anders. Marko's paranoia will do the rest."

Mia definitely has a career ahead of her as a lawyer, if not an FBI agent. "Why would Marko believe you, though? All of a sudden, you come to his girlfriend out of the blue to try to save him?"

Mia looks away from me and gazes out over the cemetery. "It's not out of the blue."

"What do you mean?"

"I know Marko better than you think. Better than I let you think."

I lean down in front of her, but she won't meet my eye.

"I slept with him, okay?" she says. "When he first came here. It lasted about two months. Then I figured out he was just using me."

I sit beside her on the wall. "Using you for sex?"

"Yes. And to get Kate."

God. "Can you tell me about it?"

Mia stands and turns toward the river, as though she can't bear to look at me while she confesses this. "When Marko first got to St. Stephen's, everybody thought he was so cool. He had this aura about him, you know? The bad boy, 'I don't give a shit about anything' aura. But he was smart, too. Anybody could see that."

She bends and picks up a blade of new grass. "He started paying a lot of attention to me. I was really down on myself back then. It was the start of senior year, and my boyfriend had just moved to Minnesota with his folks, because the tire plant closed down. Everyone else was so jazzed about the year, but I was just dead. Then . . . in walks Marko. It had more to do with Kate than anything else, even for me, probably." She turns to me at last, her eyes wet. "Because everybody expected Marko to go for her, you know? Me included. But he didn't. He wanted *me*—or pretended he did. And that made me feel really good. That's probably what made me be with him, if I'm honest about it."

"Did Marko hurt you?"

Mia nods slowly. "Not physically. But he tore me up inside. He really convinced me that he cared about me. He told me about his childhood. He said I was the first person he'd trusted or let inside since he was a boy. And . . . I did stuff with him I'd never done before. I'd only been with one guy before Marko, my first boyfriend. I was so stupid. *God.*" She turns away from me again. "Look, I don't want to talk about that part of it, okay? My point is that if I can get Marko face-to-face, I can make him tell the truth about what happened. If he killed Kate, I think he'll *brag* about it to me. I'm serious. And if he does that, Dr. Elliott might go free."

"That would only happen if you wore a wire, Mia."

She nods. "That's what I'm talking about."

"No way. You almost got killed last week. You want to put yourself into a worse situation?"

"But it's not!" she argues. "Marko has no reason to fear me. Ever since I broke off our relationship, he's been begging me to see him again. He'll believe I want to warn him, Penn. His ego's just that big."

I take her by the shoulders and look hard into her eyes. "Listen to me. We're talking about this guy because we think he may have killed one high school girl already. There's too much risk."

She gives me a smile filled with regret. "I'm not Kate, okay? The biggest risk isn't that I'll get killed. It's that I'll have to screw him."

A wave of sickness rolls through my stomach. "There's something you need to know, Mia."

"What?"

Quickly, I tell her about Ellen's confession in my hospital room. She listens with wide eyes, and when I'm done, she bites her bottom lip and looks toward the river.

"You believed her?" she asks finally.

"Yes."

"I do, too. That's exactly what Kate would do in that situation. I can just see it. She'd be *so* cruel to Ellen."

"Then you see my point. It doesn't make much sense to try to trap Marko if Ellen is the one who killed Kate."

Mia shakes her head. "I don't believe she did. And you don't either."

"But you just said—"

"I believe Ellen choked her, yes. And if Kate had died from hitting her head, I might believe she'd killed her. But she didn't, did she?"

"No," I concede, gratified to see that Mia has followed the exact logic I did. "Strangulation."

Mia nods with satisfaction. "Marko was there. I mean, who else could it have been? You know?"

"Drew."

"You never believed Drew killed her. Neither did I."

"But he could have."

Mia dismisses this with a wave of her small hand. "You know he didn't. Your gut tells you that. And my gut tells me Marko *did*."

Mine tells me the same. But can I put Mia at risk again to try to prove that? As I ponder this question, the cell phone I borrowed from my father rings. My caller ID shows DON LOGAN as the caller.

"Hey, Don."

"Penn, I've got some information you might be interested in."

"I'm listening."

"Remember we kept wondering why Sheriff Byrd was taking orders from Shad Johnson?"

"Yeah."

"I finally found out. My source at the sheriff's department told me. They're celebrating like it's New Year's over there. There and the D.A.'s office. The sheriff told my source himself."

"What did he say?"

"Shad Johnson told Billy Byrd that when he's elected mayor, he's going to abolish the Civil Service Commission. They do all the hiring and firing for the police and fire departments. I don't know how Shad could do that, but Shad says that once the commission's gone, he's going to personally hire and fire every cop in town. And he's offered Billy Byrd the job of chief."

It takes me a few moments to absorb this. "Why would Byrd put himself under Shad's thumb like that?"

"Sheriff's an elected position. Billy might never be elected again. But Shad is willing to give him the one token white position in his administration. I guess Billy figures, if you can't beat 'em, join 'em. I figure I've got about ninety days left in this job."

"I'm sorry, Don."

"Welcome to the real world, brother."

I say nothing. An idea is taking shape in my mind, and it includes Chief Logan. "Don, what if I told you we could overturn Drew's conviction?"

"I'd ask you how."

"What if I told you Marko Bakic killed Kate Townsend?"

"I'd ask what proof you have."

"Proof exists. And you can help me get it. Are you up for that?"

"Are we talking about in my official capacity?"

"Quasi-official, you might say. It would be important after the fact that you're the police chief."

"I need more to go on than that."

"Can you meet me at the City Cemetery?"

"Now?"

"Right now. And bring the smallest wire rig you've got with you."

"What the hell are you up to, man?"

"Saving Drew's ass and your job. Just get up here."

Chief Logan breathes steadily into the phone. Right now he's a man without a future. At length, he says one word.

"Okay."

I'm sitting in the passenger seat of Don Logan's Crown Victoria. Kelly and Mia are in the backseat. Kelly is checking out the wire rig Logan brought over from the police station. I introduced Kelly to Logan as a corporate security expert from Houston.

"This is old technology," Kelly says. "We use transmitters a quarter this size now."

"Do you have one with you?" I ask the rearview mirror.

"Not on this trip."

"I don't know about this scheme," Logan says. "I mean, I see the upside. But this girl's life is at risk. Let me play devil's advocate for a minute. Even if Marko tells the Reynolds girl to bring Mia to him, we have no idea where that might be. We'll be trying to follow her in two cars. If she loses us, Mia's on her own."

"Tracking device," says Kelly. "I did bring one of those in my bag of tricks. It's a GPS model. We won't lose their car."

"Okay," says Logan. "But even if we manage to stick with them, Marko will have all the advantages. He'll know the layout and the terrain. The home-court advantage, I guess I'm saying. And look at Penn: he's at half strength, if that. So, it's basically you and me, Mr. Kelly. You look like you know what you're doing, and I'm sure you do. But just the two of us?"

"We'll be fine," Kelly says with self-assurance. "Don't sweat that part of it."

"I'm just saying, if we do find out where Marko is, why don't I just call in backup and raid the place?"

"Because then we'd have a hostage situation," Kelly says. "We want Mia to walk in and out of this place under her own power."

"Plus," I add, "if we raided the place, Marko would just lawyer up, and we'd never get a thing out of him about Kate's murder."

Chief Logan nods dejectedly.

"The risk to me isn't that great," Mia insists. "If it was, I wouldn't go, you know?"

"If Marko finds that wire," says Kelly, "he won't be happy. Don't kid yourself about that."

"I've thought about it. But he *will* know there are cops all around."

"Hostage situation again," says Logan. "What then?"

Kelly looks the chief in the eye. "Then I take him out."

Logan glances at me. I nod once.

"You feel that confident?" Logan asks Kelly.

Kelly smiles. "I've been there before, Chief. Many times."

"That's not the outcome we want," I tell Logan. "We want a confession. But if Mia's in real danger, Kelly will have no choice."

Logan looks unconvinced. "I'd feel better with a SWAT team, Penn."

I glance at Kelly, and he gives me permission with a nod.

"Daniel was a Delta Force operator for eight years," I explain. "He's worth more than any SWAT team we have around here. He's the only reason I'm willing to let Mia go in there—wherever 'there' is."

Logan processes this slowly. "I see. So basically, I'm here to make this all legal after the fact."

"That's right, Don."

Logan looks at me. "What are you here for?"

"For the unexpected," Kelly says.

The chief chuckles softly. "I don't know if we're the Three Musketeers or the Three Stooges."

"The winners write history," I murmur. "We'll know which we are after this is over."

"Aw, hell," says Logan. "We don't even know if Marko will take the bait."

"He'll take it," says Mia.

"How do you know?"

She smiles in the gathering dusk. "Wouldn't you?"

Kelly laughs. "She's got you there."

CHAPTER

39

"She's been in there awhile," says Chief Logan.

It's full dark on Lindberg Street, the location of Alicia Reynolds's parents' house. Mia disappeared inside an hour ago, after calling Alicia and saying she had to talk to her about a matter of life and death. Logan, Kelly, and I have sat huddled in Logan's Crown Vic all that time, trying not to let second thoughts sway our plan. Logan and I are in the front, Kelly in back. The Reynolds house is forty yards away.

"You don't think Marko could be hiding in the Reynolds's house?" Logan suggests.

"That's a scary thought," I reply, "but no." I change positions, trying to keep my feet moving. They've been burning badly for the past twenty minutes. If Mia doesn't emerge soon, I'm going to have to get out and walk around a little.

"If Marko was in there," Kelly says, "Mia would have switched on the transmitter."

"You've got a lot of confidence in her," says Logan.

Kelly nods. "Girl has her shit together."

Earlier tonight, when Logan tried to tape the transmitter to Mia's inner thigh, she shook her head and said, "Marko's hands will wind up there, I promise you. He's that kind of guy."

"Then where?" asked the chief.

Kelly picked up Mia's handbag, pulled a knife from his pocket, and slit open the inner lining of the bag. Then he slipped the transmitter into the lining. While Logan stared, Kelly took the duct tape from him, made a loop of it, and neatly sealed the slit he'd made in the bag from the inside. He made Mia practice switching the transmitter on and off through the lining until she could do it smoothly by touch alone. Mia seemed encouraged by Kelly's professionalism.

"Where do you think Marko's hiding?" Logan asks, peering at some approaching headlights.

"Lots of possibilities," I answer, not taking my eyes off the lighted window on the side of the Reynolds's house. "He could be staying in an empty house up at Lake St. John. He could be in an empty building downtown."

"Plenty of those."

"He could be at somebody's deer camp. He could be at one of the other empty factories, like Cyrus. The bottom line is, without somebody like Alicia, we'd never find him."

Logan nods. "So, he'd be stupid to take the bait."

"Or arrogant," Kelly says.

"Good point."

My cell phone rings. I snatch it up before it can ring again. "Hello?"

"*She's on the phone with him!*" Mia hisses. "*She's got a special phone for calling him. I think we're leaving straight from here.*"

"Any idea where you're going?"

"No! Have you got the tracking device on the car?" Mia sounds panicked.

"We didn't know which car you were taking."

"Hers, I think. Shit, I don't know! She's coming. Don't lose us!" She hangs up.

"Which car?" asks Kelly.

"She thinks Alicia's, but she's not sure. They're leaving soon." My heart thumps against my sternum. "Marko's still here. Jesus."

"Put the tracker on Reynolds's car," says Logan, visibly tense.

"Not until we know for sure," says Kelly.

"It'll be too late then!"

Kelly shakes his head. "I'm gonna wait."

"If the girlfriend sees you, it's over."

Soft laughter. "Nobody's gonna see me, Chief."

Kelly gets out of the car and quietly closes the door. When I look out my window, he's vanished.

"Where'd he go?" asks Logan. "I don't see him."

"He's there. Just be glad he's on our side."

Logan leans over and begins fooling with something. The seat between us is littered with gear: walkie-talkies; the receiver for Mia's transmitter; and some of Kelly's gear, including a subnote-book computer. Lying on the floor in front of the backseat are a carbon-fiber sniper rifle and an MP5 submachine gun like the one the Asian boy was carrying last week. Both weapons are fitted with night-vision scopes.

"What are you doing?" I ask Logan.

"Making sure our radios are on the same channel. Sometimes it's the simplest thing that kills you."

The light under the Reynolds's carport goes on.

"Here they come," I say.

Alicia's white RX-8 is parked under the carport. Mia's Accord is in the driveway. Marko's girlfriend walks into the carport and stomps around to the driver's door of her Mazda. She's obviously pissed off. Mia walks out behind her, much more slowly, and opens the passenger door. She glances in our direction, but she doesn't seem to be in distress.

"Reynolds could lose us in that Mazda," Logan observes.

"Kelly's got it. Just wait."

The RX-8 backs quickly out of the driveway, then peels up Lindberg Street, its motor whining as it heads into a large subdivision lying between us and the Highway 61 bypass.

"Where's Kelly?" Logan asks.

The door to my left jerks open and Kelly leaps in. "Stay fifty meters back," he says. "Don't get in a hurry."

Logan wants to hurry, I can tell. He keeps the Mazda's taillights in sight, which makes sense to me.

"If you can see her, she can see you," Kelly says calmly, reaching over the front seat for his computer. "Trust your gear."

I wouldn't trust the local police department's gear, but this stuff belongs to Kelly.

"Have you got them?" Logan asks, barely slowing.

I look into the backseat. Sitting sideways so I can see, Kelly pulls up a city map on his screen and studies it. "Got 'em. Slow down, Chief."

Logan lets the taillights ahead wink out.

A red dot on Kelly's screen moves along the streets of Montebello subdivision, moving toward the bypass. The dot turns onto the highway and accelerates.

"Where are they?" Logan asks nervously.

"Bypass," I answer. "Now they're turning onto Montebello Melrose Parkway."

"Headed downtown?"

"Looks like it. Lots of houses before they're downtown, though. Woods, too."

The red dot sweeps down the long curving lanes that cut through the thick forest between the bypass and downtown Natchez. It passes Melrose, an antebellum plantation purchased by the federal government and turned into a National Historical Park. This part of Natchez is thick with mansions, as many wealthy planters' estates abutted in the vicinity.

Logan accelerates along the parkway. We pass a modern bank sited in the midst of the forest, then climb a hill and pass Melrose.

"They're on Main Street," Kelly says.

"Not really," I tell him. "That's the Main Street extension. They're not actually downtown yet."

"They're slowing down," says Kelly. "Stopping now."

"Where?" asks Logan.

"Can't tell," I say, thinking furiously.

"They turned into blank space on my map," says Kelly.

"Ardenwood, maybe?" I suggest.

"*Fuck*," Logan curses, and suddenly I know I'm right.

"What's Ardenwood?" asks Kelly.

"Sixty acres owned by a complete nut," says Logan. "Son of a *bitch*. We're in trouble, Penn. Mia's in trouble."

"Just get us there. This makes all the sense in the world."

"What's Ardenwood?" asks Kelly. "What the fuck are we headed into?"

I close my eyes and try to summon what I know. Ardenwood was a majestic Greek Revival mansion built by one of the wealthiest planting dynasties in the pre–Civil War South. One of the few to remain in the hands of its original family, it stood pristine through the war, Reconstruction, decay, rebirth, and then the modern city of Natchez growing up around it. A decade ago, the property fell into the hands of an heir who didn't care to live in it. An eccentric lawyer from Mobile, he preferred to let the house stand unoccupied, slowly rotting away along with its priceless contents. Last year, on a calm Sunday morning, a column of smoke began rising from the center of town. By the time the fire department arrived, a quarter of the mansion had been consumed. A crowd of hundreds gathered to watch it burn, some with tears in their eyes, others cursing the man who had let this jewel of history be destroyed for no reason. Annie and I were part of that crowd. Caitlin was out of town. All that remains now is a dangerous shell patched with plywood against the rain. That and some frightening rumors.

"A fucking nightmare," Logan grumbles, filling the vacuum. "It's an old mansion sitting on sixty acres of woods and pasture. It burned last year, and the absentee owner blamed a prowler. He's booby-trapped the whole goddamned place since then. He's got shotguns wired to the doors, spikes in the yard, crazy stuff. He's even got night-vision equipment up there. He said he's going to take care of any future prowlers himself."

"I think Marko Bakic is more prowler than he could handle," I murmur.

"The guy stays over in Mobile most of the time," Logan says. "That's one good thing."

"For his sake, I hope he's been there all week."

Logan slows the Crown Victoria, and I look left as we pass the road that leads into Ardenwood.

"I see it," says Kelly. *"Christ."*

The front acreage of the property is ten feet higher than the back, but behind the dark mass of land, a hulking black skeleton rises from between oak and magnolia trees. I can just make out the Greek Revival facade: huge Corinthian columns and an immense white capital.

"Keep driving," I say. "Kill your lights and park in the median."

The median here is forty feet wide and shaded by oak and pecan trees. We're at the edge of downtown proper, but to an urban dweller this would look like deep woods.

Logan parks, then sweeps our radios, the wire receiver, and the tape recorder into a black satchel. While Kelly grabs his weapons and gets out, I concentrate on walking without falling down. We cross the road, climb the berm we saw before, then hunker down under a large pecan tree. Logan passes out the radios.

"Now that we know where they are," he says, "how do we play it?"

"I've got to move up to the house to cover Mia," Kelly says. "You two stay here and monitor the receiver. I'll have an earpiece in my walkie-talkie, but you don't call me under any circumstance but one."

"What's that?"

"The girl needs saving. We'll use two codes: 'Red' and 'Blue.' If I hear 'Blue,' I'll try to extract Mia without harming Bakic. If you say 'Red,' I kill him."

"Understood," I say.

"Got it," says Logan. "Why hasn't she switched on her transmitter?"

"She will," says Kelly. "She's got it down."

He leans his sniper rifle against the pecan tree and shoulders his MP5. "Either of you know anything about the interior layout of this place?"

"There are usually four rooms on the ground floor and four upstairs," I tell him. "You should find a big central hall downstairs with a wide staircase, then another staircase somewhere else for the servants. I don't know how much of the interior remained intact after the fire. Even if the stairs are still there, you might not be able to put any weight on them."

"That's better than nothing." Kelly gives us both a questioning look. "The codes?"

"Blue for extraction," I answer.

"Red is dead," says Logan.

Kelly nods. "Dead as a hammer, Chief." He gives me a grin, then turns and starts to walk away.

"Hey," I call after him.

He turns and looks back.

"Don't let anything happen to that girl. She's pure gold."

Kelly smiles. "I saw that right off. Don't worry."

"Take care of yourself, too."

He waves, then turns and races off under the trees.

CHAPTER

40

Logan peers at me, his lips pale in the dark. "I'm serious about those booby traps, Penn. The owner's lawyer informed the department so we'd be aware of them. Fire department, too. He was covering his ass in case of a lawsuit."

"Fuck him. It wasn't any prowler that burned this place. It was an electrical fire. He let everything rot, and fire was the result."

"Yeah," says Logan.

As I walk over to a tree trunk to lean against it, a sharp squawk makes me jump. Then the sound of music floats through the dark. Coldplay. Then the music fades and Mia whispers to us through the receiver: *"Alicia just went inside. I'm in the car. She took my cell phone and told me to stay put. She said you can get killed wandering around this place. That's why Marko chose it."*

"She needs to stop talking," Logan says. "Marko might be watching her right now."

"That's not why he chose this place," I think aloud, looking through the trees at the dark ruin. "This is just like Sarajevo. *That's* why he chose it."

"Locals don't even think about this house anymore," Logan muses. "They pass it every day, but it might as well not be here."

"*Here she comes,*" Mia whispers. "*No Marko.*"

"He's there," I murmur. "He's waiting for you."

"This is dangerous as hell," says Logan. "It could go really wrong for that girl. Is she even eighteen?"

"Yes."

"*Come on, Mia,*" says a childlike voice—Alicia's voice. "*He's waiting, you know?*"

The sound of footsteps crunching in wet gravel crackles from the receiver.

"Are you recording?" I ask.

"Every word."

"*This is bullshit,*" says Alicia. "*I don't know what you think you're doing, but this is bullshit.*"

Mia doesn't reply.

"*I know you want him for yourself,*" Alicia goes on, her voice warbling with fear. "*Well, you can't have him.*"

"*I already had him,*" Mia says. "*That's not why I'm here. I'm just trying to keep him from spending the rest of his life in jail.*"

"*You're a liar.*"

The crunching stops.

"They're walking around the house," says Logan. "On grass. We'd have heard the porch."

"*Right here,*" says Alicia. "*Boost me up.*"

"*Through the window?*" asks Mia.

"*You see me, don't you?*"

Wood scrapes against wood. The girls are climbing through the window. Then I hear a clatter of heels on hardwood.

"*Mia!*" cries a male voice. "*So glad to see you, baby!*"

The East European accent is unmistakable.

"*Give us some space, Alicia,*" Marko says.

"*What?*" Anger now. Uncertainty with it.

"*Disappear for a while.*"

"*But—*"

"*Go.*"

The silence after this command is chilling, but then the sound of light footsteps comes to us.

"Not that way!" Marko snaps. *"I've told you a hundred times. Go sit in the front room and watch the driveway."*

"You're a bastard, you know that?"

"I know this. That's why you love me."

More footsteps, slowly fading.

Marko chuckles softly. *"So, we're alone finally. What's the big news about Coach Anders?"*

I hear a soft, sliding sound. Mia padding around the room in her running shoes? *"This place is wild,"* she says. *"Gas lantern, huh? That sheet on the window keeps people outside from seeing it?"*

"Just like back home," Marko replies. *"What's the deal, Mia? What about Wade?"*

"He's recanted his story."

"What's that mean, recanted?"

"He admitted that he lied for you. He told the police that you weren't at his house on the afternoon Kate died. The police are looking for you now."

A long pause. *"Is that so?"*

"Yes."

To ensure that Marko couldn't learn the real truth of the situation, Logan called Wade Anders and warned him not to take any calls from Marko. Logan told me Anders sounded scared shitless on the phone.

"How do you know this?" Marko asks.

"From the guy I babysit for. Penn Cage."

"Ah, Mr. Cage. I heard Cyrus fucked him up pretty good."

"He did. I saw him. But what about the police, Marko?"

"It's no big deal. I was changing my name anyway."

"Changing your name? Are you leaving town?"

"That's right. Leaving tonight."

"Are you going to come back and graduate?"

Marko laughs wildly. *"Too late for that, baby."*

"No, it's not. If you took your exams, you could still graduate with the rest of us."

"Can't do it."

"*But Cyrus is dead now. And Penn said the Asians are dead or gone back to Biloxi. What do you have to worry about now?*"

"*Cyrus has homeboys. The Asians are a gang. They believe in payback.*"

"*Is that really it, Marko?*"

"*What do you mean?*"

"*I mean . . . where were you that afternoon? For real?*"

"*What afternoon?*"

"*Don't give me that. The afternoon Kate died.*"

"*Busy. I'm a busy man.*"

"*Okay, be that way. I've just been wondering about Kate, that's all.*"

"*What about her?*"

"*Why she really died. I mean, I know better than anyone what a bitch she could be. How manipulative she could be.*"

"*So?*"

"*At the trial, the D.A. said you were having sex with her, and that's what made Dr. Elliott kill her. That he found out about it and went crazy.*"

Marko laughs again. "*No way, man.*"

Logan looks at me, his eyes shining in the dark. "He didn't do it. He didn't kill her, Penn."

"This guy is a snake. Don't believe anything out of his mouth. Let it play out."

"*You never had sex with Kate?*" Mia asks. "*I know you wanted to.*"

"*I didn't say that.*" Marko laughs softly. "*You know me, I'm a player.*"

"*You're a player, all right.*"

"*Hey, don't look like that. It's just the way I am. You know that.*"

"*Was she better than me?*"

"*A gentleman never tells, right?*"

I curse Marko's penchant for head games.

"Right," says Mia. "And you're such a gentleman."

"*Lovely Mia. Why do you care so much about Kate?*"

"I told you. I just wonder what really happened to her. I can't see Dr. Elliott killing her. He loved her."

"What about you? You loved Kate, too?"

"I hated her."

Satisfied laughter. "I thought so. Why did you hate her so much?"

"She took you away, for one thing. Without even trying."

"No way. You left me."

"You gave me no choice. But that's not really it. Kate had everything, you know? All the fucking advantages, but she never really did anything on her own. She won so many things I should have won at school, scholarships and stuff, even when my scores were higher. That SouthBank scholarship . . . it was all political. Maybe she gave out some blowjobs to get that, I don't know."

Marko snickers. "No way. You're a lot better at that than she was."

My ears prick up.

"That's not funny," Mia says.

"Forget about Kate. I didn't bring you here to talk about her. Coach Anders, either. I brought you here to see you."

"No, you didn't. I was asking about you all week, and you didn't bring me here. You only brought me here tonight because you're worried."

"Well, you're here now, okay? And I'm glad to see you."

"Are you?"

"Yeah. Come over here. You know how long it's been since we were together?"

"Do you?"

There's a brief pause. Then Marko says, "Six months."

"I'm impressed. But you haven't been lonely."

"No. You want me to be lonely?"

"Maybe. I don't know. Screw it."

"What about you? Why don't you date anybody, Mia?"

"I have a thing for somebody. He doesn't know about it. He can't be with me. He's with someone else."

A shiver goes through me. She sounds like she's telling the truth about that.

"You talking about me?" Marko asks.

"No, retard. After what you did to me?"

"Come here, Mia."

Hesitation. *"Why?"*

"Just come over here. I miss you."

More footsteps. Then the voices soften.

"You look so fucking good," Marko murmurs. *"Shit . . . feel good, too. Just the same."*

There's no conversation for ten or fifteen seconds.

"You like that?" Mia asks.

More silence.

A scream of frightening intensity bursts from the receiver. *"How can you do that? How can you touch her with me right in the next room!"*

"I want her," Marko says. *"Get used to it."*

Alicia is sobbing. Then she screams again: *"Fuck you! I'm leaving!"*

Smothered laughter. *"She'll be back in an hour,"* Marko says, *"begging me to take her back."*

"I'm not going with you to L.A., either!"

"No? Okay. Maybe Mia will go instead."

"She won't either! She's not that stupid!"

A door slams.

"Are you taking Alicia with you?" Mia asks.

"Maybe just to tide me over till I get to L.A. I'll dump her there."

"That's not very nice."

"She doesn't have to go. I made no promises."

"Marko . . ."

"I'm not a nice guy, Mia. You know that."

"Yes, I do."

"But you still like me. You don't want a nice guy."

"You don't know what I want."

"I know you want this."

"He's not going to admit anything," Logan says. "He just wants to get laid."

"At least we know he's going to L.A. now."

"Finding Marko isn't our problem now. It's getting him to talk."

Logan is right.

"We need to pull that girl out of there, Penn."

"Maybe," I say in a taut voice.

"I don't think the guy has anything to tell. I think he was just moving some dope that afternoon. That's what he used Coach Anders to cover."

"Your legs are amazing," Marko says. *"Alicia's soft in all the wrong places. Flabby, man. You're so tight. Inside and out."*

"Am I?"

"You know you are."

Mia giggles, and the sound of it stuns me. I've never heard her laugh like that.

"Are you really going to L.A.?"

"Yeah, I can't believe it. I never thought I'd miss this place. But now . . ."

"Why are you leaving tonight?"

I hear the rustle of clothing. *"What?"*

"Don't push it, Mia," I plead softly.

"I just wondered why you picked tonight. Is it because of the trial? Were you waiting for it to be over?"

Silence follows this question. And in the silence, something changes. I feel it like the approach of a predator in the dark.

"Let's go somewhere else," Marko says.

"What's he doing?" asks Logan.

"Why?" asks Mia.

"I think Alicia's still watching us."

"I figured you'd like that."

"Maybe some night. Not tonight. Just us tonight."

Footsteps on wood, quicker than before.

"Wait," Mia protests. *"Let me get my purse."*

"What for?"

"Girl stuff."

"Okay."

There's a delay, then Marko says, *"That's a cool bag. Let me see it."*

My throat seals shut with fear.

"Shit, shit, shit," hisses Logan.

"*Give that back!*" Mia protests. "*That's my private stuff.*"

Marko laughs, and then I hear a bump.

"*Hey! Get out of there!*"

The sound of Marko rummaging through the bag is like furniture being shoved around a house.

"Should we send Kelly in?" Logan asks, his voice taut.

"Get ready," I tell him.

The rummaging stops. "*Here you go,*" Marko says. "*Tampax, huh? You on your period?*"

"*That never mattered to you before.*"

Knowing laughter. "*Come on. Let's get some privacy.*"

"He didn't find it," Logan breathes. "I can't believe it."

"*Where are we going?*" Mia asks.

The hair on the back of my neck stands erect. Mia's last sentence came from the receiver at half the volume of her previous one.

"He did find it," I say.

"You think?" asks Logan.

"Her signal's fading."

"They walked away from the purse. They're making out."

I crouch and lean close to the receiver. There's a background of static now. There was none before. The voices come in and out, like someone talking on a cell phone at the edge of a tower's coverage.

"Give me your radio, Don."

"You sure?"

"Right now!"

He hands me his walkie-talkie. I press the transmit key and say, "Blue, repeat, blue. Blue, repeat, blue. Acknowledge!"

Two clicks come back to me.

Relief courses through me with the power of Cyrus's heroin.

"Kelly's going in," I say. "Thank God."

"We were crazy to send her in there," Logan says. "The Three Stooges after all."

When the explosion comes, I'm not sure whether it blasted out of the receiver or down through the trees.

Logan gapes at me, his eyes wide. "What the fuck was that?"

"Shotgun?"

He shakes his head. "Sounded like a grenade to me."

My skin goes cold. Kelly wasn't carrying any grenades.

Logan drops flat on the ground and puts his ear to the receiver. "Nothing."

"Booby trap?" I suggest.

Logan gets up and draws his gun from his holster. "I'm going up there."

I want to go, too, but there's no way I could keep up with him. "Should I call 911 and ask for backup?"

"I'll do that. You wait for the units and show 'em where to go."

I nod, but Logan is already charging up the hill, his gun in one hand and a police radio in the other. As I stare after him, one thing hits me with absolute certainty. By the time backup units arrive here, whatever is happening up there will be over. More than anything, I want to call Kelly on the radio, but he specifically told me not to. If I can help him, he'll call me. *Unless he's dead.*

There's only one contribution I can make to this effort.

Thought.

I start walking toward Ardenwood. The mansion is seventy yards away, half concealed by massive oaks and magnolias. It looks like a great ship moored in a sea of trees.

Where is Marko taking Mia? Outside? If he took her outside, the signal strength would still be strong. And if he went outside, Kelly would already have nailed him. He didn't go outside. So, where did he go? Did he throw Mia's purse into a cabinet? Down a hole, maybe? If he did, the signal would simply have dropped out, not faded gradually. Could Ardenwood have a basement? Most antebellum mansions don't, other than half-sunken "milk rooms" used to keep dairy products cool. Those were small rooms, not true basements . . .

I'm forty yards from Ardenwood now, and nothing ahead has changed. It's as though Kelly and Logan walked up this hill and sank into the earth.

My radio crackles to life.

"I found the girl," Logan says, his voice choked with emotion. "She's down. She's been hit in the neck. It's shrapnel or shotgun pellets."

I can hardly speak. "Is it Mia?"

"I can't tell. She's covered with blood. I need a light . . . god-damn it."

"Is she alive, Don?"

"She's breathing. I don't think she can talk. God, this was so stupid."

"Have you seen Kelly?"

"Nothing. I've got backup coming, though. Ambulance, too."

I walk faster—my legs won't stand a run. My heart is pounding like a kettledrum, and my jaw is clenched tight enough to break my teeth. *"Don't be Mia,"* I pray hoarsely. *"Please, God, don't let it be her."* I push my legs faster, trying to reach the house, but I can't keep my balance. I crash onto the ground, then pick myself up, so winded I can hardly stand.

"It's not her," crackles Logan's voice. "It's the other girl. She's bleeding out, Penn. What do I do?"

"It's not Mia?"

"No. This girl has a fucking ring in her nose. Mia must still be out there."

Relief rushes through me. "Where are the wounds?"

"Neck, mostly."

"Direct pressure, Don. Keep that blood inside her."

I get slowly to my feet and look up at the house. *They're not in there,* says a voice in my head. *They're gone.*

"Have you heard any motors, Don?"

"No."

Then it hits me: *It's not a basement. It's a tunnel!*

I turn to my left and walk away from the house, down the hill toward the low ground on the north side of Ardenwood. As the Civil War began to turn against the Confederacy, many plantation owners realized that the Northern armies would eventually sweep southward over their lands. Some planters had only days to prepare, but others—especially those farthest south—had months and even years. A tunnel could be used to store valuables, and then in the last extremity as a means of escape from marauding soldiers or even neighbors, a real danger to the many Natchez planters who sympathized with the Yankee cause. I've never toured Ardenwood, but I know as surely as I know my name that it has an escape tunnel.

Marko Bakic knows it, too.

Moving downhill is a lot easier than moving up. In less than a minute, I'm moving into the kudzu that lines the bayou on the north side of Ardenwood. The smell of organic decay blends with the reek of dead fish and fetid mud. It's a familiar odor. The whole of Natchez is threaded with bayous and creeks, and I came to know them well as a boy. The planter who owned Ardenwood would have known them, too—this bayou, anyway. And when he decided to build his escape tunnel, in which direction would he have told his slaves to dig?

North.

Dig in any other direction, and they'd not only have had to dig horizontally, but vertically again to come up out of the earth—unless they dug dozens of yards farther than necessary. No slave owner would waste labor like that, especially during wartime. He'd have ordered his "darkies" to dig the shortest route to safety, and that was north. Thirty yards of tunnel would have carried the diggers to the bayou where I'm standing now.

Two feet of black water simmers between the banks, with tangled tree roots reaching like fingers down into it, and long beards of moss hanging from the limbs above. The kudzu is too thick to move quietly along either bank. And walking through kudzu is the best way to get bitten by a copperhead—especially at night. Pushing through the vines that choke the bank, I step down into the water, then begin walking slowly toward the back of the mansion.

The closer I get to Ardenwood, the higher the banks rise around me. If I'm right about the tunnel, it's possible that Marko and Mia already came out of it, but all I can do is follow my instinct. I try not to splash as I slide my feet along the muddy bottom. With every step I take, unseen creatures scuttle among the roots on the banks, and shining whips uncurl in the water and glide away. *Water moccasins*. Snakes have always terrified me, but Mia is facing a lot worse than that. Tensing my exhausted leg muscles against the bite of fangs, I push steadily forward.

Ardenwood towers above me now, more like part of the landscape than any man-made thing. If there's a tunnel leading out of that ruined shell, I should be getting close to its mouth. I stop in the water and listen with the focus of desperation.

Mosquitoes buzz . . .

Wet leaves rustle . . .

A turtle splashes—

"If you make a sound, I'll kill you."

Unspeakable fear paralyzes me where I stand.

"Did you hear me, bitch?"

"I heard you."

At the sound of Mia's small voice, hope flares within me.

"Move your ass, then!"

A splash sounds behind me, much bigger than that made by the turtle. If I move now, Marko will know I'm here. I hear another splash, and then the sound of a siren floats through the trees.

"Fuck!" curses Marko. *"You lying whore!"*

"Run," Mia urges him. "You can get away. I'll just slow you down."

"If I leave you here, I leave you dead."

"Marko, please—"

"Shut up!"

The siren's getting louder fast.

"This way!" Marko says harshly.

I hear more splashing, closer to me this time, and getting closer. Marko must be less than ten feet away, yet he's still walking toward me.

He can't see me.

It's so dark at the bottom of the bayou that only the sky is visible. Only night predators can see here. I stand utterly still as the splashes get closer. Marko curses as he works along the left bank, pulling Mia behind him—at least that's what I picture from the sounds. The water washes against my leg as they pass. They only miss me because they're walking half in and half out of the narrow stream, while I stand dead in the center.

When they're ten feet past me, I turn and begin to follow them.

Marko is moving fast now, away from the direction of the road. If I don't pick up the pace, he'll lose me. If I do, he may hear me. Twenty feet ahead, two shadows walk through a column of moonlight let in by a space in the trees. Mia's shorter frame is easily distinguishable from Marko's. I move faster, fighting a stitch in my side. How long before my legs cramp? How long before I fall again, and Marko runs back and shoots me while I try to rise from the water? As I ask myself these questions, a quick series of splashes sounds behind me. I don't know what they mean, but it sounds like a horse galloping up the stream.

As I stand frozen, Marko passes through the column of light again, moving swiftly and soundlessly back toward me. In seconds, he will either pass me or crash into me. If he passes me, whatever is behind me will be a sitting duck for him. If he hits me—

"Watch out!" Mia screams. "He's got a gun!"

Three feet ahead of me, a black form spins out of the dark and fires a gun. The flame spits away from me, though, back toward Mia. Consumed by fury, I crouch in the water and hold out my father's Browning. Marko fires again, this time in my direction, bracketing the bayou with bullets. I can't fire for fear of hitting Mia.

"*Motherfucker!*" Marko screams, firing like a maniac. "*Izuzetni!*"

Then his gun clicks empty.

With all the energy left in my body, I drive my legs upward and swing the Browning in a roundhouse arc. Metal crashes into bone, and Marko goes down in the water. I raise the Browning again and drive it down hard where I heard the splash. This time I hit something softer. An explosion of air hits my face, but then powerful arms whip around my neck and drag me down into the water.

Marko is suddenly above me, trying to shove my head under the water. I've got my gun jammed into his gut, but if I pull the trigger—if I kill him—Drew will never be freed.

"Don't make me kill you!" I shout.

Marko screams in a guttural language, and the hatred in his voice sends a bolt of terror through my soul. He means to kill me, even if it costs him his life. His jerks one hand from my neck and grabs for my gun. I'm pulling the trigger when a thin red beam arcs across my eyes. A single shot splits the night, and then Marko's hands fly away as though they never clutched me in a death grip.

Mia screams.

A powerful white light sweeps across me, onto Mia, then goes out.

"It's Kelly!" shouts a voice. *"Both of you get down!"*

I drop into the water, but I hear Mia splashing toward me.

"Stop, Mia!" Kelly shouts.

"He threw his phone!" she yells back. "There's something about his phone!"

Kelly charges past me and bellows something in the same guttural language Marko used. Marko screams back at him.

"Shine your light over here!" Mia says.

Kelly steps on something in the water—Marko, I presume—then obeys Mia's order. She drops to her knees, scrabbles through the kudzu, then jumps up with a silver cell phone in her hand.

I press my hands down into the mud and slowly get up.

Kelly drags Marko to his feet and binds his wrists with thin plastic restraints. "You okay, Penn?"

"I think so."

He lifts his radio and tells Logan how to find us.

Marko groans and doubles over.

"Did you shoot Marko?" I ask.

"He'll live," says Kelly. "I had time to pick my shot."

Fear is draining out of me like bad water. "I'm glad you thought so. Shit."

Kelly shines his flashlight on his own face. The sight of his grin beneath the blond hair makes me almost giddy with relief.

"Oh, my God," Mia cries. "Oh no."

When I turn, I see her face illuminated by the faint glow of a cell phone screen.

"Look at this, Penn," she whispers. "Dear Lord."

I splash over to her and look down.

Kate Townsend is looking up at me from the screen, but her eyes are no more alive than those of a dead fish. Her face is gray, and the orbits of her eyes are dotted with burst blood vessels.

"Is she dead?" Mia asks.

"Yes," says Kelly, leaning over my shoulder.

Mia fiddles with the phone's buttons, and another photo appears. This one shows Kate from the knees up. She's lying naked on the sand, spread-eagled to show her vagina. As I stare, my stomach almost comes up. Kate's head is turned to the side in the photo, and both her nose and mouth lie beneath the surface of the brown water. Her long blond hair trails downstream.

Mia hands me the phone, then falls to her knees and vomits into the bayou. I reach down and hold her hair so that she doesn't soil it. While she retches and heaves, I hear a sound like a hammer hitting raw meat. I turn in time to see Marko crumple to the ground.

As I help Mia to her feet, Marko curses Kelly in his own language. Marko's lying flat on his back, as though pinned there by the beam of Kelly's flashlight. Kelly stands over him with the MP5, covering him with lazy grace, as oblivious to the words as to the barking of a dog. As I watch them, the echo of excited voices comes down the hill, and three flashlights appear in the distance.

"Can I go home?" Mia asks. "I don't want to be part of this anymore."

I squeeze her arm and look toward Kelly's flashlight. "You mind if I take her out of here?"

"Go on," he says out of the darkness. "Get her home. Take Logan's car. Then swallow one more of those magic pills and do what you set out to do in the beginning."

"What?"

"Get your buddy out of jail."

"Thanks, Kelly. For everything."

"Glad to do it."

As I lead Mia through the kudzu, Kelly's voice floats after me.

"Hey, Penn?"

"Yeah?"

"Before those cops get here?"

"Yeah?"

"This guy could make it, or he could be a statistic."

I stop in my tracks. The flashlights are getting closer.

"You got an opinion?" Kelly calls.

Mia squeezes my wrist. "You saw what he did to Kate," she says. "Will he even go to jail?"

"He will. Thanks to you finding that cell phone."

"Penn?" Kelly asks again.

I turn back toward the bayou. "I guess he makes it."

At first I hear nothing. Then Kelly says, "No problem. Just wanted to give you the option."

"I appreciate it. I'll see you later."

"Yeah."

With that I take Mia's hand and climb carefully out of the darkness.

CHAPTER
41

Eight hours after Marko was admitted to the hospital, I received the most surprising call of my life. Police Chief Don Logan informed me that Marko Bakic wanted to hire me as his defense attorney. I told Logan that since I had witnessed some of Marko's illegal acts, I couldn't act as his legal counsel. Logan said he'd told Marko this, but that the boy wanted to talk to me anyway.

All I had to do was take the elevator up from the first floor, where the ICU was, to the fourth, where patients recovered from surgery. Two cops guarded the door of Marko's private room. The boy lay in his bed with steel cuffs on his wrists and shackles on his legs. Another chain connected the leg irons to the hospital bed.

Marko laughed when I shuffled into the room.

"Hello, Mr. Cage. You all right?"

I nodded.

"I didn't know that was you in the stream. I just found out this morning."

"Why am I here, Marko?"

"I want you to be my lawyer."

"I can't do that."

"That's what they told me."

"So why am I here?"

He smiled enthusiastically. "I think maybe after you hear my story, you decide to be my lawyer after all."

"It's not a matter of want. I can't legally do it. But even if I could represent you, I wouldn't."

A look of mock sadness. "You don't like me?"

"No."

"You could have shot me in the stream. But you didn't."

"I wanted to make sure you'd be convicted for Kate's murder."

"I understand that. But you shouldn't hate me, man. You never walked in my shoes. You don't know how I got here."

"I know you had a tough childhood. So did a lot of other people. They didn't do the things you've done."

This amused him greatly. "Not many people had childhood like mine."

That's why I'm here, I realized. *He wants me to understand him. He wants me to hear his story and tell him he's not such a bad guy after all.* I've known a lot of criminals like that. Marko is one of those guys who, no matter what he might do, will never believe it was his fault. It would serve no purpose to hear him out, other than to gratify my curiosity about Kate's last minutes. But that was reason enough.

"Say what you want to say," I told him.

"I need a cigarette."

"I need a Ferrari."

Marko burst out laughing. "That's good! I like that."

I looked at my watch. "You've got five minutes."

"What do you think they're going to do to me?"

"Not what you deserve, probably."

"What do I deserve?"

"The Big Sleep."

"What?"

"It's a book."

"I don't think they're going to do anything," he said, like a gambler assessing the odds of a meaningless game. "Not after they hear my story. This is America, man. I've seen the talk shows. They're going to make me a cause."

He's already got it planned out, I thought. *He sees himself on the interview circuit.* "You going to do Larry King or Oprah first?"

"Yeah!" he cried, laughing even harder. "That's it! *Larry King Live*! CNN. People see me even in Croatia!"

"The meter's running, Marko."

"Yeah, I know. Okay. I come from Srebece, yeah? It's a little village not far from Dubrovnik. When I was in Srebece, I was nine years old. I had a family. Sister, brother, mama, papa. Everybody happy. Then the Serbs came. It wasn't like CNN, okay? They came at night and beat down the doors. All the houses, everybody's doors smashed. The soldiers did what they wanted, took what they wanted. Everything. Money, furniture, cars, girls."

Marko sniffed and looked around the hospital room. He wasn't laughing anymore. "When they came to our house, we were eating supper. Purple cabbage, I still remember it. When Papa got up from the table, they hit him with the butt of a rifle. Five soldiers, we had. Two older guys, three kids. All with Kalashnikovs. They beat my father to the floor. After him, my brother, Karol. Karol was sixteen. Then they took my mother and sister to the bedrooms. Three guys. Papa tried to stop them, so the oldest guy shot him in the stomach. Papa lay on the floor, holding his guts in while Mama and Katrina screamed from the back."

"Where were you?"

"One of the soldiers held me. When he let go to light a cigarette, I tried to run to Mama. That's when the old guy stuck his bayonet into my stomach. I didn't even feel it. It was like somebody knocked the wind out of me. Like a football hit me hard in the gut."

Marko began jangling his handcuffs. "The raping went on for a long time. Mama and Katrina never stopped screaming. They fought the bastards. Finally the soldiers brought them back. No clothes, blood all over them. Then the old guy said he wants a show. He tells my brother to screw my sister. You believe that? Karol says no, he won't do it. The guy says, 'Do it or I kill your mother, you stinking Croat.' Now I understand he meant to kill us all anyway, but then . . . I was a stupid kid. The Serbs did this all over the place, man. Especially to the Muslims."

"Like the Chinese in Tibet."

"What?"

"When the Chinese army invaded Tibet, they forced the Buddhist monks to kill their fellow monks. Because they're nonviolent. The Chinese made them break their most sacred vow."

Marko nods soberly. "That's it. Same thing. So this is happening, yeah? Mama tells Katrina to help Karol do sex to her, do anything they say. And Karol is trying. He's crying and doing this thing to my sister. My sister was a virgin, man. You understand this? My brother is fucking my sister on the couch. Papa is sobbing and screaming that the Serbs are animals, so they shoot him again to shut him up."

"Did they kill him?"

Marko nods. "Completely. So Mama goes crazy. Her life is over, she's watching this obscenity, and she sits down on the floor and stares at the wall like an insane person. For a second I think maybe it's going to be okay. Even though I'm bleeding all over the place, right? Then I hear a commotion outside, and about ten soldiers run through the door. They're drunk, covered with blood. They go crazy, right there. They're screaming at the first guys to kill us, that we're dogs like the Muslims. Then one of them takes out a knife, kneels down, and cuts off Papa's head."

Marko made a slashing motion with the flat of his hand. The cuffs rattled.

"He holds out Papa's head to my mother and orders her to nurse it. Put her breast in its mouth, yeah? She ignores the guy, so he shoots her. It was a blessing, believe me. Then they force Katrina to take Papa's head. She's crying, but she does what they say. They all laugh, and then someone says it's time to get back to the trucks. The old guy looks at Karol, says, 'Good-bye, dog,' and shoots him in the chest. Then they grab Katrina and drag her outside. That's the last time I ever saw her."

"And you?"

"The last guy to leave stuck me again, in the balls this time. Then he left me there to die. I tell you, man, I don't know how I made it."

"Or why."

Marko nodded vehemently. "That's right! *Why*, you know?"

"There's no answer to that."

"I guess not. Anyway, they moved me to a hospital in Sarajevo. They thought they were helping me. In some ways it was better there, other ways worse. But I learned to survive. And I got some payback."

"How's that?"

"Me and some guys, we found some Serb girls later on. One or two at a time, you know? When we finished, we'd say, 'Tell them it's for Srebece.'"

"Why did you do that?"

Marko looked confused. "Because that's what they did to us. To our women."

"The girls you raped didn't do anything to you."

More confusion. "They were Serbs, man."

"Why didn't you target soldiers instead?"

A sly smile. "We did that, too. We fucked some people up."

I walked to the window and looked out at the bypass. Cars were passing outside, the people inside them oblivious to most of what had happened in their town last night, unable even to imagine the horrors that Marko Bakic had endured in his hometown.

"What about Kate?" I asked.

Marko's face closed. "That's something else, man. That was an accident."

"What do you mean?"

"I always liked Kate. More than that, really. She wasn't like the other girls. She had something."

"You had a thing for her?"

"Yeah. From the time I first got here. But I was cool about it. Kate was that type, you know? If you let her know you wanted her, she wouldn't look at you. So I waited."

"And you slept with Mia Burke."

Another sly smile. "You know about that? Yeah. Mia's hot, too. But Kate . . . she had a dark side I liked. But she was dating that stupid football player. Anyway, I watched her for a long time. I was starting to think I'd never get my chance, but then . . ."

"She came to you for the pills."

"Yeah."

"You thought you had her then."

Marko nodded. "Cyrus fucked that up."

"So what did you do?"

"I kept waiting. I know how to wait, man. You learn to wait for water, you can wait for anything. I followed her sometimes. I even tracked her cell phone at the end."

"Like Cyrus?"

Marko laughs. "Cyrus never tracked her phone. I just told the cop that to get him off my back."

So Sonny Cross never got the truth from Marko, not even with his *Dirty Harry* tactics. "You were trying to cut Cyrus out of the trade, weren't you? You and the Asians."

"Think so?"

"You shot those people at Cyrus's safe house. You were trying to kill him."

Marko can't conceal his pride.

"That's why Cyrus's guys went to the Wilsons', to get payback."

The arrogance vanishes, replaced by a terrible bitterness.

"Let's get back to Kate," I say quietly. "Were you following her on the day she died?"

Marko raises his cuffed hands and scratches at the bandage on his shoulder. "Yeah. When the guys picked me up at Coach Anders's house, I ran home and checked my computer. I got a fix on her, and got them to drop me down by the creek. Not too close, though. They left me in front of a friend's house. I didn't want them telling Cyrus what I was doing. I went in from Sherwood Estates, not Pinehaven."

"How did you find her?" I asked, remembering Ellen's version of the story.

"I wasn't sure exactly where she was. I figured she was jogging by the water, but it had been raining, so I wasn't sure. I went down there to see."

"What did you find?"

"Kate, man. Her legs were lying in the water, and she was bleeding from the head."

"Was she wearing clothes?"

"Sure. Tennis dress."

"And a top?"

"Yeah."

"What did you do?"

Marko's eyes were fixed on the foot of his bed. He seemed to be reliving what had happened next in his mind. "I tried to wake her up. I couldn't tell if she was breathing or not. I didn't think so."

"And then?"

His eyes suddenly sought out mine, imploring me for understanding. "I got to looking at her. She was wearing that skirt, and it started getting to me. Kate was hot, man. She reminded me a little of my sister. More than a little, really."

"What did you do?"

"I decided to take a look. I pushed up her shirt. I squeezed her tits a little bit. She didn't move, but she was still warm, you know?"

I nodded as though I understood his logic.

"It made me hard, touching her, so I pulled down her skirt and went inside her."

Jesus.

"It took some work, man. She was dry like sandpaper. But after a while, I got in there."

A wave of heat passes through my face.

Marko shrugged. "What would you do, man? Like I said, she was warm. It was just like the real thing, only she wasn't moving. Some chicks are like that anyway, you know? I don't know what happened to Kate. I think she hit her head on something."

"What happened next? Was she dead at that point?"

"That's the thing, man! I did her for a while—both ways, you know? But when I was almost finished, suddenly her eyes opened up. Boom, she was looking at me! It freaked me out, because she started screaming. *Loud.* I told her to be quiet, but she wouldn't shut up. She tried to throw me off her, but I was so close, man, I just had to finish. You know that feeling?"

"Sure," I said, trying hard not to climb onto the bed and strangle him.

"I put my hands on her neck. Just to shut her up, right? Not to kill her or anything. Just to keep her quiet until I was done."

"I understand. She wouldn't shut up. So what happened?"

"Nothing, really." Marko squinted as though to see the memory more clearly. "After I came, her eyes were closed again. I think she just died, man. I don't think I even killed her. I think whatever happened before I got there killed her."

Unbelievable. "And then?"

"I heard someone coming. Moving fast. I thought maybe it was a deer, but when it got close, I could tell it was human. I ran across the creek and got down behind some bamboo."

"Who was it?"

"The doctor. Elliott. He ran up to Kate and fell down on his knees. He pounded on her chest, then started pumping it like they do on TV. But it was no use. She was gone."

"And then?"

Marko made a derogatory sound. "He was crying, screaming at the sky. I saw that all the time in the city."

"Sarajevo?"

"Yeah. After a sniper hit somebody. People cursing God, wailing, screaming at heaven. But you know what? Not one person ever got up and walked again. God didn't save any of them."

"What's your point?"

"No point, man. That's the point."

I realized I'd heard enough. The rest of the story didn't interest me. I knew without asking that Marko had been the blackmailer on the motorcycle that first night, exploiting what he'd seen that afternoon to get more money and drugs. I didn't know who'd helped him, but neither did I care enough to give him the satisfaction of asking. Marko would soon be convicted by a jury, and his fate would be up to those twelve people. It was time for me to put it all behind me. I turned away from him and walked to the door.

"Hey," he called. "You leaving?"

"Yes."

"Wait up."

I turned back. "What is it?"

"Did you fuck Mia?"

I stared at him in disbelief.

"Come on, man. Did you?"

"No."

He laughed softly. "Too bad. She's good."

I wanted to break down the steel IV stand and shove it up his ass. But I didn't. I said, "I'm sure that's true. And one day, some-one a hell of a lot luckier than you is going to spend his life with her. Somebody who earned her."

He seemed to consider this. Then he said, "Maybe so. But she'll always remember me."

I walked back to him then, fighting the urge to beat him into a puddle of wet bone and tissue. "You know what you should be asking yourself?"

"What?"

"What your mother and sister would think of you if they'd seen what you did to those Serbian girls. And what you did to Kate."

Marko's eyes radiated more hatred than I'd seen in a long time. And with that I left his room.

Two days after I left that hospital room, Judge Minor released Drew from jail under a JNOV—judgment notwithstanding the verdict. The day after that, a special grand jury indicted Marko Bakic for the murder of Kate Townsend. Just as in Drew's case, this meant that Marko had to be transferred into state custody. Deputy Tommy Burns and another deputy picked up the prisoner from the city jail and drove him downtown to the sheriff's depart-ment. Billy Byrd himself stood on the steps, waiting to greet his new charge. The deputies dragged Marko from the cruiser and jerked him erect in his irons, whereupon Marko flipped Sheriff Byrd the bird and gave him a glare both scornful and defiant. The sheriff had opened his mouth to reply when a 180-grain deer slug tore through Marko's heart, showering the sheriff with bright red blood.

The rifle shot was heard all over town. I was standing in my backyard on Washington Street, playing with Annie, when I heard what I thought was an electrical transformer exploding from the direction of the Mississippi River. Two minutes later, my cell phone rang. Caitlin had witnessed the shooting from thirty yards away. She said it looked like the bullet had come from one of the taller buildings near the sheriff's department.

Both Sheriff Byrd and Chief Logan believe that the Asians murdered Marko to prevent him from ratting out the drug traders to save himself. The joint task force issued a statement supporting this theory, adding a postscript that if the Asians hadn't done it, then Cyrus White's crew probably had. That was the story that Caitlin printed in the *Examiner.* But when I asked Drew where he was when Marko died, he told me he had taken the day off to stay home with Ellen. Mending fences, he said, for Tim's sake. Tim, of course, was in school at St. Stephen's. A day later, I managed to ask Ellen the same question, and she backed Drew's story to the hilt. But as Ellen spoke, I saw a profound disconnect between her mouth and her eyes. And I knew what that disconnect meant. Ellen Elliott will do whatever she has to do to save her family. After all, she has her own guilt to carry. But in her soul, she knows what I know now—that Marko Bakic, the boy who brutally murdered Kate Townsend, died by the hand of the man who loved her above all others.

And that is as it should be.

CHAPTER

42

Three weeks later, on a beautiful evening in May, I mounted a stage set up at the center of the St. Stephen's football field and took a seat beside Jan Chancellor. Much had happened in the three weeks following Marko's death, and thanks to Caitlin, most of it happened in public view. As a result of that publicity, Senator Brent Few, the speaker scheduled to appear at St. Stephen's graduation, begged off, pleading health problems. The senior class asked if I would be willing to speak in his place. I told them I would be proud to do so.

Three hundred chairs have been set up before the stage, and all but a few are filled. This is impressive, as the senior class numbers only twenty-one souls. When I graduated, we had thirty-two, but Natchez was larger then. I know most of the faces in the crowd, students and their families mainly. Two special chairs stand empty in the seniors' section, symbolic places for Kate Townsend and Chris Vogel. They've almost disappeared under the bouquets of flowers left there.

No chair was left empty for Marko Bakic. For the senior class, Marko is like John Lennon's assassin: He Who Must Not Be Named.

Of the bright faces shining between the royal blue caps and

gowns, one shines brighter than the rest for me: Mia Burke. Just after my commencement address, Mia will give the valedictory speech. She was scheduled to speak before me, but I asked Jan to give Mia the last word tonight. On the night we learned that Kate had been murdered, Mia told me she had some things to say to her class and to the parents. Tonight I look forward to hearing them.

Annie is sitting with my parents in the third row. She's with my parents because Caitlin is not here tonight. Last week, she flew north again, not to Boston this time but to her father's house in Wilmington, North Carolina. We decided that she's not ready for the obligations that would come with marrying me. Our parting was difficult, but mostly because of Annie. Caitlin wanted a private conversation with Annie to break the news, but I decided we should speak to her together. I still love Caitlin, and I trust her motives. But I would not take the slightest risk that something might be said which would leave Annie blaming herself for Caitlin's disappearance from our lives.

As Jan Chancellor begins her welcome remarks, I scan the football field and surrounding bowl. It seems impossible that Drew and I chased Marko across this field on a four-wheeler just a few weeks ago. But much of what happened after that night is hard for me to believe, yet happen it did. And the consequences of those events are still unfolding.

At two this afternoon, a secret meeting was held in the district attorney's office. Present were Shad Johnson, myself, and Quentin Avery. The atmosphere was tense, for Shad had not behaved gracefully after Judge Minor overturned Drew's conviction. In fact, Shad made a personal crusade of trying to convict Drew of sexual battery, which could have resulted in a sentence of forty years. For two weeks I sweated blood trying to think of a way to thwart Shad's mission. I couldn't do it. Drew's medical license had already been suspended by the state authorities, but word had leaked down from the board chairman in Jackson that Drew's future medical career would depend on the disposition of his legal case.

It was during this seemingly hopeless period that Quentin Avery earned his enormous fee. Through the tangled grapevine of the local black community, Quentin somehow learned exactly how Shad had discovered Ellen Elliot's drug addiction, and also Kate's part in it. Shad had not done this by brilliant deductive reasoning, or even by lucky accident. Three days after my kidnapping, he had received an express mail package containing the leather portfolio stolen with my car on the night of the attack at the Eola Hotel. The portfolio—which still contained Kate's flash drives, Marko's hair, and Kate's diary—had almost certainly been sent to Shad by the leader of the Asian gang in Biloxi. The gang leader had probably been prompted by Marko to send the package, in an attempt to cement Drew's conviction for Kate's murder.

Regardless of who sent the portfolio, the materials inside it gave Shad enough leads to discover not only Kate's drug activities on Ellen's behalf but also Cyrus White's obsession with Kate. Yet Shad never informed Quentin that he had any of this in his possession. Just as Quentin had predicted at the outset of the case, Shad had broken the rules—and the law—in his effort to ensure victory at trial. To withhold such evidence constituted felony obstruction of justice—grounds for disbarment—and Quentin was ready to go to war to accomplish that end. With some considerable anxiety, I sat Quentin down and explained my view of the situation: that Shad's greed had given us a magic bullet that could keep Drew out of jail. But Quentin did not lightly abandon his persecution of Shad Johnson. It took a campaign of attrition by me and my father to persuade Quentin that serving Drew Elliott to the best of his ability was a higher moral duty than ridding the city of Shadrach Johnson. In the end, Quentin relented.

When I left Shad's office this afternoon, I was in a state close to shock. Quentin had stripped more than the proverbial pound of flesh from the district attorney's backside. He had verbally flayed Shad, shaming him to a degree I thought impossible. Quentin also extracted from Shad a written promise not to seek the office of mayor in the special election. This seemed a little much, and I wondered if Quentin had done this because he was considering a run for mayor himself. But when I asked about this after the meeting, the civil rights legend just laughed.

"This town needs an idealist," he said, "not a cranky old pragmatist like me."

As I sit watching the graduation crowd, Jan Chancellor introduces Melissa Andrews, the salutatorian. A tall girl with long red hair, Melissa reads from her text without once looking up, but she speaks with genuine emotion about the pain of leaving the cocoon of her class, and her anxiety about entering a world where friends and parents will not be there to prop her up. My gaze roams over the attentive faces, then wanders to the surrounding forest. Spring has truly arrived, and with it a desperately needed air of renewal. The evening breeze blows cool and steady, and the trees encircling the stadium are alive with the pale green leaves of new growth. If Natchez were like this year-round, people would move here by the thousands.

Suddenly, Jan Chancellor's voice breaks into my reverie. ". . . a distinguished attorney who switched careers in midlife to become a bestselling author, but to the people in this town he will always be the tight end on St. Stephen's championship football team. Ladies and gentlemen, Penn Cage."

I stand and hug Jan as I walk to the podium. She showed some courage over the past month, unlike some board members I could name.

Lawyers are notorious for being addicted to the sound of their own voices, but as I look out over the crowd, I recall my basic mantra of public speaking: *Be sincere, be brief, be seated.* Using a few notes scrawled on a legal pad this afternoon, I tell the seniors the things one usually tells graduates in a commencement speech: that their time has come; that the road out of this bowl no longer leads to Natchez, but to the wider world; that the world is theirs for the taking, if they but have the courage to reach out for it. I also tell them some harsher truths: that the world they will find beyond the borders of Mississippi looks very different from the one that nurtured them to this point; that the whites among them might soon find themselves the targets of prejudice for a change; that in the real world, it *is* often who rather than what they know that will gain them advancement. I'm candid about the fact that their education has not been as thorough as it might have been, but I also promise them that the emotional grounding provided by their multigenerational families will more than compensate for this. Though it's not in my notes, I also pass along one lesson that has served me well in both careers:

"As a Southerner, you will constantly be underestimated by the people you deal with, and this tendency can work to your advantage. Learn how to use it."

Having departed from my notes, I pause for a moment and look down at Mia in the first row. She's watching me as though she expects something profound to fall from my lips, some inspiring conclusion to my thus-far-generic speech. But I don't have any pearls of great wisdom. What I do have is a sudden realization that leaves me profoundly shaken. *These kids are not coming back.* Not the best of them, anyway. As I told Caitlin over dinner at the Castle, the parents in this beautiful and unique city are raising their children to live elsewhere. Somehow, we have let Natchez slip into such a state that we cannot offer our brightest students jobs to return to, even when they want them. And that is unacceptable. I will not raise my daughter in a town that offers her no future. With this simple realization comes certainty.

I'm running for mayor.

I leave the podium after an unremarkable conclusion, but as I walk to my seat, a new energy is building inside me. I know where I'm going now.

Jan walks to the podium again and introduces a girl whom she refers to as one of the brightest individuals she has ever had the privilege to know.

Mia Burke.

Mia rises from the first row and walks uncertainly up the steps to the stage. She usually walks with such self-possession that I wonder if she's been drinking. If I recall correctly, I had a bit to drink myself on my graduation night.

Mia has to pull down the microphone to reach it with her mouth. There's a shrill whistle of feedback, then silence. Mia holds up a sheaf of paper and speaks in a conversational tone.

"I wrote a whole speech for tonight. I've been thinking about it all year long. But now, looking out at you guys, I don't want to read it. This class has been through a lot this year. Maybe too much. We lost . . . so much. We lost two great people, and we lost the last shreds of our innocence. I'm not sure we gained anything, other than experience. But I guess it's not up to us to choose when we learn what life is really about."

She looks down at the podium, seeming to gather herself. "I know a lot of parents have been freaked out by what they learned about our class in the wake of Kate's and Chris's deaths. Of course, parents in every generation have been shocked when they somehow learned the truths of their children's lives. That's the way of the world. But now, in this time and this generation, I think they're *right* to be shocked. I'm part of this generation, and *I'm* shocked. We seem to have reached a point in our society where every form of restraint has been broken down or stripped away. There are no rules anymore. In the nineteen sixties, our parents fought to achieve political freedom and liberation of the self. Well, now we've got it. We've got about as much freedom and liberation as anybody can stand. I've had a computer in my bedroom since I was five years old. I've had access to basically all the information in the world since I was twelve—not in a library, but right at my fingertips. At the slightest whim, I can view images of just about anything that piques my curiosity. And I have. But am I better for that? I don't know.

"Don't get me wrong, I like freedom. But you can have too much of a good thing. At some point you have to draw a line, agree on some rules, or all you have is chaos. Anarchy. So, I guess what I'm saying tonight is this: That's our job, guys. Our class, I mean. And our generation. To figure out where freedom stops being a blessing and starts being a curse. Our parents can't do it. They don't even understand the world we live in now. Maybe that job can't even be done for a society. Maybe it's an individual decision in every case. But it seems to me that humans given absolute freedom don't do a very good job of choosing limits."

Mia sighs deeply, then gifts the audience with one of her remarkable smiles. "Natchez is a good place to be from. But now it's time for us to go. I wish I could say something inspiring, but I guess this isn't that kind of speech. I *am* hopeful about the future. I do believe I can change the world. I just know that it won't be easy."

She waves to her class with one long swing of her hand, then walks back down the steps to join them.

There's a smattering of applause, but it soon dies. No one knows what to make of Mia's honesty. In a rather subdued conclusion to the ceremony, Holden Smith passes out diplomas to the graduates. After he's done, the seniors toss their caps into the sky as one, putting the stamp of conventionality on the proceeding at last.

I walk down the steps into the milling throng and make my way toward Mia. She's surrounded by classmates and parents, so I stand a few yards away and wait. A few moments later, I see Drew and Ellen moving toward me through the crowd. A few people gawk as they pass, but most simply go about their business.

To my surprise—and my satisfaction—Natchez remains the eccentric Southern town in which people who have caught their spouses in bed with others still attend the same Pilgrimage parties, and graciously pour punch for mortal enemies.

Ellen is wearing a designer dress, but she looks pale and drawn. She's currently participating in an outpatient rehab program overseen by a local physician. Drew is seeing a psychiatrist with her in Jackson every three days. He's been working out his grief by doing writing exercises, which he says read more like an elegy to Kate than anything else. He told me that the hardest thing for Ellen to deal with has been something I only recently recalled from the autopsy report. Kate died from strangulation, but the "bleed" in her brain caused by hitting her head on the buried wheel would probably have killed her, had she not been strangled before that could happen. So while Ellen did not in fact kill Kate, she did inflict what would have been a fatal injury. She only escaped prosecution because no one in the world knew that she had been at the crime scene—no one, that is, but the unholy pentangle of Drew, me, my father, Mia, and Quentin Avery. And none of us will ever speak of it.

After the last of Mia's well-wishers drifts away, I signal Drew to join me beside her.

"Great speech," I say, hugging her to my side.

She looks sheepish. "Not so great."

"Better than mine, anyway."

"That's true. Were you on drugs or something?"

"I was a little preoccupied."

She suddenly realizes that Drew and Ellen are behind her. She turns and gives them an awkward wave. "Hey."

"I enjoyed your speech," Ellen says. "Very much to the point."

"Thanks."

An uncomfortable silence follows this exchange, so I break it. "Drew has something to tell you, Mia."

"Really?"

He nods and smiles at her. "I want to thank you for everything you did for me."

"You already thanked me. That day I saw you in Planet Thailand."

Ellen smiles as though bursting with a secret. "We wanted to thank you in a more tangible way."

"But . . . I already got your present."

"The jewelry box?"

Mia nods.

Ellen laughs, and Drew actually blushes. "Mia," he says, "today I went down to my broker's office and opened an account in your name."

Mia nods, but I'm not sure she understands what Drew is saying. The excitement of the day, giving her speech, thoughts of the party later—all this is more than a little distracting. While Drew tries to find the right words, a girl runs up and hugs Mia, then squeals and races off to someone else.

"In my name?" Mia asks. "I don't understand."

"It's a college fund," Drew explains. "To help pay your expenses at Brown."

Mia reddens as understanding dawns. "I don't know what to say."

"Ask him how much money is in it," I tell her.

"Oh, no. My God, anything's fine. I'm serious. You shouldn't have done it. Really."

Ellen takes Mia's hand and looks into her eyes. "There's a hundred thousand dollars in it, Mia. And you deserve every penny."

Mia blinks in disbelief. Then her free hand starts to shake, and a tear escapes her eye. "I've got to tell my mom. Oh God . . . oh, my God." She leans forward and hugs Drew and Ellen at the same time. "Do you mind if I find my mom and tell her?"

"Go," Ellen says. "Happy graduation."

Mia walks away dumbfounded. As her petite form recedes into the crowd, I follow her with my eyes. Just before she disappears, she turns back and finds me. Her gaze is long and open, her eyes speaking to me as though there's no space between us. I raise my hand and open it in a motionless farewell.

Very slowly, she shakes her head and mouths the words, *Thank you.*

And then she's gone.

When I turn back to Drew and Ellen, only Drew is there. He's watching me with an empathy that raises the hair on my neck.

"You understand now," he says. "Don't you?"

I look away, but he takes my arm and squeezes hard.

"Maybe a little," I say softly.

He shakes his head, then puts his arm around me. "Let's find the kids."

We stroll through the familiar crowd, two former golden boys tarnished by the years. A few people smile and shake our hands, but more nod in silence as we pass. That's all right. I can live with my choices. Drew will have a harder time living with his, but what do people want him to do? Kill himself?

"Look," he says, pointing.

Thirty yards away, two slim figures about four feet tall walk slowly along the track that runs around the football field. One is Annie, the other Tim.

"You think maybe . . . ?" Drew says.

I smile. "I'd be okay with it."

ACKNOWLEDGMENTS

I would like to thank Susan Moldow and Louise Burke for giving me the most supportive home in publishing that one could imagine in the twenty-first century. I also thank Colin Harrison—a kindred spirit, gifted writer, and sympathetic editor—for his work on this book. Many thanks also to Sarah Knight, the Harvard girl, who acted with unerring efficiency as my liaison to the house, and who also provided some wonderful details for the book.

Special thanks to Aaron Priest, who knows this business like nobody else. "Who loves ya, baby?"

I owe a special debt of gratitude to Nick Sayers, my incomparable British editor at Hodder and Stoughton, who chose quality over commerciality and confirmed my instinct that this was the story to write next.

Thanks also to Ed Stackler, who has journeyed with me through every book from frenzied inception to ragged completion, when all I can think about is the next one. Thanks again, man.

As ever, I have relied upon many generous individuals to bring verisimilitude to my story.

For legal and law enforcement details: Chuck Mayfield, Mike Mullins, George Ward, Tim Waycaster, Jim Warren, Ronnie Harper, Debra Blackwell, and Scott Turow.

For stories about the city of Natchez: Tony Byrne, Charles Evers, J. T. Robinson, Don Estes, Guy Bass, and David Browning. My thanks to Reverend Dennis Flach for his insights into the philosophy of funeral ceremonies. Special thanks also to Ben Hillyer for his wonderful photograph of the Turning Angel. Ben has the gift of seeing things in a different way, thus transforming reality. That makes him an artist.

For insight into the black leadership crisis, the works of Cornel West.

For medical advice: Jerry Iles, M.D.; Simmons Iles.

Special thanks to Courtney Aldridge, Jane Hargrove, Jack Reed, and Geoff Iles. Thanks also to the "kids" who spoke frankly about life in a modern high school. Most of us have no idea what they deal with every day.

No matter how I try to avoid it, there's at least one factual mistake in every book. I absolve everyone mentioned above for those mistakes and take the blame myself.

ABOUT THE AUTHOR

GREG ILES is the author of nine bestselling novels, including *Blood Memory, The Footprints of God, Sleep No More, Dead Sleep, The Quiet Game,* and *24 Hours* (released by Sony Pictures as *Trapped*). He lives in Natchez, Mississippi.